Like Hal, Amadine _____ f
this tour, but for a _____ r
own ability and riddled with _____ e
looked and sounded and behaved confidently, that did not
mean that deep inside she *was*. She had much to prove, to
her critics and to herself, and America provided a perfect
opportunity.

But the skyline of New York, so beautiful a short time
ago, now looked hard and threatening. It was a daunting
reminder of the task that lay ahead and filled Amadine with
fear of failure. If she did fail, she had nothing and no one to
go back to – no home of her own, no family who would
acknowledge her, no true friends and no firm theatrical
engagement. Her whole existence was a house of cards that
could collapse and crumble to dust as easily and swiftly as it
had been built . . .

Also by Carolyn Terry

King of Diamonds
The Fortune Seekers
My Beautiful Mistress

The Pageant TRAIN

CAROLYN TERRY

WARNER BOOKS

A *Warner* Book

First published in Great Britain in 1999
by Warner Books

A CIP catalogue record for this book
is available from the British Library.

ISBN 0 7515 2631 2

Set in Jansen Text by M Rules
Printed and bound in Great Britain by
Mackays of Chatham plc

Warner Books
A Division of
Little, Brown and Company (UK)
Brettenham House
Lancaster Place
London WC2E 7EN

To the memory of my aunt,
Mary Gunson

When I am dead, no pageant train
  Shall waste their sorrows at my bier,
Nor worthless pomp of homage vain
  Stain it with hypocritic tear.

Edward Everett, 1794–1865

Prologue

They set off with such high hopes, that little band of players who gathered in New York in the fall of 1897, to prepare for a theatrical tour of America that would take them to fifty cities in twenty states in thirty-nine weeks.

A tough schedule, but most of the company were used to it, having participated in such ventures before. And for those whose first foray into the theatrical hinterland of one-night stands and jolting sleeping cars this was, the excitement of travel, the camaraderie of their companions, the envy of those they left behind and the sheer relief of having work offered more than enough compensation for any discomfort.

Of course, at the outset anyway they all wanted the tour to be a success, but their reasons varied, particularly among the upper echelons of the company. Each of that exclusive group – the English and American actors who gathered for meals and conversation in the stars' private Pullman car – had his or her own ambitions and desires, wants and needs, that the tour was intended to fulfil. The future was pertinent to the sequence of events that unravelled but, equally, so was the past that each person brought with them. No one travels completely untrammelled by responsibilities and obligations, by guilt or past associations. Attitudes can be shaped, and reactions triggered, as

much by the emotional baggage of the past as by present
aims and future rewards.

Individually, none was unduly theatrical. Indeed, in
private they were down-to-earth and rather ordinary, and
could have passed for men and women in any profession or walk of life. In public, as a group, they attracted
notice, partly because of a deliberate flamboyance of dress
and partly because of the style with which that dress was
worn, the grace of the walk and the congregation of so
many very handsome faces. Perhaps the women were more
noteworthy than the men, simply because they possessed an
assertiveness, an air of confidence and a freedom of expression that would normally, in the closing years of the
nineteenth century, have belonged only to ladies who were
aristocratic or extremely rich.

A very human group, then, with very human failings and
characteristics and, fortunately, a few virtues, although
there were times when these were not greatly in evidence.
And in New York that September it seemed that this would
be just another tour – the usual mixture of old hands and
youthful inexperience, of calm and crisis, of good and bad
houses, of getting on one another's nerves, of jealousies,
love affairs and influenza.

No one could possibly have known that this was to be no
ordinary tour. No one could have foreseen that it would
culminate in the murder of one member of the company by
another.

Chapter One

'She's here – oh my, will you take a look at that!'
The exclamation was rhetorical and aimed at no one
in particular, but contained a note of such awed and fervent
admiration that it aroused the attention of every red-
blooded male within hearing distance. To a man, they all
turned to watch the vision that had appeared on deck – all,
that is, but one who kept his gaze fixed on the creamy wake
left by the *Campania* in a blue and serene Atlantic.

Pierce Radcliffe was calculating that, with a top speed of
twenty-two knots and twin screws, the *Campania* of the
Cunard Line would overtake the American Line vessel, the
St Paul, which lay off her port bow, by early evening.
Surprising, really, Radcliffe was thinking: the Philadelphia-
based company had gone all out to win the Blue Riband
with an American-built ship, while the stately Cunarders
placed more emphasis on punctuality than on speed
records.

To his irritation the same Yankee twang interrupted his
thoughts again.

'Did you know that there used to be a Dramatic Line on
the transatlantic run? Sailing ships they were, oh, fifty, sixty
years ago, and named after great theatrical figures –
Garrick, Siddons, Sheridan and Roscius. Me, I'd name my
ship Sinclair any day.'

Radcliffe gave up the unequal struggle and, reluctantly, turned to look at the young woman who – not for the first time on this voyage, and despite his best efforts – had impinged herself on his consciousness.

Amadine Sinclair – pronounced Ama-deen to rhyme with green, to the frustration of countless lovelorn poets penning sonnets in which the name was synonymous with divine – noted actress, renowned beauty and undisputed 'belle of the voyage'. Radcliffe had witnessed her arrival aboard the liner in Liverpool and, his personal prejudices in full flow, had groaned inwardly. He knew the type, or thought he did. The advance publicity for her theatrical tour of America had contained so many references to her 'striking beauty' and 'wonderful wardrobe' that vanity and self-interest were bound to be the chief components of her 'vivacious personality'. Mind you, wonderful was not the word that sprang to mind regarding Amadine Sinclair's wardrobe: vast, yes; inexhaustible, definitely. In fact, considering that the ship was carrying her theatrical costumes as well as her personal clothes, it was astonishing that the *Campania* remained afloat.

But she was beautiful. Even Radcliffe's jaundiced eye had to concede that. She was tall, probably about four inches shorter than he, which would make her five feet ten inches in height, with a hand-span waist and a gloriously full bosom that was the object of many a man's fevered speculation, while others were riveted by the movement of those long, slim legs beneath the swish of her petticoats. However, it was her face that attracted most attention, for this was a face that one could gaze upon for hours and yet, the moment one looked away, one was compelled to look back again. The exquisite bone structure, the shining lustre of her ebony hair, the luminosity of her magnolia skin, the finely shaped lips and the cool emerald eyes with their fringe of velvet lashes, all this the dazed onlooker could assess and recall. The fascination lay in the mobility and variety of expression that enlivened this face, from the curve of that wide mouth into a warm smile, and the quirky lift of an eyebrow, to the alert and intelligent interest that Amadine took in whatever she was doing and whoever she was with. Her face was always different, its expressions fleeting and changeable as the weather in an English spring, memorable and yet impossible to remember.

And at the moment a face to which, apparently, only Pierce Radcliffe was immune. She was talking animatedly to a cleric and, as he watched, they were joined by another and another and yet another, until she was surrounded by a veritable beatitude of bishops. This hold she had over everyone, the sway she exerted over this voyage, was ridiculous. Radcliffe was waiting impatiently to go to the smoking room, where he knew a certain young man always repaired before luncheon – a wealthy young man with whom Radcliffe had business to discuss and of whose financial co-operation he cherished high hopes. However, as the fellow never missed any of Amadine Sinclair's daily constitutionals on deck, it was pointless seeking him out until his eyes were back in their sockets and his brain re-engaged.

These poor saps, why couldn't they see her for what she was? A passably pretty young woman, with an expensive taste in clothes, and doubtless a head that was as empty as it was beautiful. In all probability her acting ability was no more than average, and she had attained stardom only because she was good to look at. Steer clear while you have the chance, Pierce wanted to warn, before she ruins your life. Believe me, I know what I'm talking about. But no, they hung around in the hope of receiving a glance from those lovely eyes and took an interest in the race with the *St Paul* because Amadine was urging on the *Campania* with patriotic fervour. Frankly, Pierce could not give a damn which ship reached New York first. American-born of

English parents, he felt remarkably neutral on the subject, but the mere fact that she shouted for the British liner made him side with the American.

Ah, she was walking towards the door leading from the deck to the interior of the ship. At last.

'She's appearing at Wallack's on Broadway,' one man was saying, 'and I'm telling you to book early because there won't be an empty seat in the house.'

Radcliffe felt a smug sense of superiority. He never went to the theatre. He never had, and was confident that he never would. He had his reasons, but had never shared them with anyone so that his friends, tired of trying to persuade him, simply accepted that Pierce was not the theatre-going type. He was a transport enthusiast, at one time crazy about trains and now, at the age of thirty-four, utterly obsessed with automobiles.

Someone rushed forward to open the door for Amadine and she smiled her thanks. As her gaze swept over the crowd of admirers, it alighted on Radcliffe and for a moment their eyes met. Deliberately he composed his lean, tanned face into a mask of indifference and hoped that she would be piqued at her failure to make a conquest.

As it happened, there was another man on the ship who was able to resist Amadine's charms, and who resented her presence even more fervently than did Pierce.

The interior décor of the *Campania* was dominated by stained glass, ornately carved wood and plush upholstery in a style more suited to a baronial hall than a sleek ocean greyhound. It would be perfectly possible, decided Frank Smith as he negotiated a grand staircase that was but a distant cousin to a companionway, to spend a week on this ship and never see the sea and, on calm days, to forget entirely that one was not on dry land. Indeed, from what he had observed, this was the sole aim and object of a good proportion of his fellow passengers. As he passed the ladies' saloon, the door opened and he caught a glimpse of Constance sitting primly on an upright chair, sulking, doubtless, while Amadine held court on deck. There was going to be trouble in that direction, he could feel it in his water. Damn it, he had told Hal that to bring two leading ladies on tour, particularly a tour of such length and complexity, was courting disaster – but would he listen, would he heck! And we all know why, thought Frank grimly, as he entered the stateroom that he shared with his brother.

Edward Haldane-Smith, usually known as Hal, looked up eagerly but the spark of hope in his eyes died at the sight of Frank.

'Sorry to disappoint you, old chap,' Frank said affably, joining him at the parlour table, 'but it's only me. Amadine is corrupting the clergy again.'

'Her father was rector of a parish in Yorkshire,' his brother retorted, 'so I expect religious talk makes her feel at home.'

'There was nothing very religious about the snatch of conversation I overheard. From what I could gather, the rector's daughter had four bishops and a canon virtually laying bets.'

'About the *St Paul*, I suppose?' Hal smiled fondly. 'Amadine has decided that our victory in the race to New York would augur well for her personal success there.'

'Irrational rubbish.'

'Superstition usually is, but I have never met anyone connected with the theatre who did not believe in it, have you? And you could be a little more understanding of Amadine's position – this is her first visit to America, and she is more nervous than she cares to make out. I cannot think why you dislike her so much.'

'I don't dislike her. I just think that we don't need her, and would be better off without her.'

'Without Amadine, we would be touring with four plays,'

Hal reminded him patiently. 'Her two Pinero pieces bring the total to a much more respectable six. Good God, I have toured with Irving when he took twelve!'

Hal was the leader of the tour and its principal actor, but he and Amadine headed two individual English companies that had pooled their resources and repertoire for this American venture. Hal was accompanied by his regular leading lady, Constance Grey, and Amadine's leading man was also part of the group. A nucleus of supporting players from both companies was travelling with them, while in addition American actors were being recruited in New York.

'That's why I wanted to speak to you,' Frank remarked. 'Six plays might not seem much to you and me, but Tom is working himself up into a terrible state about it.' He paused at a knock on the door. 'That'll be him now, so you can judge for yourself.'

Tom Oldroyd, the elderly stage manager, refused Hal's offer of a seat and, clearly a bag of nerves, paced the room restlessly.

'Tom is convinced that half the scenery, props and costumes have been left behind,' Frank informed Hal. 'Of the half we have got, he is certain that most will never surface from the bowels of this ship, and the rest will survive no farther than Boston – which, as you will recall, is our first stop after New York.'

'There's too much stuff,' Tom said in a broad Yorkshire accent, 'and how I'll keep track of it I'll never know.'

'As soon as we board the special train, there'll be nothing to it,' Hal assured him.

'And two of the plays – Miss Sinclair's pieces – are new to me, which makes it even more difficult to look after all the bits and bobs,' Tom went on stubbornly.

'Those pieces are simplicity itself,' Frank exclaimed impatiently. 'No special effects, just routine scene changes, the sort of thing you've done a million times before.'

'Yes, but not among foreigners.'

'Tom, we are going to America, not Timbuctoo.' Frank's voice was rising with each sentence. 'They speak English. They are comparatively civilised. In fact, I think you might find that Boston is considerably more civilised than Barnsley.'

This dig at Tom's home town did not go down well. Tom's face reddened angrily, and Hal hastened to intervene.

'You will have plenty of help,' Hal soothed, 'particularly from Frank, who worked in America for years.'

Knowing that Frank's main job on the tour was to act as Hal's secretary and take care of financial and administrative affairs, Tom's glance was sceptical in the extreme. 'It'll still be me that has to unload the crates and boxes at the docks and see them through Customs. They'll unpack them, you know, and we'll have bits of this and bits of that scattered all over t' place.'

Frank groaned. 'We don't need to clear Customs at the quayside – the goods can be transported to the theatre and the formalities undertaken there. How many times do I have to tell you?'

At this the old stage manager stalked out of the room, leaving Hal to look at his brother reproachfully.

'He's probably gone to check the ship's manifest for the umpteenth time. Honestly, Hal, I know he has worked with you longer than I have, and I shouldn't criticise, but was he really the best you could find?'

'He is a fine fellow and, although he is a worrier, he has served me well in the past. How could I fire him at the end of last season – on what grounds?'

'On the grounds that he isn't up to an overseas tour because he is an old man and, worse, an old man who behaves like an old woman.'

'Have a little patience – this is his first overseas tour.'

'And it is your first tour as actor-manager, in charge of

your own company,' Frank said sharply. 'You need a stage manager with more experience.'

Hal smiled, but these misgivings did nothing to boost his self-confidence. Six feet tall and slightly built, he was one of the most handsome men on the English stage. Blessed with thick brown hair and melting brown eyes, his extraordinary good looks were cast in such classical mould that his profile could have graced a Roman coin, while his beautiful voice was capable of the utmost sensuality and tenderness. Aged thirty-seven, he had been at the top of his profession for some time, yet he had gone into management a mere two years ago, with extreme reluctance and only because everyone else was doing it – well, everyone who mattered – and the great actor-managers took the leading roles for themselves and left him with only second best. They were his friends – Henry Irving, Charles Wyndham, Herbert Beerbohm Tree, George Alexander, William Terriss, John Hare, Johnston Forbes-Robertson – and he did not begrudge them their success. Besides, in many ways he had been happier without the responsibility for anything but his own performance. Having taken the plunge into management, he was overwhelmed by the awful feeling that now, and on this tour particularly, the whole success of the enterprise depended on him. Yet there could be no regrets because there had been no choice: he had been standing still, and no one in the profession – perhaps in any profession – could afford to stand still.

And there was Amadine to look forward to, both personally and professionally. Hal relished the prospect of working with her, but it was on the intimate details of her imminent seduction that he dwelled during the long watches of the night. He did not know her well but recognised a challenge when he saw one, even though he was unaccustomed to encountering such obstacles. Hal was used to having everything, especially his women, his own way: his leading ladies had been swooning at his feet and into his bed for years, and he was confident that Amadine would be wooed and won without difficulty.

'One of the things I really like about Amadine,' he confided dreamily, 'is her lack of temperament. That, and all her energy and exuberance.'

'Oh yes,' Frank said sarcastically, 'it's the energy and exuberance that attracts you every time.'

'I'll take it slowly,' Hal decided. 'We will be working our socks off in New York, and even in Boston time will be at a premium. I'll soften her up gradually and then, when we board the special train, then . . . oh, boy . . .' He drew in his breath sharply.

Dear old Hal, Frank was thinking cynically; always the tall, handsome, intelligent, successful one in the family, whose rise to the top of the profession had been so smooth and easy that it was seemingly preordained. There had been a couple of rocky patches, true, but no real setbacks and through it all Hal had remained the same warm, sincere and immensely likeable man. An all-round good fellow who never did anyone a bad turn, and a generous and talented actor. Then there were those astonishing good looks. God, it was so unfair!

As he had done for years, Frank compared his own short, stocky figure to his brother's willowy grace, and judged his dark hair and thick-set features by Hal's handsome face. He had worked just as hard as Hal, had *tried* just as hard – probably harder – and yet he had barely managed to subsist as an actor. After failing in London, he had tried his luck in the States but it had been the same story there: scraping along at the bottom of the ladder, in minor roles and touring companies. All because he had not been born with Hal's looks. These days, to play the prince you had to look like one.

And then, on top of everything, he had landed in that ghastly mess in Chicago – through no fault of his own, damn it – while Hal swanned through life with barely a ripple of discomfort or disquiet. Well, all he, Frank, had to do on this tour was hold his nerve and everything would work out fine, for now and for ever, amen. And afterwards, when he had sorted things in Chicago, he would concentrate on building a fine repertory company, in partnership with Hal. He would settle for that. No more dreams of stardom – leave that to those whom fate had chosen, the Hals and the Amadines . . . The thought of Amadine reminded him why he resented her presence on this tour. Quite simply, she cost too much. Hal had been far too generous in the terms he offered her, and Frank had his own reasons for wishing to economise.

'Anyway,' Hal was saying jovially, 'I'll leave Tom to you. After all, this American tour was your idea in the first place.'

'So it was.' Frank's tone was bland, but he wondered how his brother would react to the story that lay behind that suggestion. However, it was imperative that no one knew why he had to return to the States, and that no one guessed that this tour was intended to provide the means, and the perfect cover, for the mission he must fulfil.

'You have no idea how important this tour is to me, Frank,' Hal confided. 'It can make or break me. Oh, I've had a following in the States for years, but they have only seen me with stars like Irving and Mary Anderson. Will they turn out to see *me*? I need this tour to establish myself as an actor-manager, and therefore I need personal success in America, and I need to take home enough money and reputation to launch another London season. I need this tour to be a success artistically *and* financially.'

'You and me both, brother dear,' Frank murmured, 'you and me both.'

For Constance, the bad news was that the Cunarder reached Sandy Hook – the 'finishing line' for transatlantic speed records – thirty-five minutes ahead of the American ship. The good news came when the *St Paul* swept past a virtually static *Campania* in the approaches to New York. Amadine's face was a picture, Constance noted smugly, as her fair omens sank to the bottom of the harbour.

The lull in the *Campania*'s progress allowed a launch to come alongside, and among the officials who boarded the liner was the representative of the American agent who had organised the tour. To her chagrin, Constance knew immediately that, as far as he was concerned, she might just as well not be here. He shook her hand warmly, and smiled amiably, but his eyes went straight back to Amadine and lingered there. Then he told them that, although he had arranged for the press to meet them at the pier, they had some competition on their hands.

'Because the *St Paul* will dock first,' Amadine observed wryly.

'It's rather worse than that,' the agent admitted. 'The *Fuerst Bismarck* was arriving as I left, but it's nothing to worry about,' he went on hastily, 'nothing that I can't handle, no, sir!'

'Three ships, in the space of a couple of hours, and we are the last to dock.' Hal looked troubled. 'We'll be lucky to be noticed at all, particularly if there are any celebrities on the other vessels.'

'An English cricket team is on the *St Paul*, and I think we can outshine them, don't you? But I concede we may have to push ourselves forward more aggressively than usual.' The American was eyeing Amadine thoughtfully. 'That sure is a lovely outfit, ma'am, but could you change into something with a bit more sparkle?'

Constance concealed a smile. Amadine was wearing an elegant walking dress of dark green silk, with a short matching coat and a wavy-brimmed, plumed hat, and her expression indicated that she was unaccustomed to having her dress sense queried.

'Sparkle?' Amadine repeated, with obvious distaste. 'I'm not a Christmas tree!'

'Your dress is too dark, ma'am. It will be after ten in the evening by the time we dock, and we want you to stand out in the crowd.'

With a slight sigh, Amadine complied, her departure enabling Constance to enjoy a stroll on deck with Hal and the other men as the *Campania* sailed slowly into New York harbour. It was heaven to have a spectacular view of the Statue of Liberty with her illuminated torch, while below Amadine was limited to a glance out of her porthole, and to have four men vying with each other to point out items of interest. Even at this hour the harbour was busy with ferries and tugs, the air alive with the splash of waves and the shrill of whistles and horns, lights glinting on the water and revealing a strange and fascinating skyline. Interspersed among the church spires, and beginning to dominate and overpower them, the early skyscrapers of New York were thrusting up, like darning needles stuck in a pincushion, already asserting themselves as the symbol of the power of the New World. Slipping her arm possessively through Hal's, Constance listened to his exclamations about the changes that had occurred since his previous visit here and gasped at the breathtaking beauty of the Brooklyn Bridge.

Constance was determined not to be prised away from what she considered her rightful place and to be beside Hal when they disembarked. Yet when Amadine reappeared in a stunning gown of gleaming ivory silk, worn with a three-quarter-length matching coat and a huge, feathered hat, Hal disengaged himself from Constance and hurried to her side. In no time at all, and afterwards Constance could not explain how it had happened, the *Campania* slid alongside the Cunard pier, the gangway was lowered, and the American agent was ushering Hal and Amadine towards the cluster of waiting press men.

Standing behind Constance at the rail, Frank frowned slightly. 'Something doesn't seem right. It looks awfully quiet down there in the Customs shed, but I suppose we should get our things together and try to be near the head of the queue.'

Jostled by the crowd and confused by the increasing chaos, Constance was thankful that Frank took charge. He helped her with the Immigration formalities, collected her luggage along with his own, and checked that Amadine's maid and Hal's valet were ready with the bulk of the heavy pieces. Then he went in search of Tom Oldroyd, the stage manager, and a short while later Constance found them on deck talking to one of the ship's officers.

'I'm afraid that there are no Customs inspectors available,' the officer was saying. 'Most of them are at the Hoboken pier, dealing with the *Fuerst Bismarck*. About twenty inspectors have gone to the American Line pier to start on the *St Paul*, but we're told that it is bedlam down there as well. Apparently a new tariff law has been introduced, which means more red tape and higher tariffs, and that, along with three ships putting ashore several thousand people at once, has caused the system to collapse.'

'So we could be here all night,' Frank said in dismay.

'Surely some people might prefer to leave their luggage and come back for it tomorrow,' suggested Constance optimistically, even though she did not wish to do so herself.

The officer shook his head. 'I would not recommend that. The goods would be sent to the Public Stores, and it could be three or four days before they are released. No, your best plan is to be patient.'

'Oh well,' said Frank resignedly, 'I've known more auspicious starts to a tour but still, look on the bright side, eh – things can't get much worse.'

At that moment Tom Oldroyd, who had remained silent and struggling for breath, uttered a strangled cry and collapsed, knocking Frank slightly sideways and falling heavily to the deck. Hurriedly kneeling beside him, Frank felt for a pulse while Constance loosened the old man's collar. After a few moments Frank peered closely at Tom's face, and then looked up in horror.

'He's dead.'

Dawn was breaking over Manhattan when an exhausted group roused Hal in his suite at the Waldorf-Astoria on Fifth Avenue. It took a while, and several stiff drinks, for them to come to terms with what had happened.

'I must go to the morgue later this morning,' Frank said wearily. 'Formalities . . . And there'll be messages to send to Tom's wife. Oh God, this is awful.'

'I'll take care of all that,' Hal told him. 'Try to sleep and then we'll discuss how this tragedy affects the arrangements for the tour.'

'I thought you had a press conference today.'

'Amadine can do it. She hardly knew Tom, so it will be entirely suitable for her to continue with a more or less normal programme. I won't wake her now. We'll break the news after she has had a good rest.'

'Oh yes, we mustn't disturb Amadine's beauty sleep,' snapped Constance hysterically. 'The pity is that you cannot leave her to sleep for the duration of the tour. Everything was perfect until she came along! We had no problems during our London seasons or on our tour last summer. It's her fault – she's a jinx!'

Hal and Frank smiled at each other uneasily as Constance slammed out of the room. Jinx was a word, and a possibility, that no one in the theatrical profession could entirely dismiss.

Chapter Two

The moment Jay Johnson clapped eyes on Amadine Sinclair he knew that he had found his star. In his capacity as publicity agent for Charles Frohman, the American promoter of the tour, he had assessed the company with cool professionalism when he boarded the *Campania* and, although all the group were good-looking – indeed, exceptionally so – he knew that Amadine possessed the personality, character and charisma to grab the headlines and capture the heart of America. Jay was much too focused on his own career to fall in love with Amadine himself but, as he gazed at that lovely face and alluring figure, he was one very happy man.

And the death of the stage manager was a gift from heaven. Of course, and Jay adopted a suitably grave expression, a very real human tragedy had occurred, but it was difficult to quell the excitement of knowing that the Smith-Sinclair tour was now a cinch for the front page of virtually every newspaper in the entire US of A.

This being Jay's first job as a full-time publicity agent, and a real step up from his former life as an advance man – which had entailed going ahead of a tour, arranging advertising in each town before the actors arrived – he was more than somewhat anxious to make a good impression on his new employer. The salary, which was double his previous pay, didn't hurt either, most of it being earmarked for a personal venture intended to lift Jay from the ranks of subordinate nonentities to the dizzy heights occupied by Frohman himself. Therefore Jay was throwing himself into this tour, heart and soul, day and night, yes, sir! Up at dawn, he had primed the press with details of Amadine's love affairs, particularly her reputed relationships with British dukes and earls, as well as her clothes, hairstyles and any other personal information that he could dredge from the cuttings forwarded from London.

For the press conference he had commandeered one of the public rooms on the ground floor of the hotel and ensured that Amadine's route to it included the 300-foot corridor of amber marble known as Peacock Alley. The Waldorf-Astoria had opened only recently, but already Peacock Alley was becoming the place for beautiful women to parade, watched by spectators lounging on the luxurious sofas and chairs that lined the walls on the 34th Street side. Trailing midnight-blue chiffon, trimmed with matching lace, Amadine caused a gratifying stir as she swept through the hotel. Like a medieval queen on her way to her coronation, thought Jay proudly, as he broke into a trot in order to keep up with the easy, graceful stride of her long legs.

In fact an apprehensive Amadine felt more like a medieval queen on her way to the scaffold. Thrust into the limelight at a moment's notice, and still shocked by Tom's death, the prospect of facing the New York press *en masse* filled her with dread. In London one gave a ladylike interview to a discreet reporter if one felt like it, but she had heard terrifying tales of the pushiness and forwardness of American journalists and had not expected to be thrown into the lion's den quite so soon. However, although she felt nervous and totally unprepared for the ordeal, she was damned if she would let anyone know it. Remember that you are what you seem to be, she admonished herself. If necessary, act. If that doesn't work, try bluff.

The dense crowd in the room brought a gleam of satisfaction to Jay's blue eyes, but further drained the colour from Amadine's cheeks. As with opening nights at the theatre, nausea was beginning to rise inexorably and her discomfort increased when she discovered that her place in the room was at the farthest point from the exit. Her appearance at this press conference, she thought as she sat down, could easily become famous for all the wrong reasons.

She began by apologising for Hal's absence, but was interrupted by a loud voice from the rows of reporters in front of her.

'It is being said that the old man died of shock, that there was a quarrel of some kind with a colleague in the company?'

Bloody hell, thought Amadine, this is going to be even worse than I thought! But I can't answer back or they'll adopt a malicious attitude to the entire tour and everyone in it. While she collected her thoughts, she took refuge in a classical education.

'*Ad calamitatem quilibet rumor valet,*' she murmured softly but, Amadine having perfected the art of the stage whisper, in a voice that carried clearly to every corner of the room.

Only one face registered any understanding. Pierce Radcliffe had been visiting the Waldorf-Astoria on another errand but, having caught wind of Amadine's appearance, had been unable to resist the opportunity of seeing her make a fool of herself. He was leaning against the wall near the door, arms folded, and wearing a sardonic look that changed to surprise at Amadine's lapse into Latin. 'When a disaster occurs, every report confirming it obtains ready credence.' Hm, probably a quotation she had seen somewhere and committed to memory. Actresses were notoriously good at memorising all kinds of rubbish.

'I did not witness Mr Oldroyd's death, but those who

did are certain that he died of a heart attack. I can assure you that he had no quarrel with anyone about anything.'

Would Mr Oldroyd be buried in America or in England? 'I imagine that would be his wife's decision, don't you?'

Would the tour be going ahead as planned? 'Some rearrangement of personnel and their duties will be required, but the tour itinerary and repertoire will not change.'

What was the repertoire? 'As you are aware, Mr Haldane-Smith and I head two individual companies and therefore, to some extent, we will be performing separately. He and his leading lady, Constance Grey, will present two Shakespeare productions while I and my leading man, Laurence Knight, will perform two plays by Arthur Pinero. The four of us will combine in the remaining two plays. For New York the repertoire will be Shakespeare's *Julius Caesar*, Pinero's *The Second Mrs Tanqueray* – which I took over from Mrs Patrick Campbell in London – and *The Physician* by Henry Arthur Jones. In addition to the people I have just mentioned, we will be joined here by Gwendoline Hughes, who I'm sure is well known to you, and by another American, Blanche Villard, as well as a host of American and English supporting actors.'

The assembled newsmen were scribbling busily, and certainly no one noticed the odd expression on Pierce Radcliffe's face. One of the names on Amadine's list had caught his attention and he was staring at her as if he had seen a ghost.

Don't you do Shakespeare? The bluntness of the question made Amadine wince. Not if I can help it, was the truthful answer but not one that she was prepared to give. 'There is no opportunity on this tour. *Julius Caesar* does not offer much scope for women; and, in the other play, Mrs Grey has been Mr Haldane-Smith's Juliet for some time.'

So it isn't that you *can't* play Shakespeare? It isn't that you can only do modern stuff, playing women of a certain type? Now Amadine flushed, anger beginning to overcome her nausea but, bearing in mind her responsibility to the company as a whole, she bit back her instinctive response. 'Certainly not.'

How do you like New York? 'Unfortunately my arrival has been clouded by tragedy, but I'm very excited to be here, and there are simply heaps of things I want to do and places I want to go.'

Such as? 'I want to ride on the Elevated Railway, and walk in Central Park. I want to see Washington Square – I am a great admirer of the work of Henry James – and . . .'

'Miss Sinclair wants to shop,' Jay interrupted hastily. Henry James indeed, and so soon after the Latin! The last thing they wanted was to give the impression that Amadine Sinclair was a bluestocking. 'She wants furs – good American furs – and jewellery, and lots of it.'

'I do?' Amadine turned and stared at him in surprise and dismay. Just how was she expected to pay for these furs and jewels?

This intervention led to a barrage of questions about her clothes. Yes, she ordered her gowns from Worth in Paris. Yes, that salon provided most of her stage costumes in addition to her personal attire.

Wasn't that awful expensive – all those silks, satins and sables, the velvets, beads and sequins, the silver and gold embroidery, the ribbons, lace and feathers, must add up in no time? 'I never discuss money,' Amadine said grandly, preferring to give an impression of reckless extravagance rather than reveal that the stage was currently a couturier's best showcase for his next season's line and therefore her dresses were provided at cost and often for free.

Do you have a favourite costume? 'Probably the gown that I wear in the last two acts of *Tanqueray* – it is brand-new and was ordered specially for this tour.'

'We understand that you are quite the darling of the

British aristocracy,' drawled a voice from the middle of the room. 'Could you tell us more about that?'

'There isn't anything to tell,' Amadine said between her teeth.

'Gentlemen,' Jay intervened, 'you cannot expect Miss Sinclair to name names . . .'

'There aren't any names,' she hissed.

'. . . but I'm sure she might be willing to give us one example of her aristocratic admirers and connections.'

'Oh, I'll give you more than one,' Amadine said, with a wicked smile. 'I am well acquainted with the Marquis of Granby, the Duke of Wellington *and* the Prince of Wales.' Not to mention the King's Head, the Red Lion and the Black Horse, but they might be recognisable even to this audience as public houses.

Again, only Pierce Radcliffe understood and, reluctantly, his lips twitched. Much against his will, he was concluding that there might be more going on under Amadine's bonnet than he cared to admit.

Did you get where you are today because you're pretty? It was that blunt voice again, and Amadine was sure she was going to go on hearing it in her worst nightmares. 'Good looks help one to be noticed at the outset of one's career,' she said carefully, 'but, on their own, aren't enough to keep anyone at the top of the profession.'

'You often play "bad women". Are you bad off the stage as well?' someone wanted to know.

Amadine found this so outrageous that she laughed. 'Is it because I have black hair that you believe I must be a sinner? Anyway, I don't play only women with a wicked past. If you come to my new play, *Trelawny of the Wells*, you will see that I can also portray a virtuous woman with a future.'

'But it was wicked women who brought you overnight fame,' persisted the speaker.

'My "overnight fame" is a myth,' retorted Amadine. 'Yes,

I concede that I was first noticed by the critics when I played *The Notorious Mrs Ebbsmith* and then I went on to do *Tanqueray*, but I had been in the London theatre for three years by then.'

'Not exactly a hard apprenticeship.'

'No.' Amadine had hoped that she had deflected this line of questioning, but evidently not. Everyone came back to this in the end – even her. Especially her. 'I know what you are implying – that I cannot act. That I am only . . . only . . .'

'An irresistible enchantress.'

'I suggest that you come to Wallack's and find out for yourself.' Amadine stood up and walked a few steps towards her interrogator. 'Whether I can act, or only enchant you,' she said softly, in her inimitable smoky voice, 'I can promise you a wonderful evening at the theatre.'

With that, she swept out of the room at such a pace that Jay had to run to keep up.

'Don't ever do that to me again,' Amadine flashed. 'You have made up stories about me. You have made me out to be some sort of *femme fatale*, who seduces noblemen by the score. You have made . . .'

'I have made you into a star.'

'I don't want to be a . . .' But she did. She walked on, her vivid features registering a wide range of emotions. She did want to be noticed, to be a success, but not like this. She wanted fame from recognition of her theatrical performances, not from some twisted account of her private life. My God, if they were to find out what her private life was really like!

'It's the beginning of a love affair,' Jay assured her. 'New York adores you, and cannot get enough of you. Just wait – you'll see.'

'I cannot afford any jewellery.'

'No problem. We'll hire it.'

He was shorter than Amadine, sandy-haired and blue-eyed,

with a dusting of freckles on his open, friendly face. His suits were sharp yet somehow seemed a size too small, the buttons straining across his chest. At first Amadine had been irritated by his manipulation of her, but there was something engaging about his boundless optimism, while his energy and enthusiasm for his work – his 'go' in the modern parlance – were qualities with which Amadine could empathise.

'I am not a circus turn,' she said at last, 'any more than I am a Christmas tree. I will not be put in a position where I have to act off the stage as well as on. Good God, you'll be inventing romances for me right here in New York next!'

'Funny you should say that,' Jay began, but got no further.

'No!' shouted Amadine at the top of her voice, and stalked to the elevator.

Jay smiled. If he had had one criticism of Amadine Sinclair it had been that she was too nice, too ladylike and impeccably behaved. Blow me, she hadn't been in New York for more than five minutes and already she was showing *temperament*!

That evening the tour party dined in the Waldorf-Astoria's Palm Garden, seated at a prominent table isolated from the luxuriant foliage that decorated the perimeter of the room, and, tables here being in as much demand as boxes at the Metropolitan Opera House, ogled by the cream of New York society. The level and intensity of the attention were disconcerting but, Amadine reflected, there was some comfort to be drawn from the fact that, after the assassination of her character by the press, this was as close to New York society as she was likely to get.

After dinner she pleaded tiredness and retired to her room but, instead of going to bed, she put on a hat and coat and slipped along the passage to the elevator. Emerging on the Roof Garden of the hotel, her eyes

brightened with delight. Lit by electric lamps and strings
of fairy lights, the place had a lively atmosphere; a group
of musicians played in the bandstand, over which the Stars
and Stripes fluttered bravely, and guests were packed close
together at small tables amid a buzz of conversation and
swirling cigar smoke. And the view! Skyscrapers and
church spires were silhouetted against a starlit sky, bathed
in the glow from the electric street lights that stretched to
downtown Manhattan, just as she had imagined. For years
Amadine had dreamed of such moments, and views. As a
girl she had watched the River Wharfe rush down to the
sea, and longed to go with it. She had wanted to do everything and go everywhere: to paint in Italy – even though
she could not draw for toffee; to ride a camel in the
deserts of Arabia; to pick flowers in remote jungles . . .
Oh, for the young Amadine, the list had been endless.
One of her cousins maintained that the dale, 'our dale',
was the most beautiful place in the world. How do you
know, Amadine had asked, when you haven't been anywhere else?

And now here she was, in *New York*! The enormity, and
the excitement, of her achievement was overwhelming as,
revelling in the unlikelihood of being recognised at this
early stage of the tour, she threaded her way across the café
towards a dark, quiet corner. However, her eyes fixed on
the fascinating panorama of the city, she failed to notice a
man sitting alone at a nearby table or the pair of long legs
stretched across her path. The next thing she knew she was
falling . . .

'Hellfire and damnation,' she gasped involuntarily from
a nearly horizontal, and distinctly undignified, position on
the floor.

'Quite, although I am not sure that I would have phrased
the sentiment in precisely those words.'

Amadine looked at the speaker, and groaned. 'It would
have to be you!'

'My sentiments exactly. Are you hurt?' He stood up and stared down at her.

As she began to struggle to her feet, he leaned down and helped her up. 'Everything seems to be in working order,' she said, gingerly flexing leg and arm muscles, 'but I suspect I'm in for a fine crop of bruises.'

He drew back a chair and, noticing that the incident had attracted attention, Amadine sat down on it, glad to have her back towards the other guests. Her hat had been knocked askew and she removed it, smoothing back her shining black hair. She had recognised the man instantly as a fellow passenger on the *Campania*. He had been impossible not to notice, with that towering height, crisp dark hair and clear blue eyes that seemed to see everything while conveying nothing. The fact that he had kept his distance from her, and that his sardonic expression hinted at thinly veiled contempt, also made him stand out from the crowd.

'I do apologise for my language,' she said stiffly. 'The legacy of two older brothers, I'm afraid. Tell me, do you make a habit of leaving your legs lying about for other people to fall over?'

'Do you make a habit of not looking where you are going?'

He had a curious accent, not quite American, not quite English, but somewhere between the two.

'Are you an American, Mr . . .?'

'Radcliffe. Pierce Radcliffe. And, yes, I am American.'

Amadine's eyes grew wide with astonishment. 'Pierce? Did you say *Pierce*?' When he nodded, she let out her breath in a long sigh. 'Amazing. Absolutely amazing.'

'How kind of you to say so,' he remarked drily, 'but a perfectly logical choice in the circumstances, Pierce being my mother's maiden name.'

'Fanny Kemble, thou shouldst be living at this hour!' Amadine declaimed dramatically but, as far as Radcliffe was concerned, obliquely.

'Is Fanny Kemble an actress?' he hazarded. 'An English actress, I suppose,' and he made no attempt to hide the distaste in his voice.

'Is that why you don't like me – because I am an English actress? Which part offends you – the nationality or the profession, or the combination of the two?'

'The whole world thinks you are charming, Miss Sinclair. Why should I be any different?'

'I don't know . . .'

A shiver of apprehension ran through her. Was Pierce Radcliffe a typical American? Were the reporters at this morning's meeting typical? Would all the people of the United States detest her? It was all very well for Jay Johnson to talk glibly about 'a love affair with America', but Radcliffe's coldness and the blunt questioning of the press had mined a deep vein of insecurity in Amadine's make-up. Jibes that she was a one-hit wonder who had achieved success only through her looks, and who possessed little talent, were hard enough to overcome without hitting a wall of other prejudices which were not in her power to dispel. However, Amadine's concern went even deeper: being only human, she had dreamed of enchanting the Americans but, being Amadine, she had an equal desire to be enchanted by America and its people. If Pierce Radcliffe was anything to go by, she was to be disappointed on both counts.

But he was remembering his manners, beckoning a waiter and asking her if she would like a drink. Recommending that she sample a genuine American cocktail, he guided her through the list of Manhattans, Gin Slings, Tom Collins, Mint Juleps, Sangarees and Sherry Cobblers. Having ascertained that the last-named comprised sherry, sugar, ice and orange slices, Amadine cautiously opted for that.

'Fanny Kemble was an English actress, but she and I do not have much in common,' she commented while they waited for the drinks. 'She didn't want to visit the United

States. "That dreadful America" she called it. "I do hate the very thought of America."'

'So why did she visit the United States?'

'She was acting with her father, Charles Kemble – this was in 1832 – and they needed the money.'

'Then I guarantee your reasons for coming here are the same as hers – to make money, and to impress the former colonials with your superiority.'

'I concede that we want to make money, and there's nothing wrong with that, is there?' Amadine's eyes flashed. 'From what I've heard, you Americans aren't averse to making the occasional dollar yourselves! But we certainly don't consider ourselves to be superior to American actors. The English and American theatres enjoy a continuous cross-fertilisation – the transatlantic route has been packed with players for decades, and the traffic goes both ways.'

'You cannot blame an American for assuming that a sense of superiority is intrinsic to the English character. If you had read any of the books written by your compatriots about their travels in the States, you would understand why.'

'I have read nearly all of them,' Amadine returned promptly, 'and agree that these writers did not find every-thing in your country to their liking. However, they cannot have been entirely mistaken. Certainly I did not expect to have their views on the extreme sensitivity of Americans to criticism to be proved correct quite so soon.'

Radcliffe's lips compressed into a thin line. 'So you landed in America with your prejudices preconceived and intact.'

'I have no preconceived ideas about America. I have come here with an open mind and will judge her by her performance. I was hoping that America, and the Americans, would grant me the same courtesy.'

A silence fell between them as the drinks were served, and both wrestled with their innate good manners and an overwhelming urge to walk off in high dudgeon. Yet there was something else as well; an intangible but strong sense that for some strange reason the opinion of the other person mattered.

'You are aware that the account of America written by one of those early travellers, Fanny Trollope, was coloured by the failure of the business she established in Cincinnati?' Radcliffe asked at last, with exemplary, if arctic, politeness.

'I am. Just as I am sure that you are aware that Charles Dickens's views were influenced by the copyright controversy. I suppose it was unreasonable of him to wish to be paid royalties for the sale of his books in America, instead of having his work pirated by people who thought it was cute to get something for nothing.'

'If I started to list all the sins of England, we would be here all night.'

'Doubtless. Unlike some nations I could mention, we have had several thousand years in which to accumulate a debit, as well as a credit, column. When your credit column is as long and colourful and glorious as ours, you will be entitled to criticise.'

They glared at each other, the old world quarrelling with the new, both believing they were right and that their country was the best.

'I have been looking forward to this trip,' Amadine burst out. 'I have always wanted to travel and, unlike poor Fanny Kemble, was in a frenzy of impatience to sail away from home. Washington Irving said to her: "You are seeing men and things, seeing the world, acquiring materials and observations and impressions and wisdom." That is what I want to do, and I want to do it in America. I want to love America, and for America to love me. What's wrong with that? Why do you hate me, and hate my country?'

'Hate is much too strong a word,' he said, 'but surely I am entitled to have a few reservations?'

'But you don't know me!'

'I know your country. My mother took me there when I was only a boy, and she lives there still.'

Evidently he had been unhappy about the move, but perhaps the fault lay with the mother rather than the country? Amadine, who had skeletons enough in her own family closet, was sufficiently sensitive not to pursue the matter.

'Surely you credit me with enough intelligence to have read a few American authors in my quest for information?' she suggested.

'Let me guess, *Little Women*!'

'Don't be so patronising,' she said sharply. 'That is one of my favourite books. I have loved it for years, and re-read it recently with the utmost pleasure.'

'Mark Twain, then.'

'*Life on the Mississippi*. Don't you just adore American names – Mississippi . . . Shenandoah . . .' Amadine rolled them slowly and sonorously off her tongue, and suddenly she looked across at Pierce and smiled.

Equally suddenly he saw what everyone else saw: her incredible beauty, her warmth and impetuosity, her intelligence and total lack of pretension. The moon came out from behind a cloud, highlighting her face and, as she had not replaced her hat, transforming her hair to ebony silk against the blue-black velvet of the night sky. An overwhelming physical attraction engulfed him, an almost excruciating desire to strip the clothes from that lovely body and make love to her very, very slowly – although the depth of his arousal was such that the reality of his seduction being slow was highly improbable. He wondered if she were a virgin.

This was awful. This was not in the least what he would have planned, or the outcome he would have anticipated from such an encounter. The woman was a witch. All actresses were witches.

She was talking about Walt Whitman's use of names in

his poetry, and glowing with earnestness and moonlight. This is all it was, Radcliffe thought dazedly: moonshine.

'What took you to England this summer – a visit to your mother, presumably?'

'Partly. But I also attended the automobile races in France.' A spark of genuine interest enlivened his handsome face. 'Do you realise, Miss Sinclair, that this year speeds of more than twenty-five miles an hour were reached?'

'Please call me Amadine and, no, I did not realise that. So automobiles are likely to catch on?'

'They are the coming thing,' Radcliffe assured her, aglow with the entrepreneurial spirit of the Gilded Age. 'Motor cars will be to our generation what railroads were to our fathers – a transformation in transport, a revolution in lifestyle, and an opportunity not to be missed. But at the moment the Europeans – De Dion, Panhard, Peugeot – are way ahead, and therefore although motor cars will catch on, we Americans must catch up!'

'Are you buying automobiles, or selling them?'

'I have bought one, but I'm trying to raise the finance to manufacture motor cars here in America. Unfortunately, not everyone sees the possibilities as clearly as I do.'

'Are you staying at this hotel?'

'No, I had a meeting in the bar and came up to the roof garden to drown my sorrows.'

Amadine revised her opinion of him. At first sight she had categorised him as a wealthy man, but evidently he was more impoverished than his suit, first-class surroundings and arrogant manner indicated.

'By the way,' and what made him revert to the matter he could not imagine, 'did Fanny Kemble find America as dreadful as she feared?'

'Yes and no. She loved the country and stayed, on and off, for years. She married an American, you see, and he *was* dreadful. His name,' and Amadine paused for effect, 'was Pierce Butler.'

He laughed. 'I won't judge you by your nationality and profession if you won't judge me by my first name.'

'Deal,' and they shook hands. 'You must come to see us during our tour, Pierce. If you cannot overcome your "reservations" about English actors, there will be lots of Americans for you to admire.'

Reminded of the company she was keeping, Radcliffe's face tautened. 'I never go to the theatre,' he said abruptly, and stood up. 'Goodnight.'

What a very peculiar person, Amadine thought as she slowly finished her drink, and again she hoped that he was not typical of the people she would meet here. Like Hal, Amadine needed to make a personal success of this tour, but for a different reason: she was unsure of her own ability and riddled with self-doubt. Just because she looked and sounded and behaved confidently, that did not mean that deep inside she *was*. Deep inside she was *terrified*. She had much to prove, to her critics and to herself, and America provided a perfect opportunity while presenting her with an inbuilt advantage – she was *new*, and she had been told that, in America, to be new was everything.

But the skyline of New York, so beautiful a short time ago, now looked hard and threatening. It was a daunting reminder of the task that lay ahead and filled Amadine with fear of failure. If she did fail, she had nothing and no one to go back to – no home of her own, no family who would acknowledge her, no true friends and no firm theatrical engagement. Her whole existence was a house of cards that could collapse and crumble to dust as easily and swiftly as it had been built because, without confirmation of her true talent, it had no foundation.

She must make a hit in America, she must, because she might never get another opportunity. After all, she could be *new* only once.

Chapter Three

O f the Americans who had joined the company, two had
come to the fore immediately: Gwendoline Hughes
and Blanche Villard, the oldest and the youngest respec-
tively of the select group that was gathering round the
principals. In New York Blanche, who was playing in the
Pinero pieces with Amadine, did not mix with the principals
outside the theatre, but Gwen had been assimilated immediately. On the morning of their third Sunday in New York
she was standing by the Fifth Avenue entrance to the hotel,
pulling on her gloves, when Amadine walked into the lobby.

Amadine paused for a moment, watching her. Tall and
still shapely at forty-nine years old, Gwen had abundant
brown, grey-streaked hair framing a finely boned face with
a wide mouth, clear blue eyes and a good skin. She must
have been beautiful when she was young, Amadine thought,
and she wondered why the older woman had never made it
to the very top of the professional tree. An accomplished
character actress, Gwen had suddenly abandoned her career
here in her native America and joined the Lyceum in
London, where she had stayed for four years before linking
up with Hal and Constance a year ago for a UK tour and a
London season.

'You look deep in thought,' Amadine remarked.
'Brooding about opening night tomorrow?'

'Hardly, the part of Calpurnia is not unduly taxing! No, I was reflecting on my good fortune in staying here, at the most luxurious hotel in New York.'

'Did you expect us to accommodate you in a doss-house down by the docks?'

'There is a happy medium between a doss-house and the Waldorf-Astoria! But it is typical of Hal to be so considerate – and you, too, of course,' Gwen added hastily.

'I cannot take any credit for it,' Amadine assured her, 'because I wasn't consulted. It must have been Hal's idea because if Frank had his way, I believe we would *all* be in a doss-house. He is turning into a shocking miser and penny-pincher!'

Gwen laughed. 'You're up early.'

'I'm going to church.'

'So am I. Should we go together, or have you made other arrangements?'

'I haven't decided where to go. Last week I went to St Paul's, and the week before I went to Trinity, but I thought that, this week, perhaps somewhere a little closer . . .?'

'Why not come to the Little Church Around the Corner with me? It isn't far, only to the corner of 29th Street.'

'What is the name and denomination of this church?' Amadine asked as they walked out into the sunshine of Fifth Avenue.

'I've just told you its name.' And Gwen laughed at Amadine's puzzlement. 'Officially it is called the Church of the Transfiguration, and it is Episcopalian, but everyone calls it by its nickname and it has become closely associated with the theatre.'

Gwen explained that in 1870 Joseph Jefferson, America's best-loved comedian, was arranging the funeral of his friend, an actor called George Holland. The clergyman whom Jefferson approached in this connection told him that his church did not welcome actors, but that there was 'a little church around the corner where they do that sort of thing'. 'Jefferson is supposed to having exclaimed: "God bless the Little Church Around the Corner", and the profession has had a special relationship with it ever since.' Gwen glanced at Amadine, who was smiling with pleasure at the story. 'Of course, your father is a clergyman.'

'My father died six years ago,' and a shadow fell over Amadine's face. 'I expect that my younger brother has been ordained by now, and taken over the parish.'

If Gwen thought it strange that Amadine did not know whether or not her brother had been ordained, she did not say so. 'New York churches must seem rather new and small compared with those to which you are accustomed.'

'My father wasn't exactly Archbishop of Canterbury, you know, only rector of a rural parish in the Yorkshire dales! Our church is old – fourteenth-century – but small and simple, standing in a field by the river. New York is different, that's all.'

When they emerged after the service, the streets were busier and Amadine lowered the veil of her hat over her face. Outside the lych gate Gwen hesitated. She was due at a dress rehearsal but, Hal having selected *Julius Caesar* to open their month-long New York season, Amadine was not needed at the theatre. As her leading man, Laurie Knight, had accepted Hal's invitation to play Marc Antony to Hal's Brutus – the two men were old friends, who had played and toured together on numerous occasions – Amadine had been left on her own for much of the preceding weeks.

Needless to say, Jay Johnson had seized the initiative and coerced her into undertaking publicity work. These duties had provided an opportunity to see something of New York other than the few blocks that separated the Waldorf-Astoria at Fifth Avenue and 34th Street from Wallack's Theatre at Broadway and 30th, but Amadine had disliked the lack of privacy in her sightseeing and the feeling that she was 'giving herself up as a spectacle', just as Dickens had done before her. She had gazed across the harbour from the Battery, and posed on Wall Street by the Federal Hall with Trinity Church framed behind her. She had visited the Stock Exchange, and attracted a huge crowd when riding on the Elevated Railway. And she took an energetic stroll in Central Park in order to lay a flower at the foot of Shakespeare's statue in Literary Walk.

However, this morning Amadine set off beside Gwen towards Broadway. 'I want to see the dress rehearsal,' she explained, 'because Joseph Byron is taking photographs.'

'You do realise that you, and your picture, are plastered all over the drama page of the *Times* Illustrated Magazine today?'

'Have they included a picture of Constance?'

'What do you think?'

'Oh dear.' Amadine walked on in silence for a few moments. 'And Hal?'

'They have found room to mention him, along with a rather tasteful picture, which is positioned on the page in such a way that he appears to be gazing soulfully at you.' Gwen watched for Amadine's reaction but her companion said nothing and, behind the veil, her face remained inscrutable. 'It isn't going to work,' Gwen went on slowly, 'this idea of Hal's – you acting your Pinero and him doing his Shakespeare. I can see why he did it: the combination of two companies increased the size of the repertoire, and having two sets of principals allows them the occasional night off, as well as safeguarding against illness. The theory looks fine in principle but simply doesn't work in practice. Hal is going against it already by using Laurie in the Shakespeare. And even more important, Jay – quite rightly, in my opinion – is building you into the star of the show.'

'I told him the other day that Constance ought to have more of the limelight. Damn it, the season opens with *Caesar* and I'm not in it – the public is being given a false impression.'

'But Jay is not impressed by Constance?'

'He says that she doesn't sparkle – Jay likes everyone, and everything, to sparkle – and that she looks tired and dowdy. As I said to him, perhaps she's had a hard life!'

'Lots of people have had hard lives.' Gwen's voice was uncharacteristically sharp. 'Constance's job is to entertain them so that they forget their troubles, not to remind them of her own.'

'That is more or less what Jay said.' Amadine was impressed by this consensus, and decided that a survival-of-the-fittest streak permeated America, and New York in particular. 'And Hal's profile would be higher if he didn't spend eighteen hours a day in the theatre.'

'He has to, because Frank is trying to do Tom's work as well as his own, with the result that he isn't able to give Hal support in other areas. And I predict that state of affairs won't last, any more than Hal's original concept will.'

'Are you predicting that the *tour* won't last?'

'Of course not – only the repertoire as it stands now. My dear, the public will want to see you and Hal together on the stage, every night, and preferably you and Hal in love and melting into each other's arms. At the moment you appear together in only one play out of three, and even then he falls in love with Constance. It isn't natural.'

'There isn't much that I can do about it.'

'All I ask is that you think about it and, when the time comes, be prepared for change. Flexibility is important on a tour, particularly on a long one like ours, because nothing stays the same.'

On opening night, feeling under-rehearsed and over-stressed, the entire company succumbed to nerves. Even though she was not performing, Amadine felt the strain just as much as her colleagues and arrived at the theatre in a state of considerable tension.

An awning stretched from the imposing pillared portico to the street, and uniformed attendants were assisting beautifully gowned ladies from their carriages. Society had turned out to welcome its English visitors but, as some had predicted, that society was much more interested in the Sinclair side of the partnership than in the Smith. Playing on this partiality for all it was worth, Jay orchestrated Amadine's arrival at the theatre for maximum effect and delayed her entrance into the auditorium until the rest of the audience was seated.

She looked stunning in a low-cut, short-sleeved gown of cream silk that showed off her shapely arms and shoulders, the skirt clinging to her narrow hips and cascading, in a riot of silken pleats and foaming Valenciennes lace, into a train at the back. Sitting in an ante-room, nauseous with stress, her thoughts were with the company in the dressing rooms.

'Is it going to "go", Jay?'

'Don't see why not,' he answered judiciously. 'Mind you, there are some who say this isn't a lucky theatre. Didn't do poor old Lester Wallack any favours, anyway.'

Amadine went a shade paler. She knew that the Wallacks had been one of America's first and finest theatrical families, who had founded a company that was a principal American ensemble for thirty-five years. This building had been the third theatre in New York to bear their name, and it was disconcerting to discover that it had witnessed the downfall and death of the dynasty after only five years' occupation.

'And,' Jay continued, 'I'm not convinced that *Julius Caesar* was a wise choice.'

'Now you tell us!'

'It was a favourite of Edwin Booth's,' Jay explained, 'and New York audiences were very loyal to him. One of the most famous performances of the play was in 1864, as a gala to raise money for the statue of Shakespeare in Central Park. Edwin Booth played Brutus; his brother, Junius

Brutus Booth Jr, played Cassius; and his younger brother, John Wilkes Booth, played Marc Antony.'

'Is that the same John Wilkes Booth who . . .?'

'I'm afraid so.' And Jay hurried on, the subject still being intensely distasteful to the theatrical profession. 'Still, I doubt that tonight's audience will resent Hal's usurpation of Booth's mantle. Not like they did with Macready, anyway.'

'I have a feeling that I won't like this . . .'

'As you know, Macready was an eminent English tragedian, and Edwin Forrest was his American counterpart. A rivalry developed between them, principally on the part of Forrest, who was notoriously volatile. When Macready visited America in 1849 he played Macbeth at the Astor Place Theatre, and Forrest promptly announced that he would play the same role on the same night at the Bowery. A group of Forrest's supporters wrecked Macready's performance and he decided to cancel the rest of his engagement, but was persuaded to continue. The next time he performed, a rabble descended on the Astor Place, which was guarded by police and militia. The mob attacked, and in the fracas twenty-two people were killed and more than thirty seriously injured.'

'But that's terrible! Who organised the riot?'

'The ringleader was imprisoned, but everyone believed that Forrest was the real instigator.'

'Out of professional jealousy!' Amadine was beginning to be rather grateful that the great Edwin Booth was dead.

'Mainly, but there were other factors.' Jay paused and added thoughtfully, 'Macready being English, for example.'

'Oh, great – thanks a lot!' And only sheer professionalism propelled her into the auditorium.

The theatre had been renovated recently, and the auditorium was decorated in fresh tones of cream, white, salmon pink and gold. The proscenium box, into which

Amadine was ushered, was banked with American beauty roses and a spotlight held her in its beam as she acknowledged the applause and sat down. Her heart was hammering and her throat dry as she remembered everything she had been told about the importance of New York opinion. 'New York sets the pace for all America,' Frank had said the other day. 'Its audiences are cosmopolitan; they appreciate artistic quality and have an innate eye for talent. But New York audiences are also critical and alert, and can be ruthless. Old favourites can become old-hat overnight, and nothing hackneyed will be tolerated.'

Amadine looked down at the smiling faces in the stalls below. It was terrifying to think how much rested on the approval of these people. It was even more terrifying to realise that, a few days from now, a similar group would gather to pass judgement on her.

The ovation for *Julius Caesar* was gratifying, and Hal and Laurie were called several times, Hal courteously bringing Constance with him. In a classically draped white gown and with her pale fair hair supplemented by artistically arranged false pieces, Constance looked charming and, standing together in front of the curtain, they made an exceptionally handsome trio. But somehow that did not seem quite enough. Throughout the performance Amadine had thought that she detected a lack of real warmth and spontaneity in the applause; in her opinion, that live, almost tensile link with the audience had not been made.

The critics agreed with her. Over dinner at Delmonico's, the principals toasted each other in champagne, then waited tensely for the newspapers. As they read the notices, their smiles grew fixed. They had not made the required impact. *Julius Caesar* was good, but not good enough. It was nothing to set the world on fire, nothing that New York had not seen before, in a word hackneyed.

On Tuesday night the verdict was the same, and the

night after that. The audience was polite and appreciative, but somehow analytical and oddly detached. The house was not even full. 'It's up to you to take the city by storm, Amadine,' Hal said, with a crooked smile.

Amadine fled to the bathroom, and threw up.

The part of Paula Tanqueray was not easy to interpret. Premièred four years before in London by Mrs Patrick Campbell, to wild acclaim, this complex character moves from shallow and selfish caprice to passionate recklessness and thence to true suffering and tragedy. Paula is a woman with a sordid past – the text referred obliquely to her male 'protectors', but it was clear that she had been a high-class courtesan, continually exploited and then discarded by her lovers. She attempts a fresh start in life by marrying a good man and, when she fails because her past catches up with her, she kills herself so that her husband and his virtuous daughter will not be contaminated by her influence.

Gaining sympathy for a fallen woman took courage and skill. Stella Campbell had done it, and so had Amadine, even her sternest critics conceding that she was a worthy successor to the more famous creator of the role. But the play itself took risks, and could not be guaranteed a rapturous reception. In some quarters the concept was deemed immoral, and in others the author's condemnation of Paula's 'protectors' for leading 'a man's life' aroused antagonism.

How New York would receive the work was anyone's guess. In addition to the moral question, there might be a problem with the subtleties of the settings and the British class system. A fashionable London audience recognised Aubrey Tanqueray's drawing room as a faithful reflection of their own, and equally recognised Paula as a woman who would never knowingly be invited into it, but such instant affinity and understanding might be more difficult for Americans.

All these considerations weighed on the company, and particularly on Amadine, in the days leading up to the first night. A shorter rehearsal period had been allocated to *Tanqueray* than that spent on *Caesar*, because the cast was smaller and most had played their parts before. Of the seven men, only three newly recruited Americans were unfamiliar with the play and they were taking the smallest roles. Two of the four women were being played by Americans: Gwendoline Hughes was a natural for Mrs Cortelyon, while Blanche Villard was making an excellent job of vulgar Lady Orreyed – 'flaxen, five and twenty, and feebly frolicsome' – even her version of a common prostitute trying to talk like an English lady being little short of miraculous. No, the Americans were doing fine. It was the English actress playing Ellean, Aubrey Tanqueray's daughter, who was giving cause for concern. The girl had not attempted the part before and was falling short of expectations; Ellean was innocent, but not insipid; she was a convent girl, but not colourless; she had experienced nothing of real life, but that didn't mean she had no character or personality.

Amadine was worried but, on the day that she was opening in *Tanqueray*, she had to devote precious rehearsal time to traipsing downtown to Tiffany's on Fifth Avenue. She had resented this – picking out 'baubles for the Christmas tree', as she sarcastically expressed it – and was surprised, and rather ashamed, when she enjoyed it. Such luxuries had never been top of her priorities, or within her compass. In London she had walked past Garrards or Aspreys without a pang, but now she was hypnotised by the precious stones that nestled in velvet, winked at her from sumptuous display cases or lay – cold at first, but with increasing warmth – against her skin.

Diamonds were Jay's first consideration – 'showiest stones of all, especially for the stage' – and they chose a necklace, bracelet and earrings to wear in *Tanqueray*. They dithered over a choice of emeralds or sapphires, then took both. Finally, pearls really seemed essential and the extra expense could not possibly make much difference to the total cost.

She was only hiring, not buying, the jewellery, but when she saw the boxes accumulating on the counter, Amadine panicked. 'Where can I keep them?'

'In the safe at the hotel,' Jay answered patiently.

'And when we are on the train?'

'Oh, there's bound to be a safe or some such in the Palace Car.'

'You will insure them?'

'Of course. Stop worrying.'

At the theatre, dressed and made up for her first entrance, Amadine was sick again, even though she had eaten next to nothing all day. Why do I put myself through this, she wondered, staring at her ashen face in the mirror? There have to be easier ways of making a living! Perhaps if I had been properly trained, it would be easier? If only acting was more mechanical, and I could merely turn on the talent like a tap and be certain that it would be there when it was needed. Instead of worrying that it wouldn't be there; worrying that I will go out on to the stage and find that I cannot do it – because I don't know how I do it. I don't know where *it*, the magic, comes from.

A visit from Laurie steadied her. It always did, and Amadine was beginning to realise just how much she depended on him. Taller than Hal and more heavily built, the fair-haired, blue-eyed Laurence Knight was a hugely popular artist. The female admirers of the two men tended to debate at length the vexed question of whether Hal was more handsome than Laurie, or vice versa. No conclusion was ever reached because the contest was between two very different types: the noble, refined beauty of Hal versus the clean-cut features and flashing matinée-idol smile of

Laurie. His acting ability was comparable to Hal's as well, but their personal lives were very different. The female conquests of both men were legion, but whereas Hal pursued his theatrical connections, and his leading ladies in particular, Laurie kept business and pleasure strictly separate. To everyone's astonishment, he had not made an exception for Amadine and this had the advantage of making her feel safe and relaxed with him. Forty years old, although he did not look it, and immensely experienced, his presence at her side balanced her own insecurity. To Amadine he was like an oak tree with roots planted firmly in the profession, who could withstand any storm and under whose branches she could shelter. As long as Laurie was beside her, she was safe.

Her first entrance came near the end of Act I, subjecting her to a long wait without Laurie, who was onstage throughout. Then she was on, throwing her arms around Laurie's neck, and crying, 'Dearest!' A huge wave of applause greeted her, and she and Laurie paused while it broke over them. Looking incomparably beautiful in the first of her sumptuous gowns – gorgeously beaded violet satin, which at the end of the scene she covered with a matching cloak bordered with violet ostrich feathers, and which she had teamed with her new sapphires – Amadine stood within the circle of Laurie's arms and waited until they could continue. The admiration and goodwill of the audience were almost tangible and boded well.

In Act II she wore a charming dove-grey day-dress and the pearls, at one point adding a black cloak banded and collared with sable, and a black hat. It was an act that displayed Paula's emotional fragility to the full and one during which Amadine lived on the edge, trying to show why Paula was so discourteous to Mrs Cortelyon, why she resented the removal of her stepdaughter from the house and why she threatened to return to her old life. The ovation as she left the stage was an indication that she had succeeded.

And then, for Acts III and IV, she slipped into her favourite *Tanqueray* dress of pale old-gold silk, cut square and low at the neck with elbow-length sleeves trimmed with ivory lace, tucked tight at the waist and across her hips, before draping into a lace-edged skirt and billowing back into a train. Worn with her diamonds, and with her hair piled into a chignon that became more and more errant and untidy as the play wore on, the effect was unforgettable. When the time came, when one of Paula's former 'protectors' reappeared as Ellean Tanqueray's fiancé, the situation was clear and terrible. The audience understood perfectly Aubrey's dilemma, for how could a man choose between his virtuous daughter and so glorious a creature as Paula? And, to this audience at least, Paula was real and she was a heroine – flawed, yes, but a heroine.

When Aubrey tried to encourage Paula by talking about the future, and about forgetting the past, Amadine uttered what to many was the most telling line of the play: 'I believe the future is only the past again, entered through another gate', and the audience shuddered. And they shuddered again when she killed herself. Stella Campbell had committed suicide out of sight of the audience, but Amadine did it onstage and, as Ellean said, it was 'horrible'.

Taking the applause, Amadine knew that she had not given a great performance but it had been adequate. More important, the magic had worked. That invisible link between her and the audience had been there from the start. If nothing else, she had held their attention.

Even so, it wasn't quite enough. The audience had loved every minute. The critics loved Amadine but disliked the play, and even their generous praise of the star held faint undertones of: 'Well, she is the best thing in it, but that isn't saying much.' The play was thin, they sniffed, and without Miss Sinclair's astonishing performance, *Tanqueray* would be a paltry vehicle indeed. And when they dilated on Amadine's portrayal of the woman with the less-than-spotless past, there was a hint that this was not real acting but, probably, an actress playing herself.

Failure was too strong a word for the opening of the tour. The theatre-going public of New York flocked to see Amadine, and filled the theatre every night she performed. But when Hal took stock of the situation, he knew that they had fallen so far short of the success they needed that something drastic had to be done.

At the Columbia Theatre in San Francisco, the issue of the *New York Times* containing the extensive feature on Amadine and Hal was passed from hand to hand in the greenroom and excited much comment. The pictures in particular were admired and the relationship between the handsome couple was discussed at length, the consensus being that undoubtedly they were 'close' and would soon make the attachment official.

Only one man, a newcomer to the company, failed to join in the general, and rather ribald, conversation. As soon as the names of Amadine Sinclair and Edward Haldane-Smith were mentioned, he had gone very still, freezing in the act of turning the page of another publication. No one noticed. He was comparatively junior in the hierarchy here, one of those jobbing actors who made up the numbers, filled the minor roles and never made it to the top, and as such he was hardly the focus of attention.

However, it said something for his acting talent that he was able to conceal his emotions, to continue perusing the paper he was holding and to await his turn with the New York journal with apparent equanimity and disinterest. When he did look at the relevant page, the picture of Amadine seemed to leap out at him with a three-dimensional effect and he could have drowned in that lovely face, last seen by him on a London stage three years ago.

His heart was racing uncomfortably with excitement. To be honest, he had not thought about her much recently, and he was beginning to think that he might be over her. Perhaps it was the unexpected shock of hearing her name that had brought on this reaction but, whatever the reason, the old obsession was still there and he could feel it expanding within him, ready to take over his life.

Lifting his eyes from the newspaper, he glanced round the room and had consciously to suppress an urge to inform these second-rate nobodies that Amadine Sinclair did not belong with Hal. She belonged with him – if only he could convince her . . . If only he could speak to her . . .

A visit to the offices of the local newspaper produced a copy of the Smith-Sinclair tour itinerary, with dates. There were advantages in being so insignificant that he was not required to sign a contract; after he had worked out his notice, he could reach Boston in time.

Chapter Four

Constance Grey knew that she was pretty enough, with her pale fair hair coiled neatly at her neck, her wide-set grey-blue eyes and ivory complexion, but hers was the subdued demureness of a Quakeress when contrasted with the vividness of her rival. However, comparing herself to Amadine was just what she mustn't do. Frank had said once, in connection with theatrical opinion, that everything reacts to New York – sometimes against it, true, but always *to* New York. Amadine was like that. The centre of attention; possibly the centre of the bloody universe.

The more she thought about it, the more Constance saw Amadine in terms of New York. Constance hated the place. Not only was she homesick for London and her family, but she sensed that she did not belong here, and never would. This was not her kind of environment. She was not New York's sort of person. New York was not attuned to the sick-at-heart, to the tired and defeated, to those who looked older than their years. If, like Amadine, you possessed youth and energy, Manhattan would allow you along for the ride, but even then it demanded your complete participation; relax for an instant, and New York would drop you like a stone. Constance was too mature and world-weary to conquer New York, or even keep up with it. All she could do was remind herself that New York was not America, and there were other places on their itinerary that might appreciate her more. Yes, it was cruel when Amadine received rave notices and she, Constance, was dismissed in a few polite words or, even more galling, not mentioned at all, but it did not mean that Boston or Philadelphia would be so easily seduced.

Talking of seducing . . . Hal had never given any sign of wanting her, not in *that* way. He was always friendly and affectionate, helpful with her work and understanding about her family responsibilities, but in the twenty-one months they had been together, he had never tried to sleep with her. Knowing his reputation, Constance had been surprised, but not averse to being treated with respect. She had believed that her position as his leading lady was impregnable and that if she continued to act with him, Hal would drift into marriage with her, if only because it was the obvious and inevitable thing to do. Only after Amadine arrived on the scene did Constance detect the fatal flaw in her plan. Only then did she see that Hal might, after all, be capable of a grand passion.

Constance was not strong on passion. She had met Everett Grey when she was fifteen years old, a petite pale-skinned girl with slender limbs and small breasts. Being innocent of life, it had not struck her as odd that a 45-year-old bachelor should want to possess her choice young flesh, but perhaps her mother ought to have been wiser and more protective. Admittedly her mother did persuade Grey to wait for Constance's sixteenth birthday, but on that day she witnessed the transformation of a kindly father figure – something that had been sadly lacking in her life – into rapacious lust. She endured it. She had no choice but to endure it. By the time she reached New York, Constance had been a widow for five years, but the experience of her married life had left her with no eagerness to share another man's bed. It was not physical attraction that drew her to Hal but her need for security – emotional and financial, personal and professional – for herself and her children. Constance picked up two framed photographs, of eleven-year-old Katie and nine-year-old Charlie, and pressed her lips to the glass. For their sakes, she must not give up.

But in the mirror she saw a depressing reflection of a tired-looking woman, older than her twenty-nine years – damn it, she was only two years older than Amadine! – and, there being not the slightest doubt in her mind where Hal's affections lay, that face in the mirror underlined the inevitability of his choice. Of course it would be comforting to blame Amadine, but Constance was no fool and was prepared to admit that, as things stood at present, Hal's feelings were unrequited. But how long would this state of affairs last? Amadine must fall in love with him eventually. Given Hal's looks, his eminence in the profession, his personal talent and pleasant personality, how could anyone not love him?

She was gnawed by jealousy, and frantic with worry. If she lost Hal, she lost everything – her job, as well as her hopes for the future. There was some comfort in the fact that Amadine could not encroach on her theatrical life, that her roles in the repertoire were safe and that onstage at least Hal was hers. And there was a grain of satisfaction in remembering that if her notices had been poor, someone else's had been even worse. Knowing that this tour was make-or-break for her and Hal, and that she had to fight for him, Constance began to see the glimmer of an idea. Rummaging in her capacious brown handbag, she produced the small accounts book that went everywhere with her. In this, each pay day, she entered the amount of her weekly salary and noted the sum she wired to London for the children's maintenance, household expenses and a little extra for emergencies. The accounts were neat and meticulous. Constance knew, to the last penny, exactly how much she had earned, how it had been spent and how much she had left.

Care with money had been instilled in her since child-hood. Her father had walked out on the family when Constance and her sisters were small, and her mother's only source of income had been the rents from a few slum properties. All too often Constance, as the eldest child, was sent to collect these rents, an experience that had frightened her but also focused her mind on money and its impor-tance, and hardened her to what must be done to obtain it. She and her mother agreed to the marriage with Everett Grey because he was a well-to-do playwright. The rude awakening Constance suffered on her wedding night was bad enough, but the discovery that Everett was not nearly as wealthy as she had believed was as bitter, and the resent-ment lasted longer.

After careful scrutiny of the balance in the accounts book, and considerable hesitation, Constance set off downtown to the shopping area on Broadway known as Ladies' Mile in order to buy a new dress, and then hurried back to the hotel to put it on, do her hair and coax a little colour into her cheeks. Next she opened her travelling trunk, empty of clothes now but still containing photographs of her hus-band and numerous bundles of typewritten papers – the manuscripts of Everett Grey's plays, the copyrights to which had been his only bequest to his widow and chil-dren.

Everett Grey had the luck to have a huge hit with his very first play; his tragedy was that he had never been able to reproduce the quality of that work. Two other plays had achieved moderate success but, when he married Constance, he was relying heavily on adaptations. He also relied heavily on the bottle and, when his health began to fail, he worked less and less until finally he did no work at all. Steeling her-self to beg for work, just as ten years earlier she had steeled herself to collect the rents, the 21-year-old Constance trailed round the London theatres, asking managers who knew her husband to find a place for her. Eventually she was taken on as an understudy at four pounds a month. Through hard work and determination, matters had improved since then, but Constance never relaxed her vigilance over her financial affairs, and she never ceased to look upon Everett's plays as a possible source of income.

Constance selected four manuscripts and went to Hal's suite.

A bemused Hal stared at her as she was shown into the room. He shared the suite with his brother but, as Constance had hoped, Frank was busy at the theatre and Hal was alone. Seeing Constance in a charming blue silk gown with her hair swept up into a gleaming chignon, he gaped at the transformation. He, too, suddenly remembered that she was only twenty-nine. The trouble with Constance was – or had been – that one saw her with a daughter aged eleven, and thought of her as being in her mid- to late thirties.

'Connie, you look stunning. New York suits you.'

'I don't think New York, as such, had anything to do with it.' Constance sat down on a chair opposite him. 'I miss the children dreadfully but the fact remains that, for the first time in my life, today I had nothing and no one to think about but myself. I found it an immensely novel and liberating experience, and bought a new dress to celebrate.'

Hal smiled approvingly, but then saw the manuscripts and groaned. This would not be the first time that Constance had produced Grey's work for his perusal and possible resurrection, and he was running out of ways of saying no nicely. To think that she had carted that mouldering pile of garbage across the Atlantic . . .

'Is this a bad moment for a chat?' Constance asked. 'You look frightfully busy.'

Hastily Hal gathered up the papers strewn on the sofa and on the floor around his feet. He was busy, extremely so, preparing an announcement to the company for tomorrow morning concerning some intended cast changes. The courteous course of action would be to discuss these changes with Constance, among others, in private before making a public announcement, but he had decided against doing so. Constance would not like what he had to say, but she was too much of a lady to throw a tantrum in front of her subordinates. However, the knowledge of what lay in store made him feel at a disadvantage over the manuscripts.

'I cannot stay long,' he said apprehensively. 'I'm leaving for the theatre in a few minutes.'

'Perhaps I could have a private word tonight, after the performance,' she suggested optimistically, envisaging a romantic *tête-à-tête*.

'I'm going to the Players' Club with Laurie.'

'You men and your clubs.' Constance shook her head playfully. 'Everett was exactly the same. If he wasn't at the Garrick, it was a good bet he was at the Savage, until . . .' Her voice trailed away.

Until he ran out of money, and succumbed to cirrhosis of the liver. Oh dear . . . 'The Players' Club is special,' Hal said conversationally. 'Laurie and I enjoy catching up with a lot of fellows whom we don't often see. And the premises were a gift from Booth, who died in his rooms on the top floor, so we like to pay our respects.'

'I could wait up.'

'No, I'll be tired,' he said hastily. 'Connie, if this is about Everett's plays, I really haven't changed my mind since the last occasion we discussed them.'

'Oh, those.' And Constance dismissed the manuscripts with a casual wave of her hand. 'We'll come to them in a moment, but first I have something much more important to discuss.'

Something more important than Everett's plays? There really had to be something in the New York air, or the water perhaps, that was having a remarkable effect on her.

'I have a suggestion to make regarding a possible cast

change,' Constance said in a businesslike tone, 'but you must tell me to shut up and mind my own business if I'm trespassing on other people's territory.'

'I'd be delighted to hear what you have to say.'

'One must admit that poor Ellean in *Tanqueray* did not escape unscathed from the critics.'

'That's the understatement of the century! She was so upset that she had to be virtually dragged onstage for the next performance, and her efforts in that performance were even worse than before.'

'I know. I was there – unfortunately. Hal, far be it for me to push myself forward, but would you like me to take over the role?'

'You?' Hal gaped at her. He did not know what he had been expecting, but certainly not this.

'You've forgotten.' Constance shook her head in mock reproach. 'I took over as Ellean – from Maude Millett – in the original London production of *Tanqueray* and, after watching all the rehearsals and performances here, I think I'm pretty much word perfect. One rehearsal with Amadine and the others and I would be ready. Of course I appreciate that it would be only polite to ask Amadine's approval . . .'

Thank God she raised that point and, once he was over the shock, Hal felt a real enthusiasm for the idea. 'I'll speak to her, but are you sure that this additional responsibility won't be too much for you? It means that you will be appearing in five out of the six productions.'

'So is Laurie,' Constance returned briskly, 'and he has much more to do in *Caesar* than I have. Honestly, Shakespeare was less than fair when he wrote that play. You fellows get to strut around and spout wonderful speeches, while Gwen and I shuffle on, say a few words – a very few words – and shuffle off again. It isn't tiring, if that is what is worrying you and, after all, what else do I have to do? A night away from the theatre would be welcome if I were at home, but here I'll sit in the hotel or go to the theatre anyway. I might as well work, particularly if my contribution helps the box office.'

'Spoken like a true professional.'

Constance smiled. That was exactly the effect she was aiming to achieve. She would show Hal her businesslike, professional side and soon he would be relying on her in all sorts of ways; soon she would be absolutely indispensable, and he would see what a perfect partner she would be. And a cool hand at the professional helm could easily become a cool hand on a fevered brow . . .

'Another thing,' Constance went on. 'I'm worried that Frank is trying to do too much, taking on Tom's duties as well as his own. Do remember that I have plenty of experience with accounts and financial matters, and would be happy to assist in that area.'

'I'll mention it. Thank you, Connie.'

'And now one last thing.' Constance leaned forward with an air of confidentiality. 'I'm very much afraid that you will think I am treading on your toes, but I have to say that I am worried about the content of the repertoire. The Shakespeare and Pinero are fine, but reaction to *The Physician* has been disappointing, and I really do fear that the Robertson will seem dated.'

Startled, Hal ensured that the papers he had been working on were tucked out of sight. If Constance had not read them, she must have read his mind.

'I believe we ought to think about introducing a new play if public reaction does not improve,' Constance was saying, 'and in those circumstances it could be useful to consider reviving *Lilac Blossoms*.' She patted the manuscript on top of the pile.

In Hal's opinion *Lilac Blossoms*, Grey's only hit, had been done to death and he had never liked it much anyway. 'I don't think so, Connie. Sorry, my dear, but it was written twenty-five years ago and I doubt it would transplant to the States.'

'*The Golden Apple* was produced here,' Constance said eagerly.

'I will bear it in mind, and I see you have brought *Three Guineas* as well . . .' Apt, thought Hal, because he knew that Constance needed the money such productions would bring in. As he recalled, Everett Grey had not sold the rights to his work outright, but preferred to be paid for each performance. What would Connie receive these days? Two pounds a night up to two hundred pounds, probably, and it wouldn't matter what she negotiated over and above that figure, because none of Grey's outdated stuff would play for a hundred nights. 'I'll think about it,' he said again, feeling too guilty about the axe he intended to wield the next day to refuse outright.

'I've spoken to Amadine,' Hal told Frank that night, 'and to the former Ellean, and it's all arranged. Connie will play Ellean at the next performance. So, you see, all your dire warnings were way off the mark: it is perfectly possible for two leading ladies to work together for the good of the company as a whole.'

Frank gave his brother a sceptical look, being far from convinced that all was sweetness and light in that direction. 'And you escaped from the encounter with Connie with your virtue intact?'

'Funny you should say that, because I often feel that she is likely to pounce. One would have thought that, by now, she would realise that I'm not interested.' Hal wondered why he wasn't interested. Partly it was because she had seemed older than him, and partly because he had been involved elsewhere when he began working with Constance and, by the time that affair was over, Constance had turned into his sister. She simply did not excite him physically. And professionally, with an ambitious eye on the future, Hal felt he could do better. Professionally, and physically, he had his eye on Amadine.

'By the way,' he called to Frank, his brother having disappeared into the bathroom, 'Connie wants to help you with the accounts.'

'She wants to *what* . . .?' Frank shot out of the bathroom, wiping his face on a towel. 'You didn't say that she could, did you?'

'Of course not. It's your decision, but she has a point when she says that you have taken on too much. Perhaps you should think . . .'

'I've thought,' snapped Frank, 'and the answer is thanks, but no thanks. And if I need any help, I'll ask for it.'

'Sorry, sorry . . .' Hal threw up his hands defensively.

Realising that his over-reaction might arouse suspicion, Frank made a conscious effort to calm down and smoothly changed the subject. 'Did you discuss the other changes with Amadine or Constance?' When Hal shook his head, Frank smiled grimly. 'Coward.'

'It occurred to me that this Ellean business played right into my hands – well, you'll see what I mean in the morning.'

Next day the company – except for the former Ellean, who was given permission to stay away – assembled on the stage, as ordered by a notice pinned to the board by Frank. A few chairs had been set out for the principals, but everyone else was expected to stand. Hal began by announcing that Constance was taking over as Ellean, a move that evidently met with general approval, then he paused.

'This development set me thinking,' he said soberly, 'and the more I thought, the more it seemed to me that there were other changes that could work to our mutual benefit. I stayed up all night, wrestling with the problem, and I apologise most sincerely for springing this on everyone, but I only finalised things a few minutes ago.'

Bugger me, thought Frank as he hid a smile, I didn't know Hal had it in him. First rule of management: learn to lie well. And, boy, is he learning fast!

The plays to be performed in Boston, Hal announced, would be as planned: *Romeo and Juliet*, *Ours* and *Trelawny of the Wells*. Depending on the reception there, the existing repertoire would continue until Christmas, although he was seriously considering dropping *Julius Caesar*. After Christmas the position would be reviewed again, and the possibility was that a new play might be introduced – and here Hal acknowledged Constance with a slight but significant bow. If you don't like what I am about to say, that bow inferred, just remember that you started it.

'However, with immediate effect, there will be some cast changes.' That grabbed everyone's attention all right! Even Amadine looked startled, and Constance was visibly tense. 'With Amadine's consent, I want to take over the role of Arthur in *Trelawny*.' Hal looked apologetically at the crest-fallen young man whose part he had appropriated. 'Sorry – I'll compensate you with something better later on, and your salary will not be affected.'

It was lost on no one that Arthur was the lover of Rose Trelawny, played by Amadine, and was described as a 'handsome, boyish young man'. The wryest smile was Laurie's. Having hit forty, he had decided to mature grace-fully into the meatier and more interesting role of Tom Wrench, but was now calculating that he was only three years older than Hal and just as handsome.

'You'll need all the help you can get from the paints, dear boy,' he drawled, his smile widening into a grin.

Amadine was looking with dismay at her former partner who, clearly, was devastated. She could refuse Hal's request, because technically she retained control of *Trelawny*, but in her heart she knew Hal was right. His heavyweight presence in the cast would add immensely to the play's interest and impact.

'Very well,' she agreed guardedly.

One down, and two to go. 'With regard to *Ours*,' Hal went on, 'I don't think that the pairings are right. Laurie and I will retain the same roles, but I want Amadine and Constance to change over. We'll try it at the next rehearsal and see how it goes.'

This announcement was greeted in silence by the principals, and with nudges and winks by the company. The new arrangement of the two sets of lovers again paired Hal with Amadine, and Laurie with Constance. Amadine glanced at Gwen, who was smiling at her with an 'I told you so' expression, but did not dare look at Constance.

Uncomfortably aware that Constance was gazing at him with the stricken eyes of a wounded deer, Hal hurried on to his last, and most sensitive, point.

'There are no immediate cast changes to *Romeo* but I would like you, Amadine, to study Juliet. We could consider the possibility of you and Constance alternating the role.'

Constance went white. If anything, Amadine went even whiter.

'In due course,' Hal added hastily. 'No rush.'

Constance fled to her dressing room, where she contemplated her former belief that her relationship with Hal was safe as long as she retained her hold on their stage partnership. That hold had just weakened alarmingly. To be honest, there was not much difference in length or importance of the two roles in *Ours*, but being paired with Laurie instead of Hal mattered terribly. And to think of sharing Juliet . . . oh no, it was too much to bear!

Being taken in by Hal's subterfuge, Constance believed that she had only herself to blame. You fool, you should have left well alone, she thought, and was still thinking when Hal came into the room. For a moment she knew a brief spurt of hope: he had changed his mind, he had come to tell her that everything would be as it was before – in fact better than it was before . . . But no, he had come to tell her that it was highly unlikely he could use any of Everett's plays.

'You do understand,' Constance said bravely, 'that if you don't want the plays, I must offer them elsewhere.'

'Good idea,' Hal said, with a heartiness he did not feel, 'and I wish you the very best of luck.'

During the next few days, whenever she could be spared from the theatre, Constance was to be seen doing the rounds of New York theatre managers with the same iron-willed determination that had sustained her in her search for work in London eight years before. An infinitely gallant little figure in a navy-blue suit and shabby fur wrap, carrying a carpet bag full of manuscripts, she called on Augustin Daly at his theatre across Broadway from Wallack's, on Charles Frohman at the Empire and on his brother Daniel at the Lyceum; she braved Richard Mansfield, David Belasco, A.M. Palmer and Nat Goodwin. All doors opened quickly and courteously for Constance Grey of the Smith-Sinclair tour, but closed again with equal swiftness and civility when the reason for her visit became apparent.

There was still Boston, she thought, as she replaced the manuscripts in the trunk, and after that there was Philadelphia, and Chicago . . . She was not beaten yet, not by a long chalk, not by the manuscripts or by Amadine. This tour still had a long way to go, and she would fight for Hal, and for her children's future, every inch of the way.

Constance might have felt happier if she had witnessed Amadine's reaction to Hal's announcement.

'Help me, please,' Amadine begged, in Laurie's dressing room. 'You know that I can't do Shakespeare!'

'I know that you ought to try, darling, and I also know that you cannot avoid it indefinitely,' Laurie said firmly. 'Every actress . . .'

'Yes, yes, no one is a real actress until they have done Shakespeare.'

'You are frightened of trying in case you fail. But you

won't fail – you will be wonderful. And you will confound all those critics who are so blind, deaf and brain-dead that they see only your good looks and not your talent.'

Amadine tried to smile. 'I'll try to believe that – I'll cling to that thought in the dark watches of the night when I'm sleepless with the stress and strain. But what am I going to *do*?'

'Hal will be a big help, you know. Romeo is one of the best things he does. But, if it's any consolation, I'll coach you. We can work on Juliet's scenes, in private, until the verse is second nature to you.'

Amadine's face lit up, and she threw her arms around his neck. 'Darling Laurie, you are my rock! Promise that you will never leave me!'

Laurie laughed. 'I don't know where you think I'm likely to go. You're stuck with me until next June, remember.'

Chapter Five

The lounge of the Lawyers' Club, in the Equitable Building at 120 Broadway between Pine and Cedar, was an impressive room, its immense piers supporting a vaulted roof decorated in white filigree work. At the base of every pillar was a square of banquette seats, each with its own corner table on which stood a lamp, cigarettes and matches, plus a call-bell. Seeing an arm waving to him from the middle of the room, Pierce Radcliffe negotiated an avenue of cream carpet, shook hands with his host and sat down.

'How is the bicycle business?' Oliver Morton was a youthful-looking thirty-four – the same age as Pierce – with curly dark hair and an attractive air of relaxed confidence. 'Still turning them out by the hundred, I hope?'

'By the thousand,' Pierce assured him. 'I was at the factory in Chicago last week, passing on a few refinements I heard about in England, but I'm not really needed on the manufacturing side any more.'

'Not much change in bicycle design, then?'

Pierce shook his head. 'I started at exactly the right time, eight years ago when Dunlop introduced the pneumatic rubber tyre, and the "safety" bicycle has stayed much the same ever since.'

'I thought we'd go downstairs to the Savarin for lunch,' Oliver suggested. 'My treat.'

Pierce eyed him warily. 'Most kind, but is this inquisition likely to last as long as lunch? Because if so . . .'

'Inquisition! My dear fellow, all I want to do . . .'

'I know exactly what you want to do. When I saw your father in Chicago, he made it crystal clear that he expected you to succeed where he had failed!'

The Café Savarin was a restaurant situated in the basement of the Equitable Building and, being but a block north of Wall Street, was patronised by businessmen, who could enjoy their meal while keeping an eye on the ticker-tape machine installed in the bar. The hour being comparatively early, the two men were allocated a table without delay and threaded their way across the room, Oliver stopping from time to time to exchange a greeting with an acquaintance.

'So,' he said as he sat down, 'have you raised the finance for this motor-car scheme of yours?'

Pierce glowered. 'The Vanderbilts imported some machines this summer – I'm bringing over a Panhard from France for myself, by the way – and people like Olds, the Duryeas and Henry Ford have turned out some fairly basic prototypes. It's obvious that car manufacturing is going to be a licence to print money, but everyone I approach is being damnably short-sighted. They keep turning me down flat. Same story everywhere I go. Everyone says the same thing.'

'Everyone says, "Why don't you use your own money?"' Oliver remarked conversationally.

'As a matter of fact, they do. And I keep telling them that the bicycle business is doing jolly nicely, thank you, but it is completely unrealistic to expect it to finance . . .'

'Stop being deliberately obtuse – you know as well as I do that bicycles have bugger all to do with it. These fellows have railroad money on their minds. Any financier worth his salt, in Wall Street or anywhere else, is well aware that you are worth millions.'

A shuttered look came over Pierce's face. He took a slug of whisky and leaned back in his chair, folding his arms defensively and staring past his companion's head at some object in the middle distance. This meeting was turning out exactly as he had expected. Oliver was the son of Howard Morton, one of Chicago's most eminent lawyers, who had handled the affairs of Pierce's late father for years and had grilled Pierce on this same subject only a few days before.

'They know that you are Samuel Radcliffe's son,' Oliver continued inexorably, 'and that he made a fortune from rolling stock – sleeping cars, to be precise. They know that when he died six years ago, apart from the obligatory legacy to your mother, you were his sole heir.'

'I have been saying this for six years but, as it appears both you and your father are hard of hearing, I will say it again: I will not take a cent of my father's money.'

'You see,' the other man continued thoughtfully, as if indeed he had not heard Pierce's remark, 'these financiers are entitled to be dubious about the kind of proposition you are putting to them. If you won't risk your own money, why should they risk theirs?'

'Even if I did use Father's money, I would still need additional finance.'

'You think so? With my old man handling your father's estate, I have the advantage over these rather nebulous financiers. I know exactly how much money you could lay your hands on.' Oliver paused and leaned forward. 'Four and a half million dollars, Pierce,' he said quietly but with considerable emphasis. 'I reckon you could build a fair few motor cars with that, don't you?'

Pierce did not reply, but he looked startled and his gaze swivelled from that point in the middle distance to his friend's face.

'Didn't you realise that the sum was so large? Well, I suppose I shouldn't be surprised at your ignorance,' and

Oliver gave a mock sigh, 'seeing that you never reply to Dad's letters and only sign something when he or I restrain you forcibly until you comply.'

'I do realise that I am putting your father in a difficult position, but . . .'

'Dad can look after himself,' Oliver cut in quickly, 'but why put yourself in a difficult position? Why not use the money to make your dream come true? For what it's worth, I believe you would make a terrific success of such a venture. Obviously transport runs in the family – trains, bicycles and now cars, it would be a logical progression. You could set up a factory in Chicago, or perhaps in Philadelphia – I know that you have business interests there as well. Why not Wilmington? I seem to remember that your father started out there, with Harlan and Hollingsworth, so it would be a neat case of the wheel coming full circle.'

'I will never use his money.' Pierce said it very slowly but with the most intense determination.

'Did you hate him that much?'

'Yes.'

'Do you want to tell me why?'

'No.'

After a short silence, the other man sighed again. 'There is only one cure for such obstinacy. You need a wife. No woman would let a fortune of that magnitude lie unspent and unappreciated in the cold, dark confines of my father's safe!'

'Any woman whom I married would have to love me for myself alone,' Pierce declared, with a smile.

'Then I fear you are doomed to be a bachelor. Mind you, doomed might not be the right word. Marriage can end in tears, as can plays about marriage. Have you seen this *Tanqueray* thing that's the talk of the town.'

'I've been away,' Pierce prevaricated.

'My wife and I are going this evening. Why not join us?

Can't offer you a ticket, unfortunately, but you might pick up a single seat at one of the agencies and you could dine with us. Do try!'

'I'll think about it . . .'

In the afternoon Pierce's business took him uptown, and it was at about 4 p.m. that he turned into the cigar stand at an hotel on Broadway and 43rd Street. He purchased a packet of cigars, but hesitated before leaving the shop. On the wall, beside the displays of smoking materials, were a number of theatre posters and a bank of five telephones, while emblazoned on the dark mahogany panelling were the words 'McBride's Theatre Ticket Office'. One of the posters bore a large picture of a familiar face, and advertised: 'Amadine Sinclair in *The Second Mrs Tanqueray*. Also starring Laurence Knight and Gwendoline Hughes'. Then there were several other names in smaller print, prominent among them Blanche Villard. Pierce's gaze lingered on the poster for a long time but, as he requested a ticket for the evening performance, he told himself firmly that it was only out of curiosity and because, quite coincidentally, he happened to be in the shop.

He was often in New York but, being a man who did not want the responsibility of maintaining a permanent residence there, he had opted to stay in one of the apartment hotels that were springing up in the city. Home, to which he repaired to change and to telephone Oliver regarding dinner arrangements, was the Hotel San Remo at 145 Central Park West, just north of the Dakota. Here he occupied a comfortable suite that was constantly at his disposal yet required no attention on his part while he was away on his frequent forays around America and Europe. It contained a complete wardrobe and, as Pierce kept another set of clothes at his Chicago home and yet another at his mother's English mansion in Oxfordshire, he was able to do most of his travelling unencumbered by excess baggage.

Taking his seat in Wallack's auditorium, Pierce was glad to be alone; if his feelings got the better of him, he could leave without too many questions being asked. And indeed he was surprised at the disquiet and tenseness he experienced as he waited for the curtain to rise. He tried to channel his thoughts along familiar lines, staring at a Siegel Cooper advertisement in the programme that announced: 'Prices always the lowest. Swell clothes – Swell people'. Perhaps 'swell bicycles' would sell well – theatre advertising was not an avenue he had explored. But even that failed to hold his attention and, when the curtain rose, Pierce waited in an agony of anticipation for his first glimpse of Amadine Sinclair, and for his first sight of the person who had done such irreparable harm to him and his family.

The extraordinary thing was that, having taken that initial step, he could not keep away. After avoiding the theatre all his life, Pierce now attended Wallack's nearly every night, and his next encounter with Amadine was no coincidence. He followed her from the hotel one morning, expecting her to head for the theatre, but instead she set off at a brisk pace down Fifth Avenue, covering the seven blocks to Madison Square Park so swiftly that even Pierce's powerful legs were hard pressed to keep up. At 26th Street she took a short detour to look at the Madison Square Garden building, shading her eyes against the sun as she peered up at Saint-Gaudens's figure of Diana atop the tower, before striding off again along Broadway. Intrigued, Pierce kept pace behind her. With a veil over her face, she evidently believed that she went unnoticed although in fact her height, the elegance of her costume and the grace of that long, lissom stride were causing every head to turn in her direction.

At Union Square she slowed down and began ambling along in a manner that appeared to indicate she had reached her destination. A couple of decades ago this had been the heart of the theatre district, not only because of the number of theatres clustered in the locality, but also because it harboured many of the supporting activities of theatrical production. To some extent it still did, and Amadine lingered by the windows of wigmakers and costumiers, printers and publishers, before entering Brentano's bookshop. Her absorption in the books was obviously genuine. At one point she asked for assistance or advice from one of the staff, which resulted in her nodding and keeping hold of the book offered for her inspection, but she continued to gaze longingly at the shelves.

'As, during our previous discussion, you seemed to have all the facts about America at your fingertips, I assume you are looking for fiction,' Pierce remarked, politely raising his hat.

Startled by his sudden appearance, Amadine took a moment to reply. 'For such a large person, in such a big city, you do have a remarkable propensity for popping up unexpectedly! But, as you're here, you may as well tell me if you approve of my choice.'

The book in her hand was *The Country of the Pointed Firs* by Sarah Orne Jewett, and Pierce was forced to confess his ignorance of the work.

'I hadn't heard of her before, either,' Amadine said happily, 'but now I look forward immensely to making her acquaintance.'

'You must be thirsty after your long walk. Would you care to join me for some refreshment?'

At this display of knowledge of her morning's activities, Amadine cast him a sharp, sideways glance, but she refrained from comment and merely accepted his invitation.

'Could we go to a drugstore?' she asked eagerly, after she had paid for the book and they had left the shop. 'I've been longing to see a soda fountain, but Hal has been such a slave-driver I was beginning to think I would never have the opportunity.'

Edward Haldane-Smith, and Laurence Knight, had showed to such advantage on the stage that Pierce had begun to wonder about their personal relationships with Amadine. Judging by the reaction of the women around him in the audience, the extraordinarily handsome faces, well-built bodies and beautifully modulated voices of the two men were more than enough to reduce the entire female sex to a state of swooning ecstasy, without any additional input by way of intelligence or personality. Pierce had taken little interest in theatrical affairs, but even he was aware of the accepted opinion on the relationship between an actor and his leading lady – why, those in the know hinted thrillingly that even Henry Irving and Ellen Terry were, or had been . . . Therefore, in Pierce's mind, it was not whether or not Amadine was conducting an affair, but merely which man was the recipient of her favours. She had known Laurence Knight longer, he gathered, but in his opinion Haldane-Smith had more to offer.

'I love Broadway, don't you!' Amadine exclaimed, spontaneously taking his arm as they walked along.

Pierce glanced around him at the streetcars, the horse-drawn carriages and wagons in the road, at the buildings of varied height and doubtful architectural merit that lined each side of the street, at the billboards and shop signs that advertised anything from steamship tickets to painless dentistry, and at the crowds of New Yorkers hurrying along the sidewalk. Love Broadway? Well, it was okay in its way but as far as he was concerned, and he conceded that he was prejudiced, it wasn't a patch on State Street in Chicago.

'I love the way it snakes through Manhattan,' and Amadine gave a wriggle of her hips that mesmerised the immediate passers-by, 'and links New York's past with its present, and perhaps its future! And it passes through all the different districts of the city – the financial and residential, mercantile and manufacturing, amusement and artistic –

but most of all, I love the fact that the theatre has made its home here.'

'Probably because it was paved and well lit, and safe for people to walk along in the evening,' Pierce said, in a deflating tone of practicality. 'Not to mention the first-class transport systems that have always operated here.'

Amadine refused to be dragged down to his prosaic level. 'But Broadway is romantic, in the very best sense of the word. If you stop and listen and feel,' and she paused in the middle of the sidewalk, pulling on his arm to stay his progress, 'you can sense the vibrations in the air. This is the creative pulse of America.'

Pierce stopped and listened and tried to feel, but all he heard was the traffic and all he felt was a fool.

'Philistine,' mocked Amadine, but she laughed and didn't seem to mind.

Like most of its kind, the drugstore was decked out in figured marble and onyx and, in this establishment, the long, gleaming counter was decorated with crystal-fringed lamps on marble pedestals. Amadine watched, entranced, as her sundae was prepared and, leaving his own simple soda largely untouched, Pierce watched with equal enjoyment as she consumed it.

'We leave for Boston at the end of the week,' she said between mouthfuls, 'but already I'm looking forward to coming back here and eating another of these. And I'll sit in the roof garden at the hotel again, too, only next time I'll watch the sun set.'

'New Yorkers don't watch sunsets. An indolent and comparatively pointless exercise, you see, that brings no immediate reward or tangible gain.'

'Everyone is too busy,' Amadine agreed. 'I have an impression of constant movement, and yet there is a temporary feel to everything, as if the office block being built today will be torn down next year.'

'There is no room for nostalgia in New York. Space is at

such a premium that even the most historic or charming building may have to make way for one that is more useful.'

'Being new doesn't necessarily make something better.'

And suddenly Amadine remembered that she was 'new' to New York, but that it had not been enough to bring the overwhelming, uncritical success she sought. That sensation of movement, of nothing lasting, extended beyond the finite landscape of bricks and mortar around her to the fleeting world of fads and fashions, and in her mind's eye she saw New York society surging forward, leaving behind a trampled morass of yesterday's darlings and yesterday's news. Today she was the popular favourite but, without the respect of the critics and her peers, she could soon be forgotten.

'This isn't a place in which I would like to fail,' she murmured, with a shiver of apprehension.

'You haven't failed.'

'No, but we haven't been an unqualified success, either. Fortunately we did well enough to be given the benefit of the doubt, and will be allowed a second chance when we come back in May.'

'What makes a play succeed or fail?'

Amadine looked at him in astonishment, and then burst out laughing. 'If I knew the answer to that, I wouldn't be sitting here with you – I'd be buying up a chain of theatres, organising a string of companies to put on nothing but successful shows, and preparing to become very rich indeed! Who knows what the magic ingredient is,' and she gave an expressive shrug. 'Audiences are notoriously fickle, and the most impeccably prepared and researched show can end up in Cain's Warehouse – that's a place which stores scenery, by the way, and it has become a euphemism for closing a Broadway show.'

'Presumably there are some surprising successes as well.'

'*The Devil's Disciple* is an excellent example. It opened here two weeks ago, and seats cannot be had for love or money, but I watched the rehearsals and had grave reservations about it. Beneath the religious veneer, the play is an old-fashioned, rip-roaring melodrama.'

'The star of the play must be sufficiently popular to carry it off,' Pierce suggested.

'Oh, Richard Mansfield has a loyal and enthusiastic following, but the real reason for the play's success is that it is by George Bernard Shaw and therefore, in some eyes, it must be original and brilliant. Anyway, all that is by the bye. I merely used it as an example to illustrate the fact that I am a rotten judge.'

'What made you choose acting as a profession?'

'I didn't – acting chose me. And sometimes I wish that it hadn't, while at other times I know that I could not imagine doing anything else.'

'Is your family connected with the theatre in any way?'

'Only through me, and one couldn't honestly say that they are best pleased about it.' Her tone left little doubt that this was a piece of classic English understatement.

'But your name is so unusual that it must have been contrived for an actress!'

'Amadine, and the Sinclair part, is my real name. My mother saw it on a tombstone at home. Being a rector's wife, she didn't have much to read except tombstones and the Bible!' and she laughed lightly. 'I'm afraid that my mother remains an incurable romantic. My theory is that she wanted to call my brothers Leander and Valentine, but Father stood firm and forced her to settle for James and Richard instead. And, because he had thwarted her over the boys, he gave Mother her head when it came to a mere girl.'

Her flippancy was interesting. The New York newspapers had covered her acting career fully, and he knew that it had begun six years ago when she was twenty-one years old. She had first caught the public eye in Oscar Wilde's *An Ideal Husband* when, as an understudy, she went on for several performances, and soon after she had made a success in *The Notorious Mrs Ebbsmith*, taking over the lead from Mrs Patrick Campbell. She had toured with George Alexander, playing *Tanqueray* for the first time and then, after a season with Charles Wyndham, was given her own starring vehicle in *Trelawny of the Wells*. The newspaper articles reflected what was evidently a sincere affection for her father, whom she described as a gentle, scholarly man, slightly bewildered by the fate that had stranded him in a remote parish where there were few, if any, kindred spirits among his neighbours or his flock. Of her mother Amadine said little, apart from a reference to her being the sister of an influential solicitor and, that brother having only daughters, Amadine's eldest brother was already established as his successor, while her younger brother was destined for the church.

It was at the junction of the two – her family life and her acting career – that a certain vagueness entered the narrative. New York reporters might accept that one day Amadine upped and left her Yorkshire dale and took herself off to London, but Pierce knew the country and its people, and he knew that the reality must have been rather different. He asked her about it now, suggesting that the transition must have been daunting, but Amadine dismissed it with a careless wave of her hand.

'It was just one of those silly things, a sequence of events that carried me along with it. There was nothing special about it – could have happened to anyone.' She noticed his sceptical look, and laughed. 'What do you want me to say – that I ran away from home to join the circus, or some such rubbish?'

Pierce smiled, and did not pursue the subject. Against all the odds and his preconceptions, there was something about Amadine – perhaps because she was a clergyman's daughter – that made him feel she possessed an inner and personal integrity, which would prevent her telling a lie.

Amadine Sinclair was telling the truth, but not the whole truth.

Frank Smith was by no means the most popular member of the company; indeed, in many quarters he was actively disliked but, being the Chief's brother, was treated with wary respect. He had an abrupt and authoritarian manner and, undertaking Tom Oldroyd's duties as well as his own, had turned into a strict disciplinarian whose rules and regulations rivalled those laid down by Augustin Daly at his theatre across the street.

However, his popularity – or lack of it – was the last thing on Frank's mind. He had so much work to do that personal considerations were a luxury he simply could not afford. He was a highly efficient person, able to establish routines for regular tasks, possessing an excellent memory, and reliable in emergencies, but even Frank needed sleep, and even Frank could not extend the day beyond twenty-four hours. Something had to give; opening nights could not be postponed, the company could not go without wages, and rehearsals had to be held, so it was the paperwork that was neglected.

Having had a terrible fright over Constance's offer of assistance with the accounts, he was worried that the subject would be raised again and that the overflowing mail basket belied his protestations that everything was under control. Frank conceded that he needed help, but, it being essential to maintain his grip on the company finances, such help would be hired by him on his own terms. What Hal needed, he informed his brother, was a secretary who would deal with the correspondence and so forth, while Frank concentrated on the finance and stage management – 'a well-educated young American with enough interest in the theatre to compensate for the miserly salary we will be paying'. Hal agreed and suggested that Jay might know a suitable candidate.

Jay had been away for a few days on the pretext of family affairs, although in fact he had been attending to a little private business in Philadelphia. 'I think I might know the very man,' he said thoughtfully, 'and he happens to be in New York – I bumped into him on the train from Philly today. He would be an ideal choice, if he can extricate himself from his business commitments at such short notice.'

Frank hesitated, being by no means convinced that a friend of Jay's would make the ideal personal secretary. Of course Jay was good at his job, and being loud and brash and wearing cheap suits was no impediment to his effectiveness, but this new post called for different skills and a different personality.

'Is he well qualified?' Frank enquired.

Jay looked at him reproachfully. 'Princeton *and* Harvard.'

'Surely that makes him *over*-qualified!'

'His family is loaded, and I reckon they kept sending him to school because there wasn't anything else he wanted to do. Teddy ain't exactly fizzing with get-up-and-go.'

If anything, this sounded even less promising than the prospect of another Jay, but Frank knew that he could not afford to be fussy. It wouldn't hurt to see the chap and if his family was wealthy, as Jay indicated, then it might be possible to pare down the salary even further.

'Bring him to see me after the show tomorrow.'

They were dining at Sherry's, with Amadine, Constance and Gwen after the evening's performance, Hal and Laurie having gone off to the Players' Club again. In his days as a struggling actor in New York, Frank had dreamed of frequenting places like this but now that he was here, he was less dazzled than he had expected. Oh, the bill-of-fare was as comprehensive and as expensive, the gilt traceries on walls, ceilings and mirrors as ornate, the silver- and glassware as polished, the napery as crisp and white, the glow from the red-shaded candelabra as flattering as he had envisaged. But there wasn't the satisfaction in it, not the sense of achievement that there would have been, had he got here by his own efforts instead of on his brother's coattails. Also, he would have enjoyed this dinner more if he, or rather the company, had not been paying. The party comprised only 'family' so a more modest establishment would have been entirely appropriate, but Hal insisted on his principals being seen in all the best places. Constance did not eat much, fortunately, but Amadine had a remarkably healthy appetite for one so slender, and definitely fell into the category of those whom one would rather keep for a week than a fortnight.

Having his own reasons for wishing to keep company expenses to a minimum, Frank watched morosely as the bill for food and wine mounted but then it occurred to him that, in Hal's absence, this might be an opportune moment to discuss the financial arrangements for the rest of the tour. The basics had been settled long ago, of course. Hal was to receive 60 per cent of the gross revenue, with guaranteed weekly minima depending on the venue. Out of this he had to pay all his overheads, including salaries, production expenses, and accommodation and keep for the principals. The remaining 40 per cent, which would be handled by Jay, was divided between Frohman and the individual theatres at which the company appeared.

'I was remembering the other day,' he said casually, 'that Sarah Bernhardt always insists on being paid in gold. Rather a good idea, don't you think, Jay? Some publicity in that, surely?'

Jay's sandy eyebrows nearly disappeared into the thick thatch of hair that flopped over his forehead but, after his initial surprise, he leaned back in his chair and considered the proposition.

Amadine had been preoccupied. When parting from her the other day, Pierce Radcliffe had promised to get in touch again but had not done so, and she was irritated to find that she was disappointed. However, at Frank's remark she was all attention. 'Where would this gold be kept?' she demanded, appalled.

'In that safe I told you about,' Jay answered slowly.

'This as-yet-hypothetical safe already has my jewellery in it. What do you want to do – put up an advertising poster saying: "Thieves and robbers welcome – please form an orderly queue"?'

Gwen smiled, but everyone else was deadly serious.

'America loved the Divine Sarah's gold and jewels,' Jay said thoughtfully.

'So did the thieves and robbers,' Amadine retorted. 'Didn't a bandit try to uncouple her car from the train so that his gang could make off with the loot? And I think there was an incident on one of her tours when someone was shot – fatally. And you want . . .' She stopped. It was one of those very rare moments when words failed her.

'Things like that don't happen these days,' Jay assured her.

'Tell that to the proprietor of the drugstore here who was attacked the other day by armed robbers.'

'That was on the lower east side,' Jay said, as if that explained everything.

'I do not intend that we should keep all the treasury on the train indefinitely,' Frank hastened to assure her. 'We will use the gold to pay the wages, hotel bills and other running expenses; and every so often I'll remit cash to our New York bank account, for onward transmission to London.'

'I'll be remitting Frohman's share to New York regularly,' Jay said, 'so we can go to the bank together.'

'And be shot by the thieves and robbers as you stroll down the street,' muttered Amadine, but she could see that she had lost the argument.

'Stop worrying,' Jay said automatically, receiving a withering glance for his pains. Suddenly he recalled that he really must remember to insure Amadine's jewellery.

'Amadine is worrying about her share of the profits,' Constance remarked, 'and I don't blame her. You two are welcome to put your lives in danger if it gives you a thrill, but not if my bonus is at risk.'

Constance and Laurie were employed on the basis of a weekly salary, with a bonus to be paid at the end of the tour if profits warranted it. However, Amadine was participating on a percentage of the profits, that percentage being the chief bone of contention with Frank, who considered that, in his eagerness to persuade Amadine to join the tour, Hal had been far too generous in the terms he offered. Frank fully recognised Amadine's value to the box office – the evidence was in front of him every night in the packed houses for her performances – but he also knew that if Amadine failed to collect her percentage at the end of the tour, her share would revert to Hal. And if everything went according to plan – Frank's plan – an additional injection of cash could be very useful indeed.

By the following night Frank was regretting having asked Jay to bring his friend backstage after the performance. He ought to have arranged a more businesslike interview in the office, where he could have made a more leisurely and thorough assessment of the candidate's suitability. He even began to have second thoughts about the whole idea, because it occurred to him that the man would be working closely with Hal and might gain influence that would work to Frank's disadvantage.

He was standing on the stage, talking to the chief electrician, when Jay and his protégé appeared in the wings. Frank glanced across, took one look and fell in love.

'We're staying at the Parker House in Boston?' he asked Jay the next day, knowing the answer perfectly well.

Jay, expecting a complaint about the expense of residing at that highly prestigious establishment, hastened to defend his choice of hotel. 'Anyone who is anyone stays there, and it's convenient for the Tremont Theatre. It would be difficult to change the bookings now, particularly as there was a fire at the Vendome the other day.'

'I was merely going to suggest that you should book a room for the new chap, and book him into the same hotels as us for the rest of the tour.'

Amadine was listening to the exchange with interest. 'Isn't the Parker House where Dickens stayed during his second trip to America?' When Jay confirmed that this was the case, she clutched his arm with excitement. 'Please, please, darling Jay, ask them if I can stay in the same room!'

Jay looked at her doubtfully. 'The hotel has been renovated since those days – Dickens was there thirty years ago – but I'll ask.'

'I'm not expecting the same sheets, or even the same bed! But to sleep in the same room as . . . Oh, it would be wonderful!'

That evening at dinner Jay confirmed that he had booked a room for Hal's new secretary, and also that Amadine could occupy the Dickens suite.

'Good publicity, as a matter of fact,' he remarked, 'as I'm told that Charlotte Cushman died in that very same room.'

At this mention of America's most famous tragedienne, renowned for her Lady Macbeth, as well as for playing the roles of Romeo and Hamlet, an expression of absolute bliss transfigured Amadine's face.

'I suppose it's too much to hope that history might repeat itself,' murmured Constance.

Chapter Six

They arrived in Boston at dusk, and in the rain, so that a melancholy autumn chill pervaded the air. Seen from the carriage window the narrow, twisting cobblestone streets, the lights of gas lanterns gleaming on wet sidewalks, the shop fronts glowing in the gathering darkness seemed faintly familiar and oddly atmospheric of London. Here was no Elevated Railway rattling overhead but a newly opened subway system and, there being as yet few skyscrapers, the city seemed to be constructed on a more human scale than New York, and thus more approachable. Of course this could be, and probably was, an illusion. Boston was different from New York, yes, but that did not mean that it posed less of a challenge or that its conquest would be easier. Quite the opposite, some would have said.

Their train – a scheduled service, not the special on which they would travel hereafter – had been late leaving New York, amid rumours of a tragic accident on another railroad line into the city. The matter preyed on the minds of the company, and they spent much of the journey exchanging exaggerated and colourful accounts of accidents they had witnessed first-, or at the most second-, hand. There was a palpable sense of unease, as if the occurrence of such a tragedy on the very day of their journey – and on the first leg of a railroad expedition that would cover many thousands of miles – was a sign of bad luck, just as the unusual circumstances of their arrival in New York had brought bad luck.

At the hotel, an extravagantly gabled and turreted edifice in the style of a French château, at the corner of Tremont and School Streets, Amadine temporarily forgot such misgivings in her delight in the Dickens suite. It contained the large mirror, with black walnut surround, in which the novelist had practised facial expressions for use at his literary readings; the bath into which he had fallen, fully clothed, after an especially convivial dinner; and the bed in which Charlotte Cushman had died – well, Amadine liked to think it was the same bed, even though no one was prepared to say so for certain. There was, she was told, a ghost that summoned the elevator to the third floor, where this suite was situated. Charlotte, thought Amadine with a tingle. Walking to the elevator after changing for dinner, she saw an empty car was waiting for her and entered it feeling surrounded by ghosts and thoroughly, but most enjoyably, spooked.

At the dinner table one chair was ominously vacant. 'Frank has been held up at the station,' Hal informed the group. 'A crate of props appears to be missing.'

Everyone sat in silence, thinking of Tom Oldroyd and his prophecies of doom.

'The props may not be missing,' Amadine said at last, 'and even if they are, they might belong to a play that is not being performed in Boston.'

But no one believed her. It was turning into that sort of tour.

At the Tremont Theatre next day, Frank confirmed that the missing props belonged to *Trelawny of the Wells*, in which the company was opening that night. Rather surprisingly Amadine did not seem unduly perturbed, but this apparent equanimity was due to her preoccupation with newspaper reports confirming that the previous day a train had 'plunged from the track into the swirling waters of the Hudson opposite West Point', about two miles below Garrison, New York. Twenty-three people – later amended to nineteen – had died, a number were injured, and much was made of the rescue efforts of James Corbett, the heavyweight boxer known as 'Gentleman Jim', who had taken up a stage career and happened to be on the next train along the line. Early accounts speculated that the underpinning of the track had been washed out, thus tipping the train into the river, but then another and more startling claim was made: the track had been blown up. The express car had four hundred thousand dollars in gold and jewels in its safe, a large part of the treasure being gold from the Klondike being transported to vaults in New York City, and the press speculated that a gang of desperadoes had planned a robbery.

Amadine descended on Jay, eyes blazing. 'So, nothing like this happens any more!' and she waved the paper under his nose.

'Pay no heed to that rubbish,' Jay said airily. 'Personally, I subscribe to the wash-out theory, but even if the track was dynamited, the robbery failed.'

'And the gang won't try again? And of course no other gang would dream of copying their *modus operandi*!'

'Amadine,' and Jay spoke kindly, as if addressing a child, 'we won't be carrying four hundred thousand dollars, or anything like.'

She stared at him, exasperated. 'Sometimes I think you would relish a robbery – great publicity,' and she mimicked his accent, 'and if anyone got hurt or, dare I say it, killed, why, so much the better. Just think how America would flock to gape at the survivors. If there are any survivors,' she added darkly, before stalking back to the stage.

'Overwrought,' Jay was heard to mutter as he left the theatre. 'First-night nerves.'

Of course, in one respect he was right. As the day wore on, Amadine grew paler and paler, and rushed to the bathroom at frequent but irregular intervals. However, by the time the company gathered for a dress rehearsal later that afternoon, the worst was over.

'Feeling better?' Laurie enquired sympathetically.

Amadine nodded wanly. 'I don't eat anything during the day before a first night so, even if I feel awful, nothing drastic can happen during a performance.'

'Most reassuring. By the way, the props haven't been found so we must blunder through the dress rehearsal as best we can while Frank locates replacements. So be vigilant when you sit down – there might not be a chair!'

Laurie's remark proved prescient. The chairs needed for the first act were among the missing items but, at first, their absence was a minor irritation compared to the myriad mistakes, from fluffed lines to missed entrances and bungled business, that marred the rehearsal. As Hal groaned when the awful affair was over, 'At least tonight's performance cannot be any worse'; but everyone knew that it could, and probably would, be.

Most of the cast was sitting in the greenroom, prior to going to their dressing rooms in order to change back into their first-act costumes, when Jay returned. He burst in with his usual cheery greeting but then paused, his smile freezing on his face.

'You aren't intending to go on the stage dressed like that?' he said, in an appalled tone.

The costumes for *Trelawny* were, to the contemporary eye, quaint and even bizarre but this was due, as Amadine hastened to explain, to the earnest behest of the author. Mr Pinero had decreed that the dress and décor should adhere, as closely as possible, to the fashion of the early 1860s, and therefore the actors were clad in crinoline or peg-top trousers, while the furniture on the stage was heavily into horsehair and mahogany.

'Realism is all very well,' Jay said. 'Historical accuracy may be fine and dandy, but it sure ain't very pretty.' And he stared in dismay at Amadine's immense but ugly skirt, and shapeless jacket.

'But this is *Bos*ton, Massa*chu*setts,' Amadine responded, with subtle emphasis. 'This is the Athens of America, the cultural centre of the continent, the hub of the universe. Here they don't follow fashion, because they are above that sort of thing.'

'The Proper Bostonian woman probably owns, and wears, a score of hats even more grotesque than the one on your head right now, but she doesn't expect to see her hat on the stage of the Tremont Theatre.'

Amadine glared at him, reminded sharply of his reservations about *Julius Caesar* on the opening night in New York. 'I only hope that Macready didn't incite a riot in Boston, as well as in New York,' she snapped.

'The Boston riot was down to Edmund Kean.'

Amadine gave a strangled gasp and leaned back in her chair, clapping a hand to her forehead in a melodramatic gesture of exaggerated horror.

'Kean got on the wrong side of the Bostonians during his first tour of America,' Jay began, sitting on a vacant chair and settling down to enjoy himself. 'Despite being warned that Boston theatre-goers would be apathetic in summer, he returned here for a second visit in May after a very successful winter début. The houses for *Lear* and *Venice Preserv'd* were lousy and Kean took it personally.'

'He always did,' Laurie remarked. 'He was constantly at loggerheads with audiences wherever he went.'

Jay nodded. 'One night when he was due to act Richard III, he peered through the curtain, saw that there were only about twenty people in the auditorium and refused to go on. He left the theatre and, even when told that the boxes had filled up unexpectedly, refused to return. Of course, Boston never forgave him.

'Unfortunately,' and with real regret in his voice Jay let the pause linger, 'Kean failed to realise the extent of his offence. He came back to Boston on his next American tour four years later, and again set out to play Richard III. Well, there was a packed house that night all right, but the atmosphere was unmistakable. Kean must have known what was in store for him but he went on, only to be driven off by a torrent of abuse and a hail of missiles. He tried again, with the same result, and had to be smuggled out of the theatre – and out of the city – for his own safety. Paradoxically, when the audience found out he had gone, they were even more furious. As they couldn't tear Kean limb from limb, they wrecked the theatre instead.'

'Jay, have you seen our rehearsals for *Trelawny*?' Amadine asked in a dangerously quiet voice.

'Not all the way through. I am looking forward . . .'

'So you might have missed the part where the entire plot hinges on Edmund Kean.' Jay's expression was sufficient answer, and Amadine continued: 'The part where Rose Trelawny wins over her lover's irascible grandfather by telling him how her mother played Cordelia to Kean's Lear; and she shows him the Order and chain, and the sword, that Kean wore in *Richard III* – I repeat, *Richard III* – and which Kean gave to her father. The part,' and here her voice began to rise, 'that I have to play in front of a full house of Bostonians tonight, most of whom will be well aware of that unfortunate incident.'

'It was a long time ago,' Jay scoffed. 'No one will remember.'

'This is *Bos*ton, Massa*chu*setts,' Amadine said. 'Someone will remember.'

Trelawny of the Wells was Pinero's finest work to date. Set in the London theatre world of the 1860s and billed as a 'comedietta', the piece was intended to amuse, but was full of subtleties and delicate nuances that repaid close attention.

However, from the moment a gale of laughter greeted the entrance of the openers in the first act, and each individual entrance thereafter, the Smith-Sinclair company knew that there was to be precious little appreciation of the play's finer points, and that this Boston first night was to be endured rather than enjoyed. Steeling itself to ignore this reaction to the costumes, the company carried on bravely, handling the makeshift props with cautious respect. By the time Amadine and Blanche launched into their charming rendition of 'Ever of thee I'm fondly dreaming', spirits were beginning to rise, but it was to prove a false dawn.

The first act depicted Rose Trelawny's farewell to her friends at the Sadler's Wells Theatre as she left the profession prior to her marriage. The script called for a cold collation – a joint, a chicken, a tongue and a ham, a pigeon pie, vegetables – and while Hal allowed some artificial viands, he insisted that the chicken, ham and vegetables be real so that they could be carved and handed round at the feast. Seated next to Amadine at the table, Hal decided to introduce a bit of impromptu business; he speared a piece of chicken and offered it to her playfully.

'Take it away,' hissed Amadine, but he would not be put off and, with the chicken only inches from her mouth, she had no option but to open her rosy lips and bite it with her little white teeth. Somehow she managed to swallow it, only to find that Hal was so pleased with the effect that he repeated the gesture and another, larger piece of chicken was travelling her way. 'You're making me sick,' she whispered, but his startled look revealed personal affront rather than concern for her delicate first-night stomach, and again she felt forced to take it. She chewed it slowly, trying desperately to signal to Hal that she could eat no more, when a sudden crash caused her to choke and swallow the piece whole – a piece that she was sure had gristle in it, *and* skin. Nausea rose relentlessly . . .

The eyes of all the cast and audience were riveted on the

actress playing Avonia who, after standing up in order to reach a plate of vegetables, had sat down again rather heavily. The hastily purloined chair wobbled, lost a leg and collapsed, pitching Avonia to the floor so that she landed awkwardly with her right leg twisted beneath her. In real pain, she took a few moments to recover, with the cast fussing round and trying to pass off the incident as a piece of well-rehearsed nonsense. Under cover of the upheaval, Amadine ran into the wings, hoped that no one noticed the leading lady throwing up into a fire bucket, then hurried back to her place.

Both Amadine and Avonia managed to struggle through the rest of the act and although Amadine's second rendition of 'Ever of thee I'm fondly dreaming' was noticeably less vivacious than the first, this could be attributed to the emotion of the plot. Despite a severely sprained ankle, Avonia insisted that she would carry on, and so the ripples from that incident came not from the actresses but from the props.

It was a pity that chairs were something of an ongoing motif in *Trelawny*. At the beginning of the second act Rose sat on a footstool in Sir William Gower's drawing room. 'What are ye upon the floor for, my dear?' the old man enquired. 'Have we no chairs . . .?' As a roar of laughter erupted and slowly subsided, a voice in the audience was heard to say, 'She isn't taking any chances, old chap, and I don't blame her,' which caused laughter to rise again. The next few lines of dialogue only made matters worse, but eventually the act continued serenely until Rose mimicked Sir William's 'Have we no chairs . . .?' The audience was supposed to chuckle at that point, but this audience was chuckling for the wrong reasons, and all too often it was chuckling in the wrong places.

Then a group of Rose's theatrical friends, including Avonia with a very wet umbrella, entered. The stage directions called for the umbrella to drip on the carpet, but Avonia had developed an amusing routine in which she rapidly partly opened and closed the umbrella, showering Sir William's drawing room with raindrops, which a horrified Rose hastened to mop up. Tonight, perhaps distracted by the pain in her ankle, Avonia swooshed the canopy of the umbrella up and down the shaft rather too vigorously and with a sudden click the umbrella stayed open. One of the theatre's most fiercely held superstitions had come to pass: the umbrella was up.

Sitting in the audience with Jay, Constance covered her face with her hands.

It was Laurie, as Tom Wrench, who sprang forward, grabbed the umbrella and lowered it, before handing it back to Avonia with a comic bow. The audience noticed nothing amiss. The cast was appalled.

Waiting in the wings for her entrance at the beginning of the third act, Amadine decided that this was the longest night of her life. She disliked this part of the play anyway, it being the piece where Avonia told Tom Wrench that Rose cannot act any more, that she had lost 'the trick of it'. This came too close to Amadine's secret fears for comfort, and although aware that Rose's acting powers had in fact improved, she was still glad when these exchanges were over. This evening she was also miserably conscious that all too soon she would be facing yet another confrontation with Sir William over chairs and, worst of all, the Edmund Kean section of her dialogue loomed . . .

Eventually it was over. At least the chair fiasco was unique to this night and need not, God willing, be faced again. The audience had cheered wildly, but the company shuddered to think what the critics would say.

However, even the prospect of the notices paled into insignificance compared to that umbrella. Avonia, with her painful, swollen ankle, was unlikely to act again in Boston and was considered to be immune from further harm. But Laurie, who had rushed to the rescue and handled the umbrella while it was up . . . What, the company's anxious glances asked, would happen to him?

'Blanche Villard ought to play Avonia,' Constance announced. 'She is far more suited to that part than to Imogen.'

'Maybe, but who would play Imogen?' Hal demanded.

'Constance will play Imogen,' Amadine interjected smoothly, 'won't you, Constance?'

For some reason Amadine had seen it coming. Ever since Constance had sidled into *Tanqueray*, it had been only a matter of time before she infiltrated the *Trelawny* cast, too. What's more, Amadine could understand why she was doing it: not for the good of the company, not even to put Amadine's nose out of joint, but to impress Hal. Amadine wanted to tell her that all this effort was unnecessary. There was no competition for Hal's favours. As far as Amadine was concerned, Constance was welcome to him because, although Amadine liked working with him, that was as far as it went. So far sheer pressure of work had prevented Hal from making any unwelcome advances in her direction, but Amadine had a shrewd idea that soon Hal would decide he deserved a rest from his labours and that his notion of a leisure pursuit was her. Still, cross that bridge if and when she came to it, eh? With luck he might yet decide that Constance was more worthy of him. Come to think of it, *worthy* described Hal rather well and that, Amadine thought wryly, would explain why she had not fallen in love with him, despite his beauty and many fine qualities. She could always be relied on to fall for the most *un*worthy . . .

'I would be willing to step in, if everyone felt that such a move would be helpful,' Constance was saying demurely.

'But it's asking too much,' Hal expostulated. 'You would have to be at the theatre every night . . .'

Precisely, thought Amadine, because at the theatre, every night, is where you are.

'. . . onstage every night,' Hal went on.

'Not on the evenings when Amadine is playing Juliet,' Constance said sweetly. 'If you still intend to go ahead with that . . . er . . . experiment?'

She really hopes I will fail, Amadine seethed in silent indignation. 'I think we should accept Constance's kind offer before she changes her mind,' she smiled, 'but I also think that it will take all Hal's charm to persuade Blanche to change roles.'

Hal was contemplating the pale blonde beauty of Constance as the refined Imogen, while envisaging Blanche's bright fair hair and piquant profile in the brasher role of Avonia. 'Oh, Blanche won't object,' he murmured absently.

'And the costumes will have to go,' Constance said bluntly.

'Impossible,' declared Amadine. 'Mr Pinero is adamant on the subject.'

'Then Mr Pinero must be persuaded of the error of his ways. He must be told that we are a laughing stock.'

'You tell him,' Amadine suggested, a touch of acidity creeping into her voice for the first time.

'The costumes are receiving far too much notice from the critics and the audiences,' Hal mused. 'Perhaps if Arthur Pinero appreciated that they are diverting attention from the rest of the production . . .'

'Those costumes are true to the '60s,' Amadine insisted. 'You can't change history just because it isn't pretty enough, or exciting enough.'

'In America you can,' Gwen averred.

'Well, you shouldn't. It is a very superficial approach, and panders to people's lowest instincts.' This opinion was greeted with general mirth, so in desperation Amadine turned to Frank. 'New costumes would be very expensive,' she suggested optimistically.

'I could authorise some modest expenditure on materials,' Frank said cautiously, 'but nothing extravagant, mind.'

'I'll draw up a few sketches, and speak to the wardrobe mistress about salvaging something from the existing costumes,' Constance enthused. 'And don't worry about expense – not everyone needs to be dressed in silk.'

No, but I'll bet that Imogen will be dressed in silk, thought Amadine as she promised to write to Arthur Pinero on the subject.

Knowing that Amadine had seen little of Boston beyond the theatre, the hotel and the Common, Gwen suggested that she might like to accompany her on a walk to Beacon Hill. The morning was fine, the sun glinting on the golden dome of the State House as they strolled along Park Street, but a chill in the air was a sharp reminder that winter was not far away. From Beacon Street, whose elegant and expensive row-houses were said to hold 'the sifted few', Gwen turned into Joy Street and began an ascent that left her rather out of breath so that, at the corner of Pinckney Street, she paused to recover.

'Nearly there,' she gasped, and proceeded a short way along Upper Pinckney Street before knocking on the door of a narrow-fronted brick house, the predominant feature of which was a big bay window on the upper floor. The door was opened by a small, wiry woman with greying hair arranged in a severe old-fashioned style, and whose shabby dress appeared to be of equally ancient vintage. However, her voice betrayed an innate gentility and she ushered them into her modest drawing room with perfect courtesy. Gwen introduced her as 'Miss P, who looks after my mother', before the two women went to see old Mrs Hughes while Amadine waited in the drawing room. Then, after a brief interval, Miss P reappeared and entertained her visitor with a display of beautiful manners and entrancing aplomb.

Amadine recognised the type. The rector's daughter had come into contact with every strata of society, from the aristocracy and landed gentry, through the professional classes and farming community to the very poorest of the poor, and she knew a 'distressed gentlewoman' when she saw one. With her inborn and enviable ability to adapt to any company or circumstance, Amadine immediately found common ground with Miss P and soon they were enjoying each other's company immensely. And, while she talked, Amadine was quietly reconstructing the circumstances of Gwen's mother: clearly the old lady was infirm, and Gwen was paying the impoverished Miss P to care for her, thus providing Mrs Hughes with a roof and a nurse, and Miss P with sufficient income to maintain her home.

'My mother is senile,' Gwen said sadly, when they were out in the street again, 'and doesn't know me. I just hope that there are times when a chink of light shines through the mist and that she knows where she is. She loved Boston so much, and it was always her dream to live on Beacon Hill. Although her mind has gone, physically she is very fit – she bounds up and down these slopes better than I do! – and she and Miss P go down Pinckney Street to look at the sunset,' and Gwen indicated the spectacular view ahead, as the street dipped down to the river.

'Do you have to pay some of the cost?'

'I pay all of it, because my mother has no money of her own. My parents were in the profession and, like so many of us, they did not put by.'

'Are you putting by, Gwen, for your own retirement?'

'Of course not. Are you?' Gwen laughed, but there was little mirth in it. 'I have reached the age where I would if I could, but I can't.'

'Have you a home of your own?'

'No, I live out of my trunk and keep touring. Even if I could afford my own home, I am unlikely to stay in one place long enough to appreciate it.'

'But when you retire and grow . . . old,' Amadine struggled with the word, 'you won't have anyone to look after you.'

'I know, my dear. Believe me, I know. But what's the use of worrying? There is nothing I can do about it now.'

There remained so much unsaid about Gwen's past that Amadine could not help wondering again how her friend had come to this pass. Surely there must have been a man – more than one – and marriage prospects, and career prospects, when Gwen was young and beautiful? And while Gwen contemplated her fear of growing old and ill like her mother, Amadine faced the possibility of growing old and alone like Gwen.

'You must be very fond of your mother,' Amadine said, 'to sacrifice so much for her.'

Her tone was noticeably subdued but, before remarking on it, Gwen chose to answer the implicit question. 'I am an only child. I was born here when my father had an engagement at the Boston Museum – the theatre, you know, not a museum as you know it. Those were the best days, when he was in the stock company with William Warren Jr, but he died when I was seven. Mother had to go back on the road, and I was sent to live with my aunt and uncle.' She smiled thoughtfully. 'It is strange how, in life, wheels come full circle. Mother had to pay someone to look after me while she toured, because the theatre was her only means of making a living, and now I must do the same for her.'

After pointing out houses where Nathaniel Hawthorne and Louisa M. Alcott had lived, Gwen turned into Louisburg Square and then guided Amadine into broad, green Mount Vernon Street lined with great elms.

'Henry James, and his family, stayed at several addresses here,' Gwen told Amadine. 'He called it the only respectable street in America but, then, he would. He is prone to somewhat sweeping statements! I know that you admire him, but in America he is not universally popular. His self-imposed exile in England is resented in some quarters.'

'Why should you begrudge us one of your best men? You have had plenty of ours!'

Gwen laughed, and acknowledged that she had no answer to that. 'And you, Amadine,' she said casually, 'are you fond of your mother?'

The sudden change of subject caught Amadine unawares. 'No,' she said abruptly, 'and I know that I ought to be, and feel guilty because I'm not.'

'It has always seemed to me that if a mother and daughter get on well together, it is a bonus. Such a happy state of affairs is not compulsory, and certainly not universal. There is a comment by Fanny Kemble concerning Anglo-American relations that would appeal to you: "The two nations, mother and daughter though they be, can no more understand each other than I and my children can."'

Amadine managed a faint smile. 'I don't think my mother cares for me any more than I care for her – she adores my brothers, you see. But it is her birthday tomorrow, and I wish that things were otherwise.'

'Is your mother likely to get in touch with you on your birthday?'

'She hasn't done so in recent years, but she has more excuse for her neglect than I do – she doesn't know where I am.'

'Ah.' They were strolling through side streets, zigzagging their way to Chestnut Street, and Gwen pondered this development for a few moments. 'In that case you need a husband,' she said decidedly, 'but I do recommend, most strongly, that an actress should stick with men from the profession – unless she wants to give up the stage, of course.'

'It sounds as if you speak from experience.' Amadine

waited in the hope that Gwen might elaborate but, when no further information was forthcoming, she went on, 'I am not looking for a relationship with anyone, whether in the profession or not.'

'You're mad. If I were you – young, single and gorgeous – I would be dragging Hal to the altar, kicking and screaming if necessary. He is adorable: handsome, talented *and* a gentleman. What is the matter with you, girl? Grab him before Constance does.'

'I am an independent woman, with my own work,' Amadine insisted, 'and I intend to stay that way. What sort of marriage could I have? A husband in the profession would expect me to play decorative but subordinate roles. A husband outside the profession would expect me to give up my work. All marriage offers me is a Morton's Fork of impossible choices.'

'I didn't realise that you felt so strongly about women's rights.'

'Reading Anthony Trollope helped,' Amadine said grimly. 'In his book on North America he devotes an entire chapter to the rights of women and one could not say that it is one of his most inspired passages. The general gist can be summed up in his statement that "The best right a woman has is the right to a husband". The arrogance of it!'

'That book was written more than thirty years ago,' Gwen offered in exoneration.

'You don't seriously think that male attitudes have changed? My father taught me Latin, and admitted that I learned faster than my brothers, yet still he saw no other future for me but marriage with a man in our neighbourhood.' Amadine paused, and grasped Gwen's arm. 'There is no chance that I will marry, and in addition I cannot turn to my family for help if the going gets tough. That is why this tour is so important to me, why I must be a success, and build the foundations of a lasting career.'

'Both Boston and New York have adored you.'

'They only adore how I look,' Amadine said softly, 'and the foundations of a career built on beauty are set on very shaky, shifting sands.'

By coincidence – or was it the hand of fate? – they had paused outside the house in Chestnut Street that once belonged to Edwin Booth. Gwen's heart constricted because, although she had known him only professionally, she could never think of him without pain. There were some lives that were so touched by tragedy that, to an outsider, the burden of it seemed intolerable. Gazing at the grey stone mansion, built sideways to the street, Gwen pondered whether the mixture of tragedy and glory in Booth's life was preferable to the mundane norm. What was it Disraeli had said about life? 'Youth is a blunder, maturity a struggle, old age a regret.' Gwen knew exactly what he meant.

Turning her head slightly towards the young woman beside her, Gwen wondered what the future held for Amadine. Would she follow Gwen's route to a life of regrets, or Booth's tragedy-haunted path to death and glory? At that moment the sun went in and the light darkened dramatically, casting the exquisite planes of Amadine's lovely face into sharp relief, and suddenly Gwen felt cold and afraid.

Chapter Seven

Frank had been in a fever of impatience for the moment when Theodore Wingfield Davis arrived to take up his position as Hal's secretary, although pressure of work prevented him from dwelling on it. Only when he lay awake in the early hours of the morning did he allow himself the luxury of thinking about the young man, and the even greater luxury of hope. When at last he saw the slight figure standing diffidently in the wings, his heart bumped uncomfortably but, concealing his emotions under an excess of bonhomie, Frank hurried across and seized him by the hand.

'Great to see you,' he enthused, pumping the hand vigorously. 'Have you come straight from the station?'

'I left my bag at the hotel on the way.'

'Good, good,' and, letting go of the hand, Frank slapped him boisterously on the back. 'Now, I'll introduce you to everyone.'

Amadine stood up when they came into the greenroom, and saw that the newcomer was about the same height as herself, and good-looking in a sensitive, boyish way, with regular features, wavy brown hair and hazel eyes. However, the cut of that hair and of his clothes, and a certain understated air of refinement, reeked of old money. He looked absurdly young.

'Theodore,' she repeated as they shook hands. 'Theo . . . yes, it suits you.'

'We shorten Theodore to Teddy over here,' he said, blushing.

Amadine did not think that he was intrinsically shy. In his own milieu he would display the quiet confidence of his kind, but backstage in a theatre was unfamiliar territory. Still regarding him, her head cocked slightly to one side, Amadine pronounced firmly, 'No, you are a Theo. Definitely.'

Later he was to look back on that as a crucial moment, an absolutely seminal moment, the moment when he changed into something and someone else. From then on he was not Teddy Wingfield Davis, a lawyer of respected Philadelphia stock, but Theo, companion to a band of strolling players. Somehow the bestowal of a new name brought a fresh identity. Although he would appreciate most of this only in retrospect, even now the sense of liberation was extraordinary.

'You can leave him with me, Frank,' Amadine offered, 'and I'll show him round.'

'I wouldn't dream of imposing on you,' Frank said firmly, 'besides, Theo and I have work to do – the backlog of correspondence is huge.'

The quantity of work was daunting, but after an hour or so Theo was quietly confident that the requirements of the job were well within his compass. Indeed, Frank had been correct in believing him to be vastly over-qualified for the post. The business side of the correspondence demanded few decisions by Theo – all he had to do was convey Hal's instructions to the relevant quarters and ensure that these instructions were carried out. The personal items, chiefly mash notes and begging letters, required little more than charmingly worded acknowledgements, which Theo could write in his sleep. Still, he was glad that it was Frank who was showing him the ropes. He was rather in awe of Hal, having seen him onstage in such roles as Romeo, Orlando and Leontes, as Buckingham in *Henry VIII* and as King Henry in Tennyson's *Becket*. For someone as stage-struck as Theo, it was somewhat overwhelming to meet the idol in person and he felt much more relaxed around Frank. To the other man's intense pleasure, Theo made time to watch backstage activity and in the evenings saw every performance, either from the wings or an empty seat in the house, simply soaking up the atmosphere and hardly daring to believe his luck in being here.

His first task each morning was to sort and distribute the mail. 'I never realised that there would be so many begging letters,' he commented.

'It's what they ask for that always surprises me,' remarked Amadine. 'It can be ten dollars, or a hundred thousand. Or, like yesterday, a piano.'

'Hal was asked to give a theatre,' Theo marvelled. 'Mind you, they did offer to name it after him.'

'Do people really think that we make that sort of money?' Amadine asked. 'I don't know any actors who are millionaires, do you!'

'People connected with the theatre can become millionaires,' Jay asserted with conviction. 'Producers, for example. I bet Frohman is worth a dollar or two.'

'I hate refusing to help people,' Amadine said, looking down at the bundle of letters in her hand, 'but I cannot afford to send money to everyone who asks, and how is one to know which requests are genuine? I do try to explain that to them, but . . .'

'You don't answer all your letters!' Constance exclaimed.

'Of course, don't you?' Amadine did not wait for a reply, but hurried on, 'Not everyone asks for money. I received a letter inviting me to "come to Jesus". I wanted to write back with the truth – that I had been brought up with Jesus, but that I was never entirely convinced that He wanted me around – but I thought it might sound flippant.'

'If only one could help people in other ways,' Theo said sympathetically.

'Exactly. If someone wanted practical help, other than money, or wanted advice or guidance, then I am sure we would all go out of our way to assist.'

For a moment each member of the group contemplated their own, and in particular Amadine's, stance on this question, but then the focus of attention shifted. There was a letter for Gwen, and no one could remember that happening before.

Boston was generous with floral tributes and, in Amadine's dressing room and hotel suite, American beauty roses were banked up in rows of tall, thin boxes. 'Like miniature coffins,' shuddered Constance. Amadine took to running up to Pinckney Street with the overflow of flowers, fruit and chocolates, which she bestowed on an overwhelmed Miss P, and it was when she returned to the theatre from such an excursion that she found the note from Pierce Radcliffe. She read it, but put it aside.

Commandeering Theo as guide – he knew Boston well, from his days at Harvard Law School – Amadine made an expedition to the historical district. After the Old State House, they penetrated as far as Paul Revere's home, currently occupied by the Banca Italiana and a cigar manufacturer, and the Old North Church before returning to the theatre. And to the note which, she was sorry to see, was still there.

It was still there the next day, too, and simple courtesy would not allow her to ignore it any longer. But what on earth was she to say? A straightforward dinner invitation, or a visit to another theatre, would have been easy to deal with, but a ride in a motor car . . .? 'Think of it as good publicity, even though it means you must endure my company,' he wrote, with a mixture of sarcasm and self-confidence. But Amadine was by no means sure that such a circus turn would be good publicity – she was not even sure that *any* publicity would be a good thing, not in Boston; in addition, she had not forgiven the man for doing a disappearing act in New York. On the other hand, she had never been in a motor car . . .

They arranged to meet on Saturday morning and, wrapped up well against the cold and wearing a hat with a voluminous veil to protect her face, Amadine was in the lobby of the Parker House at the appointed time. She had been waiting a good ten minutes when she heard the most awful noise – a chugging, grinding sort of noise with a few intermittent bangs thrown in – that caused the population of the Parker House lobby to pour into the street. Amadine remained in her seat for several minutes before slowly walking to the door. Oh dear, she had known this was a bad idea, but only now did it began to dawn on her just how bad.

Pierce Radcliffe was seated in the biggest, noisiest automobile she had ever seen. 'Panhard and Levassor,' he was shouting above the din to a man in the crowd. 'Eight horsepower, four cylinders, the very latest thing – next year's racing model, in fact. See, electric-coil ignition, and a steering wheel instead of a tiller. This baby will get up to speeds of . . .'

Willing hands had hoisted Amadine into the seat beside him, and she realised that the man in conversation with Pierce was taking notes – a reporter, evidently. She did not hear her name mentioned but doubtless, Pierce having stressed the value of the publicity to her, the newsman knew who she was. The crowd certainly knew, and were smiling excitedly. Only later did she question whether the most excitement was generated by her, or by the car.

'I thought we'd go for a run through the Back Bay,' Pierce said, deigning to notice her at last. 'The streets are straight and flat, and we should be able to negotiate them without too much difficulty.'

Amadine brightened. She had not ventured into the Back Bay area, and welcomed this opportunity to see the new land reclaimed from the marshy acres of the tidal flats that had formed an estuary of the Charles River.

'As long as we don't go too far,' she agreed, having to shout to make herself heard. 'I have a matinée this afternoon.'

Suddenly, and without warning, they were off, Amadine clutching on to the vehicle with one hand and her hat with the other, as Pierce aimed the car at the right side of Tremont Street. A cab horse shied and its driver brandished his whip, yelling an angry curse on this newfangled conveyance, but when the solid tyres of the Panhard had jolted over the streetcar rails, the motion of the vehicle settled down sufficiently for Amadine to relax her hold and look about her. The Common and the box-shaped kiosks of the new subway system were to her right, and what looked like the entire population of Boston was rooted to the spot in wonder at this apparition that had materialised in their midst.

'Is this a new car?' she shouted in Pierce's ear.

'Just taken her off the boat from France.'

That explained it. Pierce Radcliffe was like a small boy who opened a parcel on Christmas morning and found the wonderful toy his heart had been set on. The men she had seen driving automobiles in London had done so sedately, as if they had been doing this all their lives and there was nothing to it, but Pierce had a huge grin on his face and, although he was crouched over the steering wheel with intense concentration, had he suddenly thrown his hat into the air and yelled 'Yippee!', she would not have been surprised.

They had reached Boylston Street when Amadine became aware of the chill and tried to snuggle down a little deeper into her coat and scarves. Above them the sky was a peculiarly leaden grey, threatening rain or worse.

'Looks like snow,' she commented.

'Too early in the season for snow,' Pierce asserted confidently, shooting the car across the intersection with Arlington Street, giving Amadine a glimpse of a church so Wrenlike in its aspect that she felt a fierce stab of homesickness, and giving another cab driver the fright of his life.

'Ought the car to make this much noise?' she asked.

'Probably not,' he conceded. 'The engine needs tuning, and I think some adjustment may be required for the composition of this gasoline.'

'Can you do all that yourself?'

'Of course. I'm an engineer. I'm not intending to import these European automobiles – I want to design and build my own. This baby is just for show – and fun.'

A large drop of water landed on Amadine's nose. This was followed by another, and then another, so that by the time Pierce swung the Panhard sharp right into Dartmouth Street, the rain was falling steadily. Glad she had brought an umbrella, Amadine battled to open it as the fine Renaissance façade of the Public Library at Copley Square swirled past her to the far left. After a short distance, Pierce turned right again into Commonwealth Avenue, a broad, spacious boulevard lined by grand mansions and bisected by a central tree-filled mall that contrasted with the bare, treeless streets of the rest of Back Bay. The residences were so massive, and the styles of architecture so varied, that under normal circumstances Amadine would have enjoyed inspecting them, but at the moment she was beginning to get distinctly wet. She greeted her companion's announcement that they should make a detour along Beacon Street with dismay.

'Will this thing go any faster?' she asked, as the rain turned to sleet.

'The engine runs at virtually a fixed speed. A method of gaining power is one of the chief problems I want to crack.'

In Beacon Street he waved to three women standing at the window of an enormous mansion whose rear windows,

Amadine calculated enviously, would boast a glorious view over the river. Then, after progressing the length of Beacon Street as far as the State House, they turned down Park Street with the eastern boundary of the Common to their right and fast approaching Park Street Church on the left-hand corner. Whether the motor car was too near the centre of the road or whether the horse-drawn carriage turning into Park Street past the church was taking the bend too widely was open to debate. What was certain was that the horses suddenly found themselves confronted by this huge, noisy animal with a very strange smell, and they took fright and bolted. Within seconds there was a tangled mass of horses and carriages, wooden shafts and leather tackle, while Pierce desperately applied the brakes of the Panhard in order to avoid a serious accident. The Panhard's engine uttered a defiant bang as the car came to rest and stopped.

Then, just audible above the shouts of the people and the whinnying horses, came another bang – a sharp crack.

To her astonishment, Amadine felt herself being pulled past the steering wheel and out of the far door, so that the car was between her and the Common.

'Get down,' hissed Pierce, pulling her to her knees in the middle of the street so that they were huddled against the car.

'What on earth . . .?' Amadine began indignantly.

'Be quiet.'

He seemed to be listening, as he crouched beside her, his body shielding hers on one side and the car protecting it on the other. When the hubbub in the street died away, he stood up and stared across at the Common.

'Would you mind explaining yourself?' Amadine demanded, struggling to her feet.

'There was a gunshot, and it came from over there,' and he indicated the Common as his blue eyes raked the area.

'Don't be ridiculous. Look, if this is some sort of publicity stunt . . .'

'I don't play games with guns,' and he walked round to the other side of the car and began examining the vehicle for damage. A curious crowd gathered, but everyone asserted their belief that the noise had come from the car.

'Impossible,' Pierce said tersely. 'I had switched off the engine.'

'Could it have been the crack of a whip?' Amadine suggested.

With an exclamation, Pierce bent down and inspected some damage to the chassis, but Amadine's explanation that it might have been caused by stones in the road was discounted impatiently.

'Why should someone fire a gun at you?' she asked him.

'Have you considered the possibility that it might have been fired at you?'

By now Amadine had had enough. Turning on her heel, she walked the short distance to the hotel and had changed into dry clothes by the time her maid admitted Pierce Radcliffe to the suite.

'I suppose you'd better have a drink,' and she indicated the decanters on the sideboard. 'And you can pour me a brandy – that, and the steam heat in this place, may unthaw me in time for the matinée.'

He poured the drinks in silence, wearing that withdrawn, sardonic look she had first seen on the voyage. She was beginning to see that there were two Pierce Radcliffes, due perhaps to the English and American influences on his character and upbringing. From time to time this English reserve was uppermost, whereas in the motor car an American enthusiasm – almost exhibitionism – had taken over.

'That was a very serious incident,' he said at last, 'and I think you ought to examine the implications.'

'I refuse to believe that a gun was fired, let alone the absurd suggestion that it might have been aimed at me.'

'You ought to take steps for your own protection.'

'Such as? I am an actress, Pierce. I step on to a stage every night, and stand in front of an audience. There isn't much one can do if some lunatic decides to take a gun to the performance instead of his opera glasses. It has happened before – someone tried to shoot Edwin Booth during a performance of *Richard II* – and I suppose it may happen again. I refuse to allow such a remote possibility to affect me.'

He sighed and shook his head, as if deciding to let the matter drop. 'By the way, I must congratulate you on your performance in *Trelawny*.'

'Thank you, but obviously you were not at the opening night. Did you know that the Roman term for a theatre exit was *vomitorium*? Believe me, I gave the word an entirely new emphasis!' She considered him for a moment. 'You told me that you never went to the theatre.'

'Which only goes to prove the irresistible power of your attraction.'

'Not so irresistible that you couldn't tear yourself away from New York, without even the courtesy of a farewell note.'

'I had to go to Chicago unexpectedly. A funeral . . .'

Now Amadine sighed. A funeral was the perfect excuse – difficult to argue against, and difficult to disprove. 'Not family, I hope, or a close friend?'

'A friend of my father's, and a business associate. A man called George Pullman.'

'Of the Pullman railway cars?' When he nodded, she was surprised. 'I didn't realise that you were interested in trains.'

'My father was the railroad specialist, but trains were my first love, too. My very first job was here in Boston, working on designs for iron or steel passenger-car construction. Not very successfully, I'm afraid.'

'So are you here to renew old acquaintance, or simply to take delivery of your car, or . . .?'

'. . . did I follow you?' He smiled crookedly. 'Yes, you would think that. Well, I won't pretend that the presence of the Smith-Sinclair company in Boston was not an added incentive, but I must admit that I came here in the hope of raising finance.'

'For manufacturing motor cars, yes, I remember you mentioning the matter.'

'Boston has turned me down, of course, although I still have hopes that the Panhard may make them see sense. The women we saw in Beacon Street, for instance – their brother loaned me the wherewithal to start my bicycle business, and he has had a splendid return on it, but automobiles may be a step too far for their conservatism. All the money is in trusts, you see, and the trustees won't invest in anything that they cannot see from their office windows.'

'I can understand why some people play safe. If they have a million dollars, they want to ensure that they still have a million next year, and the year after that.'

'But if they invest with me, I can turn that million into ten, or even twenty million! We are on the threshold of the twentieth century, and there is a world to conquer and huge profits to be made.'

This mixture of idealism and profiteering made Pierce seem at his most American.

'Your approach to business, and to life, really is unique,' Amadine said slowly. 'It's as if you have a dream in one hand and a dollar in the other.'

He grinned. 'You'll get the hang of us yet.'

Another aspect of this was pushing to the front of Amadine's consciousness. She was standing in front of the Dickens mirror, idly tracing the black walnut surround with her forefinger when suddenly her eyes widened, flashed and met his in the glass.

'You used me,' she exclaimed indignantly, 'to attract attention to your automobile!'

'I said that our drive would be good publicity,' he agreed with a smile. 'I didn't say for whom.'

'Of all the nerve!'

'You didn't object when you thought I was helping with your publicity,' he said in an injured tone. 'I think it is very unfair of you to complain about helping me with mine.'

'Go away, and don't bother me again.'

'I'm going, but I repeat that you should take care. You ought to buy a gun for your own protection.'

To her exasperation, Amadine's colleagues tended to agree with this assessment although their approach to the subject was much more lighthearted.

'You are more likely to need a gun to fend off admirers than frighten off attackers,' Hal declared, hiding his jealousy of the stranger who had taken her for a drive.

'Even so, there isn't much point in possessing a gun if one isn't prepared to use it,' Constance declared.

'I have used a shotgun, but not a handgun.' Seeing the consternation this remark caused, Amadine hastened to explain. 'You must remember that I'm a country girl. My brothers taught me to shoot when we were growing up, but I'm very out of practice because I hated killing things.'

'Hartford, Connecticut, is the place,' Jay said suddenly. 'For Colt's pistols, or Sharpe's rifles. Sarah Bernhardt bought a gun there on her first tour.'

'Oh, well, that settles it,' Amadine said sarcastically. 'Anything the Divine Sarah did, I must do, with knobs on. When do we go to Hartford?'

'Two weeks from now.'

'Then I will buy a gun there – always supposing I live that long!'

When Amadine announced that a visit to Cambridge was essential to her, Theo offered – with that refined diffidence that became him so well – to arrange the matter.

The trolley to Cambridge ran along Charles Street and over the West Boston Bridge, and at Harvard Yard the narrow paths through the precincts were busy with under-graduates hurrying between the mellow red-brick façades of the college buildings. In the great Memorial Hall, Amadine and Theo stood in front of the white tablets inscribed with the names of students who had fallen in the Civil War. She had read about this chamber in Henry James's *The Bostonians*, but also had an eye-witness account of the war from Charles Wyndham, one of London's most debonair actor-managers, who had started his professional life as a doctor in London and served as a surgeon in the Federal Army. For Amadine, the poignancy of these mem-orial tablets lay not only in the tragic loss of so many young and promising lives, but also in envisaging her friend and mentor struggling to save them.

Walking up Brattle Street, Theo pointed out the home of the village blacksmith immortalised in Longfellow's 'Under the spreading chestnut tree', but when he turned in at the gate of a large, yellow-painted house set well back from the street, Amadine caught at his sleeve.

'Surely we cannot go in!' she exclaimed, restraining him as she gazed at the house that had sheltered George Washington at the beginning of the Revolution, and in which Longfellow had lived for forty-five years.

'Harvard men are always welcome here,' Theo answered gently. 'Miss Alice, Longfellow's eldest daughter, lives here and although she is away from home today, I have been assured that we may look round.'

But Amadine still hesitated, and entered the house with a reluctance that was surely caused by more than anxiety about intruding on Miss Alice's privacy. Theo watched her curiously as he pointed out the staircase featured by Longfellow in 'The Children's Hour', and, in the dining room, the portrait of the three daughters who had descended that 'broad hall stair'. He had expected Amadine, with her insatiable appetite for literature, to be more excited about this treat he had arranged, and was rather disappointed by her mixed reaction to the visit, although admittedly she brightened up in the study where the poet wrote most of his works and which was packed with items of interest.

'We'll look at the library next, and then go upstairs,' Theo suggested.

'No,' Amadine said sharply, and with a note in her voice that could almost be described as fear. 'I would prefer to leave the library until last.'

So Theo led the way to the poet's bedroom. Hardly daring to enter, Amadine ventured across the threshold and stood motionless just inside the room.

On the wall was a portrait of a young woman – Fanny Appleton Longfellow, the poet's second wife, who died in a tragic accident. Amadine began to recite Longfellow's poem 'The Cross of Snow' in her low, lovely voice:

'In the long, sleepless watches of the night,
    A gentle face – the face of one long dead –
Looks at me from the wall, where round its head
    The night-lamp casts a halo of pale light.
Here in this room she died . . .'

Her voice choked with tears, Amadine broke off and, after a last look at the picture and the bed, she turned and hurried downstairs.

Theo was beginning to understand the reason for her distress, and for her uneasiness in the house. 'We don't have to see the library.'

'I must.'

In the library Amadine looked around her, re-creating the terrible scene when Fanny's dress – a huge, elaborate crinoline, it would have been, in the 1860s – had caught fire in this room, and she had rushed into the garden, screaming with fear and pain. Her husband put out the flames as quickly as he could, but still she died. After several, silent minutes Amadine left the house and stood at the front gate, taking deep breaths to steady herself.

'I've been frightened of fire for as long as I can remember,' she confessed. 'Even as a child, reading about religious martyrs who were burned at the stake, or the Great Fire of London, gave me the shivers. Occasionally there would be a fire in our neighbourhood and I couldn't even *look*, let alone help. Something strange happens to me when I even think about fires, and if I hear or smell one I'm paralysed with fear.'

'I am very much afraid that fires will keep cropping up on this tour,' Theo said anxiously. 'There was a devastating fire here in Boston in 1872, and people talk about Chicago's Great Fire of 1871 all the time.'

'Oh, Theo, if only that were all!' Amadine gave a wan smile. 'Theatre people are great gossips and storytellers. For example, on the journey from New York it was railroad accidents that were being relived, and I can promise you that fires will be raised – only verbally, I trust – before long. By the time our friends have finished swapping stories, there will not be a theatre left unburned, or an actor left unscarred, on either side of the Atlantic.'

'And I thought that today would be a treat for you!'

'It is, and I am very glad I came.' She laid her hand on his arm. 'The manner of Fanny's death always upsets me so much that I wondered how Longfellow could go on living in the same house afterwards. I could not imagine how he endured the memories. But now I understand – the house is so beautiful that of course he could not leave, and there would have been happy memories as well as sad.'

Knowing that they were due to meet Gwen at Mount Auburn cemetery, Theo was glancing at his watch. 'We are in plenty of time,' he announced, 'but it is a long walk from here. Perhaps . . .'

'I would welcome the walk, and I'd like to look at these lovely houses.'

And so, to the relief of the man who was shadowing them, Amadine and Theo continued along Brattle Street.

Gwen was waiting inside the entrance to the cemetery, holding two bunches of flowers, one of which she handed to Amadine before setting off up the central avenue.

Bought and planted by the Massachusetts Horticultural Society, the serene acres of Mount Auburn formed a picturesque city of the dead. The groves of trees and shrubs, the colourful flowerbeds, the lakes and ponds, were connected by twisting paths that contoured the landscape, while the tombstones and crypts comprised an outdoor art museum of sculpture and memorial design. It was not at its best on a November afternoon, but its dormant beauty still shone through.

After visiting the Longfellow family graves, Gwen took over as guide, threading her way unerringly through the maze of paths. At first the incline was gentle but steady, but the final stretch of Palm Avenue was steep enough for Gwen to need a helping hand up to the top of the rise on which Charlotte Cushman was buried. The tragedienne's monument was an obelisk of white marble. It bore no epitaph, not even a date; only a name. Tall, plain and striking, it was – as Gwen said – remarkably like Charlotte herself.

'That sounds unkind,' objected Amadine.

'Oh no, Charlotte was the first to admit that she was no beauty. Indeed, her lack of looks made her success all the more remarkable in an age when a pretty face was the minimum requirement for an actress.'

'Did you know her well?'

Gwen shook her head. 'I acted with her at the very end of her career, when she appeared at McVicker's in Chicago, where I worked, but it was a tremendous experience. She had her signature roles, of course, mainly developed during the years in London that made her a star – Lady Macbeth, Meg Merrilies in *Guy Mannering*, Queen Katherine in *Henry VIII*, Romeo, Hamlet . . .'

'She had cancer, in those days.'

'Breast cancer, and she suffered dreadfully. When Charlotte played Meg Merrilies, she pounded the cancerous breast so that the genuine pain she experienced was transmuted into Meg's terrible death shriek. The effect was electrifying.'

Gwen was unsure how much of the real Charlotte Cushman she should reveal. Did Amadine, for all her hero-worship, know that Charlotte had vastly preferred the ladies to the gentlemen? Was she aware that Charlotte, in her heyday, had dressed in men's clothes, as well as playing male roles on the stage, and that she had participated in what Elizabeth Barrett Browning called 'female marriages'? Was Amadine one of the same kind, and was that the reason why she disclaimed any interest in marriage? It would explain why she discouraged Hal. In Gwen's opinion any woman – especially any actress – who repulsed Hal's advances was either a lesbian or stark, raving mad.

'Dear Charlotte,' Gwen said, and giggled.

Amadine looked at her reproachfully.

'I'm sorry, but there was another side to her. Edwin Booth hated her interpretation of Lady Macbeth, and when they did the play together and she bullied him into the murder of the king, he always wanted to say, "If you're so keen to have Duncan dead, why don't you kill him? After all, you're a great deal bigger than I am."'

'Hush, she'll hear you!' and Amadine dragged Gwen away from the grave.

'I'm sorry,' Gwen said again, still giggling. 'She was wonderful, and you are quite right to revere her. Charlotte Cushman elevated the status of American actresses beyond anything we had dreamed of until then.'

Amadine went back to the grave, laid her flowers on the

lower step of the monument and stood with bowed head. When she turned round, Theo and Gwen were disappearing round the corner into Chestnut Avenue and for a moment she was alone. Glancing at the vista from this vantage point, she was thinking that this wasn't a bad place to end up, high in this park with a view over the Charles River. In fact, she wouldn't mind being buried here herself. Today, though, there was a piercing loneliness to the place, and it was just as well that she was not frightened of phantom gunmen because anyone could take a pot-shot at her out here and get away with it.

At that moment she thought she saw something move among the trees nearby, and she stiffened, her heart thudding. However, she refused to allow herself to run in pursuit of her companions, merely lengthening her long, swinging stride and soon narrowing the distance between them. After all, why shouldn't other people be about? Yet on the curve, as Chestnut merged into Walnut Avenue, the lack of living company in the cemetery was most marked. Theo and Gwen seemed to feel it, too, and fell silent as they approached the grave of Edwin Booth.

Here was a group of three graves, those of Edwin Booth, his wife and child. The strange thing was, Gwen said, that it was his first wife who lay beside him, while the child was the son of the second wife. The baby was buried here but his mother, Mary McVicker, who had also predeceased her husband, had been buried in Chicago.

Gwen laid her flowers on Booth's grave and then, taking Theo's arm, walked away, telling him about her connection with the great actor – how she had appeared with him at McVicker's Theatre in Chicago, and how she had toured with him and Lawrence Barrett in the late 1880s. Again Amadine lingered. She had that 'I may never pass this way again' feeling, because she was a visitor not only to this city but to this country, and she did not want to hurry. She admired the circular plaque bearing Booth's likeness, and grieved over the tiny tombstone of little Edgar, who had lived for less than a day.

Around her nothing moved. The wind had dropped and the trees, branches bare and gaunt, were still against the lowering sky. Not a bird flew or fluttered or sang. As she stared past Booth's grave to the row of tombstones beyond, not another mourner was in sight. Yet suddenly the hair on the back of Amadine's head prickled, and she raised a hand to the nape of her neck. She had the most profoundly disturbing feeling that she was being watched. Alone in this remote spot, she realised again how vulnerable she was – how vulnerable anyone was – to attack, and this time when she hurried after her companions she did run.

He did not follow her. He knew their plans, having been close enough to overhear the conversation, and saw no point in rushing back to Boston in order to attend an organ recital at King's Chapel.

She needn't have run off like that, though. The gun was in his pocket, but he had no intention of using it. He'd been a fool to fire it yesterday, but the urge to do so had been irresistible; the sensation of power had been euphoric – the knowledge that he could harm her so easily if he felt inclined. Also, in a way he supposed he had been letting Amadine know he was there without actually letting her see him, and he was rather sorry that he had not hit the swell she had been with. On the other hand, he couldn't go round America letting loose at every man she talked to, or the place would be knee-deep in bodies in no time. A popular lady, our Amadine . . . *his* Amadine . . .

If it wasn't that stranger, it was this pretty boy who was hanging on her arm. And if it wasn't them, it was Hal or Frank Smith, or Laurie Knight. Good God! And, thrusting his hands into his pockets, he gave a snort of disgust. He had played with them all at the Lyceum, and they hadn't been any better than him then and they weren't any better now. So how come Hal and Laurie were topping the bill, and Frank had a cosy berth as stage manager, while he was grubbing for a living, playing poor roles in even worse productions? For Pete's sake, before San Francisco, he had been in *Australia* . . .

He smoothed his upper lip thoughtfully. The moustache was coming along nicely, and he had made a first-class job of darkening his striking, pale blond hair. He didn't want to draw attention to himself, not until he was ready, and he did not want to approach any of them at the moment, not even Amadine. There was an intense, almost sexual pleasure in waiting and planning and relishing the sensation of power. The anticipation could, and should, be savoured. Take yesterday, for instance. After firing that one shot, unseen by anyone on the Common, he had hurried across and joined the crowd of onlookers around the automobile. He was sure that Amadine had looked straight at him and that, for one glorious second, their eyes met. The more he thought about it, the more certain he was that it had been so.

Therefore he was in no hurry to confront her. His means were slender, but would allow him to follow the tour at least as far as Washington. The one-night stands were a problem, though, and when the company joined the special train next week he reckoned he would go ahead to Philadelphia and wait for them there. He might be able to pick up a bit of part-time work to tide him over. Of course, the best, the absolutely ideal thing would be to find a way of boarding the train . . .

Chapter Eight

Helping Amadine to study Juliet, Laurie was more astonished by her lack of self-confidence than by her excellent progress. That soft, smoky voice spoke the verse with such intelligence and emotion that she was, he told her sincerely, a natural for Shakespeare. His only criticism was that she would strive for too much realism in her performance. When she wailed that she was too tall and too old to play Juliet, he replied caustically that, yes, perhaps her physical appearance was more suited to sirens such as Cleopatra, but she could always try *acting* the part!

However, Amadine also had an unfortunate tendency to seek the meaning of the text, and all too frequently Laurie was unable to enlighten her. Eventually he was forced to confess that, famed for his interpretation of Shakespearian roles as he was, he often had not the foggiest idea what he was saying. He got by on technique and sheer bluff, combined with the fine presence, rich voice and romantic vigour he brought to the stage.

Laurie's background and education contrasted sharply with the advantages Amadine had enjoyed. While Amadine had been educated by a governess, in the company of her wealthy cousins, Laurie had a working-class background. The only son of a stage-struck mother, he was pushed on to the stage when he was a child and, being beautiful *and* talented, soon progressed to playing Mamillius, and Puck, or one of the young princes in *Richard III*. But his progress in the theatre resulted in a lack of schooling, and he was self-conscious about his poor education. His reluctance to go into management was only partly because he did not want the additional responsibility, and owed much more to his conviction that he was not clever enough to do it. Secretly Laurie was terrified of educated women like Amadine, who would find out that he was nothing but a trumped-up working-class boy with a pretty face but very little brain, and so he socialised with people who would not find him out: labourers, with whom he shared a drink; barmaids, who were easily seduced; people of his own kind, who were captivated by his handsome face, cultivated manner and cosmopolitan air. His colleagues were kept at arm's length, Laurie maintaining relationships with them on a purely professional level because in this area he could earn respect.

This idiosyncracy of Laurie's was well-known, even if the reasons for it were not understood and so, when Amadine broached the subject of the trip to Salem, he was surprised.

'Darling, you know perfectly well that it isn't my sort of thing,' he said breezily, but with an underlying current of caution.

'You must come, just this once,' she coaxed. 'It's our last chance to have a day out before we board the train on Sunday.'

'Which is all the more reason for going our separate ways – once we are on that train, we'll be sick of the sight of each other in no time.'

'If you won't do it for me, do it for Hal. He has been cooped up in the theatre ever since we landed in America, except for a few evenings at the Players' Club and several official receptions. He needs a break, and if you are one of the party he will have no excuse to cry off.'

Laurie did not want to go, but was too loyal and good-natured to refuse.

There was a raw chill in the air that Thursday when they set out, with an icy sleet knifing from a sky of uncompromising grey. Winter had arrived, and Amadine warded off the cold with the sable coat she had been persuaded to buy in New York, while Constance was wrapped in a distinctive hooded cloak of brown woollen tweed, banded and collared with beaver. They travelled by train to the little town of Salem, a few miles north-east of Boston on the coast of Massachusetts where, Theo had ascertained, carriages would be available to take them farther afield if they so desired.

'Because,' Theo informed them, 'much of the witchcraft hysteria, and the events connected with it, took place in Salem Village, now called Danvers, and it would be too far to walk there.'

As Amadine's chief interest was the connection of the writer Nathaniel Hawthorne with Salem Town – and bearing in mind the threatening weather, the early dusk and the need to return to Boston in time for the evening performance – further adventuring seemed unlikely. However, during the journey there was little doubt that the attention of the group centred on the witch trials, so Theo recounted again the basic facts of the story.

In 1692 a circle of young girls gathered at the parsonage in Salem Village in order to listen to tales of voodoo and black magic related by Tituba, a slave from Barbados. In this Puritanical and isolated place, such stories had a disturbing effect on the girls and one of them – the daughter of the minister – began behaving strangely. One by one her friends followed suit, until the whole group was having 'fits' and was deemed to be bewitched. Under interrogation, the girls named the witches who were tormenting them, and by the time the hysteria had run its course, 150 local men and women had been accused, of whom five died in prison, nineteen were hanged on Gallows Hill in Salem Town and one was crushed to death.

'And those wicked girls were making it up?' Constance gasped.

'One cannot be sure exactly how it started,' Theo said cautiously. 'Perhaps they blamed others in order to save their own skins – in the social and religious atmosphere of Salem at the time, they ought not to have been dabbling in the occult. Certainly, once they had started the ball rolling, the girls were caught up in the hysteria. What is astonishing is that so many sober ministers and magistrates believed them.'

'Do any of you believe in witches?' Constance asked the group in general, and was answered by an immediate chorus of dissent. 'Yet large numbers of people used to believe, and perhaps some still do.'

'My father maintained that the ceremonies and other features of witchcraft were simply the customs of ancient, pre-Christian faith,' Amadine said thoughtfully. 'For instance, it used to be supposed that witches could metamorphose into animals or birds, and many pagan gods were believed to be shape-shifters.'

'Did you come across any of these old customs in the country?' Constance enquired.

'I knew several wise women who used herbs and plants for medicines, and gypsies who told fortunes, and who sold love charms to village girls or fair winds to sailors. And there are many farmers who observe the old rituals connected with the harvest and the other seasons.'

'But surely rituals of that kind fall into the category of superstition, rather than witchcraft,' Constance argued.

'One is an extension of the other,' Amadine suggested. 'Take horses, for example. In the olden days horses were believed to be at special risk from wicked witches, and in our village there was a man who could calm intractable animals merely by whispering in their ears. Yet we happily embrace the horseshoe – shaped like a crescent, symbol of the witch goddess of the moon – as a good-luck charm.'

The discussion was developing into a sparring match between Amadine and Constance, and their companions were as interested in the contest as in the subject matter.

'Are you saying that superstitions can work both ways – for good or bad – depending on one's point of view?' Constance tried to think of another example. 'Like black cats – in the theatre we are very superstitious about black cats, and I've known other people who are afraid to have one cross their path.'

Amadine nodded. 'Because it might be a witch who has taken on the form of a cat. Yet, to some people, a black cat is lucky. There is an old folk rhyme that says: whenever the cat of the house is black, the lasses of lovers will have no lack.'

'Equally,' Constance continued, 'there were good and bad witches, although one always hears about the wicked, not the white, ones. They are depicted as horrid, malicious creatures, who conjured up storms, floods and pestilence, who afflicted their victims with disease and madness, who bewitched children, set fire to houses, blighted crops and soured the beer. Why was that, do you think?'

Amadine allowed a slight pause to ensue as she considered her answer. She was beginning to see where the conversation was leading, and it was a destination not much to her liking. 'I imagine that it has always been easier and more convenient to blame witches for one's misfortunes than admit to any fault of one's own,' she said sharply.

Constance was equal to the challenge. 'I imagine a witch to be an ugly, old woman, living alone with her black cat. Yet I don't see why – she could be young and beautiful . . .'

She looked meaningfully at Amadine, and so did everyone else: at Amadine's long, lithe body, gleaming black hair, green eyes and sable coat.

'Just because the clergyman's daughter started the Salem hysteria,' Amadine snapped, 'doesn't mean that I am a witch, or that I'll denounce anyone else as one.'

Her colleagues smiled, but a slight unease remained. Constance had not mentioned the word jinx, but she had not needed to – everyone, including Amadine, was fully aware of the bad luck dogging the tour.

The weather, and the landscape, was growing bleaker. Snow had been falling, and the trees and streams were black against the untrodden whiteness and a sky of iron. At Salem the temperature was several degrees lower than in Boston, and a freezing wind was blowing in from the sea. Amadine, swiftly recovering her spirits, speculated optimistically about using a sleigh but it appeared that the streets were passable, with care, to foot and carriage traffic. Theo had arranged for two conveyances to meet the train and, in order to irritate Constance, Amadine sat beside Hal and exerted herself to be at her most charming.

They drove to the harbour, once the centre of Salem's flourishing maritime trade, from where the town's prosperous merchants despatched their fleets to find coffee, tea and spices, wine, silk and ivory. Now the wharves were silent and deserted, for the trade had moved to larger and deeper harbours, but the Custom House still stood, with its wide granite steps and great gilded eagle over the door. It was here that Nathaniel Hawthorne had worked as Surveyor of the Port of Salem, and which he described in the introduction to his masterpiece *The Scarlet Letter*. Apart from Amadine, only Hal had read the book and they were delighted to find that they could enter the office Hawthorne had occupied.

'Look, there's the tin pipe in the ceiling,' Amadine exclaimed.

'Which "forms a medium of vocal communication with other parts of the edifice",' Hal quoted.

'And the stove with voluminous funnel . . . the desk and the stool . . .'

They were talking in a sort of shorthand and sharing a pleasure that excluded their companions. Unsurprisingly, it was Constance who tried to break the intimacy.

'You acted in a version of *The Scarlet Letter*, didn't you, Hal?'

'In London, a few years ago,' he agreed.

Amadine gazed at him thoughtfully. 'Oh, you would be wonderful as the Reverend Mr Dimmesdale – with your looks, you could seduce the most virtuous Puritan!'

Hal smiled and preened a little, even as he disclaimed such powers amid much chaffing from his fellows. Laurie did his share of the teasing, although he had no idea who Dimmesdale was. It was only by the utmost concentration on the conversation that he gathered that the scarlet letter was a red badge of shame, an A for adulteress, which the mother of an illegitimate child was forced to wear on her gown.

'I've never understood why Hester Prynne paraded through the streets wearing that letter, for years and years, instead of moving to a place where no one knew her,' Hal commented. 'Isn't that what you would have done, Amadine?'

'I would not commit that particular sin in the first place.'

But that aroused a chorus of disbelief and disdain, which even a reminder that Amadine was the rector's daughter could not quash, and it was in argumentative mood that the company re-entered their carriages and drove to Hawthorne's birthplace, as well as other houses in the town where he lived and worked. Their last stop before luncheon was The House of the Seven Gables that had inspired the eponymous novel and Hal, for whom this excursion was bearing unexpected fruit, succeeded in guiding Amadine away from the others. The house being privately owned, they could not go in but stood facing the sea and the 'rusty wooden house, with seven acutely peaked gables . . . and a huge, clustered chimney in the midst'.

'It is easy to see how the house inspired such a Gothic tale,' Hal commented.

'I don't agree that the story is Gothic,' Amadine declared, and they argued good-naturedly over the finer points of the novel until Hal drew Amadine's arm through his, retaining hold of her hand for as long as he dared.

'I do like stories that finish with the young lovers driving off to marriage and a new life together, don't you?'

'Not to the exclusion of everything else,' Amadine replied cautiously. Genuinely enjoying Hal's company today, and impressed by his literary knowledge, she did hope that he would not spoil things by becoming too personal.

'Of course the other theme in *Seven Gables* is inheritance, of property in particular. I suppose a religious person such as yourself has strong views on the subject?'

'You make me sound so disapproving! And, no, I don't have strong views on the subject, possibly because I have no property to inherit.'

'I do. Have property, I mean.'

Oh Lord, he was getting personal. 'It doesn't seem to take up much of your time and attention.'

'I haven't inherited it yet – Father is hale and hearty, thank God – and when I do, I'll probably put my brother Harry in charge of the place. He's a real stop-at-home fellow, like my sister, who has kept house since Mother died. Funny, isn't it: Frank and I rush round all over the shop, and those two cannot be prised from their shells.'

'Perhaps Frank would like to be in charge of the place.'

Hal shook his head. 'Frank chose the theatre and, besides, he is younger than Harry. Strict order of precedence, you see, so Frank has to earn his own living.'

'Where is this property?'

'Sussex. I usually go down in August for a few weeks'

rest and relaxation. You ought to come with me after the tour – you'd like it down there and,' here Hal squeezed her hand, 'it would like you.'

Like hell it would, thought Amadine. That sister, so happily running the house, would hate me on sight. 'Has Constance visited?'

'Good God, no.' Hal sounded positively alarmed at the idea. 'The family have met her, though. I coaxed them up to town for a first night but they, and my sister in particular, didn't take to her.'

Poor Constance, thought Amadine compassionately, desperately trying to make a good impression on Hal's people, while the Haldane-Smiths warily eyed a widowed actress with two children. Oh, how Constance would have loved to be able to leave the children in Sussex with Hal's sister while she toured ... Feeling mean and guilty about her own behaviour in appropriating Hal so deliberately, Amadine glanced over her shoulder and saw Constance watching them from some way off. The expression on her face clearly indicated that, appropriately for Salem, she wished Amadine would go to the devil.

Laurie was wishing that he hadn't come. It wasn't that he minded being stuck with Constance, or that he was offended by her obvious preference for Hal – quite the contrary, in fact. No, Laurie was out of his depth; listening to Hal and Amadine's intellectual conversation made him feel inferior and uncomfortable because, having nothing to contribute, he could not join in. To make matters worse, little Blanche Villard was making sheep's eyes at him. Including her in the expedition had been Gwen's idea. 'Blanche is lonely,' Gwen had asserted. 'She has no friends of her own age and status in the company, so I think I will adopt her.' Which was all very well, but the girl from Baltimore was making it quite clear that she would prefer Laurie to look after her. Oh, she was being very polite and attentive to

Gwen, but she didn't fool Laurie for an instant. He had been in this situation on countless occasions, and it was another reason why he avoided socialising with his colleagues – the complications, and the repercussions, could be endless.

Gloomily Laurie sat down to luncheon and listened to the comments ricocheting around him. He wondered if it was possible to learn the art of conversation.

'I have just realised that you are the spitting image of the 1840 Osgood portrait of Hawthorne,' Frank was telling Theo.

'Unfortunately the resemblance ends there,' Theo smiled ruefully.

'Does that mean you have literary aspirations?'

'I write a little,' Theo admitted. 'Plays, and a bit of poetry.'

'Have any of the plays been produced?' And when Theo answered in the negative, Frank asked, 'What sort of stuff is it?'

'I am greatly influenced by the Philadelphia School of Dramatists,' Theo said eagerly, 'being from that city myself.'

Frank had heard of this group of gentlemen playwrights who adorned Philadelphia in the first half of the nineteenth century. Several plays – notably Boker's *Francesca da Rimini* – had been moderately successful but, and it was an awfully big but, Frank knew that the group had usually produced romantic tragedies in blank verse. He groaned inwardly and, had the aspiring dramatist been anyone other than Theo, would have discouraged further discussion. However, Frank recognised that here was the opportunity he had been seeking. His relationship with Theo, which as yet hardly merited the term, was inordinately delicate. Men with his homoerotic tendencies dared not reveal their feelings, and went to such great lengths to conceal their inclinations that time and patience were needed in order to discover whether the object of one's desire shared one's sexual identity. Not only must Frank guard against making the wrong overtures, but he must ensure that his own inclinations did not become public knowledge. Therefore what he needed was a set of circumstances where he and Theo could be alone, in a situation conducive to closer intimacy.

'I would be delighted to look at your work,' he offered, 'if you brought any manuscripts with you.'

Theo did not confide that the hope of such a development had been the driving force behind his readiness to accept a comparatively lowly and poorly paid position. All the same, he hesitated fractionally. Recognising their intellectual superiority, he would have preferred Hal or Amadine to read his work, but . . . any port in a storm, he thought, and Frank was proving to be his sheet anchor in this strange new world. 'I would be very grateful for your advice,' he said warmly.

Frank was thinking ahead, to the train journeys and hotel rooms spread in glorious profusion over the forthcoming six months, and to the vision of him and Theo working on the scripts, heads bent close together until the sexual chemistry could be denied no longer and . . . 'Let's keep this between ourselves,' he said in a low voice. 'Hal is terribly busy, and he tends to be touchy about new plays – for one thing, Constance is always nagging him about her husband's ghastly trash. You and I could go through your stuff, decide on one play that has possibilities, and whip it into shape before presenting it to Hal.'

Laurie was listening to the general ribbing of Gwen about a letter she had received.

'Come on, admit it, someone sent you a mash note,' Amadine teased.

Gwen went pink. 'As a matter of fact, it does appear that one is never too old to attract a little attention.' Then, under pressure, she admitted that her correspondent lived in New York – 'so, seeing that he only wrote after I left

New York, he isn't very keen to meet me' – but that he travelled on business from time to time, and hoped that his itinerary might coincide with that of the tour.

'What did you say in reply?' Amadine wanted to know.

'I haven't replied, and I'm not sure that I will. Anyway,' and Gwen tried to divert attention from herself, 'why all this fascination with my mail? The affairs of you young people are much more interesting.'

'Theo received a letter this morning,' Blanche remarked quietly.

Laurie noted, with hope in his heart, that as she spoke Blanche's attention was focused firmly on Frank. With any luck, she had sensed that he, Laurie, wasn't interested, and was seeking romance elsewhere. Still, it would be odd if she had a fling with Frank, because Laurie had sensed friction between them.

'In a charmingly feminine hand,' Amadine was corroborating. 'Out with it, Theo.'

'A girlfriend in Philadelphia,' Constance speculated.

'She isn't my girlfriend. She's my wife.'

There was a clatter of spoons, a few choking noises and a thunderstruck silence.

'You're married?' Amadine gasped at last. 'But you are so young!'

'I'm twenty-eight. I just look younger.'

There was another pause as everyone struggled to adjust their view of him.

'You are a dark horse,' Frank chaffed bravely. 'Why didn't you mention this before?'

'No one asked. And I didn't want to make an issue of it, or you might have decided that a married man was unsuitable for the position. I did so want the job.'

It means nothing, Frank tried to convince himself. Lots of homosexual men were married. For God's sake, *Oscar Wilde* was married . . .

*

After luncheon Gwen left the room with Amadine and, to his dismay, Blanche attached herself firmly to Laurie and ensured that she sat beside him during the afternoon drive. They were to follow the route believed to have been taken by the condemned 'witches' from the gaol to their place of execution on Gallows Hill.

'The witches are why I came,' Blanche confided.

'Me, too,' Laurie agreed politely.

'I wouldn't tell this to everyone, but that business this morning – about the novelist an' all – was right over my head. I'm afraid that I'm not as clever as Amadine and the Chief.'

Laurie's depression deepened. Blanche's wide-eyed innocence and air of naïvety didn't cut any ice with him. That young lady was as sharp as a tack and her pretence of being stupid could mean only one thing – that she thought *he* was stupid. Blanche was trying to attract him by bringing herself down to his level. She had found him out. Already.

'I like the way you appreciate things in your own quiet way,' Blanche went on. 'It's what I call real English reserve – the behaviour of a real English gentleman.'

And that is what I call over-egging the pudding, dearie, Laurie thought wearily, but he roused himself sufficiently to smile and be polite. Mustn't rock the boat, not this early in the tour.

The two carriages were travelling slowly and with extreme caution. Instead of turning to slush, the snow was now hard and compacted, freezing into a treacherously slippery surface. After some distance they took a right-hand turn and then a left, before stopping to allow the company to disembark and look up at the grim outline of Gallows Hill.

'It's higher and steeper than I expected,' Hal said doubtfully. 'The snow might make the climb too difficult.'

'Are you sure this is the right place?' Amadine asked

Theo. 'The condemned people were brought here in carts, weren't they? You couldn't drag a cart up there.'

Theo assured them that this was supposed to be the very place, and accordingly Amadine set off in a determined attempt to reach the summit. But the slippery slope defeated her, and soon she was taking one step forward and two steps back while the others laughed at her predicament. Then, pausing halfway up the first gradient, something caught her eye.

'The children are sledding,' she called out, slithering back to ground level. 'They'll lend us a sled if we give them a big enough tip!'

No one else displayed any great enthusiasm for the idea but, as usual, there was something about Amadine's exuberance that towed the others along in her wake. In a few minutes she was using her charm on the schoolchildren and persuading them to allow her a turn on one of their sleds. As they talked, a sled came coasting down the slope, gathering speed on the smooth, frozen surface, its runners rattling over the ice.

'I haven't done this since I was a child,' Amadine exclaimed eagerly. 'Who is coming down with me?' None of her companions moved or spoke. 'Well, don't all rush at once,' she said sarcastically.

One of the schoolboys, a tall youngster of about fifteen, stepped forward and offered to take her down on his sled.

'Cowards,' she threw over her shoulder as she and her escort began the climb to the top of the slope.

The great thing about this adventure, she thought as she settled down on the sled and the boy took his seat behind her, was that this youngster had not the faintest idea who she was; he was merely being polite and kind. Mind you, if she became really famous he would be able to dine out on the story for the rest of his life, but at the moment there was just the silence and the slight warmth and pressure of his body behind hers. It wasn't a sexual pressure, of course, but even if he hadn't been a mere boy, she doubted if she would have experienced such a sensation. That sort of thing didn't happen to her any more. And then suddenly she remembered the closeness of Pierce Radcliffe's body against hers as they crouched beside the car the other day, and she was swamped by a rush of desire. She had not felt it at the time but she did now, in retrospect. Then the flood of warmth was gone as quickly as it came, because the sled jerked forward and an icy wind was rushing past her face . . .

At the bottom they screeched to a halt and Amadine sprang up, kissed her embarrassed hero and mollified him by slipping a handful of coins into his pocket.

'I thought better of you,' she scoffed to her companions. 'I thought that you would have more gumption.'

Her mockery was so clearly lighthearted, rather than intended to goad anyone into action, that perhaps it was her use of that old northern expression that struck a chord. Or perhaps Laurie felt that physical activity was something he could contribute. Whatever the reason, he walked forward and towed the sled to the top of the run.

He was halfway down when the problem became apparent. Whether the steering was defective, or he couldn't get the hang of it, or whether the sled was unbalanced with one heavy man at the back instead of two smaller people of more equal weight, was never resolved. All anyone knew was that the sled veered out of control, bumped out of the ruts worn in the slope by previous runs and shot across a patch of virgin snow. Then, with a dull thud, the sled and Laurie smashed into a tree.

He lay motionless, his body twisted at an unnatural angle, as bright-red blood stained the snow.

Chapter Nine

No one mentioned witchcraft, curses or jinx. Even Constance said only two words – '*the umbrella!*' – during the ghastly train journey back to Boston. Someone else remembered that, that very day, the Boston *Daily Globe* had printed a letter from Fanny Davenport, the noted actress who had been appearing at the Boston Theatre, in which she lauded the emergency hospital for its treatment of a severely ill member of her company. 'I bespeak for the Boston emergency hospital the warm and hearty support of all members of my profession,' Fanny concluded. Yes, but they had not intended to show their support by bringing another patient to its doors.

While Amadine cradled Laurie's gashed head and tried to stem the bleeding from the appalling lacerations to his face, Theo and one of the local boys fetched a doctor. Carefully he straightened the misshapen legs and bound them with splints, before bathing and bandaging Laurie's head. It seemed probable that the arms and upper body were injured, but in the gathering dusk and freezing cold it was difficult to tell. The train to Boston being due, the best plan seemed to be to move Laurie to it and thence to the Boston hospital, so they improvised a stretcher on which to carry the unconscious man.

Even in a time of such trouble, business matters had to be

considered. Laurie appeared in every play in the Boston repertoire. Hal decided to change that evening's bill and put on *Romeo*; the alteration to the schedule would entail some swift scene-setting, and it was to be hoped that all the cast could be located, but it was the play in which Laurie could be replaced with minimum upheaval. The plan also freed Amadine to stay at the hospital with Laurie, so that there would be a familiar face beside him when he woke – if he woke . . .

When Hal arrived at the hospital after the performance, Amadine was sitting beside Laurie's bed. His broken legs and broken nose had been set, and the gashes to his head and face had been stitched, but he had not regained consciousness.

'Suppose his spine is injured,' Amadine said suddenly, 'and that, even if his broken legs mend, he never walks again.'

'I'm sure it won't be as bad as that.' Hal tried to sound convincing. 'Laurie's a tough old bird, for all his matinée-idol smile and occasional actor-ish flourishes.'

'Remember that wonderful bit in his Romeo, when he swings up to the balcony? His athleticism is such an integral part of his acting. Suppose . . .'

'Stop supposing. There's nothing we can do but wait.'

'And his face . . . Oh, Hal, it looked so dreadful, all cut open on one side and his nose bent. Laurie relies on his looks. We all do. Damn it, why couldn't it have happened to me!'

Hal could have told her that she was more important than Laurie to the overall success of the tour, but he knew that these sentiments were unlikely to help. 'Good house tonight,' he remarked, more to pass the time than impart the information. 'We offered refunds, due to the change of bill, but no one asked for them.'

'You'll have to recast all the plays again.'

'I know.'

After another lengthy pause, she said, 'Will this tour ever run smoothly?'

'Of course it will.' He moved his chair closer to hers and put his arm round her, drawing her head on to his shoulder. 'Go to sleep. I'll wake you if Laurie comes round,' and as she closed her eyes, he pressed his lips to her forehead. He dozed.

'If I'd known it would bring you two together, I might've had an accident sooner.'

The words, and the sight of one blue eye peering through the bandages, catapulted Amadine out of her chair and on to the bed. She began kissing what little of Laurie's face was visible.

'Are you all right? Do you recognise us? Does it hurt? Darling Laurie, it was all my fault and I'm so terribly sorry.'

'Stop babbling, darling. Of course I recognise you, and of course it hurts.' Laurie tried to move, and winced. 'It hurts everywhere.'

'But that's good, that's really marvellous! The more it hurts, the less chance there is that your spine is damaged.'

Hal had gone to fetch a nurse, and Amadine was relegated to the corridor while Laurie's reflexes were tested and he was given something for the pain. When Hal rejoined her, he was smiling.

'The dear old fellow is a mass of lacerations and bruises but, other than the legs and nose, nothing appears to be broken. And he can feel the pain in his legs, so there is every chance he will walk again.'

But, relieved though she was by the news of Laurie's condition, Amadine's fears for his future did not abate. She remained deeply concerned that any permanent loss of mobility, and scarring to his face, could seriously affect his acting ability and limit the roles he could play. Not wishing to depress him, she was cheerful and optimistic during her visits to the hospital and outwardly devoted her efforts to arranging matters for his comfort after the company left Boston. Dreading the necessity of leaving him alone in a city of strangers, Amadine had a brainwave in the shape of Miss P of Pinckney Street. After checking that Gwen had no objection to the plan, she arranged for a delighted Miss P to visit Laurie at least twice a week and to send Amadine regular reports on his progress, and insisted on leaving a handsome sum to fund cab rides for Miss P and little gifts for the invalid.

Even with these arrangements in place, leaving Laurie in the hospital was one of the hardest things Amadine had ever done. She was racked with guilt, and refused to believe Laurie's assurances that she was not to blame and that his own clumsiness had caused the accident. Also, Amadine relied heavily on Laurie during her performances, and his own uncomplicated approach to acting helped her through the torment of her self-doubt. She had called him her 'rock'; now his invaluable support was gone.

'Do one thing for me,' he said, as they parted. 'Play Juliet for me.'

'I would prefer to play Juliet with you! And we will, won't we! Let's make it a promise.'

Laurie tried to smile, but his facial injuries contorted his mouth into a grotesque grimace. 'Can't promise, darling,' he said, with a brave attempt at jauntiness that tore Amadine apart. 'It could be character parts for me from now on.'

Frank spent the better part of Saturday night loading scenery, props and costumes into the freight and baggage cars at the front of the special train. Apart from the obvious necessity of ensuring that nothing was lost or left behind, the fact that all the paraphernalia would be unloaded and reloaded many times in the months ahead meant that it was vital each item was properly labelled and stowed in its appointed place. In this area Theo's meticulous eye for detail was invaluable, and he duly received his reward. Theo was the first, if unwilling, beneficiary of Laurie's absence from the tour: he inherited the stateroom that Laurie was to have occupied in the men's car.

This, a standard Pullman 12 + 1 sleeping car was situated behind the baggage car. Like the other carriages, it was of wooden construction and the exterior was painted a dark olive green, richly ornamented in gold stencil work. The men's wash- and smoking-room was situated at the front, then came the twelve open sections of two double berths each, with the stateroom and another communal washroom at the rear. The Brussels carpet was patterned in crimson and gold, the window and berth curtains were of crimson velvet and the seats – which formed the lower berths at night – were covered in crimson plush with a gold leaf pattern, but the real glory of the interior was the elaborate use of rare and beautiful wood. This car was panelled in walnut and teak, with raised mouldings of amaranth flowers, while the panels on the undersides of the upper berths were decorated with inlaid work of rosewood, tulip and amboyna. Lit by ornate silver-plated Pintsch gas lamps, heated by steam, and furnished with every amenity from small portable tables to ice-water coolers, these cars were considered the height of luxury by some, and denounced for their 'barbaric splendour and gloomy magnificence' by others.

Theo felt a proprietorial pleasure as he looked round the little crimson and gold stateroom that was to be his home for the next few months, except during longer stays in the bigger cities, where hotels would be used again. He had been perfectly ready to muck in with the other men, but he was accustomed to privacy and therefore was grateful to Hal for this privilege. He did not know that Hal had suggested he might share the room with Jay, and that it was Frank who had protected Theo's privacy. The publicity man was left to sleep in the open section, in the berth nearest the stateroom door and the vestibule connecting the men's car with that of the women immediately behind.

The women's car was furnished in similar style except that the carpet and plush seats were of sage green with a gold flower motif, and the berth and window curtains were of sage green and gold damask. The woodwork was mainly of dark mahogany, finely carved and highly polished, and the upper-berth panels and partitions were inlaid with satin, ebony and other fancy woods carved in the popular pineapple pattern. However, the layout of this car varied in that there was a stateroom and communal washroom at each end. The stateroom at the rear had been allocated to Gwen and, helping the older woman with her luggage after travelling with the principals to the station, Blanche Villard manoeuvred herself into the berth nearest to Gwen's door.

At the front of the car, Constance sat down in the other stateroom and looked around her. She was swamped by a sudden wave of loneliness and depression, which even unpacking the photographs of her children, and placing them in a prominent position on the little dressing table, could not dispel. Nothing about the tour was turning out as she had hoped and expected, professionally or personally. Leaving aside her feelings for Hal, she was disappointed that there were no kindred spirits among the company with whom she could be friends. If only there had been another young mother with whom she could have shared her worries about the children, her joy when a letter from London reported good news, and shopping expeditions for little gifts to take home. Of course, this situation was no one's fault, and she could not accuse her colleagues of forming bosom friendships from which she was excluded. Constance's loneliness came from within, from a feeling of being different, of being unable to relax in a carefree fashion as the others did. More specifically, as she perceived Amadine did.

Constance was consumed by jealousy, eaten away by envy, of Amadine. At times – fortunately few and short-lived – she even resented her children because she felt that their existence was offputting to Hal, and that they cramped her style and weighed her down. Always she was faced with Amadine, free as a bird, with no ties or responsibilities, concerned only with her own career, appearance and relationships. Every woman could look that good, Constance thought furiously, if she had only herself to think about, if she had that much time and money to spend on herself.

Somehow the stateroom encapsulated her situation. The problem lay not in the accommodation itself – it promised to be comfortable in a cosy, compact sort of way – but in its location. Constance was isolated at the front of the women's car, while Amadine occupied a sumptuous stateroom in the private Palace Car at the rear of the train – a room that was immediately adjacent to Hal's.

Hal had brooked no argument on the subject when Frank, foreseeing that such blatant favouritism would cause ill-feeling, proposed that Gwen should vacate the second stateroom in the women's car in favour of Amadine.

'Leaving the Palace Car room for you, I suppose,' Hal had said, with uncharacteristic sharpness. 'Certainly not. Amadine has seniority, and a right to the private accommodation.'

Frank eyed his brother speculatively. 'Couldn't be that you have an ulterior motive?'

'Damn right I have an ulterior motive. I want that woman so much it hurts, and I'll take her to bed before this tour is over, if it's the last thing I do.'

'It seems to me that she hasn't shown much interest in sex,' Frank remarked. 'Perhaps the rector's daughter is virtuous.'

'Then I'll marry her. In fact I am seriously thinking of doing exactly that.'

'If she'll have you.'

Hal laughed. He was in buoyant mood, feeling that real progress had been made with Amadine in Salem, and that the intimacy of the Palace Car would provide the perfect atmosphere, as well as the perfect opportunity, in which to consummate the relationship.

'I never had any trouble with my other leading ladies,' he asserted confidently. 'Well, correction – there was occasional unpleasantness when I had to persuade the lady that marriage was definitely *not* a good personal or professional move.'

'What about your rival – the chap with the motor car?'

'History,' Hal declaimed, with a dismissive wave of his hand. 'I don't suppose it amounted to anything in the first place.'

'I hate to spoil this idyll, but you do realise that I will be sleeping in the Palace Car as well?'

'In that single room off my stateroom? Oh . . . but wouldn't you prefer to share with Theo?'

Frank went bright scarlet, and then deathly pale. 'Why do you say that?'

'The single room is little more than a cubicle – probably designed for a child, or a servant. Isn't it beneath your dignity?'

'Of course not.' Reassured that Hal remained in ignorance of his sexual preferences, Frank hastened to emphasise another aspect of the matter. 'And before you tell me that three's a crowd, bear in mind that the presence of a chaperone in the Palace Car adds considerably to the propriety of the situation.'

'That's true.' Hal thought for a moment, and then sighed. 'Yes, of course, you are right. I only hope that you are a sound sleeper – better stock up on earplugs of some kind to be on the safe side!'

Frank remained unconvinced that this would be necessary, and breathed a sigh of relief that his own sleeping arrangements were finalised to his satisfaction. However much he might desire to share a bedroom with Theo, his first priority must remain control and supervision of the safe.

Except that there wasn't a safe. This unpalatable fact was discovered by Amadine as she prowled round her little domain while her maid dealt with the unpacking.

Private Palace Cars were not standardised but produced to individual requirements, custom-built for the moguls of the gilded age or for rental customers like the Smith-Sinclair company. This was Amadine's first experience of this very American phenomenon, and she was delighted by the opulent furnishings and clever use of space.

At the front, just beyond the vestibule leading to the women's car, was the accommodation for the crew. Next came the kitchen and pantry, where a glowing fire shone on polished pots and pans, and where silver-bright saucepans and steamers swung on hooks on the dresser. From there one entered a large open room, which extended the full width of the car and doubled as parlour and dining room. Panelled in mahogany and satinwood, with gorgeous inlays on the white mahogany ceiling, the dominant colour in the room was gold, from the gold silk tapestry curtains and hangings to the rich cream and gold carpet. Containing an extension dining table covered in a silk tapestry cloth, dining chairs upholstered in gold plush, comfortable chairs and sofas elegant with lace antimacassars, a sideboard with silver and glassware, and an upright piano, the room was large enough for informal rehearsals.

Amadine's stateroom lay beyond this area, decorated tastefully in pale gold and cream, with bedstead, dressing table and wardrobe of French walnut, mirrors of heavy French glass, and a washbasin and toilet of white porcelain. It was adjacent to Hal's room which – and Amadine risked a quick glance inside – proved to be identical to hers except for crimson drapes and bedcover, and the door leading to Frank's cubicle. Beyond the sleeping area was the observation room with an exterior platform.

But there was no safe and, with her jewel boxes burning a hole in her bag, Amadine hastened to impart this information – at the top of her voice – to Frank and Jay. To her astonishment, neither man seemed unduly put out by this disclosure.

'Can't do anything about it now,' Jay said laconically, 'but we can pick up something suitable in Portland tomorrow.'

'A metal box would do,' agreed Frank, 'as long as it is fireproof, and has a stout lock.'

'And is too heavy for a man to lift and carry away,' Amadine contributed in a voice heavy with sarcasm. 'Obviously a steel safe, bolted to the floor of the car, hasn't been invented yet.'

'This is America,' Jay exclaimed impatiently. 'Of course it has been invented. But we don't need anything quite so sophisticated.'

'Or expensive,' added Frank.

'Let's hope your frugality doesn't turn into a false economy,' Amadine said ominously. 'And in the meantime I think the most secure place for my jewellery is under my pillow or secreted about my person.'

Both men watched her as she walked away.

'She may be right,' Frank said at last. 'I don't believe anyone will gain access to her jewellery there, for all Hal's optimism.'

In Portland the next day, as an icy gale roared in from a grey and angry Atlantic over the rugged coastline and picturesque villages of Maine, Frank found time to walk along Congress Street and locate a suitable safe. It was only a small safe but reassuringly substantial, and sufficiently heavy to require the services of a boy with a handcart to convey it to the train.

What with the unfamiliar movement of the train and the overpowering steam heat, Amadine had not slept well. She rose early, eager for fresh air and exercise, and happened to be in Congress Street in search of Longfellow's birthplace when she spotted the little procession trundling along the road. Battling into the teeth of the gale, she hurried after Frank, the boy and the handcart and was in time to supervise the installation of the safe, which had been dumped in the parlour of the Palace Car.

'It's splendid,' Amadine declared, 'but I don't think you should leave it there. Too many people will be wandering in and out of this parlour, and the safe would be easily found by an intruder.'

'The train is never left unattended,' Jay pointed out, 'even when most of us are at the theatre.'

Frank had been following the argument while his fertile brain weighed up the situation. 'The safe ought to be less conspicuous, if only for our own peace of mind.'

'Then where . . .?' Jay began, but Amadine was already walking down the passage, past her own stateroom. Outside Hal's door, she hesitated.

'Go in,' Hal invited, 'but there isn't a spare inch of space.'

By now Constance, Theo, Gwen and Blanche had arrived and were watching events with interest.

'This is the perfect place,' Amadine proclaimed triumphantly, indicating a gap in the very basic furnishings of Frank's cubicle.

Willing hands – although, judging by the frown on his face, Jay's hands might have been slightly less willing than the others – moved the safe to its new home. Frank surveyed it, and the entire proceedings, with the utmost satisfaction. Thank you, Amadine, he murmured to himself. I couldn't have organised it better myself, and it was so much better coming from you.

· 'The only snag with a second-hand safe,' he said smoothly, 'is that it has only one key. I do hope that there are no objections if I keep it.'

'Now, hey, hold on just a minute there.' An expression of real anger crossed Jay's face. 'That safe is as much my responsibility as yours. My share of the takings has to be placed in it, and I'm entitled to a key!'

'Children, children,' Hal intervened. 'If there is only one key, one individual must be in charge of it. I do hope, Jay, that you don't think my brother would make off with your takings! I do assure you that I have no fear of him making off with mine. Let Frank keep the key. The pair of you can lock away the money at night, and unlock it again in the morning when you take it to the bank.'

'I think that, on these visits to the bank, Amadine ought to ride shotgun,' Constance remarked, 'armed with that pistol she intends to buy.'

The newcomers soon began to feel the pressure of the series of one-night stands – Portland, Concord, Worcester, Springfield, Hartford – although old hands adjusted quickly to the routine. The intense cold of the New England winter contrasted sharply with the steam heat in theatres and the train and, with so many people constantly in close proximity, an early crop of coughs and colds attacked the company. The steam heat became a bone of contention: the English contingent found it too hot, but the Americans complained if the temperature was lowered. Amadine in particular was affected by the heat and, on the night they left Hartford, got out of bed and wandered into the parlour.

'Can't you sleep?' Suddenly, and soundlessly, Hal was beside her. 'Sorry, I didn't mean to startle you.'

He reached up and lit one of the Pintsch lamps, keeping the flame low so that only a dim glow illuminated the room, and then he looked at her. She was wearing a thin shift of ivory silk that clung to her body. Over it, for decency's sake, she had flung a filmy negligée but it hung open, revealing the rapid rise and fall of her bosom and the narrowness of her hips. The shift was cut low over her breasts, but Hal had seen as much flesh before, in her stage costumes – one of her *Tanqueray* gowns definitely verged on the risqué. The difference now was that he knew, as he saw her nipples pressing against the thin silk, that she was naked beneath that flimsy covering, and they were alone . . .

Naked himself beneath his navy-blue robe, Hal turned his back on her for fear that his desire should become all too evident.

'Drink?' His voice was husky as he busied himself at the sideboard.

'I'll have a Scotch if there's any ice.'

He went to the ice-box in the kitchen, and when he returned it was not only the faint flush on his face that had subsided. Rather to his relief, she had wrapped the negligée more closely around her.

'So,' he said, sitting down beside her on the sofa, 'are you pleased with the way *Trelawny* has been playing in the country areas?'

Amadine nodded. 'It was good of you to take over as Tom Wrench, and give "Arthur" back his old role.'

'Tom is the better part – I can quite see why Laurie chose to do it. Of course Arthur does have the inestimable advantage of spending his time very close to you,' and his eyes smiled at her over the rim of his glass.

He was so good-looking that a girl had to pinch herself to ensure that she was awake and that he was real. Just as aware of him as he was of her, Amadine tried not to think about what lay beneath the blue robe.

'But they are still laughing at the costumes, and I can see why,' she went on. 'Constance is right – the frocks, and us, are simply not glamorous enough. I haven't heard from Pinero, but let's go ahead and change them anyway.'

'Do you want to be involved in the designs?'

'Except for my own dresses, no. This is a terrible admission, but that side of things doesn't interest me. I'm all in favour of delegation.'

'We'll delegate the *Trelawny* costumes to Constance, then.'

'Please don't put it like that,' Amadine said in alarm. 'I think I'm unpopular enough in that quarter as it is.'

'The stateroom . . .'

'Let's just say that I don't think she would be too happy if she could see us now.'

'Oh, I don't know – devoted to her children, and all that.'

'Modesty becomes you, Hal, but you do know, or should do . . .'

'Honestly, my relationship with Constance isn't the same as it was with my other leading . . .' He broke off, grimacing.

'It's all right, dear, your reputation has preceded you,' Amadine said drily.

'But yours hasn't – you don't have a reputation.'

'Every nice girl should be without one.'

'One can have a reputation for virtue.'

'Not in the theatre,' she said with conviction, 'not if one is unattached.'

'In that case, perhaps you should attach yourself to some lucky man forthwith.'

'Are you offering?'

'Yes.'

Amadine looked deep into his eyes, and then smiled slowly. 'You are a shocking flirt,' she said lightly, 'and what's more you are a flirt who has been drinking too much.'

'If you say so.' Hal stood up, took her empty glass and refreshed it with whisky and ice. Resuming his seat, he leaned his head against the back of the sofa, and smiled at her.

His throat was so beautiful and his robe revealed a deep

V of such magnificent chest, covered in a matt of fine dark hair, that she had to fight an urge to lean across and kiss that warm flesh. The temperature in here was still too hot, and rising . . .

'This steam heat is intolerable,' she said huskily, 'but it only has to be endured for another day or two before we reach Philadelphia, and then it's hotels for several weeks.'

'Mmm.' Hal's tone was noticeably unenthusiastic. In hotels, unless a miracle happened, he would not enjoy this kind of access to Amadine. 'Thinking about the next few weeks, and about Constance, I'm afraid that we must put her nose even further out of joint.'

'Juliet.' Amadine took an extra large gulp of Scotch.

'I know that you were studying with Laurie. Do you think that you are ready to rehearse with me?'

No, she wanted to scream, but . . . 'I am ready to go through my paces, as if understudying Constance, but whether I can produce a performance of my own – well, I'm not sure that I'm qualified to judge.'

'Then you must allow me to be the judge.'

She looked at him and knew that, in this area, she trusted him completely. 'Yes,' she said simply. 'When do we start?'

'Now.'

'It's rather late,' she prevaricated, 'and I've had a lot to drink.'

'There are one or two aspects of the play that lend themselves to private, late-night rehearsals. Look, if you are so warm, take off this robe,' and he untied the ribbon and pulled the garment from her. 'And, as Juliet, you'll need to wear your hair loose.' With practised ease, he loosened the thick braid into which Amadine's hair was plaited at night, and ran his fingers through the ebony mass that gleamed on her pale shoulders. He caressed the nape of her neck, his touch tender yet sure and, as a tremor ran through her, Amadine was reminded of his reputation and his expertise. 'And this is something else we can practise.'

Amadine started to say no, but his lips smothered her protest, pressing against hers with cool tenderness. She knew that she ought to push him away, but there was something tentative about Hal's touch, almost experimental, as if he was half-expecting rejection and was ready to withdraw like the gentleman he was. Much to her surprise, Amadine was inclined to allow the experiment to continue. When she felt the gentle probing of his tongue, her lips parted almost of their own volition and her own tongue slid into the silk of his mouth to entwine with his.

Her arms slipped round him, feeling the hard musculature of his back through the silk robe as Amadine found herself responding and, almost involuntarily, returning his kiss. When he withdrew, she opened her eyes and glared at him with a mixture of disappointment and indignation, only to see him gazing down at her with an expression in his eyes she had never seen before.

'I'm not sure that I remember Romeo and Juliet kissing like that in the play,' Amadine said dazedly.

'They do in my production. A lot.'

Hal kissed her again. But this time, encouraged by her lack of dissent, his mouth was harder and more demanding, and whereas before his hands had lain lightly on her shoulders, now they began an erotic exploration of her body. A warmth began to flood through her, a strong tide of desire centred on her most feminine and private place, which remained, as yet, untouched and shrouded in the folds of her shift. Her breathing quickening, she slid her hands beneath his robe to caress the smooth skin of his back as, with his mouth still devouring hers, Hal pulled down the straps of her nightgown. Drawing in his breath sharply and deepening his kiss, he tightened his hold on her so that the softness of her bare breasts pressed against his hard chest, and again Amadine felt that ache of longing yawning inside her.

She had not expected to want him at all, let alone to want

him this badly. She did not love him. This was physical desire, and she had not known that lust could be separated from love and experienced in this way. Perhaps she was aroused because it had been so long – oh God, *so* long – since . . .

He tore his mouth from hers and pushed her back against the sofa cushions. 'You do want me, don't you . . .'

Not a question but a statement, and how could she refute it? The evidence was right before his eyes, in the hardness of her nipples, and the thudding of her heart, which was clearly discernible in the pulse at her throat and the throbbing of her left breast. Hal bent his head and took the rigid peak of her right breast in his mouth, the sensation so exquisite that Amadine cried out softly. Her body arching beneath his, she pressed his head against her and entwined her fingers in the thick brown hair at his neck. But then she felt his hand ruching up her skirt, baring her legs and beginning to travel to her knee and beyond . . . If she didn't stop this now, it would be too late.

'No,' and she pushed his hand away from her thigh.

'You don't mean that.'

'I do, and I should have said it sooner. I apologise – it was not my intention to tease.'

'But, darling Amadine, I can tell how much you want me,' he said persuasively. 'Your whole body is melting into mine.'

'I don't deny that I was attracted to you, but it isn't enough, and it isn't right.' Amadine rearranged her night-gown, and sat up. 'I don't sleep around, Hal. I'm not Paula Tanqueray.'

'Of course you aren't,' he hastened to assure her. 'Perish the thought. But this is different, surely you can see that!'

'I can see that, if we can reproduce even a fraction of this passion on the stage, our *Romeo and Juliet* will be a sensation.'

And with a murmured goodnight, she vanished into her

room, leaving Hal to take his painfully throbbing flesh into his own bed and, uncomfortably aware of Frank's proximity, obtain his own relief. He remained optimistic: he had lost tonight's battle, but would still win the war. Frank was wrong – the way she kissed proved that the rector's daughter was not virtuous, even though she was trying very hard to be.

Amadine's frustration was less easily assuaged and she lay awake for a long time, sure that she had done the right thing but filled with regret that it had to be so. And she wished heartily that she could sleep because it had been a busy day, what with buying a gun.

Jay had taken charge of the proceedings, and the men from the *Courant* and the *Times* had been riveted by his highly embellished account of Amadine's near-death experience at the hands of a gunman in Boston. By now, Amadine was too inured to his methods to correct the story – she had heard that truth was one of the first casualties of war, and was learning that it was also an early victim of this tour.

Escorted to a suitable practice ground, Amadine was instructed how to load and fire the gun. She had not held a firearm for years, and did find the little pistol more difficult to handle than she expected, but she mastered it soon enough and impressed her audience with her coolness, her quick grasp of the mechanics, and the accuracy of her aim.

'Is it loaded?' Constance enquired, as the company inspected the pretty pearl-handled pistol that Amadine admitted choosing for its looks rather than its performance.

'Yes, but the safety catch is on.' Amadine showed them how it worked.

'You ought to keep it in the safe,' Constance observed doubtfully.

'It isn't much use to me there, is it! No, I'll keep it in my bedside drawer and, as far as I'm concerned, that is where it will stay.'

In the darkness Amadine stretched out a hand, opened the drawer and groped for the distinctive shape of the gun, merely to reassure herself that it was in its appointed place – not that it would ever be needed . . . or fired . . .

Chapter Ten

Before leaving Boston, Theo had purchased a typewriter and, in his spare time, was learning how to use it. Rather to his surprise, Constance was familiar with the machine, having assisted her husband with the typewriting of his plays, and offered to share her expertise. Ensconced in his stateroom, Theo was banging away at the keyboard with the forefinger of each hand when Frank came in.

'You look like a newspaper reporter,' Frank laughed, as he sat down.

'I hope I write better than a journalist!'

'Come, come, that's a bit hard! Some of the best dramatists began their professional lives in newspaper offices.'

'Not in Philadelphia,' Theo averred with conviction.

'You might be allowing Philadelphia, and its School of Dramatists, to influence you too much.' Frank, who had been wading through Theo's stock of manuscripts, tried to find a way of letting him down gently. 'One of your disadvantages, Theo, is that you are more sophisticated than the average audience. I'm not. So, trust me when I say that, by and large, American audiences are conventional. They want the square deal, and for virtue to conquer. Forget subtlety and veiled meanings – think big hearts, terse dialogue and fast action.'

Theo had suffered rejection of his work before but had managed to alleviate his dismay, to some extent anyway, by believing that no one had actually read his manuscript. This criticism was therefore harder to bear.

'Isn't there anything in my work that you like?' he asked wistfully.

'Heaps of things,' Frank lied heartily. 'Too many to mention.'

'But there isn't a play that we could knock into shape for Hal, as you suggested?'

Frank had tried to find one. My God, had he tried! But it was no good – there wasn't a theme, a character or even a line that was rescuable. 'Some of this is very promising,' and he patted the pile of manuscripts encouragingly, 'but its style and content are dated. We're nearly in the twentieth century, remember! Of course fashions change, but I would recommend that you stop using blank verse.'

At this Theo looked even more crestfallen.

'It's just that Shakespeare does it better, old chap!' Frank hastened to console. 'And perhaps you could differentiate between the characters more: aim for a strong, easily recognisable *type*. You are being too democratic with your people – very American, I'm sure! – but while equalising all classes and conditions of man in dress, intelligence and behaviour might be excellent for society, it makes frightfully bad theatre.'

'I do see that.' Theo tried to be more positive in his thinking. He had wanted advice and criticism, and he mustn't whinge because the message was not the one he wanted to hear.

Frank was rising, reluctantly, to his feet. 'Perhaps we could continue this conversation tonight? I'd like to leave you with this thought – try to invent a really dramatic plot, and remember that in America a play needs a star artist. Preferably a woman.'

'Oh Lord.'

'There's nothing new in this world, Theo. Remember what Sheridan said:

Through all drama – whether damn'd or not –
Love gilds the scene, and women guide the plot.'

'But I'm much more comfortable with men,' Theo groaned.

Oh, Theo, Frank thought as he returned to his own quarters, I was so hoping that you would say that.

That evening the train was in a siding at Newark, New Jersey, when Frank quietly made his way down the dark central aisle of the women's car, negotiated the linking vestibule and knocked softly on Theo's door. Ahead of him the men's car, also in darkness, resonated with deep breathing, the occasional snore and, here and there, a whispered voice, in a world redolent of male flesh and temptation. The steam heat was high again, and Theo was sitting at the table, naked to the waist. He had his back to the door and, as Frank went into the room, was leaning forward over the papers on the table in a posture that revealed an inch of buttock cleavage. For Frank, already mesmerised by the curve of Theo's back and the unexpectedly powerful shoulders, the glimpse of that valley, and the way the trousers stretched tight over the tautness of Theo's bottom, was almost too much to bear.

'Don't you hate walking through the women's car?' Theo asked. 'I have to run the gauntlet nearly every night. Sometimes they're only half-dressed and I get really embarrassed, but they don't seem to give a damn.'

'A shameless bunch of hussies. Don't let them intimidate you! And look on the bright side – you won't have to run the gauntlet tomorrow night.'

'No, I'll be at home tomorrow night.'

Theo's voice was steady, but he did not sound overjoyed at the prospect. But, Frank chided himself cautiously, this was probably wishful thinking on his part.

'In a way it's a pity that we are returning to hotel life for a while,' Frank remarked. 'We are just beginning to form a cohesive company, to unwind with each other and let down our defences. For instance, have you noticed that Hal and Amadine seem to be hitting it off?'

'Are they . . . you know?'

'I don't think so. Why? Do you fancy Amadine yourself?'

Theo sat bolt upright. 'Of course not!'

'Why not? She is the most extraordinarily beautiful woman.'

'But I'm a married man!'

'I wouldn't be surprised if, even in Philadelphia, there are a few married men who would like to take Amadine Sinclair to bed.'

Theo thought about it for a moment. Amadine *was* lovely, and intelligent, and many other things besides, but he had never considered the possibility of making love to her. He supposed that was slightly odd, but perhaps it proved how much he loved his wife.

'I guess she isn't my type,' he said.

Frank had brought a flask of bourbon, and he sloshed some into two glasses before asking casually, 'What is your type?'

Theo's hesitation appeared to indicate that he was not a man who made a habit of discussing women with his friends over a drink. Having bluffed his way through countless conversations of this kind, Frank was acutely attuned to the vibrations, but in this instance he was at a disadvantage in that he was not accustomed to socialising with a man of Theo's background.

'My wife has brown hair and blue eyes,' Theo said awkwardly, 'and is very pretty. Not in the same way as

Amadine, though. Susannah's beauty is . . . well, less obvious, if you know what I mean.'

Which, coming from a man who spent his leisure time writing blank verse, wasn't exactly the start of a sonnet.

'I only asked because, should you devise a play for a star actress, I feel it might help to have a particular actress in mind,' Frank said smoothly. 'You could do a lot worse than use Amadine as a model.'

'And base the hero on Hal?'

'It would make sound commercial sense. Hal and Amadine are the actors to whom you have immediate access, and who would – no question – read the play and give it fair consideration.'

'I don't want to be too commercial. I'm not doing this to make money.'

'The producers and actors will want to make money,' Frank said, rather sharply. 'You must give the public what it wants, not what you think it ought to have.'

Theo felt like the new boy at school who knew nothing and no one, and who ought to be grateful if an older boy, like Frank, offered to show him the ropes. And Theo was grateful. Really, he was. It was just that Theo was not sure that this was a school he wanted to attend, let alone a school in which he wanted to flourish and come top of the class. Talk of commercialism went against Theo's idealistic nature. In this he was possibly somewhat un-American, the majority of his compatriots managing to combine the two ideologies without difficulty, as in Amadine's analogy of 'a dream in one hand and a dollar in the other'. But then Theo had never been without a dollar in both hands, and in both pockets as well. His substantial private income allowed him to think of playwriting as a civilised hobby. It was artistic excellence that Theo sought. He wanted nothing less than to write the great, the definitive American Drama.

'Have you considered the Civil War as a background?' Frank asked.

'It has been used before, of course, most recently by William Gillette in *Secret Service* – an appalling melodrama, in my opinion.'

'His primary objective is to entertain,' murmured Frank, 'not to preach or inform.'

Theo finished his bourbon and looked at his companion. He often found it difficult to think of Hal and Frank as brothers. The two men were so different physically and, as far as Theo could see, in most other ways as well. What Frank lacked in height and presence, he made up in raw energy and a powerful physique. There was strength in those broad shoulders and in those capable hands with their short, stubby fingers – workman's hands, thought Theo – and even Frank's hair, darker and coarser than his brother's silky locks, possessed a wiry springiness and vitality.

'Could you spare me some time when we leave Philly?' Theo asked diffidently. 'I'll have my hands full until then, what with work and family commitments.'

'I'll look forward to it.' Frank stood up, to take his leave. 'Shall we have the pleasure of meeting your wife?'

'I'm not one hundred per cent certain of the domestic arrangements – it's Emily's birthday, you see.'

'I thought that your wife's name was Susannah.'

'Emily is my daughter.'

It means nothing, Frank groaned again as he tossed on his bed all night. *Oscar Wilde* has children . . .

The Davis town house in Philadelphia was a three-storeyed mansion in Walnut Street at Rittenhouse Square, and here Theo entered a familiar world of dark panelling and ornate ceilings, of vast rooms crammed with heavy furniture, pictures and porcelain, of Aubusson carpets and Florentine chandeliers. He hurried up the stairs and along a passage to his bedroom. Then he ran to the baby's room, before returning slowly to the head of the stairs. There was no doubt about it: not only were both rooms empty, but they had that intangible air of having been unoccupied for some time.

'If it isn't the return of the native,' a voice drawled behind him. 'Welcome home, Teddy.'

He had become so accustomed to being addressed as Theo that for a split second he did not respond. Then he swung round with an exclamation. 'Thank God you're here. Where the hell is everyone?'

It being Sunday morning, Robert Davis, Theo's elder brother, was still in his nightclothes and, before answering the question, he led Theo to his bedroom and rang for coffee.

'Bit of a late night,' he explained, 'or, rather, an early morning.'

'Where are Susannah and the baby?'

'Didn't she tell you? They went to Chestnut Hill several weeks ago.'

Some years earlier their father had purchased a stately home in the affluent suburb of Chestnut Hill as a summer house and weekend retreat, but gradually it became the family's principal residence. One reason for this was the delicate health of their mother, who loved the quiet life in the country, and another was the semi-retirement of their father, who these days rarely put in an appearance at the office. However, this attachment to the place did not explain Susannah's presence there.

'Mother isn't worse, is she?' Theo asked in alarm. 'Did she need nursing?'

'Mother is fine – she'll outlive us all. No, Susannah just upped and went.'

'But she knew that I was coming home this weekend.' Theo looked perplexed. 'She can't have forgotten.'

'Oh, I guarantee she hasn't forgotten.' Robert regarded his brother quizzically as a servant brought in the coffee. 'Doesn't it occur to you that she might be trying to tell you something?'

'Susannah said she didn't mind if I travelled with the theatre tour for a few months.'

'Teddy, Teddy, surely you realise that there is a world of difference between what women say and what they mean!' Robert groaned in exasperation. 'They talk in code, and you have to learn the key.'

'Unfortunately I don't possess your natural aptitude for these things.'

'Why did you marry Susannah?' Seeing the startled look on his brother's face, Robert hastened to rephrase the question. 'I mean, why her in particular? A pretty boy like you had plenty to choose from.'

'I loved her, of course.'

'Of course.' Robert struggled to keep the scepticism out of his voice. 'And the family were delighted. Mother and Father adore her – she is the daughter they never had – and it's wonderful how Susannah seems to prefer their company to that of her own parents. She looks set to become a phenomenon: a woman who, instead of turning into her own mother, turns into her mother-in-law.'

'I think it's a good thing for everyone, and especially for Emily, that they get on so well together.'

'Of course,' Robert said again, 'and now, much as I am enjoying this reunion, I recommend that you drive posthaste to Chestnut Hill, where I predict that, even as we speak, the carpet is being paced, a frown is furrowing the fair Susannah's brow and even angelic little Emily is on the receiving end of her mother's tongue.'

'Are you coming too?' Theo asked optimistically.

'Good God, no. I'm not going out there for only a few hours, and I don't want to stay overnight because I have a nine o'clock meeting in the office tomorrow morning. It may have escaped your notice, little brother, but when you trotted off on your theatrical jaunt, your workload devolved on me.'

'You were frightfully decent about it, or were you speaking in code as well?'

Robert laughed. 'I was never more astonished in my whole life than when you calmly announced your plan that day. I didn't think you had it in you.'

'Am I so feeble?'

'Not feeble, merely . . . conformist. You do what is expected of you.' Robert seemed about to elaborate on this statement, but changed his mind. 'No, you have my blessing, Teddy. I do think that it might have been better had you expressed your individuality *before* you became a husband and father, but better late than never.'

Theo smiled at him affectionately. He had spent a good proportion of his life wishing that he was more like Robert – so tall, handsome and debonair, so clever, charming and capable. Theo felt that he never quite lived up to his brother's example, no matter how hard he tried. The only thing he had done that Robert had not was marry – not that this had influenced Theo's decision to marry, not at all, of course not. But marriage was the one area in which Robert had resisted all pressure put on him by the family: he had insisted that he would not tie himself down too young, that he would have a jolly good look at the entire female sex while he had the opportunity, and that he would have a jolly good time while he was doing so.

'I'll see you tomorrow,' Theo said from the doorway.

'You'll be returning to the city so soon?'

'I have work to do. I am expecting to be very busy all week.'

'But what about Susannah and Emily?'

'I'll bring them back here with me, of course.'

'Of course,' Robert said, yet again, but his eyebrows twitched and they remained arched in an expression of cynical scepticism for some time after his brother had gone.

On the journey to Chestnut Hill, Theo managed to convince himself that his brother exaggerated Susannah's disaffection, but then found something else to worry about.

Suppose Emily had forgotten him? He had been gone only a month, but suppose she did not recognise him? Theo was not used to children, and he had no comprehension of the extent of a one-year-old girl's memory and understanding. He only knew that he adored her.

And when he entered the house, it was not his wife whom he swept into his arms but this beautiful bundle of warm, scented skin, silky curls, laughing eyes and rosebud mouth. Whether or not Emily recognised him as her father, he could not tell but, to his delight, she beamed at him, tugged happily at his hair and chortled as he bounced her up and down. This last activity not meeting with general approval, the little girl was removed speedily to the nursery and Theo was left to face his wife and parents without the safety valve of the child's presence. The conversation was so stilted, the atmosphere so heavy with disapproval, that Theo could hardly believe that this was his home and his family. A gulf had opened between them that had never existed before.

'Your absence has been difficult to explain, Theodore,' his father said. 'We thought it best to let it be known that you are working on a case for a special client. In New York.'

New York. Because, Theo thought, Philadelphians despised the place and avoided it as much as possible.

'Perhaps,' his father continued, 'you would bear that in mind should you meet any of our friends and acquaintances during your stay.'

'Are you so ashamed of me?'

No one answered. No one would talk about it. Come to think of it, no one here had ever talked about anything. This family never quarrelled or confided. Emotion was kept under strict control, and unpleasantness swept under the carpet. Perhaps, like Robert, his father did and said all the right things, while quietly living a secret life of his own. It was possible, Theo thought, darting a glance at his father's granite profile. What was certain was that he, Theodore, had embarrassed everyone by doing something they did not like or understand, and doing it openly.

'Robert has been very busy,' his father was saying. 'I trust you will manage to call at the office and put in a few hours there?'

Theo was acquiescing hastily, because he recognised an order when he heard one, when Susannah murmured something to his mother and left the room. He hurried after her and, in the bedroom, took her in his arms. She went rigid, but did not pull away.

'Darling, you said you didn't mind if I went away for a while. But you do mind, don't you, and I'm so terribly sorry.'

'If I had said I minded, would you still have gone?'

'No,' Theo said firmly, 'but in that event I guess I would have minded! It looks as if one of us is doomed to unhappiness over this business.'

'And naturally it is you who gets what he wants.'

'As I said to you at the time, I will be gone for only a short while.' Theo propelled her to the bed and sat down beside her, holding her hands in his. 'It means so much to me, or I wouldn't ask you to make this sacrifice. To see the theatre from behind the scenes, learn about stagecraft and talk to people about my work – it's the opportunity of a lifetime! You used to be interested in my work.'

Indeed, before they married, Susannah had sat patiently for hours, listening to extracts from his plays, but she had looked upon him as a poet, as a charming, slightly unworldly versifier. More to the point, she had believed he would be this versifier only occasionally, and that for most of the time her husband would be the Philadelphia lawyer with exquisite manners and impeccable family connections. She had expected that she and Teddy would simply repeat their parents' lives – that was what the aristocracy of Philadelphia *did*. They perpetuated; they did not change. And they certainly did not change into scapegraces who ran off to the decadent, dubious, world of the theatre, wrote letters describing the most peculiar people and places, and referred to actresses by their first names.

'Please don't go back to them,' she begged, making it sound as if he had joined a gang of villains. 'Stay here with me and Emily. It's so lonely without you.'

'You should be in town, not stagnating out here. There are heaps of parties you could go to.'

'I don't want to go to parties on my own.'

'I must continue with the tour,' Theo said gently. 'They are relying on me, and I cannot let them down. Please, try to understand. Give me these few months, then I will come back to Philadelphia and we will carry on exactly as before.'

'Who is relying on you? That Amadine person, I suppose.'

He laughed, and kissed her cheek. 'Darling, there is nothing going on between me and Amadine, or between me and anyone else. On that you have my absolute word.'

He seemed sincere, and Susannah was inclined to believe him. Teddy had never been a flirt. He had always been straightforward and rather serious, treating the young women of his acquaintance with the utmost respect and transparent honesty.

'Now, tell me all about Emily,' he said. 'I want to know everything she has done and said.'

'Said!' Susannah smiled pityingly at his ignorance. 'Being only twelve months old, her vocabulary is somewhat limited . . .'

Talking about their daughter restored some semblance of peace and normality. At dinner, with Susannah and his mother discussing arrangements for Emily's birthday party the following Saturday, Theo sensed a slight thaw. Then he realised that he would have to ask Hal for the day off on Saturday, and suddenly his thoughts whirled across the city to his new friends. Frank would be at the theatre, moving in the scenery and other effects. Hal and Amadine would be in their suites at the Hotel Stenton, as would Gwen and Jay, although they qualified for less expensive rooms. Blanche was not provided with hotel accommodation, and she would have hastened to secure a room at a decent boarding house. It was another world, and although Theo knew that he did not belong there, he was not sure that he belonged here either.

'Are you listening, Teddy? You look miles away.'

'What? Oh, yes, of course I'm listening. I was just thinking that I must obtain your theatre tickets tomorrow. Which days would you like to come?'

'We will not be attending the theatre,' his father said firmly.

'Not even once? But it's such a good bill – *Julius Caesar* . . .'

'Thank you, Theodore,' his father interrupted, 'but no.'

'I wanted you to meet my friends,' and Theo saw by their faces that this was why they would not go.

'I didn't want to press you about the theatre in front of the others,' Theo said as he undressed, 'but which nights do you want to go?'

Susannah was already in bed, lying on her back, staring at the ceiling. 'Father made it clear that we aren't going.'

'He made it clear that he and Mother are not going. I didn't realise that he spoke for you as well.'

'He does speak for me.'

'But I must be at the theatre myself most evenings, and if you don't come with me, you'll be lonely at Rittenhouse Square.'

'I'm staying here.'

'I finish work late at night,' Theo protested in dismay. 'I'll only reach Chestnut Hill after you are asleep.'

'Obviously the best thing is for you to stay at Rittenhouse Square during the week, as long as you are here for Emily's birthday.'

Theo turned off the light and climbed into bed, lying motionless for a few moments while his mind adjusted to this unexpected turn of events. Philadelphia – dear, predictable old Philly – was springing a few surprises, and Theo wasn't at all sure that he liked them. Beside him, equally motionless in the darkness, Susannah was waiting for him to make love to her, and he heard her sigh softly. She was usually a sweet-natured girl, obedient and biddable, but Theo was sure that the sigh – doubtless involuntary – was a sign that she wanted to get this over so that she could go to sleep. Actually, he felt much the same about the activity himself, but knew that he would do what was expected of him. Or try to.

He rolled towards her and stretched out a hand, which encountered the mound of one of Susannah's breasts under her nightgown. She was petite with a very shapely body, a true hourglass figure with large breasts and a tiny waist, or so it seemed from what little Theo had seen. He had never seen her naked. Susannah was nearly always in bed when he came into the room and, if she did have to get up to go to the bathroom, ensured that she was encased from head to toe in voluminous folds of white cotton. Theo pulled up her nightgown, and fumbled under his own nightshirt as he moved on top of her. To his horror he realised that he had no reaction; his body was limp and disinterested. He tried to enter her, but was too soft and slithered out again.

'Sorry,' he gasped. 'Must have had too much to drink.'

Desperately he reached down and held himself, masturbating until he produced an erection, and slipped inside her as quickly as he could in case he lost it again. As usual, the sensation was highly pleasurable and although it took him a bit longer than usual to achieve orgasm, he really didn't mind.

Afterwards he helped Susannah to rearrange her gown and lay listening until her even breathing indicated that she was asleep. He was aware of a niggling concern over his lack of arousal, and was very much afraid that something awful had happened, and that he did not look upon Susannah as truly his wife any more. If so, it was Robert's fault – all that talk about their parents treating her like a daughter, and of Susannah turning into his mother. For God's sake, she was beginning to seem like his sister! He had been genuinely distressed when she refused to leave Chestnut Hill but, all things considered, if it wasn't for Emily, he might almost feel relieved.

Quite honestly, he did think that his family – with the honourable exception of Robert – was over-reacting to his temporary change of lifestyle. Good Lord, if they were like this over the small matter of the theatre, what would they be like if he did something really dreadful?

Feeling indignant and guilty in turns, Theo gave up the unequal struggle for sleep and crept out of bed. After carefully negotiating the corridor in the dark, he lit the lamp in the nursery and sat down beside the cot.

Emily was sound asleep, a tiny thumb stuck in her mouth. Incredibly long dark lashes fluttered on round pink cheeks as she sighed and stirred but, as Theo held his breath, she did not wake. An immense wave of love engulfed him, and it was hard to remember that he had not felt any great pleasure when Susannah had told him of her pregnancy. He had taken it for granted and been rather embarrassed by the fuss, and in particular by the coarser comments of his brother Robert and his friends. But the moment Emily was born, the instant he saw her for the first time, everything changed. He was besotted. At last he understood what love really was, a completely uncompromising, unquestioning love that had no beginning and no end, but simply *was*.

Tiny and helpless though Emily was, Theo did not think in terms of nurturing and protecting her, for the affluence and influence of his family provided their own security against the onslaught of a cruel and wicked world. Gazing at his sleeping child, Theo's thoughts were of her natural progression through the stages of Philadelphia life until she took her rightful place in the forefront of society, as befitted her family's position and unblemished reputation. And he knew that he would do anything for her – anything that would ensure her happiness, her well-being and her future.

In need, and Theo tenderly stroked her cheek, he would even die for her.

Chapter Eleven

Amadine managed to slip away on her own on Wednesday afternoon, while the company was engaged in a matinée of *Julius Caesar*. By then she had familiarised herself with the elegant, charming city and its colonial and revolutionary connections, and she had gazed at the vast bulk of the City Hall, visited Ben Franklin's grave and strolled along Elfreth's Alley. She had seen the Arch Street Theatre, once managed by the redoubtable Mrs John Drew – whose grandchildren, Lionel, John and Ethel Barrymore, were now coming to prominence in the profession – as well as the Walnut Street Theatre, which was probably the oldest theatre in America. Indeed, the city had a rich theatrical history and boasted a large number of playhouses of varying size and architectural merit. For instance, the Broad Street Theatre, where the Smith-Sinclair company was appearing, was an extraordinary confection in the Moorish style, with its domes and minarets, and its façade boasting a series of arches and elaborate balconies, providing a startling contrast to the staid dignity of the street.

Jay had been guiding her footsteps in the direction of well-known department stores, such as John Wanamaker's, and Strawbridge and Clothier, but on this particular afternoon Amadine sought solitude and she therefore took a cab to Fairmount Park. This park, and its famous

Waterworks, was a popular local attraction, but today the road from the city centre was almost deserted. Although Philadelphia was free of snow, the sky was overcast with the threat of rain and Amadine sat in a gloomy half-darkness that suited her mood admirably.

Most people would consider that she had little cause for complaint: her performances were greeted rapturously by a generous public, and she knew that her colleagues had little enthusiasm for appearing without her. But Amadine did have a problem – her old enemy, and greatest asset: her looks. Although she appeared to be oblivious of her effect on people, in fact she was fully conscious of the reaction she provoked. It was just that she was used to it, admiration having been a part of her everyday life for as long as she could remember. However, there was no vanity in her: Amadine was enough her father's daughter to know that her beauty reflected no merit on herself, and to do penance for the undeserved advantages it brought.

Unable to overcome her conviction that her looks were solely responsible for her theatrical success, she knew that one answer was to have the courage to take a role as a plain woman – if she could disguise her beauty sufficiently, and if she could find a producer willing to finance such a risky venture. Clearly this was not possible during the American tour and so she must find another short-term solution.

The carriage had reached the large, beautifully land-scaped park on the banks of the Schuylkill River to the north-west of the city and, although the broad expanse of grass and thickly wooded slopes were not unduly inviting on this winter afternoon, Amadine stopped the carriage short of her destination. Telling the driver to wait for her there, she left the park and walked slowly towards the river.

Behind her, and beyond a curve in the road, another hired carriage stopped and a man dismounted. Despite the remoteness of the spot, he paid the driver and dismissed him, and then, at a discreet distance and with his hat pulled down over his eyes, he followed her.

One thing was certain, Amadine reflected: Juliet was not the answer to her dilemma, although rehearsals were going well and she believed that she could give an adequate performance. If she must do Shakespeare, there were other parts she would prefer to play. Hal was hinting again that he might drop *Caesar* from the repertoire, and put a new play into rehearsal after Christmas, and Amadine knew she must ensure that Hal chose the play she wanted. Reviewing the Shakespeare canon, she decided that the choice lay between Cleopatra and Beatrice in *Much Ado*. Of the two plays, *Much Ado* was probably easier to stage in the existing circumstances and the casting fell perfectly into place – or it would have done, if only Laurie had been here to play Claudio as he had done countless times before.

She reached a narrow path that followed the bend of the river, and turned along it. The area was deserted and, out of sight of the cab driver and in the silence, suddenly she experienced again that prickly sensation in the nape of her neck that she had felt at Mount Auburn, as if she was being watched or followed. Abruptly swinging round on her heel, Amadine looked around her, searching every tree and bush for signs of movement, but she saw nothing . . .

It was pure luck that had impelled him to seek cover in a small grove of trees at the precise moment she turned round, or perhaps some sixth sense had warned him that she was aware of his presence.

That she *was* aware of him, that some invisible signal was pulsing between them, was encouraging and exciting. And it wasn't his imagination that this was happening, because he was sure the same thing had occurred at the cemetery in Boston. It proved that the bond between them did exist, and it changed everything.

He had left San Francisco on an impulse, his thinking

muddled and with no clear plan of action, but now he knew exactly what he wanted to do. Pulling his hat even further over his eyes, more from sheer habit than fear of being recognised, he left his hiding place and set off after her.

The Waterworks complex was very striking, constructed in a mellow golden stone and in the classical tradition, its pillars and colonnades looking more like Greek or Roman temples than industrial buildings. A low balustrade guarded the edge of a terrace on which Amadine stood as she contemplated this charming scene.

There had been no further intimacy between her and Hal, Amadine having ensured that the opportunity did not arise, but that intriguing tingle of attraction and desire was providing both a personal and professional stimulus. She was still amazed that the attraction existed. Not being one to fall for a pretty face – she had made that mistake before, and once was more than enough, thank you very much – she had anticipated being immune to Hal's obvious, and numerous, charms. She had not expected him to be so pleasant and supportive, so intelligent and so good at his job. Gwen was right: Hal was a great catch. For an actress with Amadine's aspirations, he could be a once-in-a-lifetime opportunity.

Amadine realised that she was being swayed not only by Gwen's opinion but by her situation, alone in her middle-to-old age, struggling to maintain herself and an invalid mother. Gwen had been beautiful once so there must be a story there, of bad luck and broken dreams . . . Amadine did not love Hal, but what was love anyway? In Amadine's experience, it was a short-lived conjuring trick – there one minute, gone the next. Perhaps a relationship built on affection and mutual advantage would be sounder and would last longer. So far, so good, but she had a strong suspicion that Hal would want to marry her. As marriage was a step too far for Amadine, would he be content with a less formal relationship and, even more to the point, could she go through with it?

Amadine was, and always would be, the rector's daughter. She had been reared by a virtuous man, a High Victorian who taught right from wrong, and preached of sin and guilt. His influence might be diluted by the theatre and by his daughter's common sense, but it was not eradicated. Amadine saw the choice starkly, and in simple terms: if she could not marry Hal, then the alternative was to 'live in sin'. Of course, in her line of business, there were plenty of precedents. Among her contemporaries, Ellen Terry's love life was a very tangled web, while Mrs Patrick Campbell was rumoured to be no saint, and this state of affairs had done their careers no harm. Perhaps the public liked, even wanted, its favourite actresses to be . . .

A hand touched her shoulder, and she screamed.

Pierce Radcliffe had also checked into the Hotel Stenton, at the corner of Broad and Spruce Street, immediately adjacent to the Broad Street Theatre, for the duration of his stay in Philadelphia. His proximity to the principals of the Smith-Sinclair company was no coincidence and this morning he had loitered inconspicuously, or so he hoped, by the elevator on an upper floor of the hotel until his quarry appeared. Tipping his hat politely, he had boarded the elevator behind her and, leaning against the wall with his arms folded, had studied her covertly during the descent. However, he must have been looking at her oddly because she glanced at him warily, and hurried out of the elevator as soon as the doors opened. He must be more discreet, he thought wryly, or he would be acquiring a reputation . . .

After transacting some business, and lunching in the city, Pierce returned to the hotel in the early afternoon and enquired after Amadine. Undoubtedly the desk clerk, who had hired the cab for Amadine, would not have divulged her whereabouts to a stranger, but Mr Radcliffe was a regular guest and a good tipper.

'Fairmount Park!' Pierce exclaimed. 'Alone?'

When informed that Miss Sinclair had been alone when she left the hotel, Pierce's frown deepened. He was in no doubt that the Boston gunshot had been real and, although he had no proof that Amadine had been the target, he felt profoundly uncomfortable at the prospect of her wandering about an area as exposed as Fairmount Park. Presumably even Philadelphia had its quota of crackpots! However, if he set off to the Waterworks now, he shouldn't be far behind her.

It was a comparatively simple matter to locate Amadine's carriage, waiting where she had left it, and for the driver to point out the direction she had taken. As he strode off in pursuit, Pierce was both worried and angry. He had told her to be careful but, no, she must go wandering off on her own. Frankly, he didn't know why he bothered with her – this woman deserved to come to a sticky end! Yet when he could see no sign of her, his anxiety grew. On this grey afternoon, under a lowering and rapidly darkening sky, the only person in sight was a man who emerged suddenly from a grove of trees in the middle distance. Even if more people had been about, this figure would have attracted Pierce's attention, for there seemed something oddly furtive in his movements, as if – in his dark coat with the collar turned up, and with his hat pulled low over his eyes – he had been hiding in that clump of birch and hickory. Probably wanted a pee, Pierce thought, but he quickened his stride nonetheless.

Rounding the bend of the river, Pierce glimpsed a flash of movement far ahead, a figure that might be Amadine, and at the same moment the man looked back and saw him. After a fractional hesitation, the stranger struck away to his left, away from the river, and disappeared into another thickly wooded section of the park. Pierce was just close enough to catch an impression of a pale, thin face that contrasted with a dark moustache.

Amadine was standing dangerously close to a low balustrade, and Pierce drew in his breath sharply when he saw how easy it would be to creep up behind her and . . . His footsteps rang out on the stone flags of the terrace, but she seemed lost to the world and did not look round. He tapped her gently on the shoulder. She screamed, and pulled away before swivelling to face him.

'Oh, my God,' and she put her hand on her heart. 'You frightened the living daylights out of me!'

Pierce apologised, and guided her firmly away from the edge of the terrace.

'I could have fallen in,' she complained, 'and died of hypothermia. No, on second thoughts, in these clothes I would have been weighed down by the water and drowned.'

'Nonsense. I would have dived in to rescue you.'

'Without the presence of a posse of newspaper reporters, and your precious Panhard as a photogenic backdrop? I doubt it!'

'Your cynicism does not become you.'

'That isn't cynicism, it's realism, and since meeting you I've been honing it to a fine art.'

'You are holding a grudge over an imagined slight on my part connected with our Boston excursion,' he said sadly, and with a mock sigh. They were walking back along the same path, and he was careful to keep his body between hers and the trees.

'There is nothing imagined about it,' Amadine retorted. 'Where is that beastly contraption of yours anyway? Obviously it isn't here or I would have heard it, and you couldn't have sneaked up on me like that.'

'I left her in Boston,' he said regretfully. 'Winter is rather too far advanced for driving long distances.'

'If a motor car isn't any use in bad weather, mightn't you have discovered a design flaw?' Amadine asked sweetly.

When this failed to elicit a response, she glanced at him and found that he was staring hard at the grassy slope and trees to their right.

'Were you aware of being followed when you came along here earlier?'

Her head jerked back towards him and her eyes widened. She had begun to assume that he had been responsible for that creepy sensation. 'Certainly not,' she lied robustly.

'A man was following you. He lit off into those trees when he saw me, but who knows, he might have pushed you into the Schuylkill *and* not bothered to dive in. Tall chap, pale face, dark moustache. Ring any bells?'

'No, which is amazing considering the fine detail of that description!' Uttering a sound that verged suspiciously on a snort of disgust, Amadine lengthened her stride and bristled with indignation. She believed that Pierce was playing a game of his own. First he 'rescued' her from the phantom gunman of Boston, now he frightened off the phantom stalker of Philadelphia. What sort of idiot did he take her for! 'You'll be saying that it's the same person next,' she said, pursuing her own train of thought, 'but just because you follow me here from Boston doesn't mean that anyone else is likely to.'

'Oh, I followed you here, did I? Well, I suppose I shouldn't be surprised that you jump to that conclusion, modesty being your middle name!'

She flushed with embarrassment and anger – at herself. He was right. It was unpardonably arrogant of her to make such an assumption.

'However,' Pierce conceded, 'looking like you do, it's an understandable mistake to make.' But, he wondered reluctantly, was it a mistake? At the outset Amadine Sinclair had not been his chief interest in the theatrical company but, if he were honest with himself, he had to admit that things had moved on a bit. Each time he saw her, on the stage or off, things moved on . . .

Rain began to fall, the first few drops followed by a steady downpour. Seizing her hand, Pierce ran towards a row of boathouses nearby, and they hurried up the path of the first one and into the shelter of the porch.

'It rained on us in Boston, too,' Amadine panted. 'Do you think the gods are trying to tell us something?'

'Only that the way you treat me is enough to make the heavens weep.'

There was a wooden bench at the back of the porch, and Amadine sank down on it and began to laugh. 'How do you want me to treat you?'

Pierce sat down beside her and stared into her eyes. A strand of raven hair had escaped from beneath her hat, and very gently he smoothed it back from her face and tucked it behind her ear.

'You don't really want me to answer that,' he said in a low voice, 'not here . . . not now . . .'

Even in the gathering darkness his gaze was magnetic, and Amadine found herself swaying towards him, her whole being concentrated on the thin, hard line of his mouth. But, with their lips only inches apart, there was a sudden commotion on the path outside – the sound of hooves, the jingle of harness and a shout.

With a muffled curse, which he changed quickly to a rueful laugh, Pierce wrenched himself away and stood up. 'Of all the darnedest times for a pair of drivers to show some initiative, this takes the cake! Madam, your carriage awaits.' He escorted her outside, and handed her into the vehicle. 'May I accompany you?'

'I think I will be safest alone,' Amadine replied, 'despite the threat from phantom stalkers.'

Pierce Radcliffe's Philadelphia was very different from Theo's. He had been born in the city, and received his first schooling here but, although by that time his father had made money, a *nouveau riche* family could never scale the

social heights occupied by the Davises and their ilk. Not
that this lack of recognition troubled Samuel Radcliffe, but
it was a source of considerable disappointment to his wife.

Samuel was an uneducated cabinet-maker and coach-
maker who, after emigrating from England with his wife,
worked in the car shop at Harlan & Hollingsworth of
Wilmington, Delaware. A superb craftsman with a driving
ambition, he saw early on the potential for sleeping cars,
and the profit to be made from operating as well as building
them. As he anticipated, the railroad companies soon tired
of the wearisome detail of bedding, porters and fussy passengers, and began contracting the work out, while sharing
the profits. Samuel Radcliffe was ready for the start of this
concession business, with a fleet of cars and the organisation to run them, and his fortune was made.

Unfortunately, Catherine Radcliffe was regretting her
marriage. The daughter of a village schoolmaster, she had
fallen in love with Samuel's good looks and forthright
manner, only to discover that they had nothing in common.
In addition, she did not settle in America as happily as
Samuel did, was lonely without her family and old friends
and depressed by her apparent inability to have a child. To
help with the family finances, she taught at a school in
Wilmington, the work having the added advantage of keeping her occupied during Samuel's increasingly frequent
absences. Then, at last, after thirteen years of marriage, she
became pregnant and persuaded Samuel to move to
Philadelphia, a city that she felt provided a more suitable
background for her gentility and the future of her child. At
the same time, more and more of Samuel's business was
centred on Chicago, which he loved, but his 'dynamic
atmosphere' was Catherine's 'noisy vulgarity', and she
steadfastly refused to move there. While too young to
analyse the situation, Pierce grew up with an awareness
that the contrasts between the two cities somehow mir-
rored the differences between his parents, and he was torn

between the two. The boy had no difficulty in deciding which place he preferred – Chicago won every time – but then came the cataclysm when, without any warning or explanation, his mother swept him off to England.

After avoiding the city for years, because the memories were painful, Pierce now saw a Philadelphia to which his mother had turned a blind eye: a city that was one of the premier manufacturing centres of the world. Here was the home of Baldwin's locomotives, the Cramp shipyard, Midvale Steel, Disston saws and Smith Kline druggists. Philadelphia made tools and hardware, textiles and lace, musical instruments, cigars, Derringer pistols and Stetson hats. They brewed root beer and published everything from bibles and encyclopaedias to the *Ladies Home Journal* and the *Saturday Evening Post*. Pierce's business interests took him to numerous sectors of the city, and meant that he was in and out of his hotel at irregular hours. It was towards the end of the week that a third member of the Smith-Sinclair entourage attracted his attention.

Jay Johnson, publicist *extraordinaire*, was a type Pierce recognised instantly. The only barrier the Jays of this world recognised was that which separated success from non-success and, having been placed on the wonderful American highroad of life, the only slogans they knew were: 'It's up to you' and 'The sky's the limit'. For them, the end justified the means and while they could easily envisage the goal, their grasp of the ethics that ought to pertain in achieving it was very weak indeed. What puzzled Pierce was the presence of such a man in the Smith-Sinclair company. These types tended to be self-employed, because their first and foremost priority was to make a lot of money for themselves. Surely the opportunities for financial self-aggrandisement on a sufficiently large scale were decidedly limited in such an environment? Pierce was no expert on the theatre, but he felt fairly certain that a mogul like Charles Frohman would keep his minions on a pretty tight rein.

In his peregrinations around Philadelphia, Pierce caught sight of Jay several times, in a variety of venues but always with the same man: a big, fresh-faced fellow of exactly the same type as Jay himself. A real couple of heroes, Pierce thought to himself, and he wondered vaguely what they were up to. Then he happened to be in the lobby of the Stenton one evening and to overhear Jay talking to Theodore Davis. Jay was explaining, at length and in considerable detail, that he could not attend the theatre that night because he was feeling unwell. However, after Davis had gone, Jay hightailed it to the bar. Having nothing better to do, Pierce followed.

Within minutes Jay was joined by his fellow buccaneer, and a short but intense discussion ensued before Jay was called to the desk. He reappeared with another man, and the atmosphere changed immediately: intensity became expansiveness. It was as though Jay was transformed into Charles Frohman before one's very eyes. When the group left the bar, Pierce followed them again and noticed the conspicuous manner with which Jay handed in his room key at the desk, as if emphasising the fact that he was staying at this expensive and highly reputable establishment. Then they walked up Broad Street to Walnut, crossed over to the north-west corner and entered the Bellevue Hotel.

Pierce had to eat somewhere this evening, and he might as well dine in the excellent Bellevue Restaurant as anywhere else. Besides, his curiosity was thoroughly aroused. Something was going on, and, as Jay's activities could affect the Smith-Sinclair tour and its participants, Pierce wanted to know what it was.

Chapter Twelve

'We have the theatre,' Jay was saying, 'and the star. The scenery and costumes can be obtained in a jiffy. What we need now is the book and the music.'

'And it's a revue you have in mind – like *The Passing Show*, which was on at the Casino a while back?' The newcomer, a sharp-faced young man from New York, was doing full justice to the free meal while he absorbed the details of the planned production.

'*The Philadelphia Girl*,' Jay declared. 'It can't fail. Imagine the scene: William Penn returns to his beloved city at the end of the nineteenth century, and finds that a few changes have been made. You could put in one or two bridging sequences, showing the transition from the old to the new – a few high-stepping chorus girls in Quaker bonnets wouldn't go amiss.'

'Who is the star?'

'Nancy Loring,' Jay announced proudly, but untruthfully.

The New Yorker whistled softly. 'Hey, not bad. I like it, gents, I like it. So, how much are you paying for the book?'

'My associate deals with the money,' and with that same expansive air that Pierce had noticed earlier, Jay waved a hand in the direction of his friend.

'This production,' Bill Stewart emphasised, 'is gonna be

a great success. We want it to have everything – laughter
and tears, songs and dance, and plenty of pretty girls.
Consequently we thought it only fair to offer you a piece of
it – seems kinda selfish to keep all the action for ourselves.
So . . .'

'. . . you thought you'd offer me a measly percentage, and
kid me into writing the book on spec.' The New Yorker
shook his head sadly, and carried on shaking his head in a
manner that indicated no deal. 'I gotta live. I gotta eat. And
so has the musician. I take it you want me to find the musician?'

'We thought you would probably know a guy in New
York who you could work with,' Jay said.

The man nodded. 'Sure I do. Look, here's the deal. I'll
take a percentage of the box office – we'll talk figures in a
minute or two – but I want two hundred and fifty bucks up
front. I'll write the book and when you've okayed it, I'll find
the music man and give him a hundred bucks advance out
of mine.'

Jay and Bill looked at each other. 'You got it,' Jay agreed.
'What's two hundred and fifty dollars in the great scheme
of things!' and he gave a casual shrug.

'How long will you need for the book?' Bill asked.

'I'll have the outline ready in the New Year. As soon as I
get the go-ahead from you, I'll write the script and start on
the songs with the music man.'

'And at that point we can organise the casting, scenery
and costumes.' Jay lit a cigar and nodded sagely.

'How does an Easter opening sound?' Bill enquired tentatively.

The New Yorker finished his wine, accepted a cigar and
thought for a moment. 'Sounds good,' he said at last. 'No
reason why you can't rehearse the first half of the show
while I'm writing the second. I'll catch up with you, don't
you worry.' Some skirmishing over percentages ensued, but
eventually the deal was settled and the New Yorker looked

at his watch. 'Gotta go – I'm catching the last train back to New York. So, if I can see the colour of your money, I'll be off.'

Bill produced a cheque book, an absolutely magnificent item with his name embossed in gold letters on the outside, and each individual cheque gilt-edged. The New Yorker eyed it warily. It looked impressive, but he had lingering doubts about the account holders. They seemed to know what they were talking about and they must have money – you didn't stay at the Stenton and eat at the Bellevue on fresh air – but there was something about them . . . The *suits* – too shabby and badly cut . . . Still, it didn't do to judge a man by his tailor. He would go ahead with the book for *The Philadelphia Girl*, but . . .

'Cash, please, gents,' he said.

'I'm sure the management here will cash our cheque,' Jay said smoothly.

The management obliged, and if they thought it strange that the cheque was drawn on a bank in a town about as far upstate as one could go, they refrained from saying so.

After the New Yorker had left, Bill took out a handkerchief and mopped his brow. 'Why the hell did you agree to give him two hundred and fifty bucks?' he yelped. 'Are you sure that the bank will meet that cheque?'

'Calm down, for God's sake,' Jay hissed. 'There's a thousand dollars in that account – *my* thousand dollars – so quit complaining.'

'But we need that stake. Somehow, and I do hope you've got a few bright ideas on the subject, it has to finance this entire enterprise.'

The Philadelphia Girl was Jay's idea. Pierce Radcliffe – still sitting at a nearby table – was an excellent judge of character, and he had been spot on in his assessment. Jay Johnson was sick and bloody tired of lining other men's pockets, and had decided to win a piece of the action for himself. This was the golden age of opportunity in the

United States. All around him men were making immense fortunes – out of steel, railroads, mining, publishing, finance, you name it – and Jay was determined not to miss out. One of the carriages on this gravy train had his name on it, and he had decided that if he didn't make a move now, it might be too late.

His father was a newspaper editor in Ohio, and an inveterate theatre-goer, who took young Jay to every show within a reasonable radius of their home town. When Jay was fourteen, he persuaded his father to let him work in the printshop of the newspaper and then ran away to be a tramp-printer, travelling from town to town and from paper to paper. At twenty, he went to New York and landed a berth in the composing room of the *World*, but within a year he had talked his way into a job as a reporter on the *Dramatic News*. His next stop was Fiske's *Dramatic Mirror*, which proved as short-lived as everything else in his life. He grew restless again, and became an advance man for theatrical tours.

An advance man travelled ahead of a touring company, and arranged all the publicity and advertising at every town where his company had an engagement. He carried with him a clean shirt and a toothbrush, and about a hundred-weight of posters, of various sizes and shapes, which advertised his troupe. His days were spent drinking with local editors and persuading them to print his stuff, and fighting running battles over pasting up his posters in prominent positions. His nights were passed sitting up in a day-coach, because his expense allowance did not run to Pullmans, and most mornings he faced a repetition of the previous day's struggle. And all for fifty dollars a week.

But Jay knew that this was the best education he could have for a career in the theatre. Many of the important producers had started this way – Charles and Daniel Frohman among them. An advance man knew every theatre manager in every town in the country, and he knew what type of entertainment would 'go' in that town and how much money it would make. So when Jay Johnson created, and got behind, *The Philadelphia Girl*, he wasn't just blowing off a head of steam. He really knew what he was talking about. He had the theatrical pedigree. What he didn't have was the money.

His thousand-dollar investment was the result of some uncharacteristic frugality, and a lucky bet. It was now or never, he had decided, knowing that he might never accumulate such riches again, and he had approached Bill forthwith. Bill was the best bluffer in town, and his sudden loss of nerve tonight was so untypical that Jay was confident the lapse would not recur.

'I need another drink,' Bill declared.

'Not here, not at these prices,' and Jay called for the bill. With the same flourish that had accompanied the presentation of his room key to the desk clerk at the Stenton, he paid in cash. 'Now,' he said to Bill as they passed Pierce's table, 'we can cash a cheque here again – if you get my meaning.'

Pierce certainly got his meaning. He had not found out the nature of their business, but he sure as hell had discovered how they intended to finance it. Jay Johnson and his confederate intended to fly a few kites.

The principles of kite-flying needed no elucidation between the two friends. Opening that out-of-town bank account had been a tacit agreement that such tactics might be necessary, although the procedure had not been openly discussed. Now, as they sat over their drinks in a far more modest establishment than either the Stenton or the Bellevue, the financial arrangements for their venture could be postponed no longer.

The system for kiting cheques was simple but demanded meticulous care and, as Jay would be continuing his work with the Smith-Sinclair tour, the responsibility would be

Bill's. When he needed money for costumes, scenery or salaries, and the bank account was bare, he had to cash a cheque – in a shop, hotel or restaurant, like the Bellevue tonight – and pay cash for the goods or services. Before that cheque could reach that remote, out-of-town bank, he would cash a bigger one and wire money to the bank to meet the first cheque. So far, so simple: the tricky bit was ensuring that each cheque cashed was for a bigger sum than the previous one – so that there was enough money to wire to the bank *and* pay another batch of bills – and keeping track of a confetti-like mass of cheques flying round Philadelphia, and upstate Pennsylvania, all at the same time. It would take only one mistake, and for the bank to cotton on, for the whole house of cards to come tumbling down.

'I'm living cheap on this tour,' Jay said, 'all accommodation provided and plenty of free meals, so I can wire you most of my salary.'

'I can chip in a few bucks before the New Year, but after that I'll have my hands full with the show,' Bill said apologetically.

'You'll need a stage manager to oversee the cast and rehearsals, while you look after the finance and such.'

'We need a theatre and a star first.'

They were a couple of cheerful, confident chancers, and the original conception of this show had been the most exciting and stimulating idea they'd ever had. However, the theory was becoming reality and, despite their alcohol intake, the effect on Jay and Bill was very sobering indeed.

'Your first choice is still the Gayety?' Jay asked at last.

'It's comparatively new – opened five years ago – and is the largest theatre on the Rialto.' Bill was referring to the 200 block of North Eighth Street, between Race and Vine, which was developing into a bustling theatrical and business district. 'And it will be available after Christmas.'

'Let's take a look at it tomorrow, and close the deal if we like it.'

'Sure, why not!' There were plenty of reasons why not, but a casual insouciance was returning to spur them on. 'And there is just the small matter of Nancy Loring,' Bill continued, remembering that Jay had promised the services of this splendid artiste.

'We'll ask her. She can only say no.' Jay produced a piece of paper and a pen, scribbled a few lines in a bold hand and pushed the paper across the table.

Bill read it – a telegram offering Nancy Loring the lead in this as yet unwritten revue at one hundred and fifty dollars a week – and pushed it back again. 'Send it,' he said.

'You send it,' and back across the table it went again.

They stared at each other, like boys in the school playground saying: 'I dare you . . .'

'I can't send it,' Jay went on in a reasonable tone of voice. 'If Frohman finds out I'm involved in a stunt like this, he'll skin me alive and we won't have my salary to rely on.'

Bill muttered an expletive and pocketed the slip of paper. 'At least give me the quarter for the telegram.'

Miss Nancy Loring replied promptly, wiring her acceptance of the offer and asking when rehearsals started. Jay and Bill shouted '*Yes!*', then stared at each other in silent consternation. The ball was really rolling, and now there was no stopping it.

Despite Susannah's chilly assurances that his staying at Rittenhouse Square would cause no offence, Theo felt morally obliged to make several visits to Chestnut Hill and then he fulfilled his father's expectations by going into the office. To his weary consternation, Theo found that he was looking forward to leaving the city. He thought longingly of the convivial evenings in the Palace Car, of late-night discussions with Frank over a bourbon or two, and of simply becoming his own man again, instead of this puppet who tried so anxiously to fulfil other people's expectations.

Thank God for Robert who, with his robust common sense and uncomplicated normality, seemed to be the sole preserver of Theo's sanity. Yet, in the end, it was Robert who tipped the scale and caused Theo to search his soul.

The two brothers were driving back to the city on Sunday evening after spending the weekend at Chestnut Hill, celebrating Emily's birthday.

'You are a lucky dog, Teddy, enjoying easy access to all those gorgeous actresses! I suppose you couldn't arrange an intimate *tête-à-tête* between me and Amadine Sinclair?'

'No, I certainly could not!' cried Theo indignantly. 'Our young ladies are precisely that – *ladies* – and none more so than Amadine. Good God, Robert, the very idea!'

'All right, all right, keep your hair on. Can't blame a fellow for trying,' and Robert sighed regretfully, because he had been to the Broad Street Theatre several times and had admired Amadine no end. 'On second thoughts, it might be as well not to have any other distractions this coming week,' he mused in a more thoughtful tone, 'because it is just possible . . . er, are you sleeping at Rittenhouse Square tomorrow night?'

'Of course.'

Robert grimaced. 'In that event, I shall have to plead for your discretion, old boy. I may be entertaining a friend there that night, and I wouldn't like it spread about.'

'Oh Lord, Robert, you aren't taking one of your floosies there!'

'No,' Robert said sharply. 'She certainly isn't a floosie. She's . . . Look, just keep out of the way, Teddy, and say nothing to anyone.'

After this, most men would have been unable to resist turning up at the house early and hanging around in order to spy on proceedings, but it was sheer coincidence that Theo came home from the theatre at the precise moment a carriage drew up at the door. A woman, wrapped in a cloak with a hood covering her head and most of her face, emerged from the vehicle as the front door was flung open and Robert appeared. Evidently the servants had been dismissed and Theo waited a few minutes, to give the pair time to clear the hall, before quietly letting himself into the house.

A lamp was burning in the big drawing room to his right, and Theo tiptoed softly to the adjoining music room, which would provide a ringside seat. He could hear voices, but the conversation was very indistinct and, as soon as he glanced into the room, he could see why. Robert and the woman were kissing, but it was an embrace such as Theo had never seen before and certainly had never experienced. Their murmurings were inarticulate and then, as Theo watched, Robert wrenched off the woman's cloak and flung it aside before pulling her to him again. Theo recognised her. She was the wife of Robert's best friend.

As his muddled brain came to terms with this development, Theo's next thought was to wonder how long the affair had been going on, but their panting, broken sentences made it clear that this was their first romantic encounter.

'I've wanted you for years,' Robert was groaning, 'since the first moment I saw you.'

'I know,' she said hoarsely. 'I was beginning to give up hope. I thought he'd never go away and give us an opportunity . . .'

They were pressed hard against each other, grinding their bodies together, but it was their faces that fascinated Theo. They were virtually unrecognisable, the cheeks so flushed, the eyes glazed, the swollen lips devouring . . . Robert was tugging at her dress, and suddenly she was naked to the waist, full breasts spilling into his eager hands, and Theo realised that, in readiness for this, she was wearing nothing underneath her gown. Her neck arched, and she gave a deep cry of pleasure as Robert's mouth travelled down her throat and fastened on her breast. But then, and

Theo froze in shock, her hands were fumbling at Robert's groin, unbuttoning his trousers and, sinking to her knees in front of him, she took him in her mouth.

After what seemed an eternity, Theo forced himself to move. Burning hot and, to his shame, in a state of considerable arousal, he crept up the stairs to his room. Lying on his bed fully clothed, he tried to compose himself.

He had not known such passion was possible. To him, sex was a moderately agreeable duty, and he had assumed that it was thus for everyone. Or, judging by the boastful, coarse remarks of some men, that it was a game, a conquest that brought quick physical pleasure. But now Theo was scorched by the heat pulsing from those two bodies, and he was certain that at this moment they were coupling on the drawing-room carpet, because their need for each other was too great for them to make it up the stairs to a bedroom.

Theo closed his eyes, and gave a deep, shuddering sigh. It wasn't only Robert's passion that came as a revelation; it was the woman's. Her response to Robert's lust, her uninhibited participation in the experience, provided so immense a contrast to Susannah's passive acquiescence that Theo was crushed. Is that how it is supposed to be, he asked himself? He tried to imagine Susannah behaving like that, but it was impossible, the leap of imagination required was too great, and at length he began to believe that it was Susannah's fault that the physical side of his marriage was unsatisfactory. If she did things like that, and involuntarily his hand pressed against his groin, he might enjoy it more.

But it was not likely that Susannah would ever be so uninhibited. Why *had* he married her? Bleakly Theo came to a very different conclusion from the one he had given his brother only a few days previously: he had married Susannah because it had been expected of him. She was the daughter of an old family friend, and the match had been – well, not planned exactly, but cultivated since they were children. Theo hadn't minded. He sort of drifted into it because it seemed the right thing to do and, yes, he must admit that the fact that he became the centre of attention, and received all the parental approval instead of Robert, might have had something to do with it. What a pity he had not realised this at the time.

And it was even more of a pity that, having experienced nothing of passion so far in his life, he felt so certain that now he never would.

He could easily have rejoined the tour in Baltimore the following Monday morning and spent another weekend at Chestnut Hill, but Theo made his excuses to his family and went straight to the train after the theatre on Saturday evening. His stateroom was tiny compared to his rooms at Rittenhouse Square and Chestnut Hill, but it was all his – no woman's clutter taking up most of the space – and here he could please himself what he did: what time he came to bed, how long he sat over a book and how late he put out the light. With a sigh of relief Theo unpacked his small valise, and placed a photograph of Susannah and Emily on the table. He hesitated. On second thoughts he didn't want Susannah watching him, and he replaced the picture with one of Emily on her own. After surveying his little domain with satisfaction, he jumped off the train and walked forward to the freight cars where, as he expected, Frank was talking to one of the stage staff. Frank, who was carrying a cash box, saw Theo and his face lit up.

'I didn't expect to see you until tomorrow.'

'I wondered if you needed any help, moving stuff from the theatre.'

'Not at the moment, thanks,' Frank assured him. 'The props and costumes are being packed, and we'll shift them down here first thing in the morning. Shouldn't take long – the theatre staff will help, and they are old hands at it.'

'Oh, good.' Theo hovered uncertainly. 'I don't suppose you feel like a drink? You'll be too tired, I expect . . .'

'I'd love a drink,' Frank said quickly. 'Just give me a sec to lock away the cash, and I'll be right with you.'

When Frank entered the stateroom, Theo had two glasses of bourbon ready.

'Cheers,' and they clinked glasses. 'Frank, you have no idea how good it is to be . . . here.' Theo had corrected himself hastily. He had been about to say how good it was to be home.

Frank had locked the cash box in the safe, along with Jay's bag of gold and bills. As usual they had gone over the accounts with the theatre manager during the day, and divided the box-office receipts on the agreed percentages. The cash would remain in the safe on the train overnight, and be transferred to the safe in their Baltimore hotel the following day, whence it would be taken to the bank on Monday morning. After topping up the float he carried, because company salaries were paid on Saturday mornings and the hotel bill had to be paid, Frank would wire a lump sum to the company's account with a New York bank, ready for transfer to London at some future date. Jay would wire his share of the takings to Frohman's account in New York.

They were settling into a routine. The Monday morning banking of the receipts had become an unvarying rule, and was particularly important after an engagement such as the two weeks in Philadelphia when a considerable sum of money was involved, but sometimes they also banked on a Friday.

On this particular Monday morning, in Baltimore in December, Jay removed one hundred dollars from his employer's share of the receipts and, with a lingering sigh of regret, handed over the balance to be wired to New York. The hundred dollars, representing his salary, he wired to Bill's upstate bank.

Frank had sat up half the night doing the accounts. He really did not have the time to devote to this drudgery, but dared not delegate the task to anyone else. To date he could account for every last cent. The books were in immaculate order, matching the cash in the float, the sums wired to New York and the receipts for cash paid out. These last items were chiefly hotel and restaurant bills, cab fares, food for the Pullman kitchen, costume materials and salaries. All the company were paid in cash on a Saturday morning, with the exception of Amadine, Hal and himself who, if they wanted any money for personal reasons, simply asked for it and signed a receipt. Their main recompense would come at the end of the tour when the spoils in that New York account were divided.

But Frank had his eye on the calendar. The time was coming when a few financial adjustments would be needed, because Chicago was only five weeks away.

Chapter Thirteen

In Baltimore, Maryland, it was Blanche Villard who was flung into the bosom of her family for a brief, and not necessarily welcome, reunion. As she trudged up Charles Street, stopping every so often in order to transfer the weight of her bag from one hand to the other, she tried to recall how long it had been since her previous visit. She had come home for a week last year, she remembered, and the year before that she had been here with the Coghlans on tour. On that occasion, as invariably happened when Blanche came to Baltimore to work, she was mysteriously struck down by 'illness' and could not appear for the duration of the company's stay in the city. Well, it isn't going to happen this time, Blanche said to herself defiantly. I'm going to act, and I don't care if I am recognised.

The neat little city was built on the slopes of a steepish hill that plunged down to the harbour, its serried ranks of nearly identical streets presenting repeated vistas of compact red-brick row-houses, of two or three storeys, even the most modest adorned with gleaming white marble steps. Blanche turned into just such a street, dumped her bag on the sidewalk outside one of the houses and took a deep breath.

She was of medium height but so slender and small-boned that she appeared petite, while her corn-blonde hair and doll-like china-blue eyes gave a false impression of innocence. This was a very shrewd young woman who played on her youthful looks by knocking five years off her age – she was twenty-five – for professional purposes, and by playing the *ingénue* on and off the stage. Having composed herself sufficiently for the forthcoming confrontation, she picked up the bag, mounted the marble steps and opened the front door.

The house was very quiet, and a quick inspection of the downstairs rooms confirmed that they were unoccupied. With a sigh of irritation, Blanche went to the foot of the stairs and called, 'Mama, are you there?' There was a scuffling noise overhead, followed by the sound of a door opening, and then a head of tousled blonde curls peered over the banister.

'Dodo, what a lovely surprise!' and a middle-aged woman, wrapped in a fuchsia-pink robe, lumbered down the stairs and clasped Blanche in her arms.

Blanche suffered the embrace dutifully before disentangling herself. 'It shouldn't be a surprise – I wrote you I was coming.'

'Next week. You said next week.'

'I said today. I definitely said . . . Oh, it doesn't matter.'

The physical likeness between them was so strong that there was no mistaking them for anything but mother and daughter. They shared the same blue eyes and thick fair hair, although the older woman's was duller and streaked with ash-grey. Her complexion, too, was pinker than the porcelain of her daughter's, and her formerly shapely figure had run to fat, which bulged in unattractive folds beneath the frills and flounces of the garishly coloured robe. Dora Hamilton exuded an air of cheerful vulgarity utterly at variance with the slightly pinched refinement that Blanche was careful to cultivate.

'I take it *he* isn't back,' and Blanche jerked her head in the direction of the upstairs rooms.

'Of course he ain't, and I'm not sure I'd take him back if he dared to show his face,' Dora retorted.

'You'd have him back quick enough if he waved a wad of dollar bills under your nose,' Blanche said caustically.

The 'he' in question was Blanche's stepfather. Her own father – Dora's social superior by a very large margin indeed – had died when she was only a baby, and for many years Dora and the little girl had lived an uncertain and peripatetic life, dependent on the charity of the disapproving Hamilton family. The only expense they had not seemed to begrudge was the girl's school fees, and eventually Blanche was sent to one of the very best boarding schools in the area – presumably because if she learned to speak and behave properly, she would not disgrace the Hamiltons in public. They kept the appalling Dora on a strict financial rein, giving her just enough to live on, and just enough to ensure that she recognised her dependency and thus moderated her behaviour accordingly.

Dora was undeniably common, rather brassy, blowsy and loud, but always good-natured. She bore the Hamiltons' frostiness without complaint, and had tried various ways of improving the family's finances, although invariably her half-hearted efforts ended in failure. Everyone, and particularly Blanche, had been taken by surprise when she remarried. She had had several offers over the years and had refused them all but suddenly, and not long after Blanche left Baltimore for New York, Dora ended seventeen years of widowhood. Unfortunately she made a bad choice.

'It isn't likely, is it?' Dora said, in response to Blanche's last remark. 'He only married me because he thought he was marrying Hamilton money and, when he found out different, he vamoosed. For good. I know that, and so do you.'

'You ought to find out where he is, even if it's only so that you can divorce him.'

'Divorce? Are you mad – can you imagine what the old lady would say?'

'If you are still married to him, you can't marry anyone else,' Blanche pointed out.

'I don't want to marry anyone else. I've had two husbands, and both were a disaster. And don't look like that, Dodo, because your father *was* a disaster, even if it wasn't altogether his fault. No, I'll manage. The old lady has reinstated my allowance – I'm using the Hamilton name again, and she don't want it brought into disrepute – and you're a good girl, Dodo, and send me what you can. Also,' and Dora sighed, 'I'm thinking of going back to Strouse Brothers.'

This firm of garment manufacturers produced men's suits and overcoats in a fine building at the corner of Paca and Lombard Streets, and had employed Dora briefly before her second marriage.

'I'm extremely glad to hear it,' Blanche replied roundly. 'I don't think you should rely on handouts from Grandmother – it isn't the American way.'

'It's an allowance, not a handout, and it's no more than I deserve. And don't you go talking to the old lady and rubbing her up the wrong way, because I can't manage without my allowance, and that's final.'

Dora stomped into the kitchen, and Blanche grimaced at her mother's retreating back. That attitude wasn't going to make things any easier.

Over tea Blanche told her mother about the tour and the people she was working with – give Dora her due, she was always interested in her daughter's work, and in the theatrical life. In fact she was a touch envious of this exciting existence, and listened entranced to descriptions of the gorgeous gowns worn by Amadine Sinclair.

'And is your understudy ready to take over this week?' she enquired.

'I am acting my own roles this week,' Blanche said, meeting her mother's eyes steadily.

'But you can't,' Dora wailed. 'It will be the end of everything! They'll cut us off without a cent. I'll starve – don't you care if I starve, Dodo?'

'Listen to me,' Blanche said firmly. 'For years we have been pretending to Grandmother and my uncles that I am a teacher in New York, and whenever a tour comes to Baltimore, I feign illness so that there is not the slightest possibility of my being recognised on the stage. I have gone along with this deception because you insisted on it, but I can no longer allow this situation to damage my career.'

'How can dropping out of the cast for one week, because of a *very serious illness*, damage your career?'

'Because my colleagues know that I have been in perfect health throughout the tour so far, and they also know that I live in Baltimore. Something tells me they might smell a rat, and I'm simply not prepared to risk it.'

Dora's eyes began to brim with tears. 'You promised me that you wouldn't do this.'

'I did not promise. What you must understand is that this tour is my big chance – it's my stepping stone to the big time, to important roles and beautiful frocks. Look at me,' and Blanche stood up and pirouetted in front of her mother. 'Do you think that I want to spend the rest of my life dressed like this?'

Dora eyed the tailor-made woollen costume and neat shirtwaist that her daughter was wearing. 'You look lovely. You always do. I wish that I could afford clothes like that.'

'They cost every dollar of Grandmother's last birthday present.'

'You spent all that money on clothes?' Dora gasped in horror.

'In my business, appearances are everything. The more successful you look, the more successful you will be. In these clothes I look a cut above the chorus girls and supers, but I don't even begin to enter the same league as Amadine Sinclair, or even Constance Grey, come to that, and she's no fashion plate. But I will, Mama, I will be in that league, or die in the attempt!'

'It won't be you who dies,' sobbed Dora. 'It'll be me.'

'Don't be silly,' Blanche said sharply. 'Have I ever let you down? No, and on this occasion I'm not letting down the company, either. I've got too much riding on this. I've been sucking up to these people ever since I met them in New York – I've carried bags, soothed shattered nerves, kept quiet like a good little girl, and piped up with appropriate compliments right on cue. I've been accepted as one of the principals – well, almost – and I'm sticking to them like a limpet. If I play my cards right, they might take me back to London with them.'

At that Dora began to cry in earnest.

'Not for ever,' Blanche assured her hastily, 'but the experience would be invaluable. Mind you, there might be circumstances that could persuade me to stay over there . . .'

The extremely handsome face of Laurie Knight swam into her mind, and she heaved a silent sigh of regret. Blanche had harboured high hopes of Laurie, but was forced to concede that he was unlikely to rejoin the tour in time for her to make herself indispensable to his private and professional lives.

In New York, at first sight, her initial interest had been in Frank Smith, but that didn't last long. She soon found him a rude, overbearing disciplinarian who would not have lasted five minutes in the job had he not been the Chief's brother. He had introduced a rule that no one was allowed out of the theatre after reporting for a performance, and had supplied a book for everyone to sign when they arrived. In Boston he had extended the rule to rehearsals, a dictate of which Blanche soon fell foul, and Frank had reprimanded her publicly, in front of junior members of the company. He even threatened to institute a system of fines. Fines! Just who the hell did this guy think he was? But Blanche had been around a bit, and she knew that Frank

Smith thought he was Augustin Daly. Well, she had news for him – he wasn't no Augustin Daly. What he was was a right royal pain in the . . . But, him being the chief's brother, one couldn't say so. One couldn't even hint. She was almost a principal, damn it, and did not deserve to be treated the same as a super, particularly when she was putting herself out to give Avonia her best shot. Having much preferred her original part, that of Imogen, in *Trelawny*, Blanche felt that her generous co-operation in switching roles entitled her to more respect.

As if all that was not enough, Blanche had a shrewd suspicion that Frank was one of *them* . . . She had seen his face that day in Salem, when Theo said he was married, and she had watched him carefully ever since. The idea made Frank even more repulsive, because Blanche hated men like that. She thought what they did was disgusting.

The only remaining unattached man in the company whom Blanche deemed worthy of her notice was Hal himself, but he was the greatest catch of all and she did not seriously think that she could aspire to those dizzy heights. The competition was awesome. It was common knowledge that he was crazy about Amadine and, in the unlikely event of Amadine refusing him, Constance Grey would be the next contender. Still standing after doing her pirouette, Blanche gave herself an appraising look in the mirror before sitting down. I'm prettier than Constance, she thought. I'm *younger* than Constance . . .

'I do not believe that I will be recognised in Baltimore,' she maintained, and began ticking off points on her fingers. 'One, I am known as Blanche Villard, not Dorothea Hamilton. Two, my grandmother has not been to a theatre in living memory. Three, my uncles and family friends have not clapped eyes on me since I was a schoolgirl. I don't see that there can be a problem.'

'You hope.'

'*You* hope,' Blanche countered. 'Frankly, I don't care.'

'You may not care about my allowance, but you'll be sorry when the old lady cuts you out of her will!'

'I have more chance of marrying the next King of England than of being mentioned in Grandmother's will!'

Dora smiled in spite of her distress, and blew her nose. 'A Baltimore girl married Jérôme Bonaparte, and he became a king.'

'And his big brother, Napoleon, annulled the marriage, so I wouldn't call it a happy precedent,' Blanche retorted, laughing. 'But a title would be nice, wouldn't it, and really one in the eye for Grandmother! But, on the whole, I think money would be better.'

Life's vicissitudes had not completely crushed the romantic in Dora, and she sighed wistfully before dragging herself reluctantly back to the present. Then she stared thoughtfully at her daughter. 'Knowing you, you'd probably get both – money and a title – if you wanted them badly enough,' she said. 'You were never one to let anything, or anyone, stand in your way, were you, Dodo?'

In her room a little later, preparing to make a duty visit to her grandmother, Blanche reflected on the truth, or otherwise, of her mother's observation.

She acknowledged the underlying barb. Dora had been aghast when, soon after leaving school, Blanche had insisted on going to New York. Not only was Dora terrified of being left on her own, but she had expected her daughter to find work in Baltimore and contribute to the household expenses. Dora had been looking forward to it. A few dollars sent from a meagre pay packet, after paying for board and lodging in the big city, wasn't the same thing at all. Besides, as long as Dodo conducted herself like a lady, there was always the chance that the Hamiltons might relent, acknowledge her fully as granddaughter and niece, and maintain her – and her mother – in style. However, Blanche had remained unmoved by the tears, recriminations and general prostration. She knew that if she was to have any life of her own she must leave Baltimore, and where better to go than New York?

The theatre had not been part of the plan. The possibility had never entered her head. She had a little money, hoarded from birthday presents over the years, but work was not hard to find for such an attractive, well-spoken young lady, and the girl took a job as a shop assistant in order to eke out her savings while she found her feet. Her first lodgings were not to her liking and, as her circle of acquaintances grew, she moved to another boarding house near Union Square which happened to cater chiefly for actresses. She was in her element immediately, and before long had enrolled for the drama classes run by Dion Boucicault at the Madison Square Theatre. Everything was proceeding splendidly – Blanche, as she was now called, had a real talent and a genuine enjoyment of the work – when disaster struck. Boucicault died suddenly in the middle of the course and, unlike fellow student Maxine Elliott, Blanche was unable to find a job in the theatre straight off. It was back to the shop floor, until at last she landed a small part in Charles Frohman's Comedians company, in a production starring Georgiana Drew Barrymore, and she was launched on a theatrical career. She was also launched on a life of lies and deceit, as she and her mother tried to conceal her true profession from the rest of the family.

The strange thing was that, the moment she had won this job with the Smith-Sinclair company, she had had the oddest sensation – an absolute conviction – that an era was coming to a close. This job was a step up. From now on she was in a different class: no more obeying the 'rules of the house' in shabby lodgings; no more borrowing, or lending, clothes for auditions; no more 'Mr Frohman isn't seeing anyone this week', 'Mr Palmer is out of town', or 'No casting today, leave your name and we'll call you . . .'

Her friends had been impressed. 'You got the Smith-Sinclair tour? May I *touch* you!' and they had made a hilarious show of treating her with awe and kissing the hem of her garment for luck. When she received good notices for *Tanqueray*, the girls were genuinely and generously pleased for her and, her birthday happening to fall during the company's final week in New York, clubbed together for a cake and some wine. They were all so kind and Blanche was grateful but, while they made much of how they were looking forward to her return, Blanche's own thoughts were very different.

Standing with a glass of wine in her hand, accepting their congratulations and good wishes, her resolution had been razor-sharp and etched diamond-hard in her head.

'I am not coming back here,' she had said to herself, looking round the dingy room in the shabby boarding house. 'I don't care what I have to do to ensure it, but I am never coming back.'

Few cities had adopted the row-house to such an extent as Baltimore. Space being restricted by hilly terrain and the harbour, row-houses had been built here from the time of the earliest settlers as a means of housing a growing population in a small area. They varied in size, from two to four storeys, but formed an astonishing link between the lives of all Baltimore's citizens because virtually everyone, rich or poor, lived in one.

That said, the house that Blanche approached on this cold Sunday evening proclaimed its superiority to Dora's humble home with a display of effortless elegance. Situated in charming Mount Vernon Place, and boasting four storeys not counting the basement kitchen, the Hamilton residence was built in the Italianate style. The red-brick façade was enlivened by decorative window and doorway frames in white marble; ornate cornices projected from the flat roof and, of course, the ubiquitous white marble steps gleamed in the lamplight. Throughout the city in summer, Baltimore people sat on their marble steps and gossiped or just watched the passing parade but, Blanche knew, that never happened here. Grandmother Hamilton's steps were worn smooth by the knees of housemaids who scrubbed them several times a day, but no *derrière* had ever dared to defile them.

The interior of the house had remained unchanged in every detail for as long as Blanche could remember, and so had its occupants. This evening her grandmother received her in the parlour, a murmur of voices from the second floor indicating that the bachelor son of the house was entertaining friends in the library, where Blanche was more accustomed to sit. Furnished with heavy mahogany, lace curtains and antimacassars, with an arrangement of silk flowers under a glass dome on the mantelshelf, the parlour had an oppressive and distasteful formality. Sitting on the edge of her chair, her spine stiff, Blanche had her back up in a more metaphorical way as well. One of these days, she vowed, she would tell these people where they could go, and what they could do when they got there. However, until then, for Dora's sake . . .

'I do hope that I have not called at an inconvenient time, Grandmama,' she said demurely, 'but I only arrived today, and wanted to see you as soon as possible.'

Grandmother Hamilton still wore mourning for the husband who had died more than thirty years ago. Her high-necked black silk dress was edged with a dainty white collar, a white linen cap covered her severely styled silver-grey hair, and apart from her wedding band, her only adornments were a simple pearl brooch and a mourning ring of pearls and black enamel. The immense family Bible stood open on a wooden stand beside her chair. Blanche stared at it warily. She had assumed that the Bible lived in the library upstairs, but evidently it went where her grandmother went. She wondered if it contained a family tree at the front and, if so, if her name was in it. There was some satisfaction in contemplating the dilemma that this entry, or its omission, must have presented.

'*You* are always welcome, Dorothea,' Mrs Hamilton said.

The emphasis, underlining her antipathy to the girl's mother, was not lost on Blanche. She saw, suddenly and clearly, that, but for Dora, she would be gathered into the bosom of the Hamiltons without delay or demur. An unprecedented surge of loyalty to her mother swept through her, or was it resentment at not being accepted for what she was?

Her grandmother's fingers were drumming on the arm of her chair.

'I'm sorry that I didn't arrive in time for church,' Blanche ventured, in deference to her grandmother's strict and unvarying allegiance to the Episcopalians.

The drumming increased in intensity. 'A most unedifying spectacle,' the old lady muttered, 'and very upsetting indeed.'

Blanche's eyes widened, and she leaned forward slightly in concern. 'I'm sorry . . .?'

'Not you, child,' and the impatience in the voice was matched by the abrupt wave of a thin hand. 'At church, this evening, we were *invaded*!'

'By the Presbyterians or the Catholics?' Blanche enquired, struggling to keep a straight face.

'By *actors*,' Mrs Hamilton intoned in a sepulchral tone.

'How many actors?'

'I was assured that there was only one.' Mrs Hamilton sniffed, and looked sceptical. 'If so, I can only say that it seemed like a lot more than one at the time. Why us, I asked – and still do ask. Why was our church singled out for this . . . this *pollution*?'

At that moment Blanche would have given her chances of an inheritance, her mother's allowance and a year's salary to explain the mystery. Amadine had asked for the name of an

Episcopalian church and Blanche had promptly advised her to attend Christ Church in St Paul Street, explaining its easy access from the Stafford Hotel at the corner of Charles and Madison Streets, where Amadine and the other principals were staying. She had even toyed with the idea of accompanying Amadine, in the hope of giving her grandmother a heart attack in front of the best Baltimore society, but Dora had put paid to that little pipedream.

Looking at the luxury surrounding her, Blanche remembered all the reasons that had driven her from Baltimore eight years ago. She had grown up angry and humiliated by the Hamiltons' rejection but, above all, she had been confused. What was she, who was she and where did she belong? At school she had mixed with girls who were the social equals of the Hamiltons, and so she could not ask them to visit her at her mother's home during the holidays. She noticed that, alone of her group, she was not invited to the best parties, which meant that she would not meet the best-connected young men. The final straw came when, lacking Hamilton support, she was not invited to the Bachelors' Cotillion, a social snub that she could never overcome. Feeling superior to Dora's shabby lodgings and inferior to the Hamilton mansion, Blanche decided that she must get away on her own and simply be herself.

Towards the end of the visit, Blanche could not resist returning to the subject of the theatre. 'Did that actor belong to the English company that is touring here?'

'I believe so. She was handsome, I must admit, and most beautifully dressed. I am told that she seemed to know her way through the service without recourse to the book.'

'If she is who I think she is, her father was a clergyman. He died,' Blanche added as an afterthought.

'Knowing his daughter's way of life, the poor man will not be resting peacefully.' Mrs Hamilton looked at Blanche suspiciously. 'You are remarkably well informed.'

'There was a piece about her in the newspaper,' Blanche

replied glibly. 'Grandmama, I always thought Baltimore was proud of its connections with the theatre – with the Booth family in particular.'

The old lady's thin lips compressed into an even harder line. Junius Brutus Booth had indeed made his home on a farm near Baltimore, and had lived in the city during the winter months. His numerous brood had gone to school here, and many of the family – the infamous John Wilkes among them – were buried at Greenmount cemetery. However, the fact that Junius Brutus married his children's mother only after living with her for thirty years was hardly likely to endear him to Mrs Hamilton. Even more important, she had poignant memories of the Civil War, the military occupation of Baltimore and the assassination by John Wilkes of the President, as had many of the older inhabitants of this essentially southern town. Any reference to John Wilkes Booth, however indirect, touched a very raw nerve.

Blanche saw the expression on her grandmother's face, and felt the chill in the atmosphere, but misunderstood the reasons for it. In fact, as far as Mrs Hamilton was concerned, history was repeating itself. It was always the same. Just as one was beginning to warm to Dorothea, who was a good-looking girl and could have been an asset to the family, she said or did something so stupid or insensitive that one was reminded, sadly but inexorably, of her mother.

'I will not detain you further,' and Mrs Hamilton rang for the butler to show her granddaughter the door. 'Are you staying in Baltimore for Christmas?'

'No. I . . . er . . .' Blanche floundered for an excuse as to why a schoolteacher would not be on holiday at Christmas.

Mrs Hamilton was not listening. 'Doubtless we will see you during your next visit to the city,' she said, and presented a pale, finely lined cheek that allowed the faintest brush of Blanche's lips before it was withdrawn again.

Blanche found herself on the white marble steps, with the

door closing firmly behind her and facing the long walk home alone. She stayed there, at the top of the steps, looking up at the starlit sky and at the immense column of the Washington Monument in the little park to her left. The street was silent and deserted. All I need is some money, Blanche thought dreamily. It doesn't have to be a fortune, just enough to secure a small house for Mama and bring her a modest monthly income. Then, *then*, I can be free of all this.

Wrapping her coat more warmly around her, Blanche walked to the end of the road and turned right at the Monument into Charles Street. She glanced across at the lighted windows of the Stafford Hotel and hesitated, wishing that she dared go in and find out if the others were still up. Better not – she hadn't been invited. She had not been accepted completely by the principals, and yet she no longer fitted in with the lower echelons of the company. The story of my life, she thought with a bitter smile. I never belong anywhere. Neither one thing nor the other, that's me. And she wondered if it would always be like this.

She told her mother that the old lady had not been in a good mood, and had not appeared pleased to see her. She did not report the various references to the theatre that had punctuated the discussion, and also failed to mention – for fear of her mother having hysterics – that in her role as Avonia she spent much of the third act of *Trelawny* in tights.

On Wednesday morning Blanche, who was only walking-on in *Romeo and Juliet*, accompanied her mother to Lexington Market. After shopping for provisions among stalls piled high with Maryland produce and the bounty of Chesapeake Bay, she made her way east along Fayette Street towards the Holliday Street Theatre, which lay near Peale's Museum and directly across from the City Hall.

The trouble with Fayette Street, she thought resignedly,

was that someone was always digging it up or building something along its borders. She could not remember a time when the street had not been obstructed, and today was no exception. Construction work between St Paul and Calvert had necessitated fencing off the sidewalk, and pedestrians were being directed along a narrow boardwalk. To make matters worse, a convoy of delivery wagons had dumped their loads of building materials in the road immediately adjacent to the wooden path, so that one's passage was even further restricted. If one met someone coming the other way, one had virtually to waltz with them, there was so little room to pass. Then, to her irritation, a man came towards her who made no attempt to move out of her path. Impatiently she caught hold of her skirts and tried to sidle past him, but he deliberately blocked her way.

'Dodo,' he said softly. 'Or should I say Blanche Villard?'

Raising her eyes to his face, Blanche felt as if her feet were nailed to the boardwalk. She could not move, despite the pushes and shoves of the other pedestrians trying to pass. She looked at the man, in silence, for what seemed an eternity and knew that, despite all her brave words, she could not wear Avonia's white tights in Baltimore. With *Trelawny* due to be staged on Friday, she had two days in which to find a foolproof reason for not appearing.

The man who confronted her was her long-lost step-father.

Chapter Fourteen

While Blanche gazed longingly at the lighted windows of the Stafford Hotel, the principals had been sitting late over an excellent dinner of soft-shell crab and terrapin. They were laughing at a story Hal was relating about the English actor-manager Herbert Beerbohm Tree, who had stayed at this hotel earlier in the year during his own American tour.

'He is king of the epigram,' Hal declared, as the mirth subsided. 'He comes out with a seemingly succinct remark, such as "The only man who was not spoiled by being lionised was Daniel", but says it in such a way that everyone knows he really means "Daniel and Herbert Beerbohm Tree".'

'With Herbert, you certainly wouldn't echo the sentiments of the American critic who reviewed a certain King Lear,' Frank remarked. '"He played the king as though under momentary apprehension that someone else was about to play the ace"!'

'No one ever trumps Herbert's performances,' agreed Hal, laughing. 'A shrinking violet, he is not.'

'Stop it,' Amadine protested, smiling despite her protest. 'I did *A Bunch of Violets* with him four years ago, and he was absolutely sweet to me.'

Everyone looked at her, and then at each other, with exaggerated expressions and exclamations of surprise.

'And some of his epigrams are true, or at least I hope they are,' Amadine persisted. 'Realising that I lacked self-confidence, he used to say to me, "Genius is an infinite capacity for not needing to take pains." He really believes that acting is more a matter of temperament than training.'

'But, Amadine, darling,' Hal expostulated, 'don't you see that Herbert was still talking about himself! He has to believe that, because I don't think he has had a day's training in his life.'

Amadine, who was due to play Juliet for the first time this week and who was growing increasingly nervous at the prospect, glared at him. 'Thanks, Hal,' she said sarcastically. 'I would have liked to believe it, too.'

'Did Mr Tree appear at the Holliday Street Theatre here, as we are doing?' Gwen asked hastily, but no one could remember. 'There has been a theatre on that site for a hundred years,' she said affectionately. 'I think that this is the third building – the previous one burned down about twenty-five years ago, and was rebuilt by John Ford.'

'The number of theatre fires one hears about over here is astonishing,' Hal exclaimed. 'But I think it's wonderful that they are usually rebuilt, and quickly, too.'

'Oh, it isn't only theatres that catch fire,' Gwen assured him. 'I'm afraid that our towns and cities have a habit of going up in smoke.'

'Only once have I been in a theatre during a fire,' Hal said reminiscently, 'and that was in New York when I was with Irving on his second tour here. We were doing *Hamlet* and, at the end of the Players Scene, an over-heated spirit torch set some draperies alight. Irving was magnificent. The man never missed a beat, and continued with the scene while the stage staff ran round with buckets of sand and water. Unfortunately his sang-froid was not shared by a young man in the audience, who panicked and ran up the aisle. I shall never forget the sight of Bram Stoker seizing him by the collar and frogmarching him back to his seat. Is there something wrong, Theo?'

During these latter exchanges, Theo had begun to look extremely uncomfortable and had been darting anxious glances at Amadine.

'Theo is being his customary considerate self,' Amadine explained. 'In Boston, I confided in him my ridiculous – even paranoid – fear of fire, and he is worried in case I am unnerved by the current subject matter. Sweet of you, Theo, but I'm fine. Honestly.'

All the same Theo deemed it diplomatic to change the subject. 'Who was with you on that tour, Hal?' he asked. 'Was Laurie there, or William Terriss?'

'Not Laurie.' Hal frowned in an effort to remember. 'And not "Breezy Bill" Terriss, either – he stayed at the Lyceum while we were away, and did *Romeo and Juliet* with Mary Anderson.'

'Another of the great Juliets,' and Amadine grimaced. She knew that comparisons were odious, in Shakespeare especially, but it was another of those instances where the gap between the theory and putting that theory into practice was virtually unbridgeable.

'I was in love with Bill Terriss for years,' Constance sighed dreamily. 'I thought he was the most handsome man I had ever seen and, when I went into the profession, I was dying to act with him. But then I found out that he does everything with Jessie Millward and, despite the fact that he is married to someone else, I do mean everything!'

The chuckle that went round the table contained no malice. Terriss and Millward were an established theatrical couple, and it was generally assumed that Mrs Terriss turned a blind eye to the relationship.

'They are an excellent match in every respect,' and Hal's gaze lingered on Amadine, 'and the arrangement works well for everyone.'

'Did your friend enjoy the outing to Walt Whitman's

house, Amadine?' Constance cut in quickly, with what seemed like a change of subject but wasn't. As she had expected, Hal's expression changed immediately.

Having told no one that Pierce Radcliffe had accompanied her on the Camden ferry in Philadelphia, Amadine regarded her thoughtfully. 'I didn't ask,' she said, the note of finality in her voice discouraging further discussion.

'If he isn't the intellectual type, he might have been bored to tears,' Constance persisted, 'and you must have formed some view of the man's character.'

'Oh, I'm an excellent judge of a man's character,' and Amadine paused before continuing, with a deceptively sweet smile, 'and of a woman's, too.'

The veiled hostility between the two women escaped Hal's notice. He realised that Constance had spoken lightheartedly of her youthful mash on Terriss, but was wondering if there was any possibility of his old pal Bill helping him out of a hole here. If Bill could give Connie a decent berth next season, it would be the answer to Hal's prayers, because he did not want to act with her again. Not now that he had worked with Amadine.

Next morning Amadine entered Constance's dressing room, and shut the door behind her.

'Do come in,' Constance said sarcastically, 'and make yourself at home.' She was sewing the hem of a silk frock in a delicate shade of forget-me-not blue. 'And do forgive me if I don't stop working, but some of us are trying to make the new *Trelawny* costumes ready for Chicago. Of course,' she continued pointedly, 'if everyone lent a hand they could be ready for Pittsburgh.'

'You wouldn't want to wear a dress made by me – it would fall apart at the seams in no time, on the stage, and at the most dramatic and inconvenient moment. Besides, I don't accept that, just because I wear a skirt, I ought to be sewing one. I'll guarantee that you haven't asked Hal to pick up a needle and thread.'

'Now you're being silly.'

'No, I'm being a leading lady. Which is what you ought to be, instead of trying to win friends and influence people by being Queen Bee of the sewing circle.'

'Look here,' angrily Constance laid down the silk, 'you ought to be grateful. *Trelawny* is your starring vehicle, not mine, and the least you could do is show some interest and appreciation of the efforts being made to improve it.'

'But I do,' Amadine responded in the same dangerously quiet voice she had used throughout. 'I have merely delegated my interest to Ida, who is a much better seamstress than I can ever be.'

'Sending your maid to do your share of the work doesn't count,' scoffed Constance, 'particularly when it forms part of her duties anyway.'

'That is where you are wrong.' An edge entered Amadine's voice. 'Ida is my personal maid and dresser. Her wages are paid by me, not by the company. If her duties are to be disputed, Constance, I might have to remind her that they don't include ironing your dresses and combing your hair.'

Constance flushed. 'Not all of us are fortunate enough to be able to afford a personal maid. You might remember that some of us have other responsibilities, which leave no room for luxuries.'

'Oh, I do remember. After all, you never allow us to forget it.'

As soon as she said it, Amadine hated herself, but for some reason Constance brought out the worst in her. The poor young widow struggling to maintain her orphaned children was a pathetically gallant figure, and arguing with her made Amadine feel guilty. It was as if Constance's personal tragedy ought to excuse any self-centredness or bad behaviour, yet this didn't altogether succeed, not with

Amadine anyway. She was discovering that being touched by tragedy did not necessarily make someone into a nice person. 'Virtue is not always amiable', as John Adams had said.

'I didn't come here to argue,' Amadine went on, with an attempt at restraint. 'I merely wanted to say that I did not appreciate your remarks about my personal life at dinner last night. What I do, and with whom, is no one's business but mine.'

'Then don't flaunt your relationships in other people's faces,' snapped Constance, who was thinking of Hal, not of Pierce.

'I know what you are trying to do, Constance, and I am surprised that you aren't being more subtle about it.' Amadine perched on the arm of a chair and, with her superior height, stared down at her adversary. 'You are hoping that Hal will lose interest in me in the face of American competition or, even better, decide that I am too promiscuous to be taken seriously.'

'I certainly think that he deserves better than you.'

'Hal doesn't think so. And all you have achieved so far is the arousal of his jealousy to fever pitch – he's been pestering me with questions about my friend all day. You see, the more promiscuous I am, the more Hal would like it. Let's face it – the man has slept with every leading lady he has worked with. Except,' Amadine added thoughtfully, 'you and me.'

'He discussed me with you?' Constance was horrified.

'Hal is like all men – he can be as free with his tongue as with other parts of his anatomy. The point is that he hasn't slept with me because I have not allowed him the privilege.' Amadine leaned forward slightly, and looked into Constance's eyes. 'Can you honestly say the same?'

'That is none of your business.'

'I agree.' Amadine stood up. 'Just as my relationship with him, or with any other man, is none of yours.'

'I take it as a compliment that Hal has never forced himself on me. He didn't marry any of those other trollops, did he?'

'He hasn't married you, either.'

'You intend to have him, don't you? I see it now – your mystery American is a diversion to make him jealous and, silly me, I played right into your hands.'

'There's such a thing as being too subtle, Constance, and you are going from one extreme to the other. Do be careful or you might goad me into having him, if only to save him from you!' But Amadine did not seek victory over Constance, merely a cessation of hostilities, and now she offered a truce. 'Just stay out of my affairs, Constance. I am not trying to take anything from anyone – I don't play those games.'

'Do you love Hal?' Constance asked at last.

'Why should I tell you?'

'Because I do love him.'

'He isn't merely the obvious answer to your problems? Because,' and Amadine stared hard at the other woman, 'Hal deserves better than that.'

'You haven't answered my question.'

'I can't, because I don't know the answer. I don't love him now, but who is to say what tomorrow will bring? It's easy enough to love a man today and find out the next day that you made a mistake, so why not the other way round?'

With that Constance had to be content, and the two leading ladies repaired their relationship sufficiently to continue working together. However, Constance discerned the ring of truth in Amadine's observations on love, and she began asking herself the questions that many others – Hal and Pierce chief among them – had been asking: how many men had there been in Amadine's life, had she slept with any of them and what had prompted her to make her way to London and the stage?

*

In this connection Constance had an advantage over the likes of Hal and Pierce: she was on excellent terms with Ida, Amadine's personal maid and dresser. Ida was a tall, brown-haired Londoner, plain of face, determined of manner and hotly pursued by Hal's valet, whom she treated with scorn. Although loyal to her mistress, she liked Constance and accordingly there was no difficulty in leading the girl into a good gossip over the sewing.

Ida described Amadine as a woman besieged on all sides by admirers, but who never allowed herself to be compromised. Any man who visited her London flat or hotel suites was never alone with her – either other guests were present, or Ida was within earshot. Yes, she did go out with men unchaperoned, but only to public places.

Had she ever entertained men alone in her dressing room? Yes, but only with the door open.

Had she visited Mr Haldane-Smith in his hotel suite? Yes, but only for informal rehearsals, and Mr Frank and Mr Theo were in and out all the time.

What about the train? Ida hesitated. Well, she said at last, she couldn't say about that. She didn't know nuthin' about what went on there. Which confirmed Constance's fears: the train, the proximity of Hal and Amadine's state-rooms in the Palace Car, was her own – and Amadine's – Achilles' heel.

No, Ida did not know how Amadine had come to take up acting. No, she never saw any letters from family or child-hood friends. No, she did not post any letters from Amadine to family or friends in Yorkshire.

This American, Mr . . .? Miss Amadine referred to him as Mr Panhard because of his motor car, Ida volunteered. 'How droll,' smiled Constance, who was beginning to despair of finding out anything new. Amadine must receive letters from her admirers, she suggested desperately. Hundreds, Ida agreed, and some of them said things you wouldn't believe. Miss Amadine dropped those straight into the wastebasket although, in Ida's opinion, she ought to take some of them to the police. There are people out there, Ida said darkly, who ought to be locked up.

'Amadine wouldn't take such things seriously,' Constance opined, 'just as she didn't believe someone tried to shoot her in Boston.'

'But Mr Panhard took it seriously – I heard them talking afterwards. Miss Amadine thinks he's taken leave of his senses, 'cos apparently he tried to tell her that she was being followed in the park in Philadelphia.'

So someone could be trying to harm her, Constance mused. Now that is interesting.

On Tuesday the post brought such unexpected good news that Constance believed her luck was turning. A London manager was interested in reviving *Three Guineas*, one of Everett Grey's earliest plays, and wrote offering generous terms. She rushed to wire her acceptance of the offer, then drafted a more detailed letter.

'May I borrow the typewriter?' she asked Theo, in his office at the theatre.

Theo sighed. It was difficult to refuse people who had helped him to master the intricacies of the machine, but Constance was not the only person who asked for the favour and he was falling behind with his own work. However, he told her to go ahead.

Constance hurried to the post office as soon as she was finished, being careful to enter the time of her departure from the theatre in Frank's book – people like Blanche might rail against the rule, but Constance fully approved of disciplinary measures, and believed in setting a good example by obeying regulations herself. In celebratory mood, she decided to treat herself to tea and cake and ventured into a tearoom where the homeliness of the low ceiling and delicate plasterwork, the shelf around the walls displaying china pots and plates, the framed engravings, rose-back chairs and the fire burning in the grate persuaded her to sit down. Pulling off her gloves, she noted the unqualified respectability of the other patrons, most of whom were women in white shirtwaists and warm skirts, with their coats draped over a spare chair. There was one elderly man sitting alone at a table in the corner, reading the *Sun*, and another young man at a table near the door. Constance did not recall seeing him when she came in, and thought it likely he had entered immediately after her.

The atmosphere was very pleasant and the tea, when it arrived, was excellent. Warmed and refreshed, Constance could almost imagine that she was in London, and that she would be going home to the children this evening. A wave of homesickness engulfed her, for this would be her first Christmas away from them. Her eyes blurred with tears as, feeling the heat of the fire, she began to take off her coat.

'May I be of assistance?' and skilful hands whisked the coat from her shoulders and laid it across a chair.

Turning, Constance saw the young man from the table near the door. Close up, he was not as young as she had thought; his dark hair and moustache contrasted with a fair, pale complexion, blemished here and there by the red spidery squiggles of broken veins. However, he was still an attractive man, with a tall, upright bearing and an exceptionally charming voice.

'Thank you,' she said.

'Thank *you*,' he returned, bowing. 'I am a great admirer of yours, Mrs Grey, and it is a privilege to meet you.'

Constance was taken aback. Unlike Amadine, she was recognised in public only rarely. 'You speak with an English accent.'

'Because I am English,' and he smiled, his pale blue eyes crinkling at the corners.

'Do join me,' Constance said impulsively. 'The waitress can bring your tea to this table.'

This was soon accomplished, although not without a

slight hauteur on the waitress's part, and Constance realised that she, of all people, was offending the rules of respectability by allowing herself to be 'picked up' by a stranger in a tearoom. For once, Constance did not care what other people thought. She wanted to talk about home, and she was delighted when, after introducing himself as George White, her companion declared himself to be a Londoner born and bred.

'I know Regent's Park very well,' George said, after she had described her marital home there. 'My parents used to live in that area, but my father died young – he was an Army officer, killed in the South African war – and my mother was forced to move to less expensive accommodation. We went to live in genteel poverty in Highgate and my mother is still there. I've offered time and again to move her to a more suitable address, but she is determined not to be a burden, as she puts it.' He shook his head. 'Bless her heart, as if she could ever be a burden!' And he smiled at Constance, that same smile which crinkled his eyes at the corners in the way he knew women loved.

It was all nonsense, of course. His father had been a publican, keeping a shabby house in Woolwich near the Royal Dockyard and the Royal Artillery Barracks. After his father's death, his mother took over the licence and she still carried on the business, with the help of a barmaid who had been waiting for the past fifteen years for George to marry her. But George had told this story before, and he told it well. His 'my mother is my best friend and greatest love of my life' performance had always been one of his best.

'This is such a pleasure and a privilege,' he said, in his most winning way. 'I first saw you at the Haymarket in *The Dancing Girl* – oh, how long ago was it? You were just a girl then, not that you look a day older today!'

'It was six years ago,' Constance replied, glowing at the

compliment. 'And I'm afraid that I was very much a beginner, and completely outshone by Julia Neilson.'

'On the contrary, your fair beauty was the perfect foil to Miss Neilson's dark good looks, and the contrast contributed a great deal to the success of the production. I went to everything you did after that, when I was in London.'

Constance was flattered – who wouldn't be? – but a small part of her remained wary and unconvinced by the notion of a man following her career with such interest. 'What brought you to Baltimore?' she enquired.

'I'm on my way home, after working abroad for several years.'

'What sort of business are you in?'

'Oh, I do a bit of this and a bit of that,' he replied vaguely, 'but I used to be in the profession.'

Constance stared at him, seeing him as if for the first time. She ought to have realised: the poor complexion was the result of constant applications of greasepaint and, probably, injudicious consumption of alcohol; the shabby clothes hinted at a lack of success with the 'this and that', and in the profession as well.

'Ought I to know you from somewhere?' and her enquiry had an icy edge.

He sensed it, and tensed slightly. 'I doubt it. I've been working in Australia and San Francisco recently. Before that I did most of my work at the Lyceum, with some seasons at the Criterion, the Garrick and the Royal Court.'

Walking on, Constance thought. I imagine George White does, or used to do, a very pretty line in messengers and first attendants. And the hair looks dyed, she thought, he must be going grey.

'Is that the time? I must be on my way,' and she gathered her things together.

He stood up, in order to help her on with her coat. 'I'm on my way back to London, but if you needed anyone to fill a gap on the tour, I could delay my departure.'

'I'm sorry?' Constance could not believe that she had heard aright.

'I can turn my hand to anything – I've played the lead in many provincial productions – or I could help out behind the scenes.'

'Oh, I don't have any say in that side of things. You'd have to speak to Frank Smith, but I doubt that there are any vacancies. Goodbye, Mr White,' and, after ostentatiously paying her own bill but not his, Constance sailed out.

He squeezed another cup of tea out of the dregs of the two pots, and lingered over it by the warm fire, ignoring the acerbic glances of the waitress.

It had been a mistake mentioning the profession so soon but, the whole object of the exercise being a berth on the tour, he'd had little option. That berth, with its proximity to Amadine and a free bed on the train, was becoming vital because his money would not last for ever. Since leaving Boston he had been working as a waiter in Philadelphia, but the wages were not much more than subsistence level, and taking cabs to follow Amadine was expensive.

His failure with Constance Grey rankled, and proved how careful he must be in his approach to Amadine. It was essential to make the right impression at their first meeting, so he needed to corner her in a location where he could put his case without interruption and where she couldn't scream the place down – or, if she did scream, no one would hear. The urge to make direct contact with her had become impossible to resist, and he had started writing to her: enigmatic letters, in disguised handwriting, full of hints and hidden meanings. He liked to imagine her touching the paper he had touched, and pondering on his words, but even that was no longer enough and his latest letter had described, in fairly graphic detail, the two of them in bed together. He got an erection just thinking about it, and knew that he would write again. In fact, sometimes he felt that thinking and writing about it was more exciting than actually doing it.

Perhaps he had failed with Constance because he had acted on impulse. He had been hanging around the theatre in Holliday Street, seen her hurrying out of the stage door and followed her. Yes, that would be it. Not thinking it through or planning a strategy was a much more likely explanation than the unpalatable possibility that he was losing his touch. Still, in his seedy hotel room that evening, he subjected himself to close scrutiny in a cloudy, cracked mirror. He had been wearing his good suit, otherwise he probably would not have spoken to her, but he had to admit it had seen better days. A gift from a lady, he recalled with a self-satisfied smile, on one of those interminable provincial tours. In those days his leading ladies had always been generous in their appreciation of his . . . er, services.

He frowned at his reflection, aware that he was not looking his best. It was the hair, he decided. It was all wrong: too dark, dull and lifeless. His hair had always been beautiful – the colour of flax and the texture of silk, his lovers used to say as they caressed it – but it was so recognisable that he must disguise it, and this shade was too dark against his fair skin. Red might be a better choice for his colouring, a rich auburn; he would make a start on it tomorrow.

In the meantime, what to do about the tour? Reflecting on Constance, he concluded that one problem was her age. She was too young. He was – horrible to contemplate – forty years old, and even in his heyday his main appeal had been to older women. His claim to have played leading roles in the provinces was genuine, but he had achieved this in a succession of companies led by ageing actresses who rewarded him for his performance in bed. It looked as though he must tread this road one more time – the last time, if things with Amadine went according to plan . . .

Amadine was due to play Juliet for the first time on the

Wednesday of their Baltimore engagement and, determined to be sweetness and light, Constance went to the theatre during the day to see how the final dress rehearsal was progressing.

As usual on these occasions, Amadine was white as a ghost and had hardly eaten for the past forty-eight hours. She was losing weight on this tour and her costumes were being taken in as often as a bride's wedding gown, but it was galling to note how the pallor and extreme slenderness suited her. Her skin was a luminous ivory against the ebony of her hair, and her eyes glittered like emeralds in that perfect face. Cheekbones you could cut yourself on, Constance thought with a sharp stab of envy, and she clung like a drowning man to the straw of hope that, beautiful though she was, Amadine was no Juliet. The pounds she was shedding were falling off her waist and hips, and were not detracting from the shapeliness of her shoulders or the fullness of her breasts. Amadine was altogether too voluptuous and sensual to portray the innocence of Juliet – which is how Constance interpreted the role – with any realism or conviction.

In a spirit of co-operation and generosity, she had purchased a little gift for Hal – a necktie of grey silk – and had drawn a good-luck card to accompany it. Constance was no mean artist, and her depiction of Hal as Romeo, with a Juliet whose long tresses had a centre parting and were half black and half blonde, was wickedly clever. While Hal was occupied with the rehearsal, Constance slipped into his dressing room to leave the items there for him to find later. Hal was not a tidy person, and the dressing table was so littered with greasepaints, notes and cards that she looked in vain for a space on which to place her offering. The only answer was to move some of the clutter from the centre of the table and, rather gingerly, Constance pushed a tube of greasepaint in one direction and a handwritten letter in the other. She gave the missive a cursory glance, thinking it strange that Theo was not dealing with it, but to her surprise her own name seemed to leap from the page. Quickly she checked that the corridor outside was deserted, and then she read the letter.

Then she read it again.

Replacing it, and the tube of greasepaint, in their original places, she picked up her gifts and hurried to her own room, where she shut the door and sat down. She was shaking, and white from shock.

Hal was writing to William Terriss at the Adelphi Theatre in London. The two actors were old friends and the first part of the letter contained the usual enquiries after Bill's health and that of Jessie M, and the profitability or otherwise of the current production. The second section was a rueful account of this tour and its chapter of accidents, particularly that which had befallen Laurie, but ending with a paean of praise for Amadine. The third section asked Bill if he could fit Constance Grey into his plans for next season.

Her heart was racing, pounding so uncomfortably that she pressed her right hand to her chest and tried to draw a deep breath. She had collapsed on to her dressing stool, and was staring at herself in the mirror. She looked lovely; even at a moment like this her face glowed with a charming serenity beneath its smooth cap of pale blonde hair. When she let down that hair, and skilfully applied her stage make-up, she could deceive an audience into believing that Juliet was fourteen years old.

But it was not enough. It was not nearly enough. Hal did not want to perform with her any more, and was discarding her like an old sock. Worse, she was an object of pity, to be passed like a parcel around London managements as Hal called in old favours. And all because of Amadine.

Wrenching her gaze from the mirror, Constance looked at the photographs of her children that always stood on her dressing table, and the enormity of what she had to lose hit her like a physical blow. Hal had been so sweet with the children; they could have been a family – she might even have had another baby – as well as a leading professional couple. It would have been so perfect, and now what was she facing? Relegation to the second division, and a life of loneliness and financial hardship.

She gave way to a storm of tears, remembering, as she cried, another epigram of Tree's: 'Hell is desire without hope.' But she had not sunk quite that low, not yet. There was still a ray of hope somewhere, wasn't there?

Romeo and Juliet was a triumph. Constance did not watch the entire performance because she simply could not bear it. How did one compete with that? How did one compete with that flawless portrayal of a girl who – with Amadine using her looks to advantage – is oblivious of her charm, and then gradually becomes aware of her sensuality.

The answer was that one couldn't fight it – not in a fair fight, anyway . . .

The morning after her début as Juliet, Amadine awoke feeling wonderful, and ravenously hungry. There was something to be said for enduring all that misery, she decided as she tucked into breakfast in bed, because it was so glorious when it stopped. With the breakfast, Ida had brought in a pile of letters and messages of congratulation and Amadine read them slowly, her pleasure evaporating slightly as she remembered that she had to repeat her performance that evening.

Then one letter made her sit bolt upright in bed. Neatly typed and purporting to be from one of the supers at the theatre, it begged her to spare the writer a few minutes of her time. 'I am so sorry to bother you, but I am in dreadful trouble and do not know where else to turn. I will go to the theatre at ten o'clock in the morning, and wait in case you come.'

This was a plea that the rector's daughter, already riddled with guilt at ignoring begging letters, could not refuse. Amadine jumped out of bed and, calling for Ida, began to dress.

In the cab, she ordered the driver to make a brief detour to the corner of Fayette and Greene. She was learning to seize her opportunities on this tour, and she had no intention of leaving Baltimore without seeing the grave of Edgar Allan Poe. Considering the lack of time at her disposal, she was glad the handsome white memorial was situated immediately inside the churchyard gate and she circled it solemnly, pondering on Poe's macabre tales, which sent shivers of delighted horror through her. The murder stories were her favourites and it seemed oddly fitting that the author's own death, on a visit to Baltimore when he was only forty years old, remained something of a mystery.

Alone in the deserted churchyard, it was not difficult to imagine the horror of being murdered; with another of those delicious chills running through her veins, Amadine tried to decide what, if she were murdered, she would prefer: for her death to remain a fascinating mystery, or for a detective like Poe's Auguste Dupin to solve it. Smiling at these flights of fancy, she returned to her carriage.

The stage door of the theatre was open, but there was no sign of the doorkeeper. The signing-in register was lying on the counter, open at today's page, but Amadine's was the first signature to be entered and she decided to go up to her dressing room and wait there. The front-of-house staff would be at work in the auditorium and box office, and the stage staff would be due shortly, but at the moment an eerie hush hung over the cavernous backstage area. Her footsteps echoed on the stairs and in the long corridors, and for the first time since coming to America she was aware of the cold inside the building, for the steam heat had not been turned on.

Leaving the door open, she sat down and, to pass the

time, began leafing through some of the mail that Theo had given her yesterday and which she had not had time to read. Everything continued to be very quiet, but once she thought she heard a scuffling noise and went to the door to investigate. The corridor was still deserted but several bundles of rags caught her eye, one at the far end of the passage and one near the top of the stairs. She did not think they had been there when she arrived, so presumably the cleaning staff must be around. Looking at her watch with what she considered justified irritation, Amadine went back to her letters.

I hope that this girl isn't pregnant, she thought idly. What shall I tell her to do if she's pregnant and not married? Oh well, the way things are going I won't have to tell her anything because it looks increasingly as if she's got cold feet and isn't coming. Which reminds me that my feet aren't exactly scalding hot. She got up and stamped, and walked around a bit, to get her circulation going. She coughed. Oh Lord, don't let me catch a cold, she prayed. The last thing I need is to lose my voice.

She coughed again, and now she noticed a funny smell.

It was the smell of burning, and she saw that not only had the door been pushed shut, but curls of smoke were drifting under it.

Amadine ran to the door and flung it open, only to reel back from the sudden rush of flames and smoke. The whole corridor seemed to be on fire but, peering through the smoke, she managed to discern that there appeared to be two main centres to the conflagration: one on either side of her – one blocking the way to the stairs, and the other blocking the way to the end of the passage and the fire escape.

She was trapped.

Chapter Fifteen

The panic was as suffocating as the smoke. Amadine closed the door and leaned against it, gasping for air, her inability to breathe due as much to her terror as to the increasingly oppressive atmosphere in the room. Against her shut eyelids, she could see the blaze on the other side of the door, but it merged in her mind with a stable fire she had witnessed long ago. She could hear the high-pitched whinnies of the terrified horses, and she could hear the screams of Fanny Longfellow as she ran from the house in a ball of flame.

Somewhere, deep inside her, in some mysterious well of her being, she had always known this would happen, that God would send her this trial one day . . .

Think, Amadine, *think* . . . She took a deep breath, or at least the deepest she could achieve, and felt the hot air in her mouth and passing down to her lungs. You can do something about that for a start, she admonished herself, and hurried to fling open the window. After several welcome breaths of cold, fresh air, she began to scream for help. In the voice that, a few hours before, had reached the back of the gallery in the 1,800-seater auditorium, Amadine shouted: 'Fire!'

Her dressing room was located on the equivalent of the third storey of a regular building and, as she shouted,

Amadine was gauging the distance to the ground. She would jump rather than burn alive but, as the cool air calmed her senses, she realised that she would be more mangled than poor Laurie if she did so. The window looked on to the faceless brick wall of the neighbouring building, which was separated from the theatre by a narrow alley, but that thoroughfare only provided access to the back yards and no one was in sight. There wasn't even a drainpipe down which she could shin.

Perhaps if she took off these voluminous skirts, she could make a dash for it through the flames and out the other side. But which way should she go – left to the stairs or right to the fire escape? Leaving the window open, Amadine, thinking more clearly now, went to the wash basin, soaked a scarf in cold water and tied it over her nose and mouth. It was a struggle to open the door – it was sticking and the handle was hot – but, heaving at it with her full weight, she succeeded. And immediately wished that she hadn't.

The corridor was a wall of flame, licking its way relentlessly towards her. The faint crackling noise had increased to a dull roar and the rush of heat was so intense that it hurt her eyes. Even through her protective scarf she could sense how soon her mouth, windpipe and lungs would be scorched if she didn't get out of here. She *thought* – she couldn't be sure – that the blaze looked worse at the fire-escape end but, backing into the room again and battling to close the door, she wondered if it made much difference. She very much doubted if she could find the courage to run through the flames, when she had no idea how far the fire extended.

Hurrying back to the window, she took in fresh gulps of cold air and began shouting again. The room behind her was filling with smoke, and wisps were spiralling past her out of the window. The fire must have started in two places at once, she thought confusedly. The dressing rooms farther up the passage must be well alight by now, and the contents . . . The costumes! My God, the costumes would be destroyed!

Suddenly, and irrationally, it seemed terribly important to save her costumes. Ida always insisted on unpacking the full trunk of dresses when the engagement was for a week or more, and on ironing them all and hanging them on a rail. Amadine seized her precious *Tanqueray* gowns and hurled them out of the window, anxiously watching as they ballooned slowly to the ground. Thank goodness it wasn't raining or snowing, and the dresses settled on a dry and comparatively clean surface. She ran back to the rack for another armful and tossed them out, too, and it occurred to her that, if she had to jump, the garments might provide a soft landing. But, for the most part, the dresses were too light and filmy to settle in one place, and floated to rest over too wide an area to allow that. Surely the stage staff must have arrived by now, she thought dazedly, but they wouldn't have any reason to come up here and by the time they noticed the fire, it might be too late.

Doggedly she went back to the dress rack and lifted off her *Trelawny* costumes. She would not mind losing these, but the new dresses were not ready. Oh Lord, she did hope that the new dresses were safe – all that work by Constance and the other girls, what a tragedy if it was wasted . . . Not such a tragedy as *you* being wasted, she thought. She did not want to die. Last night she had come a step closer to being recognised as a serious actress, a 'proper' actress, and she did not want to die before she had built on that and achieved her dramatic ambitions. Clutching the armful of dresses, she stood motionless while she tried again to clear her mind and devise a way of escaping.

She was still standing there a few moments later when the door burst open, and a grotesque figure lurched through the flames towards her like something straight out of Edgar Allan Poe.

Frank and Theo had taken a streetcar downtown from the hotel, and walked together from Charles Street to the theatre. Theo was raving about Amadine's wonderful performance the previous night, declaring that he had seen Juliet for the very first time.

Frank's feelings towards Amadine were ambivalent but, in all sincerity, he had to agree. 'Not only that, but she brings out the best in Hal. It's as though she spurs him on to greater things. He's done Romeo a thousand times, but never better than last night.'

'It's the sexual tension between them,' Theo declared 'You can *feel* how much he wants her.'

'Not much acting needed there,' Frank responded, with a grin. 'The point is: how much was *she* acting? And if Hal has his way, and has her, will the sparks still fly between them onstage?'

'I hope so. They could be one of the greatest professional couples the theatrical world has ever seen.'

It was true. On the stage Hal and Amadine were terrific individually; together they were sublime. Being fond of his brother, as well as dependent on his professional success, Frank wanted what was best for him and had to concede that Amadine was the best. On the other hand, with Chicago only thirty-two days away and with money much on his mind, Frank was conscious that Amadine was a luxury he could not afford. At this stage of the tour, her drawing power was essential to the company finances, but even Hal's future glory in the theatre could not be allowed to alter the fact that Amadine could not be allowed to claim her share of the profits at the end of the tour. That money was earmarked for Frank's own survival.

'It's a bit early to be bestowing laurel wreaths,' he said

cautiously, as he and Theo approached the theatre. He pushed open the stage door. 'Bloody hell!'

The air was thick with smoke, and stringent with the acrid smell of burning. Seeing the doorkeeper's booth empty, Frank swore again.

'If that fire has caught hold, I'll have his guts for garters!'

'The stage staff?' Theo shouted, holding a handkerchief to his mouth.

'I told them to come in late. They've given a hundred and one per cent this week, and I'll need them all day tomorrow to set up *Trelawny*.'

'So there's no one here?'

'Doesn't look like it.' Frank was straining his streaming eyes into the gathering gloom. 'But let's check,' and he located the register. '*Amadine* . . . Oh, no . . .'

Theo peered over his shoulder to see her signature in the book, appalled as he remembered her fear of fire. 'Why would she be here, and where would she go?'

They looked at each other. 'Dressing room,' they said simultaneously, and began to grope their way towards the staircase. The closer they went, the more obvious it became that they were heading for the heart of the fire.

'It's silly for both of us to go,' and Frank pushed Theo back. 'Call the fire brigade, but first throw some buckets of water over me.'

'Frank, you cannot possibly go into that fire!'

'Hurry up, man, and don't argue. Help me to locate the nearest tap, and if we can find a blanket as well, so much the better.'

They did find a blanket and soaked that with cold water, too, and as Theo ran off to fetch help, Frank tied a wet handkerchief over his mouth and nose, pulled the blanket over his head and shoulders, and started up the stairs.

The lower treads were safe and solid and, judging by the almost impenetrable gloom, the flames had not reached the upper flights. It began to dawn on Frank that he ought to have checked the rear of the building but, even had he thought of it, if Amadine had not escaped that way, he would have lost precious minutes before retracing his steps to his present position. Now the angry orange glow of the fire began to penetrate the smoke and, trying to hold his breath, he could see the flames in the dressing-room corridor.

He knew that he could not hesitate for long, not in this heat, and with his blanket and clothes drying sufficiently to catch alight. As it was, the little bit of his face that had to be exposed felt as if it were blistering, and his eyes were sore and streaming. He tried to remember which door was Amadine's and then, after taking a deep, scorching breath, put his head down and ran into the fire, through the fire, counting the doors until he came to what he hoped was the right room, and threw his weight against the door. It could not have been closed properly because it flew open and he hurtled into the room, and saw, to his overwhelming relief, that Amadine was not only alive but on her feet and apparently intact. But instead of being pleased to see him, she screamed, and it was only afterwards that he realised what a strange sight he must have presented. The impetus of his abrupt entry sent him reeling to his knees, and he let go of the blanket.

'Frank! Are you all right?'

He stood up quickly, and closed the door behind him. 'A bit singed, but otherwise I'm fine.'

In fact his hands were badly burned from holding the blanket in place, his eyes were streaming, one of his trouser legs was smouldering and he could barely breathe. He went to the wash basin and poured cold water on his leg, too preoccupied to notice the pain.

'Theo is calling the fire brigade, so we should have you out of here in no time.'

She was looking at him with a very odd expression on her face. 'You came through the flames? Just for me?'

'What do you mean, *just* for you?' Frank was at the window, looking down into the alley. 'Someone had to find you – you might have been lying unconscious somewhere.'

'Thank you.' She wanted to say more, but went into a violent spasm of coughing. Flames were creeping under the door, and smoke was billowing past them out of the window.

'Try not to talk. Ah, there's Theo.'

Theo and the box-office manager were running down the alley and, with a wild display of sign language, Theo indicated that the fire brigade was on its way.

'My dresses.' Amadine tried to scream the words, but only managed a croak. However, the costumes were conspicuous in the unsalubrious alley, and Theo and the box-office manager removed them to the safety of the lobby.

A crowd was gathering, gazing up with eager eyes at the two faces at the window. They'll be sorry when it's over, Frank thought. They'll be sorry if we get out of here alive. And he was pleased in more ways than one when the fire trucks arrived and the officers ordered the crowd out of the alley.

'Can you manage to climb out of the window?' he asked Amadine, as a ladder was leaned against the wall.

'I'm afraid of fire, but I'm not afraid of heights,' she answered, with a strained smile, and began gathering up her skirts in readiness.

'I don't suppose you have a pair of trousers?'

'No, but I don't think this is any time for false modesty, do you? If anyone down there gets a cheap thrill from seeing my stockings and bloomers, they're welcome to it.' She coughed again, feeling a tight, searing pain in her chest, and at that moment, with a roar, the fire burst into the room.

A fireman was climbing the ladder, but Amadine did not wait for him to reach the top. With Frank's help, she clambered on to the sill and swung first one leg, then the other on to the rungs. To a cheer from the men on the ground, she began the descent as quickly as she could, so that Frank could follow her to safety. Her legs were trembling, but they gave way only when she at last reached terra firma. A fireman caught her before she fell and, as she was half-carried out of the alley, she was able to turn her head and see that Frank was out of danger.

The Baltimore Fire Department announced that a full inspection of the building would be carried out during the afternoon but, long before then, Hal cancelled the evening performance. Even if the theatre was pronounced safe, the smell of smoke and the damage to costumes made it impossible to proceed. The only person in his element was Jay, organising press conferences at which he paraded Theo as his star eye-witness, while whispers that Baltimore was the thirteenth stop on the tour circulated among the company as persistently as the smoke still drifting in the theatre.

Hal divided his time between the theatre and the hotel, where the two fire victims had been ordered to bed. Both were suffering from the effects of smoke inhalation, while in addition Frank's burned hands and leg required attention. Even though he could raise no more than a whisper, Frank was protesting that he ought to be at work, and that all the fuss was unnecessary – like his heroics, he said, because a simple call to the Fire Department would have sufficed.

'You didn't know that when you went in.' Hal looked at the reddened skin of his brother's face, the singed hair and sore eyes, and at the bandaged hands lying limp on the coverlet. 'When I think how close I came to losing the two people who are the dearest in the world to me, I . . .' His voice shook.

'Some tour, eh, Hal? Perhaps the gossip is right. Perhaps she is a jinx.'

'I won't have that sort of talk,' Hal said fiercely, 'not even from you!' and, leaving Frank to sleep, he hurried to the room next door to check on Amadine.

Physically she seemed in better shape than Frank, although Hal suspected that shock would soon set in. Propped up on pillows, and resting her voice, she communicated by gestures and scribbled notes.

'Do you still have the note that asked you to go to the theatre?'

Amadine shook her head. 'Left it at the theatre,' she wrote, 'so gone up in smoke.'

'It wasn't signed? No . . . Would you recognise the handwriting?'

'Typed.'

Hal grimaced. 'And you say that the fire seemed to start in two places at once, at each end of the passage?'

A very nasty suspicion was forming in his mind, but he hesitated to share it with her. For one thing, he feared that her recovery was more fragile than it seemed; for another, his suspicion was so ludicrous, so preposterous and fantastic that it made no sense.

Amadine was writing furiously. 'Promise not to tell anyone about letter – I feel such a fool.' With a mixture of reluctance and relief, Hal promised.

Now that the danger was over, Amadine felt very strange – feverishly alert and wide awake. She wanted to talk and talk, and was frustrated by the need to care for her voice. Feeling that she could walk from here to New York without difficulty, she had already tried to get out of bed once, only for her knees to buckle and an irate Ida to come running and order her back to bed.

The doctor gave her a sedative, but Amadine did not rest easy. Tormented by dreams of fire, she tossed and turned in a bed that seemed ringed by flame and from which she could not escape. She muttered under her breath, and occasionally tried to call out.

'O! she doth teach the torches to burn bright . . . And fire-eyed fury be my conduct now! . . . fiery-footed steeds . . .'

Ida, fearing damage to her mistress's voice, was relieved when she awoke. However, to the maid's surprise, when told that she had been talking in her sleep, Amadine grew agitated and gripped her arm tightly.

'What did I say?' she whispered.

'It was bits from the play mostly. I couldn't make it all out.'

Amadine relaxed her grip and sank back on to the pillows, but she refused another sedative and tried to stay awake. She was in a nightmare of fear and flame, and now she was afraid to sleep in case she blurted out things she did not want anyone to hear.

Later in the day the Fire Department had good news, and bad news, for Hal. The good news was that the fire, although fierce, had been confined to the dressing rooms and, unlike the devastating blaze of 1873, had not damaged the fabric of the theatre. The building was declared safe after the electrical company confirmed the wiring in the auditorium and stage area was unaffected. Hal immediately announced that the Friday and Saturday performances would go ahead but, due to Amadine's indisposition, with a change of programme.

The bad news was that the Fire Department suspected arson. Close inspection of the debris indicated that the fire had started at each end of the dressing-room corridor, a fact that Hal affirmed agreed with Miss Sinclair's observation. At that point Hal found himself impaled on the horns of a dilemma. Did he tell the Baltimore authorities about the letter which, he very much feared, had lured Amadine to the theatre? He had promised Amadine not to tell, and was fairly certain that she would not mention it, but perhaps his greater responsibility to her demanded that he bring it into the open. But what would happen if he did? Hal returned to the hotel and examined the matter from every angle.

From what he had seen, and from what the authorities had said, the chances of identifying the arsonist were slim. The evidence, if any, had vanished in the fire. So if he did mention the letter, what would happen? The entire company would be interrogated, that's what would happen. If someone had lured Amadine to the theatre and then set fire to the place, the charge would be attempted murder. It did not bear thinking about. Not only must Hal consider the effect on the company, which was demoralised enough, but also he must weigh the effect on Amadine.

In the end, that factor settled it. While on the one hand it might be better to warn her, on the other hand he could not bear to frighten her. So Hal said nothing and, with no motive and no additional evidence, the Baltimore authorities were unable to pursue the investigation.

Hal took it very much to heart, for he could not help wondering how much of the company's misfortune was due to his lack of management experience. In all honesty he did not see what he could have done differently, and he did not see what he could do to ensure that nothing untoward happened in the future. Except keep an eye on Amadine. Day or night. Preferably both.

In the meantime he had to face a really embarrassing interview with Constance, who joined him in the parlour of the suite after visiting Frank's sickbed.

'Frank insists on going to work tomorrow,' she remarked as she sat down. 'I suppose it's a good sign that he feels well enough to say that, but I would have thought such a move was most unwise.'

'Short of chaining him to the bed, I don't know how to stop him. Stubborn as a mule is our Frank, and convinced that he is indispensable.'

'Apparently you have decided that the show goes on tomorrow but, may I ask, which show?'

'Amadine cannot perform for several days . . .'

'You cannot send on an understudy for either *Tanqueray* or *Trelawny*,' Constance interrupted in a practical tone of voice. 'All things considered, our only option is for you and me to do *Romeo and Juliet*.'

Hal looked at her gratefully. 'I wasn't sure how you would feel about coming to the rescue.'

'We are a team,' Constance protested indignantly, and smoothly switched the conversation to practicalities. Hal's dressing room, her own and Gwen's were among the casualties of the fire. 'For obvious reasons, my Juliet costumes weren't there,' she said piously, 'so they are intact, and it occurred to me that we could alter some of Laurie's outfits for you. Gwen and I will help the wardrobe mistress – there were a whole host of people along that corridor, I'm afraid. Oh dear, more expense, and on top of the new *Trelawny* costumes, too.'

'I haven't dared to ask about them.'

'No need to worry – most of them are right here in my hotel room, so that I could work on them while you were busy with your other Juliet. Oh, talking of which . . .' and she produced a package and a card that she handed to him. 'I intended to give you a little gift yesterday, but only found something this morning. Just as well, really – you might have left it lying around in your dressing room, to be destroyed in the fire.'

Looking at the grey silk necktie and charming card, Hal was touched. Connie had her faults, but she could always be relied on in a crisis.

'You're looking very pleased with yourself, Dodo,' Blanche's mother remarked.

'Not pleased, exactly. Just relieved.'

Yesterday – was it only twenty-four hours ago? – her

stepfather had taken her firmly by the arm and propelled her into the nearest bar, where he had the gall to order a drink and expect her to pay for it.

'Does my mother know that you are back in Baltimore?' she had asked.

'What makes you think I ever left?' He grinned as his gaze swept approvingly over her svelte little figure. 'But no, Dora don't know I'm in town. There are a few people I'm avoiding, and Dora never did know how to keep her mouth shut.'

'She told you about me, didn't she?'

'Of course she told her ever-loving husband about her little girl in New York, *and* what that little girl did for a living.'

'I'll kill her,' Blanche said without emotion. The person she was furious with was herself: she ought to have known that Dora would confide everything to this ghastly man. And he was the person she would like to kill: dropping him from the top of the Shot Tower would be an absolute pleasure. 'So,' she said in a conversational tone, 'what will it take to stop you telling my grandmother about me?'

'A thousand bucks.'

'Do I look like Mrs Vanderbilt?'

'Let's call it seven hundred and fifty, then.'

'Let's call it complete crap.' Blanche looked at him dispassionately. She was feeling the exact opposite of dispassionate, but was a remarkably good actress. 'You know that I don't have access to real money.'

'As soon as I saw you were at the Holliday Street,' he remarked, 'I got me a ticket for Saturday night.'

Trelawny. If he saw her in Avonia's white tights, the price would go up.

'I realise that I have to buy your silence,' she said, turning to go. 'I will meet you here on Friday, and we'll discuss the price when I've had time to think things over.'

The fire changed everything. With only her walk-on role

in *Romeo and Juliet* to face the following day, Blanche was able to plan her strategy coolly and calmly.

'I will pay you five hundred dollars,' she said without preamble, when she met him again, 'but you must understand that I will need time to accumulate such a sum.'

'How much time?'

'Here is fifty dollars,' and, with sinking heart, she steeled herself to hand it over. It was all she had, and in all probability she would have to sleep in the street in Washington. 'I'll save the rest during the tour, and pay you when we return to Baltimore at the beginning of April.'

'April! I could be dead by then!'

One can live in hope, Blanche thought uncharitably, but knew in her heart that she would not be that lucky. There was something indestructible about him, from that greasy hair to the dirty fingernails and the bad, beery breath. How her mother could have endured him for five minutes, let alone . . .

'Take it or leave it,' she said boldly, calling his bluff. 'I'm only a jobbing actress and I'll have to beg, borrow or steal the money as it is. I can't do it any quicker.'

He did not like it, that was clear. He had seen an opportunity for a quick profit and did not want to wait. However, four hundred and fifty dollars was worth waiting for, and it was logical that she would not have that sort of cash handy.

'If that's the best you can do,' he said grudgingly.

That fifty dollars bought her time. When she returned to Baltimore in April, Blanche trusted that either fate would have found her a fortune or another solution to the problem would have presented itself.

At the theatre that Friday, Hal was trying to be optimistic and to lift the spirits of the company. 'I remember,' he said, during a little address to all the cast and stage staff, 'what Lillie Langtry said when her theatre burned in New York. She believed it to be an omen of future good fortune that the fire was extinguished before it obliterated her name on the sign across the front of the building. Now, we have the theatre itself still standing . . .' He caught sight of Jay, who was brandishing a piece of paper in order to attract his attention. 'Yes, Jay?'

'Didn't you say the other day that you knew this William Terriss feller?'

'Of course I do. All the English contingent on this tour know him.' Hal allowed his irritation to show. 'What of it?'

'He's dead. I thought you'd want to know.'

'*Dead?*'

'He's been murdered.'

As tumult broke out among the English company, Hal grabbed the wire from Jay, then buried his face in his hands. It took all his strength to get through that terrible day, and to give a passable performance that night. By the time he, and the other principals, returned to the hotel for a late dinner, more details of the tragedy had emerged.

They sat round the table: Hal, to whom Breezy Bill Terriss had been friend and inspiration; Frank, who had known him well; Constance, who had admired him for years; Gwen and Theo, who had seen him act many times; Jay – and Blanche, invited to the meal by Gwen – who knew him by reputation; and Amadine, who had been told of the tragedy during the day and who came downstairs to join them.

The previous evening Terriss had arrived at his private entrance to the Adelphi Theatre in London when a cloaked figure leaped out of the shadows and stabbed him repeatedly. Terriss collapsed, and died soon afterwards in the arms of his mistress and leading lady, Jessie Millward. But for the Smith-Sinclair company, as for many others who mourned in England that night, the horror went yet farther and deeper. Terriss's murderer was an actor, who believed, quite wrongly, that the great star had kept him out of work and then stopped his benevolent money.

'Bill . . . killed like a rat in an alley, by a member of the profession!' A muscle twitched in Hal's cheek.

They looked at each other, pale and unsmiling around the table, and then their gaze dropped to the virtually untouched plates of food in front of them.

'I'm sure,' and Amadine's voice was only a hoarse whisper, 'that such a thing can never happen again!'

Chapter Sixteen

The nightmares were receding. Amadine's bed was no longer ringed in flame, the crackle and roar of the fire were muffled and her room smelled sweet again. She had thrown out every garment she had worn that day and felt, at long last, that she had washed the smell of smoke from her hair. Her voice was growing stronger, enabling her to feel confident of playing *Tanqueray* for the final three nights of their Washington engagement.

Only concern about the cause of the fire stood between her and a complete recovery and, as the days passed, Amadine began to doubt the evidence of her own eyes and to attribute that searing vision – of the fire starting at both ends of the passage simultaneously – to the panic she had experienced at the time. She had been questioned at length by the Baltimore police, but had not told them about the letter and, judging by their silence on the subject, Hal had kept his promise not to mention it. Had the letter been a hoax, luring her to the theatre so that an attempt could be made on her life? Amadine could not believe it; at heart she remained a down-to-earth Yorkshire woman, who was not easily scared. She made only one, temporary, concession to her personal safety: when she left the train in Washington, she removed the pistol from her bedside drawer and placed it in her handbag.

She had been disappointed that Pierce Radcliffe had not rushed to her bedside in Baltimore but decided not to bear him a grudge and, when he invited her to dinner in Washington, she dressed with particular care. In a gown of black velvet, very plain but of exquisite cut and quality, its texture enhancing the sheen of her skin and matching the ebony gleam of her hair, and with diamonds sparkling like stars at her throat, wrist and ears, she made an entrance into the dining room of the Washington hotel that had even the sophisticates of the capital choking on their soup or watching, forks suspended in mid-air, as she glided to her seat.

Pulse racing, Pierce stood up as she approached. This was becoming a habit. He tried to stay away, but was drawn back to her time and again, and on each occasion the shock of her incredible beauty was like a physical blow. It was as if a hard fist punched him in the solar plexus, leaving him winded and gasping for breath. He tried to believe that he scheduled his business commitments to coincide with the theatre tour because of his other, and originally predominant, interest in the cast, but it wasn't true. As she drew closer, his gaze never left the perfect oval of her face, dominated by the cool green eyes and the lovely line of her lips, the planes and contours strengthened by the severity with which her hair was drawn back. There was the slightest suggestion of a dimple in her chin. But then, taking her black-gloved hand and raising it to his lips, he saw the bracelet. And when she took her seat opposite him, the diamonds flashed at that lovely throat and at the tips of those delicate ears.

He reached across the table and held her wrist, his fingers tracing the raised outline of the gems. 'Very pretty,' he said, in a voice as hard as the stones. 'A gift from an admirer?'

Amadine jerked her hand free. 'What business is that of yours?'

'None, but it could be the business of the man's wife and children.'

'So not only do I have a lover who showers me with expensive baubles, but he's married as well! Are you mad?'

He had spoken from the heart, but without thinking, and realised he had gone too far. 'I do apologise. Please,' because everyone in the restaurant was riveted on her every move, 'let's not make a scene.'

'But making scenes is what I do best.' Amadine was so furious that she was damned if she would explain that the diamonds were borrowed, and that they were the same gems that she wore in *Tanqueray*.

'I really am very sorry. I cannot imagine what I was thinking of.' In fact Pierce knew exactly what, or who, he was thinking of, but freely conceded that he must have suffered a brainstorm by mentioning it. 'Let's start again. It is a great pleasure to see you, Amadine, and I am so glad that you were free tonight.'

She took a sip of wine, and forced a smile. 'Hal and Constance are doing *Romeo* this evening, while I rest my voice. So you, Mr Radcliffe, are supposed to entertain me with amusing conversation, not irritate the hell out of me!'

'I read about the fire, and came as quickly as I could.'

'Did it make the newspapers in New York and Boston? Oh, Jay will be thrilled! This tour makes its own publicity – deaths, accidents, fires, we hit the headlines without even trying. Just imagine what we could achieve if we really put our minds to it!'

Sensing how brittle she was behind the flippancy, Pierce tried to coax the story out of her. Amadine admitted that she, and the Baltimore authorities, suspected arson, but she did not tell him about the letter.

'So it was sheer coincidence that you happened to be on the premises at the time?' Pierce asked, gauging her reaction carefully.

Amadine shrugged. 'I suppose so.'

He did not believe her. 'Is there anyone, in your past or present life, who would want to harm you?'

Amadine laughed. 'I have no enemies,' she asserted.

'You are a very beautiful woman,' he said gently, 'who must have aroused many emotions in many people.'

'And never the right emotions in the right people,' she responded with a wry smile. 'But I suppose there must be women who envy me, and women in the profession from whom I have taken a role that was important to them; and there have been men who wanted to . . . know me better, and whom I refused. However,' and she met Pierce's gaze levelly, 'there are no lovers, married or otherwise.'

'Not even Haldane-Smith?' Pierce was unable to keep the sharpness out of his voice. 'Not for want of trying, I'll be bound!'

'That's beside the point,' Amadine retorted. 'Any hurt I may have inflicted was unintentional, and could not possibly warrant the death penalty.'

'Perhaps someone has become obsessed with you as an actress, but the difficulty with that theory is that it doesn't fit all the attacks. If one tries to get inside the head of such a person – and that sure ain't easy – one can envisage him as the stalker in Philadelphia, trying to get close and talk to you, in the belief that if he does meet you, you will fall in love with him. Killing you is hardly likely to be on the agenda, unless . . .' Pierce stopped himself just in time – he had been about to say: 'unless you turned him down.' He thought quickly. 'Could you leave the tour, and go back to London?'

'Certainly not.'

'It would be the safest move.'

'I'm not running away. I'm English!'

The relevance of that eluded him, but evidently it had the utmost significance for her. 'Assuming that you have experienced nothing like this before, the odds are that this fellow is an American, and it seems unlikely he would pursue you across the Atlantic. Of course, it would be better still if you gave up the stage.'

'Back in my little box! Good God, you're just like all the others.'

'Box?'

'One of Henry James's more successful images in *The Bostonians*. For a man who, I sense, disapproves of the women's movement, it is remarkably perceptive. A female character in the book is explaining why women want freedom, for the lid to be taken off the box in which they have been kept for centuries. Men think it's a comfortable, cosy, convenient box, with nice glass sides so that the women can see out, and they want to keep the lid on and the door locked. Typical!'

'How does suggesting that you give up the stage, for your personal safety, put you back in this imaginary box?'

'The stage is how I make my living. Take that away from me, and what else is there but marriage and that box! Even my father who loved me, and my mother who didn't, could see no farther than that and contemplate no alternative. My mother wasn't even happy in her own box, but she still tried to sentence me to mine!' Amadine's expression was animated, and her eyes glowed with the intensity of her feeling. 'I am out of the box, and I am never going back. If freedom means facing the occasional lunatic with a gun or a box of matches, so be it. It is a price I am prepared to pay.'

'Bravo,' and he applauded softly. 'You are wasted speaking other people's words on the stage. You ought to write, and speak, your own.'

'Stand for Parliament, you mean, or for President?' she said sarcastically. 'Somehow I doubt if the time is right, but I admit to believing that women could run the world just as well as men, if not better. "When I look around me at the world, and at the state that men have brought it to, I confess I say to myself, 'Well, if women had fixed it this

way I should like to know what they would think of it!'
When I see the dreadful misery of mankind and think of
the suffering of which at any hour, at any moment, the
world is full, I say that if this is the best they can do by
themselves, they had better let us come in a little and see
what *we* can do. We couldn't possibly make it worse,
could we? If we had done only this, we shouldn't boast of
it. Poverty, and ignorance and crime; disease, and wicked-
ness, and wars!"'

'You've won my vote,' Pierce said, laughing with admiration.

'Sorry to disappoint you, but that was Henry James
again – verbatim, I'm very good at remembering my lines.
I agree with every word of it, but giving expression to
others' inspiration is what I do best. Cobblers should stick
to their lasts.'

'Are you cobbling on Christmas Day?'

She nodded. 'We have a matinée of *Tanqueray*, and in the
evening Hal has arranged dinner for the entire company.' A
faint look of disappointment crossed his face. 'I have to be
there,' Amadine said, 'although, come to think of it, there
might be some who would prefer it if I stayed away.'

Pierce raised an eyebrow quizzically.

'They think I'm a jinx,' she explained, 'the bringer of
bad luck, the harbinger of doom.'

'Superstitious nonsense.'

'There's an awful lot of that about in the theatre.' But
Amadine smiled and looked more cheerful. It was strange
how a good argument with Pierce Radcliffe lifted her spirits. Heaven alone knew why, but a few insults from him
were becoming preferable to all the compliments and syco-
phancy heaped on her elsewhere.

Pierce was feeling a heightened anxiety for her safety.
More than ever he feared that somewhere out there was
an unseen enemy. Indeed, if one weighed the facts and
looked at this series of disturbing incidents from every

possible angle, it seemed likely that there was more than one.

Next morning Pierce requested a meeting with Hal, but only after convincing Theo that the interview concerned Amadine and the Baltimore fire was he granted an audience. Waiting on a sofa in the corridor outside the Haldane-Smith suite, and wishing to conceal his presence from Amadine, he hid behind a newspaper. Uncharacteristically he turned to the theatre page, and read a review of the previous evening's presentation of *Romeo and Juliet*. Oh dear . . .

Washington was giving the production the thumbs down. Romeo received grudging approval, but the attack on Juliet was scathing. Pierce was surprised, as he had seen Constance Grey in the role several times and did not think that she was that bad. However, it seemed that the Washington critic had seen her play the part before, and more importantly he had made the short journey to Baltimore the previous week and seen Amadine in the role. In his opinion not only did Constance fall far short of Amadine's performance, but she failed utterly even to emulate her own former and comparatively paltry efforts. Her leaden, and embarrassing, performance had dragged down Edward Haldane-Smith to depths never previously plumbed.

Pierce was sitting there, wincing, and hoping that Constance Grey had not seen the review, when Haldane-Smith's door opened and the lady herself rushed out. Her appearance dishevelled and her face streaked with tears, she ran up the corridor and disappeared into her own room. Oh *dear* . . .

Vaguely Pierce wondered if such unfavourable comparison with Amadine was grounds for murder, but decided that Constance could hardly blame Amadine for her own shortcomings. Anyway, she looked the type who would shoot her mouth off rather than a gun.

Then he was ushered in to meet Edward Haldane-Smith for the first time.

Hal was not having a good day. The appalling reviews had come as no surprise to him – he had been there when the crime was committed, so to speak – but coping with Constance over breakfast was guaranteed to upset his equilibrium for the rest of the day. At times like this he was inclined to wonder why he had hired her in the first place. The simple answer was that she had been available; and when they came to work together, she had been competent, pliable and non-argumentative. Hal, groping his way into management, had been grateful for small mercies. However, the mercies were becoming smaller all the time. Her Juliet last night had been a travesty – a pouting schoolgirl trying to be sexy, and failing miserably. Constance wasn't sexy. She never had been, and she never would be; but she had seen Amadine's Juliet smouldering into sexual maturity, and decided that whatever Amadine could do, she could do better. God, it had been ghastly!

What he was going to do about her, he did not know. Even without Amadine, he did not think that he could continue to work with her. *With* Amadine, it became a total impossibility. As he could no longer rely on Terriss to provide a solution, the situation was grim. Constance had gone from leading lady on his arm to millstone around his neck in a mere four months.

So this Radcliffe chap hadn't picked the most propitious moment for a chat. Hal had a shrewd idea who the fellow was, and as soon as Radcliffe came into the room these suspicions were confirmed. This was Amadine's mystery admirer, no question. Telling himself that it was no bad thing to meet, and assess, the competition, Hal shook hands and prepared to listen to what the man had to say.

'Amadine did not mention the stalker,' he said a few

minutes later, 'and I must admit that we tended to treat the gunshot in Boston as something of a joke.'

'I felt it important to ensure that you were in possession of all the facts.'

Hal frowned. The man's attitude was a bit bloody condescending, but happily a means of retaliation was at hand. 'Did Amadine tell you about the letter?' he enquired smoothly, and knew by Radcliffe's grim expression that both of them had the satisfaction of imparting information, and both suffered the chagrin of knowing that Amadine had not confided fully in them.

'I wonder what else she hasn't told us,' Radcliffe said drily.

'I have no idea, but I do know that she would take great exception to us talking about her behind her back,' Hal retorted, showing off what he believed was his more intimate knowledge of Amadine's character.

'Then she mustn't find out,' Pierce observed levelly, 'because we must discuss ways of ensuring that Amadine is not put at risk again.'

'You may leave that to me.'

'Her employer cannot be responsible for her twenty-four hours a day.'

Pierce and Hal were eyeing each other warily, taking the measure of the other man and trying to be polite, but wondering about the precise nature of Amadine's relationship with him.

'I am her partner, not her employer, and I will do whatever is necessary,' Hal said at last.

'Does that include intercepting her mail?' Pierce asked, expecting Hal to be affronted by such a proposal.

'Yes, as a matter of fact it does.' With a smirk of satisfaction, Hal rang for Theo and asked him to bring in several letters that had been abstracted from Amadine's postbag. 'Naturally we have been absolutely honest and open with Amadine about this procedure,' he said suavely, 'but I will admit that we have not told her about these.'

Pierce looked at the two letters that Theo handed to him. Both were written on cheap notepaper, one in an uneducated scrawl and the other in carefully printed capitals; and although they conveyed the same message, one was expressed in clearer, more grammatical language than the other.

'There's no name and address – hardly surprising, given the contents – and they don't seem to be written by the same person,' Theo commented.

'Although both describe in fairly explicit detail what they would like to do to Amadine.' Hal grimaced with distaste. 'In fact, one of them seems to have imagined doing it so often, he is virtually reminiscing about it.'

'Have they written before?' Pierce asked.

Theo nodded. 'According to Ida, yes.'

'Do all actresses receive this kind of filth?'

'None of my female colleagues has ever mentioned anything quite as bad as this,' Hal replied.

'From the point of view of the ladies in the profession, I am very relieved to hear it but, from Amadine's point of view, I was hoping that they were all in a day's work.'

'I shall be glad when we board the train again at the weekend,' Hal said, with malicious pleasure, 'and I can watch Amadine's every move. She and I share the private car, you know.'

Pierce had not known, and found the information disconcerting. Being a seasoned campaigner himself, he was aware that, in the art of seduction, opportunity was everything. And opportunity Haldane-Smith undoubtedly had – along with his good looks, his charm and his profession. The image of him and Amadine cocooned in that warm, private world of the Palace Car, while the rest of the company slept, was not something on which he cared to dwell.

He produced a business card and offered it to Hal. 'My

home and business addresses in Chicago. Someone there will always know where I am if you need me.'

'Oh, I don't think we'll need you, any more than Amadine needs you,' and Hal walked into the adjoining room without taking the card.

Apologetically Theo took the card and put it in his pocket. He did so only out of sheer politeness, because he was sure that Hal would endure any amount of torture before he used it.

Gwen was talking to Blanche in the hotel lobby and, as she approached, Amadine saw her surreptitiously pass a bundle of dollar bills to the younger woman, who pocketed it with a grateful smile.

'We'll give Constance another five minutes,' Gwen decided, 'but after last night . . .'

'. . . and today's papers,' Amadine added.

'. . . it is doubtful if she will come.'

But Constance did come, wearing that distinctive hooded cloak, and a brave smile, and the four women set off into a frosty, wintry Washington.

'Aren't we paying Blanche enough?' Amadine asked Gwen in a low voice.

'She needed a loan, to pay for her lodgings. Apparently she asked Frank for an advance on her wages, but he refused.'

'Frank is my hero, for obvious reasons, but I understand that he can be a bit tightfisted with cash. How much does Blanche need?'

'Fifty dollars. I gave her twenty, but . . .'

'I'll give you fifty dollars later today, and you can reimburse yourself and pass on the rest to Blanche. Don't tell her it's from me – she might be embarrassed. Did she say why she had run short of money?'

'She had to give all her wages to her mother in Baltimore.'

'And you felt sorry for her because you know the feeling!'

'I cannot guarantee that Blanche will repay you.'

Amadine shrugged. 'It's all in a good cause.'

They were walking along E Street and turned into 10th, and there it was: Ford's Theatre where, in April 1865, an actor called John Wilkes Booth assassinated President Abraham Lincoln. Gwen had warned the English visitors that there was not much to see, but Amadine in particular was anxious to visit the scene of an act that had such a devastating effect on American history, and on the American theatrical profession.

The building being empty, Gwen had arranged for a caretaker to admit them and, as soon as they were inside, the visitors realised why Gwen had been lukewarm about the expedition. The interior of the theatre was an empty shell, piled with debris and clearly unsafe. However, Gwen tried to give an idea of how the theatre would have looked, indicating the location of the box occupied by the President, from which Wilkes Booth jumped down on to the stage after the shooting.

'It was never used as a theatre again after that night,' she explained. 'The government bought it from John Ford, and turned it over to the War Department for use by the Record and Pensions Bureau, and the Army Medical Museum. But four years ago part of all three floors collapsed into the basement.'

'Was anyone hurt?' Amadine asked.

'Twenty-two clerks were killed, and sixty-eight injured,' Gwen replied soberly, '*but*,' and she paused dramatically, 'it happened on 9 June 1893, at the very moment when Edwin Booth's coffin was carried out of the Little Church around the Corner in New York, after his funeral.'

The eerie coincidence made Amadine's skin prickle. 'John Wilkes was Edwin's younger brother?'

Gwen nodded. 'And, according to my mother who worked with him, the handsomest man of his day and a fine actor. Unfortunately he sided with the South during the Civil War, and became possessed by the insane conviction that Lincoln was a tyrant who had to die.'

To the growing interest of her audience, Gwen asserted that Booth was not the only person at Ford's Theatre that night whose life was tainted by insanity. Ten years later Mary Todd Lincoln, the President's widow, was judged insane and admitted to a sanatorium. The other occupants of the presidential box that fateful night, a Major Rathbone and his fiancée, Clara Morris, also came to a tragic end: the major murdered Clara in 1883, was declared insane and was committed to an asylum, where he still languished.

'And there was another victim who is never spoken of, except by the profession. President Lincoln and his party had gone to see Laura Keene in *Our American Cousin*, a hugely popular piece that had been in her repertoire for years, and after the assassination she, and most of her company, were arrested for conspiracy. The President had been killed by an actor in a theatre, that actor had escaped and the authorities assumed that the company was in on the plot.'

'While they knew nothing about it?' Constance asked.

'They merely happened to be there at the time. Imagine the situation of Harry Hawk, who was alone on the stage when Booth dropped down from the box. Harry knew the man; he knew him very well. He knew Booth was in Washington – Booth had been hanging around the theatre all day. So, being in the middle of his soliloquy and having no idea that the President had been shot, Harry would merely think: what the hell is Booth doing onstage?'

'But the police thought he should have stopped Booth getting away,' Blanche said.

'Laura Keene called for calm, and went up to the box to help the dying man, but it does seem that the company was reluctant to name Booth as the assassin. When questioned, Laura maintained that she did not know who had shot the

President, but said that "The man who leaped from the box was Wilkes Booth."'

'She couldn't know who fired the shot if she didn't see it,' Amadine averred.

'The company was cleared of any involvement, of course, but Laura's career never recovered. The taint of that night, and a lingering residue of suspicion, was never eradicated. She was ruined – financially, professionally and physically – and died of consumption eight years later at the age of fifty-four.' Gazing at the ruined building, Gwen said softly, 'Laura Keene's life ended here, just as surely as did President Lincoln's, but no one remembers that. After all, she was only a woman. She was only an actress.'

Amadine looked up at the ceiling, which still showed remnants of its former glory, and down into the basement where lay the boards on which Lincoln, Wilkes Booth and Laura Keene had trodden. In her mind's eye she tried to reconstruct the events of that night. She saw Wilkes Booth walk through the Circle and into the presidential box, shoot the President and struggle with the major, before leaping to the stage, catching his heel in the draperies and falling awkwardly, injuring his leg. She saw him brandish the dagger with which he stabbed the major, declaim '*Sic semper tyrannis*' – thus always to tyrants – and limp from the stage, to hurry past the members of the company and mount his horse, which was being held by one of the stage staff in the yard.

She started the sequence again, running it through her mind until she came to the moment when Wilkes Booth held the derringer to the President's head and pulled the trigger.

'How could anyone do that?' she asked. 'How could anyone hold a gun to a man's head, and kill him?'

'You're the one with the gun,' Constance riposted. 'You tell us.'

Amadine opened her bag and pulled out the pearl-handled pistol. With the eyes of all four women riveted on it, the gun gleamed ominously in the dull, winter's light.

'Don't do that!' Gwen gasped in horror. 'Not here – not here, of all places!'

This tour was being a happier experience for Gwen than for most of the company. She liked and respected her colleagues, she found most of her roles rewarding and, although she had her personal problems, she was accustomed to them and able to live with them, as one tolerates a nagging spouse or uncongenial neighbour. And in addition to these old friends – because a role such as the Nurse in *Romeo and Juliet* was a very old friend indeed – Gwen had a new interest. The admirer who had written to her from New York continued to correspond, and she had decided to reply to his letters.

Clearly Nicholas Lang was an educated, cultivated man with a deep interest in, and knowledge of, the theatre, but he vouchsafed few details of his life, age, marital status or business affairs. Gwen imagined him as elderly, tall and spare, with a distinguished air and a mane of silver hair. As he had written openly and provided a name and address, she decided that he was a widower, and also that he was a professional man – a lawyer, perhaps, or Wall Street financier. She was sure that he was very dignified, very refined and very, very rich. After all, if one had an admirer, he might as well be the best!

Certainly his business allowed him to travel; the letter received in Boston commented on her New York appearances, while that addressed to Philadelphia praised her performance in Boston, so that now, each night she went on, she wondered if he was in the audience.

However, the letter she received in Baltimore was different. Mr Lang began by reminiscing over some of her early New York appearances. He remembered her Maria in

Twelfth Night with Stuart Robson and W.H. Crane; and the year before that he had seen her playing Celia in *As You Like It* with Adelaide Neilson and Henry Miller. During that same season she had played the Nurse for the first time, to Neilson's Juliet, and he compared her interpretation of the role then with the way she played it now, seventeen years later. Gwen's original Nurse had been young and attractive, energetic and romantic in her participation in the lovers' conspiracy, and these days Gwen was reluctant to alter her approach. She covered her greying hair with a wig of chestnut curls, applied rouge to her pale skin, and only the thickening waistline betrayed how altered she was from that radiant young actress of long ago. Admittedly she had not been sufficiently radiant to play the leading roles in New York, but she had been attractive enough to want to maintain the illusion now.

For an illusion it was, and an illusion was what Nicholas Lang was seeing on the stage. When he closed his letter by saying that he hoped they could meet soon, face to face, Gwen looked at herself in the mirror and knew that it could never be. She wrote immediately, and truthfully, to tell him so.

'You would be totally disenchanted, if we met. I am no longer young, and am very different from the woman you see on the stage. To wear a wig and rouge in real life would be demeaning. Anyway, a dab of paint and a few chestnut curls would not be enough to make you admire me – quite the opposite, probably! Oh, this situation makes me feel that being an actress is a curse, because one must always disappoint; one can never be as beautiful or as entertaining as one is on the stage. I hope that you will continue to write because I enjoy hearing from you, but we can never meet.'

After posting it, she felt depressed. He was unlikely to write again and, although the correspondence had been short-lived, its absence would leave a hole in her life. It was in sombre mood that she made her customary pilgrimage to Rock Creek cemetery, in order to visit a family grave. Recently there had been another reason why she made the journey: an exceptionally beautiful sculpture by Augustus Saint-Gaudens, commissioned by Henry Adams as a memorial to his wife. Gwen made her way to it as soon as she had paid her respects at the family plot.

The seated figure of a woman was clothed in flowing draperies, with a hood pulled forward round her face, and one bare arm raised so that her hand rested softly near her cheek. The entire figure exuded an extraordinary aura of tranquillity, but it was on the lovely face, shadowed by the hood, that Gwen's gaze lingered. Eyes closed, the expression on that face was an enigma. To Gwen it conveyed a deep peace and spirituality, as if the woman was communing with her innermost thoughts and had achieved a calm acceptance of whatever might lie in store for her. She seemed separate from the world, entire within herself, and yet enduring, a rock against which all the storms of the universe could beat and she would not break.

Unconscious of the cold, Gwen gazed at that face and drew inspiration from it. And so absorbed was she that the man's voice made her start with surprise.

'They call this figure Grief, I am told.'

Very tall, with black hair and piercing blue eyes, he looked faintly familiar, but she could not place him and therefore answered with some reserve. 'It is also known as Death, and Peace or Nirvana, but I think she can be anything one wants her to be.'

'Yes,' he said thoughtfully. 'Henry Adams is reported as saying that the interest in the figure is not in its meaning, but in the response of the observer.'

'The spirit of this memorial is as admirable as the beauty of its execution. Not many men would commission a sculpture in memory of a dead wife, without insisting that it be a likeness of her and that it bear a fulsome inscription. Yet here we have an anonymous face, and not a word – not even a name.'

'Perhaps Adams trusted the sculptor to create such a great work of art that his wife's name would be remembered for ever, because of her association with it.'

Gwen glanced at him again. She had seen him at the hotel, she recalled, in the elevator. 'Clover Adams was a lucky lady,' she remarked, 'to live on in this beautiful figure, and to have had a husband who loved her so much that he made it possible.'

'Yet she committed suicide.'

'It seems extraordinary, doesn't it! She was a woman who seemed to have everything. She had wit – she was friendly with Henry James, and is supposed to have remarked that it wasn't so much that he bites off more than he can chew, but that he chews more than he bites off! She had a position as one of the most exclusive society hostesses in Washington; wealth . . .'

'Are rich people less likely to commit suicide than poor people?' he interposed.

'You might as well ask if money buys happiness! No, of course I don't think that.'

'So what drove Clover Adams to drink potassium cyanide in her own photographic studio?'

'Hereditary melancholy seems to be the accepted explanation,' Gwen said slowly, thinking that for someone so well informed on the facts of the case, he asked an awful lot of questions. 'Her father committed suicide, and not long after Clover's death, her sister was killed when she threw herself in front of a train.'

'Suicidal tendencies run in the family, eh? Now, there's a thought! I trust that they are not prevalent in your family, Miss Hughes.'

Hostility had replaced neutrality, and his antagonism was almost palpable. 'Thank you, no,' she said, turning to face him square on. Her heart began to thump, and her throat was dry.

'Would that I could say the same,' he said softly. 'But I think there are many reasons why people feel that they cannot carry on. Unrequited love, for instance. Or a love that dies on one side but burns as fiercely as ever on the other.'

Gwen stared at him steadily, but said nothing.

'Or guilt.' Expressionless, he returned her stare. 'Guilt has so many forms and so many sources that it must have propelled many people in front of trains, don't you think?'

'I try not to think.'

'This memorial to Clover Adams was put up in 1891 – the very same year . . .' and Gwen understood his meaning perfectly. 'Perhaps I should commission Saint-Gaudens to create a male equivalent, and erect it in a certain cemetery in Chicago.' And with a courteous tip of his hat, he turned and strode away.

It wasn't suicide, it was an accident, Gwen thought confusedly. She watched his retreating back. So that was what Pierce Radcliffe looked like. And suddenly there was no peace anywhere, not even in the sublime figure in front of her, who seemed to avert her face and withdraw her blessing.

Chapter Seventeen

What with Christmas in Washington and New Year in Cincinnati, no one noticed that Ida Norris was unusually preoccupied. Moreover, those with whom she came into regular contact had preoccupations of their own, and the one person who hung on her every word and movement was in no position to judge her mood. Walter, Hal's valet, remained locked in the throes of unrequited love but, as Ida never spoke to him unless forced to do so in the course of her duties, he did not realise that she had gone very quiet with everyone else as well. His ignorance was merciful, because Ida's air of distraction had a simple and time-honoured cause: she was in love.

George White, as he was still styling himself, had experienced a change of heart. After his failure with Constance Grey in the Baltimore tearoom, he had intended to use his charm on Gwendoline Hughes, calculating that, at her age, she would be grateful for the attention, while his past liaisons with older women had stood him in very good stead.

In fact, it had been an older man who had shown him the way out of his father's Woolwich pub. Very good-looking in those days, with his fair hair and blue eyes, George had been taken up by a West End gentleman who cruised the dockland bars. The man was an obvious homosexual, but

George was breezily confident of repulsing unwelcome advances, while maintaining the relationship for as long as it suited him. Through this patron he obtained an entrée to theatrical circles, and for five years the decorative qualities of his 'pretty boy' looks were used in a variety of walk-on parts. He was twenty-three when he met the first of the ageing actresses who took him under her wing, and into her bed, and with whom he toured the provinces for two exhausting years. A pattern was established: after each spell in the provinces he would return to London, determined to win advancement on the West End stage; inevitably he failed, and after a couple of seasons was back on the road with another middle-aged Black-Ey'd Susan, Peg Woffington or Lady Teazle, who was past her prime but still disconcertingly vigorous in bed.

Therefore George felt on firm, tried-and-tested ground with Gwendoline Hughes, but still he hesitated. It was humiliating to have to admit that he had always been as dependent on his looks as a chorus girl, and frightening to realise that time was not being kind to him. Then he thought of Ida. At that moment, naturally, he did not know her name, but was a sufficiently seasoned touring actor to know that her job, and therefore she, existed. His resources had dwindled to the point where he could not afford tickets for the theatre, but he had seen the company perform in Boston, and had hung around the stage door in several cities, so he knew everyone by sight. To George, Ida was an instantly recognisable type: the neat but shabbily dressed East Ender, who saw everything that was going on behind the scenes, and who longed to have some glamour and romance in her own humdrum life. With a renewed surge of optimism, he prepared to play Gentleman George to the hilt.

He bumped into Ida, literally, in the street in Washington, and helped her to pick up her parcels. Next he affected great surprise at seeing her again in the lobby of the hotel and, in his most upper-crust English accent, invited her to share a pot of tea. He pretended even greater surprise at her connection with the theatre, but was careful to evince more interest in her than in other members of the company.

'I dabbled a bit myself in my youth,' he said airily. 'The family disapproved, of course, but it was tremendous fun.'

As with Constance, he let her think that he was in America on other business, but on this occasion he bided his time before leading up to his true objective. George could be very charming and, smitten instantly with his convincing air of sophistication, Ida departed Washington with the utmost reluctance. He had hinted that he might be in Cincinnati but cleverly kept her waiting, and only put in another appearance in the great coal and steel city of Pittsburgh. For Ida, the sun broke through the canopy of smoke that shrouded Mellon's empire, and the massive blast furnaces and ovens of Carnegie's fiefdom.

Ida thought Pittsburgh was beautiful. She walked with George in a park on the heights above the city, and slipped away to meet him late in the evening, thrilling when he put an arm around her as they watched the flames of the furnaces burning fiercely against the night sky. 'Hell with the lid off', some people called it, but Ida thought she had died and gone to heaven.

'This may be goodbye,' he said, with infinite regret, on the tour's last day in Pittsburgh. 'My work here is finished, and I ought to go home.'

'Must you go?' Ida exclaimed in dismay. 'The tour isn't nearly over yet, and it would be so nice if you . . .' She stopped, not wanting to seem too forward.

'It would be very nice,' George agreed sadly, 'but, unfortunately, when the work finishes, so does the salary.'

'I thought you were rich,' Ida said, 'being so posh.'

'Is that why you go out with me?' he teased. 'I'm sorry to disappoint you but, although my family is very rich, and very posh, I am *persona non grata* in that quarter.' Seeing the lack of comprehension in Ida's eyes, he explained: 'I'm the black sheep, as you might say.'

Ida glowed with love and good intentions. She would redeem him. With her beside him, he would be a changed man. 'Isn't there other work you could do, which would mean you could stay?'

'I've tried to think of something, but . . .' and he shrugged and shook his head.

'If only you could come with us.' And then she thought: why not? Several men had left the tour after the Baltimore fire, and therefore it was possible that replacements might be needed. 'But you wouldn't be interested in joining the tour,' she said, believing that it would be beneath his dignity.

'My dear, I would even shift the scenery if it meant I could be near you.'

Gazing into those tender blue eyes, Ida struggled to keep her mind on the business at hand. 'I'll speak to Mr Smith about it, but I'll have to choose the right moment because he's so busy. Next week we're at Columbus, Dayton and Indianapolis, but then we have two weeks in Chicago. Meet me in Chicago,' and she clutched his hand, 'and I'll tell you what he says.'

'Sweet of you to want to go to all that trouble for me, but I'm afraid it's no good, old thing. The money won't stretch as far as Chicago.'

Ida opened her bag. Having little time or incentive to spend money on herself, she had saved most of her wages and thus was able to peel off a number of dollar bills from an impressively large roll. George's eyes widened appreciatively as he pocketed the money and promised to meet her in Chicago. He had definitely done the right thing in choosing Ida, who was a good-natured if gullible girl; and he would do the right thing for her, by ensuring that she kept her job.

Because George's objective in his pursuit of Amadine was changing, evolving, crystallising . . . After that headlong dash across America in order to stake his claim, and to convince her that they belonged together, he had begun to enjoy the game for the game's sake. Now even his sexual fantasies were less vivid than the overwhelmingly attractive vision of himself as the power behind the throne. Not only would he be the focus of Amadine's personal life, but he would be her professional manager as well, arranging her theatrical appearances, the sole conduit to Amadine through whom everyone else must work. Ah, all that power and money, and Amadine, too; now *that* did make the game worth the candle, and worth playing cautiously.

When he had read about the fire in Baltimore, he had been concerned in case she had been scarred by burns but, thankfully, it appeared she had escaped unscathed. The newspaper reports had speculated about arson, but if someone had set the fire deliberately, it certainly was not George. He intended Amadine no harm. Quite the contrary: Amadine's continued health and strength were all-important to his future plans. She might need a bit of sense knocking into her, and showing who was master, but it was not in George's interests to inflict permanent physical damage.

Of course, if Amadine didn't see reason, and didn't cooperate, that would be different . . .

'You think this tour needs more *zip*!' exclaimed Amadine, in an uncooperative tone, when Jay cornered her. 'I would have thought that this tour, and everyone concerned with it, had had enough zip to last a lifetime!'

'It's been eventful,' Jay conceded.

'But not eventful enough for you!'

'We've had plenty of publicity, but it's been all doom and disaster.'

'There's nothing people like more,' Amadine said firmly.

'They are queuing at the box office in the hope of seeing one of us meet a very sticky end on the stage.'

'We need a change of mood, for the New Year. Look, it's winter out there,' and Jay waved a hand at the window, 'and we need something that'll warm the cockles of America's heart.'

They were sitting in the observation room at the rear of the Palace Car, where Amadine had been studying Shakespeare. She laid down the book and stared at the frozen landscape of Ohio, revealed by the panoramic windows of the car. She was way ahead of him.

'The answer is no,' she said flatly. 'Hal and I are good friends, and nothing more.'

'Isn't there just the teeniest hint of romance?' Jay asked wistfully.

'Jay, my sweet, this is real life,' she expostulated. 'You can't write in a romance merely because you think it would suit the leading actors. I've told you before – I act on the stage, but not off. Besides, I don't see that anyone would care if Hal and I are lovers or sworn enemies.'

'Of course they care. Surely, after all these months, you don't need me to tell you that the American public is fascinated by everything you say, do, wear and think. They love you, and they love Hal, and what they want more than anything is for you and Hal to love each other.'

'And what is the intended climax – oh, dear, not a happy choice of words in this context – to this grand passion?'

'A wedding would be nice.' And, ever the optimist, Jay beamed at her.

Amadine leaned back in her chair, and surveyed him with a wry grimace. 'Tell me, Jay, is yours a new profession, or one that is well established in America?'

'It's bang up-to-the-minute,' he said proudly. 'I'm putting my own stamp on this: I'm probably the first proper publicity agent in America – in the world, even – but where I lead, others will follow, yes sir!'

'I can hardly wait,' Amadine murmured.

'You see, over here we don't have kings and queens and such, so we have celebrities instead.'

'You want me to marry Hal because it would be good for business?'

He nodded. 'It'll be the trend one day. It'll be the way things are done in the entertainment business, believe me.'

'Oh, I do believe you. I'm seeing the future, and it appals me! So, what happens when Hal and I go home after the tour and find that we loathe each other?'

Jay looked surprised. 'I don't think you would loathe each other but, if it did happen, you divorce. Obviously,' and he shrugged his shoulders.

'Divorce,' Amadine barely breathed the word. 'Don't you realise that marriage is a sacrament? For better or worse . . . until death do us part . . . That isn't dialogue, it's a vow before God.'

'Suppose you make a mistake, and marry the wrong person?'

'You have to live with the consequences, particularly if children are involved. You have to tell yourself that God has a purpose, and if that purpose doesn't happen to suit you, tough! And if you are unhappy, you have to examine your conscience and accept that you are atoning for your sins.'

This was all becoming too deep for Jay, and his expression showed it.

Amadine laughed humourlessly. 'Never forget that I am the rector's daughter and that, among other things, I was brought up to believe in the sanctity of marriage. I have betrayed my father – along with his teaching and my faith – more than enough by taking to the stage to earn my living, without selling my integrity down the Swanee for the sake of the box office!'

Oh well, can't win them all, Jay thought philosophically as he beat a hasty retreat. Forget Amadine's unreasonable attitude, and think about *The Philadelphia Girl*. This year it's Broadway or bust. It's the starry way, the primrose path, to wealth, more wealth and happiness.

Admittedly the old year had ended on a somewhat downbeat note. He had dashed back to Philly in order to check on progress and ascertained that the theatre had been booked, a stage manager had been hired and the writer had confirmed that an outline of the book was nearly ready. Unfortunately the bad news was the amount of money spent by his partner on reaching this stage of the proceedings. Jay could understand that Bill felt he should be seen in all the best places, so that word would spread that money was no object, but considered that he was taking his role as budding entrepreneur a mite too seriously. In fact Jay had begun to wonder if Bill was the right partner, and the right man, for the job. Still, there wasn't a darned, tootin' thing he could do about that now. He must just exercise as much control as possible from the wintry fastnesses of the Midwest, where the tour was now headed.

Then in Pittsburgh, when the new year was only a few days old, he had received the outline of the book, together with the first scene, which was written in full so that they could get the flavour of the thing. And it was stunning. It was so good that Jay wanted to leap on the nearest table and launch into a snappy little dance number himself, out of sheer exuberance.

Instead, he had sauntered to the telegraph office with commendable restraint, and wired his acceptance to the writer in New York and his enthusiasm to Bill in Philadelphia. He was filled with euphoria. He really did believe that happy days were here to stay.

Amadine closed the book on her knee – the text of *Much Ado* – and chastised herself for handling the encounter with Jay so badly. She had no right to expect others to share her moral code, while she had been most unwise to reveal so much of her true feelings. Fortunately Jay was not the most introspective of people and he was unlikely to start analysing the conversation, but it was with an air of determined normality calculated to dispel any false impressions that Amadine left the observation car and walked back into the parlour. There she found only Frank and Theo, sitting at the table, talking about plays.

'I must have read every American play in print,' Theo said, after telling Amadine about his literary aspirations, 'but I'm still searching for inspiration.'

'Have you read any of Bronson Howard's plays?' Amadine asked. 'I was in an English adaptation of his *Saratoga* – we called it *Brighton*. It's been in Charles Wyndham's repertoire for donkey's years, but is still hugely popular.'

Theo nodded. 'And also I've been reading Boucicault, Daly and Belasco. I've even,' he added gloomily, 'studied Clyde Fitch.'

'You will learn much more about playwriting from them than you would by studying the literary giants,' Amadine declared. 'It is extraordinary how great novelists like Mark Twain, Bret Harte and Henry James cannot write for the stage. Three years ago Henry James was devastated when his *Guy Domville* failed in London, and the failure was made worse by the huge success of Oscar Wilde's *An Ideal Husband*, which opened on the same night.' Amadine paused, and sighed. 'Poor Oscar,' she said softly.

There was a moment's embarrassed silence at this mention of the unmentionable.

'I do envy you, Theo,' Amadine exclaimed suddenly. 'It's all still to do – the great American drama still has to be written. Just think how lucky you are compared to the poor English dramatist, who will always have to play second fiddle to Shakespeare!'

Enthusiasm began to burn again in Theo's breast. 'I wondered if there were any American stories that appealed to you, or characters who you would like to portray,' he said eagerly.

So Theo wanted to write a play for her. It was very flattering, but . . . 'Have you considered Fanny Kemble?' Amadine asked cautiously. 'English actress from great acting family – her aunt was Sarah Siddons – comes to America to tour. Marries a Philadelphian, and has two daughters, but the marriage is unhappy and ends in divorce. Imagine it: divorce in 1849! She had to return to the stage, and give public readings, in order to maintain herself, but her real claim to fame was her *Journal of a Residence on a Georgian Plantation*, which described a visit to her husband's plantation and the lives of his black slaves.'

'Which would be very difficult to dramatise,' Frank said doubtfully.

'That *Journal* had an impact on British public opinion second only to *Uncle Tom's Cabin*, and that has been dramatised,' Amadine shot back.

'I think the stage version of *Uncle Tom* owes much to Mrs Howard's portrayal of the little black girl, Topsy,' Frank smiled, 'who had no idea where she came from and insists: "I 'spect I growed."'

'American audiences just love actors who play the same part over and over again,' Theo agreed, 'and Mrs Howard's Topsy was one of them. In addition there was Frank Mayo as Davy Crockett, Denman Thompson as Joshua Whitcomb in *The Old Homestead*, James O'Neill as Edmund Dantes in *The Count of Monte Cristo*, Joseph Jefferson as Rip van Winkle, Maggie Mitchell's *Fanchon, the Cricket* and, oh, there are heaps more.'

'I still don't think that the slave plantation would "go",' Frank said, 'particularly in the South.'

'Are we only concerned with box office?' Amadine demanded.

'No,' said Theo.

'Yes,' said Frank simultaneously, and decisively.

'In that case, there must be romance,' Amadine declared.

'And an impediment to that romance,' Theo said, 'and I can overlay the story of the lovers with some of the dominant characteristics of American life.'

'Most of all you need to show them behaving nobly,' Amadine argued, 'accepting the worst that Fate can throw at them and showing courage in the face of disaster.'

'The Civil War,' Frank insisted. 'I've said so all along.'

Amadine thought of *The Bostonians*, in which Henry James's New England heroine is wooed by a Southerner. 'No, the other way round,' she said, thinking aloud. 'Southern belle and Yankee man.'

'Southern belle and Yankee Army officer,' supplied Frank.

'Barbara Frietchie,' murmured Theo. He was thinking of John Whittier's poem based on a supposedly true incident: that when the victorious Confederate army of Stonewall Jackson marched through the town of Frederick, Maryland, all the houses displayed Confederate flags except that of the Frietchies, where Barbara defiantly waved the Stars and Stripes. 'No, that wouldn't do,' he sighed. 'Barbara is believed to have been ninety-six years old, and bedridden, at the time.'

'So make her twenty-five years old, and in love with a Yankee,' Frank said impatiently.

'But that would be tampering with history,' Theo protested.

Amadine was torn, remembering her previous opposition to such deviations but also relishing the prospect of this role. 'Couldn't you adapt the story, and call the heroine by another name?'

'Everyone knows that name.' Theo, too, was torn by a conflict of interests, wishing to keep his integrity intact but fascinated by the vision of Amadine as a Southern belle in a low-necked crinoline. And Hal would make a perfect Yankee captain. He began to weaken. 'Poetic licence,' he decided in justification, 'and, come to think of it, Whittier must have used a bit of that, too.'

They began to bubble with ideas, and the Palace Car became peopled with the ghostly characters of their imaginations. Barbara and her Yankee captain were joined by Barbara's brother, a Confederate soldier wounded at Gettysburg and on the run from Yankee search parties; and by a jealous lover, the boy next door who had been expected to marry Barbara. Dramatic incidents sprang easily to mind: the Yankee captain pretended not to see Barbara's brother and sent the search party away; a Southerner attempted to shoot the captain, and Barbara shot the gun from his hand. Theo's head was spinning, with excitement and euphoria, and the feeling that this was *it*. This time he really would get it right. He could hardly wait to start.

Lingering in the Palace Car for a few moments after Amadine had gone, he laid a hand on Frank's arm. 'I don't know how to thank you – I've never been so happy in my life!'

Somehow – and afterwards Frank could not decide how it had happened – they ended up with their arms around each other. It was not a lovers' embrace, more a fraternal hug, but Frank's heart hammered with excitement. He was becoming closer to Theo, he was sure of it.

For Theo that conversation was a turning point. Wishing to work quietly, uninterrupted and without jeopardising his official duties, he began to get up early in the morning and work on the play in his room before breakfast, bribing the Pullman porters to bring him plenty of hot black coffee. His progress was amazing. At times he seemed to be watching Amadine and Hal on the stage and merely writing down what they said and did, and he could hardly write fast enough to keep up with them. He lived in constant fear that one day he would wake up and this strange, inspirational creativity would no longer happen.

Like Amadine and her acting, Theo was afraid that the magic would disappear.

Several nights later Amadine slipped a negligée over her nightgown and opened the door of her stateroom. As she had expected, Hal was sitting at the parlour table in his dressing gown, his head bent over a pile of paperwork but, abandoning his work with alacrity, he poured drinks and sat down beside her on the sofa.

'I do believe that there might be something in the power of positive thinking,' he said, with his most disarming smile, 'because I have been sitting here, absolutely willing you to join me.'

'If you are planning on willing me to do certain other things, I wouldn't count on increasing your success rate,' Amadine said drily, 'because this is a business meeting.'

Those melting brown eyes slid over the diaphanous silk and lace that barely concealed her curves. 'With your perfect fashion sense and innate gift for dressing for the occasion, just what sort of business did you have in mind?'

'I wanted to discuss the repertoire.'

Hal's expression indicated that he considered this as good an excuse as any for her presence. 'I intend to drop *Caesar*. It's no fun without Laurie and, frankly, I misjudged the mood of the audiences. America wants romance.'

'Particularly if that romance is between you and me.'

'Is that what you want?' Hal pressed a little closer so that their thighs touched.

'Not if it means changing roles with Constance again,' Amadine declared, deliberately misunderstanding him, 'which rules out continuing with *The Physician*.'

'And *Ours* is creaking at the joints, which leaves us with the Pinero and *Romeo* – if you are prepared to do Juliet from time to time.' He sighed. 'I think I've hauled Connie back on to the right tracks, but she isn't a patch on you.'

'Can we afford to put on something new?'

'As long as the costumes and scenery aren't too lavish. The new *Trelawny* costumes are paid for, and nearly ready, and the fire-damaged stuff has been replaced. It would be no bad thing to put a new piece into rehearsal – a company tends to be stale at this stage of a tour and a new challenge keeps them on their toes. I've been giving this some thought and, in my opinion, the Americans look to us to do classic English plays . . .' He began outlining his ideas on the direction they should take.

Amadine stood up and walked round the table to face him, fully aware of the alluring figure she made with her hair loose around her shoulders and her body gleaming through the silk of her gown.

'"I wonder that you will still be talking, Signior Benedick: nobody marks you."'

Hal stopped speaking, looking startled, and then he smiled. Jumping to his feet, he faced her across the table. '"What! my dear Lady Disdain, are you yet living?"'

Launched into the scene, the cut and thrust of Beatrice and Benedick's dialogue crackled between them so effortlessly that they might have been acting together in *Much Ado* for years. Perhaps this Benedick did sound a trifle too rueful when he declared: 'But it is certain I am loved of all ladies, only you excepted', but he had been bounced into this exchange with very little warning. When Hal and Amadine completed the scene, they burst out laughing and threw their arms around each other.

'It's perfect,' Hal said against her hair. 'I'll cast it first thing in the morning.'

'If only Laurie were here to play Claudio . . . Oh, Hal, I am so afraid that he will never work again!'

'I have a plan for Laurie which I wanted to discuss with you, but . . .' The laughter left his eyes as he stared down at her, and his grip tightened. Then he bent his head and kissed her.

She had expected this to happen and been prepared for it,

but now Amadine found that nothing could altogether prepare one for the sweetness of Hal's kiss. The pressure of his lips was so persuasive, the intertwining of his tongue with hers so pervasive, that her senses swam. Yet, even as he pushed her back to the table in order to steady them against the swaying of the train, part of Amadine's mind remained detached. Even as those beautiful hands caressed her and turned her to flame, she knew that this was lust, not love. And even as the hardness of his erection pressed into her groin, she knew that although it felt wonderful, it still did not feel right.

Amadine pulled away. 'I'm sorry, but I can't.'

'Why not?'

'This isn't us – it's Beatrice and Benedick . . . Paula and Aubrey . . . It's Romeo and Juliet, for God's sake, but it has nothing to do with you and me!'

'That isn't true.' He was not giving up, standing close to her and holding her by the shoulders.

'It's a theatre thing, and it has made me understand how and why you have ricocheted from leading lady to leading lady all your life. I'm even beginning to see that I am capable of doing the same thing! If you and I went to bed together tonight, no doubt the experience would be most enjoyable, but we would still part company at the end of the tour, and start the process all over again next season with someone new.' Amadine looked at him sadly. 'Our work spills over into our private lives – the romance, the physical attraction, goes with the territory.'

'Not this time,' Hal insisted. 'This is different.'

'I'll bet it is always different.'

'Marry me, Amadine. Please, please, marry me!' His grip on her shoulders tightened. 'I have waited years to find the right woman, and the right actress, with whom to share my life and career, and you are that woman. Please, marry me and work with me. I can offer you financial security – my home in Sussex . . .'

Amadine was standing motionless, watching him. He sounded so sincere, and yet she still felt that she was taking part in a play.

'. . . and professionally you would have an equal say in the content of the repertoire – we would pick plays that show you to advantage, even if there wasn't such a good part for me. Oh, Amadine, darling, I have such plans! We bring out the best in each other on the stage, and together we can scale the very heights of the profession! And I want to include Laurie in our company – like you, I'm worried that he may be permanently injured, but you and I could look after him.'

Dear, darling Hal, saying all the right things, and pressing all the right buttons, but . . . 'I don't love you, Hal,' she said slowly.

'My love for you is strong enough to make the relationship work,' he said eagerly, almost as if he was relieved that this was her sole objection.

She reached up and stroked that impossibly handsome face. Poor Hal – of all the women who must have longed to hear him make this proposal, and who would have jumped at the chance, he had to choose her. 'I am very honoured, Hal,' she said softly, 'but I cannot . . .'

He silenced her with a finger pressed to her lips. 'Don't answer too hastily,' he urged. 'Think it over, please!'

Amadine sighed. It would be best to disappoint him now rather than let him live in hope, but she had not the heart to be too cruel. 'Very well, I'll think about it.'

He smiled and tried to kiss her again, but the gesture became a mere brush of his lips as he sensed her resistance. Suddenly his face darkened.

'Is it Radcliffe?' he asked harshly, grasping her wrists. 'Is it him you want?'

'No,' she answered truthfully. 'No, he isn't the reason why I cannot marry you.'

Pierce Radcliffe, Amadine admitted as she lay awake

through the night, was not even the reason why she could not have a casual affair with Hal. She wished fervently that she was not what she was, and that, like other women, she could leap lightly into bed with Hal. Her body wanted to do it but, just as she began to succumb to temptation, her mind lowered a portcullis and said no, this does not feel right. But would it ever feel right, with any man, at any time, anywhere?

The routine for handling the box-office takings had not changed, Frank transporting money from the theatre, and to the bank, in a steel, velvet-lined cash box that was a familiar sight to everyone in the company. Not only did Frank carry it openly, even conspicuously, in the street several times a week, but it lay open on the table when he paid the wages. However, although no one would have noticed anything amiss or detected anything different in his demeanour or deportment, something had changed since the company left Washington: on each occasion that the box was carried to the bank, it contained several hundred dollars less than it should have done.

Only Hal, Amadine and Frank himself were entitled to money from the cash float on request. Frank made the necessary book entries, and kept a signed receipt so that the sum could be taken into account when the profits were divided at the end of the tour. Starting in Richmond, Frank took three hundred dollars from the box; he allocated one hundred dollars to himself and signed for it; and then he forged Hal's signature on a receipt for the other two hundred dollars. Next time it was Amadine's turn. Happily, unlike Constance, Amadine was not the type to keep a meticulous account of her finances and he was fairly certain that she would not have the remotest idea how much she had signed for, any more than she would be able to tell the difference between her own genuine signature and the forgery. Indeed, Frank had been delighted to meet her request for fifty dollars in Washington – although he might have been less pleased had he known that the money was destined for Blanche – because the more odds and ends of cash that Amadine requested, the less likely she was to query the final sum.

So much had happened on this tour that it was hard to remember that his rendezvous in Chicago had been the reason why the enterprise had been mooted, developed and finally launched. Now that the moment was almost upon him, he was overwhelmed with nervousness. Still, his cache of stolen dollars was growing at a satisfactory rate, and he had worked out a sound strategy. In the end, they were bound to be reasonable men, he thought optimistically.

Amadine stood with her nose pressed to the window of the observation room, and thought that she had never known winter until now. She had grown up in a harsh, unrelenting landscape where the snow fell thickly on the tops and drifted down the dales, to barricade the narrow lanes and cut off the village from the outside world, but she was awed by the vastness of the frozen Midwest. Longfellow's lines hammered in her head to the clickety-clack of the train:

> O the long and dreary Winter!
> O the cold and cruel Winter!
> Ever thicker, thicker, thicker
> Froze the ice on lake and river,
> Ever deeper, deeper, deeper
> Fell the snow o'er all the landscape . . .

She had never realised how huge this country was, and how isolated the homesteads, towns and villages. Sometimes she saw the small-town people gazing at the train as it rattled past, and she could imagine how some of them longed to be aboard, because once she had been a small-town girl with a yearning to travel. How glamorous the actors' lives must seem as they moved from place to place, yet there were those aboard who longed for a home, a family and a settled life.

And she, what did she long for? She did not know but, when the train drew into Chicago and Pierce Radcliffe was standing on the platform, her heart somersaulted. Her companions – Hal, Frank, Constance, Theo, Jay, Gwen and Blanche – either smiled or glared, according to their personal reaction to Pierce's presence, and in the flurry of their arrival it occurred to no one to think ahead to their return visit to Chicago in six weeks' time. A return visit that one of them would not live to see.

Chapter Eighteen

Not since New York had Amadine felt such pressure to succeed. After a mere twelve hours in the city, her hotel suite was heaped with bouquets and nosegays, chocolates and books and she had received invitations to balls and dinners, luncheons and soirées, from the cream of Chicago society. The courtesy and the friendliness were overwhelming and, as first-night nerves set in early, Amadine was terrified of being a disappointment and of letting people down. However, even more daunting than the warmth of Chicago's welcome was the theatre in which the company was to perform.

Ushered up the grand staircase to the balcony of the Auditorium Theatre, Amadine and her colleagues had walked slowly, and in stunned silence, treading on mosaic floors made up of fifty million tesserae, resting hands on bronze railings, gazing at ivory and gold stencilling on the walls, pausing by marble fireplaces and immense pillars on carpeted landings, the magnificent detail of the architecture held together by the ongoing motif of powerful arches. As the group entered the balcony, the main body of the theatre was in darkness but, at a softly spoken word from the manager who was escorting them, the lights were switched on. With an audible gasp, Constance sat down suddenly, while Amadine grasped the back of the nearest seat for support.

Above them, the great barrel vault of the ceiling was spanned by a series of arches, ornamented with gold-leaf and set with scores of carbon-filament lights that twinkled like diamonds. And those lights illuminated the most colossal auditorium that any of them had ever seen.

Amadine was tense as she listened to the manager explaining that, designed as an opera house, the stage was one hundred feet wide by seventy feet deep and was the largest in the country. It could be extended, and the floor of the auditorium raised, to form the country's biggest ballroom. The orchestra pit was flexible: the first four rows of seats could be removed, and a full orchestra fitted in. This was the first new building in America to be lit by electricity, and the first to be fully air-conditioned.

'Excuse me,' Amadine interrupted in a strangled voice, 'but how many people does the theatre seat?'

'Four thousand two hundred,' was the proud reply.

Which was fine for grand opera, with a stage full of people and everyone making a lot of noise, but for Amadine's intimate drawing-room dramas . . .? She sat down beside Constance and they looked at one another, old rivalries temporarily forgotten.

'However,' the manager continued, 'the size of the auditorium is flexible, too. We have a mechanism for closing off the two galleries above us, which reduces the size of the house to three thousand people. And we can drop a curtain midway up this balcony, which reduces the size of the audience by another seven hundred.'

Amadine was looking at the stage, trying to imagine making herself seen and heard in that vast, empty space. The colour was draining from her face, and was destined to be gone for some time.

'Lower the reducing curtain,' the manager said, in a perfectly ordinary tone of voice, and the most extraordinary thing happened. Two vertical panels began to descend from the rigging loft, one on each side of the stage, and then it became apparent that they were joined at the top. When in place, the effect was like a square frame set within the proscenium arch, reducing the size of the stage opening by approximately thirty feet in width and five feet in height.

'How did your staff know that you wanted the curtain lowered?' Amadine asked, staring at the stage which, she admitted, was now a suitable size for her Pinero pieces.

'They heard me give the order,' and the manager laughed at the incredulity on her face. 'This theatre isn't just big, and beautiful to look at. The most marvellous thing about the Auditorium is its perfect acoustics. Eleanora Duse has stood alone on that stage and *whispered* D'Annunzio's lines, yet she could be heard in the top gallery, which is the equivalent of six storeys above her.'

However, these words of comfort and encouragement failed to restore the roses to Amadine's cheeks: not for one moment could she consider herself in the same class as Duse.

That first evening in Chicago she dined with Pierce in the dining room on the tenth floor of the hotel, which, being part of the same Auditorium complex as the theatre, reflected a similar style of architecture. Here were blue-and-yellow stained-glass windows, ceilings stencilled in dull gold on a white ground; here, above all, were those powerful arches, exemplified in this dining room by the massive curved vault of the roof, which began at floor level, and by the five arched trusses that divided the ceiling into bays, each arch decorated and studded with lights. Everywhere Amadine looked, she saw echoes of that theatre and she trembled.

Then, as she was bracing herself to do justice to that colossal and incredible jewel, and not to let down the people of Chicago, Pierce applied more pressure by announcing that he would be attending the *Tanqueray* opening and had a reservation for all the other plays, too. From the moment he had greeted her, Pierce exuded an indefinable air of belonging here. He seemed more relaxed, conveying the impression that, although he might hang up his hat in many other places, this great prairie city by the lake was home. Amadine sensed that he really wanted her to like Chicago, perhaps even to love it as much as he did. He was proud of the place and she knew instinctively that it was important he was proud of her performance here. As if she didn't have enough to worry about already.

During rehearsals for *Tanqueray* the next day, Amadine decided to trust the Auditorium Theatre – to trust the perfection of its acoustics and sightlines; to trust the assertion that everyone, no matter where they sat, could see and hear everything that was happening on the stage. On that basis, she decided to under-, not over-, play; to simplify her movements, despite the awesome vastness of the place, and to use soft, subtle inflections in her voice instead of straining to project to the back of the balcony.

And the irony was that, that night, Amadine felt closer to her audience than ever before. In that colossal space she achieved an intimacy with the people in the darkened Auditorium that ought to have been impossible, and she gave the greatest performance of her life. As the audience rose to acclaim her, with Mrs Potter Palmer and Marshall Field leading the applause from their boxes, Chicago took Amadine to its great and generous heart. Here, it said, is America. Forget New York – it may be big, exciting and successful, but New York is a world city, it is not America. Chicago is big, exciting and successful, too, but it has retained an accessibility and sense of its roots that makes it a quintessentially American place. There is a magic here, which blows off the lake and sprinkles an enchanted dust over the city, and makes Chicago, and the Auditorium Theatre, special.

'It can always be like this,' Hal said softly, leading her forward for yet another curtain call, and reminding her subtly that he was still waiting for an answer to his proposal of marriage.

'No, it's this theatre . . . I wish that I could fold it up and take it with me wherever I go.'

Such was the warmth of their reception that, for the first time on the tour, an impromptu party took place on the stage. Champagne was produced from the bowels of the Auditorium cellar, and Chicago society flocked to meet the stars. Hal watched sourly as Pierce steered Amadine through the crowd, introducing her to the great and the good, until Jay intervened by taking her to meet some of the newspaper men – and women, because the drama critic of the Chicago *Daily News* was Amy Leslie. To Hal's relief, Pierce Radcliffe then left the party, apparently without saying goodnight to Amadine or having a personal conversation with her, and so restored was Hal's good humour that he even found a few moments to congratulate Constance on her performance.

In fact Constance's performance that night – both on the stage and at the party – had been one of the best and bravest she had ever given, for her smile concealed a host of troubles. Two letters from London had been waiting for her in Chicago and, opening Nanny's letter first as always, she learned that her son was ill. Nanny sounded quite matter-of-fact about it, assuring her that it was only influenza but that Charlie was feverish and therefore he was confined to bed.

Constance was anguished. If Charlie was ill, he needed his mother. He needed her calm voice, her soothing hands on his fevered brow, and her hugs of reassurance. Equally, she needed to be near him and to be reassured that truly it was not a life-threatening illness. He could have died since the letter was posted! It was dreadful to be so many thousands of miles away and not know what was happening at home.

Christmas had been a terrible ordeal, because she had never been apart from the children at this time of year before and missed them badly. Then, the other day, Hal had announced that 'Amadine and I have chosen *Much Ado . . .*' Oh, they had, had they! And just how, when and where did they discuss this idea, as if she didn't know. Constance already lay awake at night, envisaging the intimacy of the Palace Car, and now she felt she had proof that her worst fears were being realised.

She was perpetually up one minute and down the next, not on a train journey through the United States but trapped on a nightmare funfair ride. Take the past few weeks: no sooner had the fire destroyed Hal's letter to Terriss than the Juliet reviews came to haunt her, bringing with them the fear that Hal would write a similar letter to someone else. Then she re-established herself as Juliet, in the hope that Amadine would not want to face the part again, only to be told that she would be sharing it after all *and* that she must play second fiddle in *Much Ado*. How could she compete with that? Amadine, as Beatrice, would act everyone else off the stage.

But there was the production of *Three Guineas* in London to cling to – and that was when Constance opened the second letter.

The writer's name was familiar. Constance recalled her husband talking about him, and that there had been some sort of quarrel between them, but she could not recall the details. The letter enlightened her. When she finished reading it, she was shaking with fear and anxiety and the sheer unfairness of it all. Was nothing ever to go right?

The letter referred to an old dispute over the authorship of *Three Guineas*. More than twenty-five years ago, the writer maintained, he and Everett Grey had collaborated on a translation of a French play, which the writer had staged in London. Then Grey decided to make a free adaptation of the main plot, assuring his friend that the finished play would bear so little resemblance to the original that the adaptation could still be staged. When *Three Guineas* was produced, this man wrote to Grey detailing all the similarities in the plot and demanding a share of the profits. Grey refused, and the argument raged for months, both men enlisting the opinions of third parties and, according to this man, most people siding with him in the dispute.

'Mr Grey promised to pay me fair compensation, and I have the correspondence to prove it. However, he never settled on a mutually acceptable figure and never paid me a penny. When he died, *Three Guineas* no longer being in production, I decided to let the matter drop, but now I hear that the play is to be staged again in the West End. I was planning a revival of my original piece, but obviously I am now prevented from doing so and shall be out of pocket. I intend taking steps to claim not only my rightful share of the proceeds of the new production but also the monies owing from previous productions.'

Surely he cannot do that, thought a panic-stricken Constance. Surely I cannot be responsible for debts incurred by Everett before we were married! That's ridiculous, as well as being totally unfair. Probably her best course of action would have been to strike a deal with the man, and pay him the lion's share of the proceeds of the current production in return for waiving his other claims, but Constance simply could not bring herself to do that. The windfall of this production had been unexpected, but she had seen the promise of that money and she could not let it go. Instead she tried to think of ways of fighting the claim, of proving this man wrong or establishing that she was not responsible for her husband's old debts. However, there was nothing she could do about it now: she needed Everett's old correspondence, and she needed legal advice. It crossed her mind to ask Theo's opinion, but she was uncertain whether American law would be the same as English law in this respect. She wished that she dared to confide in Hal, but did not want to be a burden or seem unable to cope.

Walking, talking and smiling through the party, Constance could not decide what to do and, in the end, she did nothing. If she could spin this out for long enough, she reasoned, she could deal with it when she returned to London. By that time the proceeds of *Three Guineas* would have been paid into her bank account, and possession was nine-tenths of the law. Besides, she defied any man to win a court case if she took the witness stand against him: not only was she a poor widow with two young children, but she was a fine actress, even if she wasn't Amadine Sinclair.

Out of the corner of her eye Amadine saw Pierce leave the stage area and, with a sharp pang, her enjoyment of the evening went with him. Deeply disappointed that he should depart so abruptly, she pleaded tiredness and went to change out of her *Tanqueray* gown. The weariness was not just an excuse but suddenly all too real, as slowly, and reluctantly, she edged closer to the realisation that her success meant nothing if Pierce did not endorse it. The praise lavished on her by others was merely empty words if he did not admire her. Tonight she had given the greatest performance of her life, and he was one of the reasons why it had been great.

Not needing to venture outside into the bitter cold of the Chicago night, she did not bother to dress properly, merely slipping on her evening gown over the minimum of underwear. Wrapping herself in a black cloak, she left the theatre unobserved and entered the lobby of the adjoining hotel. Suddenly there he was, leaning against the wall of Mexican onyx, and he took her arm and propelled her towards the elevator. It was empty – either the operator was off-duty or had been bribed to make himself scarce – and Pierce pushed the buttons before saying, 'Perhaps we could meet for breakfast in the morning?'

'Not here – I'd like to get away from the others for a bit.'

'Henrici's,' he said. 'Seventy-one West Randolph. Will ten o'clock be too early, in view of your late night?'

Amadine shook her head and tried to think of something witty to say, but his blue eyes were pinning her to the side of the lift.

'Do you realise,' he went on, in an oddly detached tone of voice, 'that this is the first time you and I have been alone. Really alone. We have met on the decks of transatlantic liners, in countless restaurants, in your hotel suite with your maid only inches away, in a bookshop and a soda fountain . . .'

'There was the park in Philadelphia,' she reminded him, 'and the boathouse. We were alone there . . .' Her voice trailed away as she recollected the detail of that encounter.

'So we were, and we were interrupted . . .' Pierce pulled her towards him, and the light in those blue eyes made it clear that he intended to carry on from where that meeting had left off. His dark head bent towards hers and at last, at long last, his lips met hers.

And at that precise moment the elevator shuddered to a halt and the lights went out.

'Did you arrange that?' Amadine spluttered indignantly.

'No,' he murmured, not letting go. 'But it only goes to show that there is a God.'

For a split second Amadine was sufficiently alert to pray that the elevator was stuck between floors, and that the doors would not open suddenly to reveal them to a watching world, but she did not dwell on the matter because Pierce Radcliffe's lips – firm and cool, and totally familiar in that they felt exactly as she had imagined they would feel – had the power to banish conscious thought. Then she heard him draw in his breath and, as his arms tightened around her, his tongue slid into her mouth and began a serious invasion that transported her into very unfamiliar territory.

Afterwards Amadine was to be bitterly ashamed that she

did not ask him to stop, and horrified that she did not even consider asking him to do so, but now, clasped close against that lean, hard body, she wound her arms around his neck and kissed him back. His hands were sliding under the cloak, feeling the warmth of her flesh through the silk of her gown, discovering her lack of lingerie. One hand found an expanse of bare back and caressed it lightly, sending such shivers of delight through her that she experienced real disappointment when the hand withdrew. In fact a small gasp of protest did escape into the mouth still clamped firmly on hers and, to her even greater disappointment, Pierce pulled away from her. Then, to her relief and intense excitement, she felt him pushing aside the folds of her cloak and his hand slid inside the bodice of her dress.

The silence and the darkness rendered them anonymous and invisible, yet Amadine could picture him clearly, while being glad that he could not see her. In a state of tense, almost anguished anticipation she waited for him to touch her breast. As his fingers stroked across it and cupped it, and then lifted it free from its silk prison, he gave a muffled groan and sought her lips again. Now he was more demanding, his tongue entwining with hers with an urgency and intimacy that imitated the closer coupling they both so ardently desired. His thumb was rubbing her nipple and then, without warning, he tore his mouth from hers and fastened it to that erect, rock-hard point.

Amadine arched back against the wall of the elevator, her breathing ragged as she pushed up her exposed breast, urging it farther into his mouth. The darkness was not only her friend but an enhancer of her passion, for she was conscious only of sensation, of the loving, sensuous swirl of his tongue on her flesh before he took her nipple between his lips. With a groan, Amadine buried her hands in his hair, pressing his head closer, feeling that she had reached the dizziest heights of delight. She was wrong.

A hand was tugging at her skirt, pulling it up and then

burrowing beneath it, so that Amadine's next sensation was of Pierce's fingers sliding up her silk-stockinged leg. He reached the garter and paused, the suspense of waiting for his next move tearing a moan from deep in Amadine's throat. Then, very slowly, those fingers ventured on to the smooth flesh of her inner thigh and lingered there, smoothing and caressing, before creeping inexorably upwards.

Here Amadine knew that she ought to call a halt but, on the contrary, was quite sure that she could not bear it if he stopped. The fingers slipped under her drawers, into that hot, moist crevice, and began to explore with a devastating, and experienced, intimacy. The explosion of desire was too much. Amadine abandoned any last, ladylike inhibitions to which she might have been clinging, and let out a deep groan of longing. This was marvellous, wonderful, but it wasn't enough . . .

'Pierce, please . . . please . . . I want . . .'

And then she shuddered, her body vibrating against the side of the lift, but it was not the earth that had moved beneath her. The elevator lurched, and suddenly the lights flared into life. In a split second of sheer horror, Amadine's half-open glazed, green eyes met Pierce's burning blue stare, and then she erupted into a flurry of activity. In seemingly a single movement, she covered herself with the black cloak while tucking a stray breast back into place and pulling down her skirt. To her overwhelming relief, the elevator travelled up to the next floor before the doors opened, and she was able to exit with her dignity, and reputation, intact. In silence Pierce accompanied her to her suite, raising her hand to his lips as Ida opened the door.

'I'll see you at Henrici's,' he said, 'at ten.'

The utter awfulness of what she had done, or allowed to be done, entirely dominated any pleasure she had felt in her personal success at the theatre that evening. To face Pierce across a breakfast table was surely an impossibility. At least a dozen times during the night Amadine decided not to meet him, yet nine-thirty in the morning found her enquiring the way to West Randolph Street and setting off into a freezing temperature and a biting east wind.

Following what was to become a regular route, she walked briskly up Michigan Avenue as far as Monroe; then along Monroe, passing under the iron girders supporting the 'El', or elevated railway, at the intersection with Wabash, to State. The neat grid pattern of the streets making it easy to find her way, Amadine strolled up State Street and stopped to buy a newspaper from a boy standing at the corner of State and Randolph outside Marshall Field's famous department store. Then she had to negotiate the teeming traffic of wagons, carriages and trolley cars in State Street in order to cross over to West Randolph. By this time she was torn between the hope that Pierce would not come and the equally deep dread that he might not come, because in either event humiliation seemed inescapable. At Henrici's bakery and restaurant, the sight of the back of his head bent over a newspaper, and his broad shoulders in an immaculately cut dark suit, caused her heart to give one of those sickening little lurches that indicated pain or pleasure, or both.

'I hope that you slept well?' he asked politely, as she sat down.

'Not all that well,' she admitted, aware that she looked pale and tired.

'Too much excitement last night,' he declared. As colour flooded into her face, he continued calmly: 'To have the entire audience at the Auditorium on its feet and shouting for more must be a remarkable experience.'

Somewhat relieved, Amadine felt the flush begin to fade. However, as she stared at him, she could have sworn that the slightest suspicion of a smile tugged at the corners of his mouth, and she could almost believe that he was teasing her. 'The reaction of the audience was certainly the highlight of my evening,' she retorted.

'After all that applause, what else could you possibly want?'

One of his eyebrows twitched. Definitely. And Amadine was sure that he remembered, as clearly as she did, what she had been saying when the lights in the elevator came on.

'I certainly do not want to know what the papers are saying about me this morning,' she announced, in a brave attempt at changing the subject. 'Good or bad, reviews are a most offputting experience – bad reviews for obvious reasons, and good because it is easy to be influenced by them, and either become over-confident or tilt one's performance in a direction the critic has mentioned.'

The smell of freshly baked bread and coffee reminded her that, yesterday being a first night, she had not eaten for thirty-six hours, and the buttering and consumption of a bread roll helped to fill a few awkward moments. Pierce folded his newspaper and pushed it aside, mesmerising Amadine with the movements of his hands. She could not take her eyes off them, except to lift her gaze to his mouth, remembering where those hands and lips had been and what they had been doing. And the really awful thing was that she caught him looking at her, and she was sure he knew what she was thinking. Never before had she felt so vulnerable, exposed and at such a disadvantage.

'Shouldn't you be making bicycles or something?' she enquired, hoping to be rid of him.

'I am free this morning and entirely at your disposal.'

Those long, sensitive fingers slowly rolled a piece of bread into a ball and placed it in his mouth. Oh God . . .

'I could show you something of Chicago,' Pierce offered. 'Of course, the lake and the shore are hardly at their best in January, but the river is always interesting. Or we could look at the skyscrapers in the Loop.'

'The what?'

'The Loop is the colloquial name for the downtown area, called after the route of the El, which forms a rectangle in the city's business and financial districts. Alternatively, would you like to go to the stockyards?'

'Definitely not!' Amadine shuddered. 'The very thought of those poor animals being slaughtered is enough to make me vow never to eat meat again.'

'Then I suggest we go back to your hotel . . .' and he paused. Amadine trembled. '. . . and to the observation tower on the roof. It provides a spectacular view of the city and is a popular tourist attraction.'

Amadine agreed. 'I didn't realise that it was Chicago which give birth to the skyscraper, and that the first was built here in 1884 . . .' And she succeeded in initiating a conversation about modern architecture that saw her safely through to the end of the meal.

Later, she was both disappointed and relieved when he made it clear that he would not be attending that night's performance, but she found herself agreeing to meet him at the same time, same place, the following morning. Again, after breakfast, Pierce escorted her back to the hotel, following the same route past the newspaper boy outside Marshall Field's, and leaving her in the lobby of the Auditorium. However, on this Wednesday morning, Pierce had no sooner seen Amadine safely into the elevator when another member of the Smith-Sinclair company approached him.

'I was hoping to see you,' Gwendoline Hughes said. 'I am going to the cemetery this afternoon and, if Washington is anything to go by, I dare say that your visit might coincide with mine.'

Abruptly abandoning his schedule, Pierce travelled a few miles south of the city to the Pullman Car Works, and the company town built by George Pullman for his staff. Believing that a pleasant environment created better and happier workers, Pullman had constructed a model town of brick houses, schools, libraries and tree-lined streets, but had retained such total control of the facilities – particularly house rentals – while pay levels plummeted, that discontent and strikes ensued. However, the place was peaceful enough today as Pierce walked past the 60-acre timber-drying yard, his agile brain computing the capital tied up in that vast quantity of wood, and made his way to the car shops, or construction sheds.

Built in 1881, these Pullman works had no childhood memories for Pierce, nor were they part of his association with his father. When Pierce visited Chicago as a boy with his parents, his father still ran his own business and only in 1879, four years after Pierce's mother took him to England, did Samuel Radcliffe sell out his company and patents to George Pullman in exchange for cash and a large tranche of Pullman stock. But Pierce knew that Samuel had haunted these works, coming here nearly every day, if only to smell the wood and the paint just as his son was doing now. Pierce had not inherited his father's facility with wood, and had no training in working in wood as his father had, but he could still love the feel and smell of the stuff, and appreciate the craftsmanship in the carving and marquetry of the panels being prepared for the cars.

As he wandered slowly round the shop – nodding to the occasional worker who recognised him, and pausing to watch a car-painter lift an elaborate six-foot-high stencil into position and begin tracing the outline on to a panel – he could imagine Samuel's eagle eye for detail picking out the delicate nuances of a design, and even see his father seizing the tools and executing a carving himself. That was the Samuel he had adored as a child: the businessman for whom no detail was too trivial and who had made a fortune by his own wits and expertise, and the artist with an unerring eye and deep love of beauty. Unfortunately, Samuel's appreciation of the beautiful had strayed beyond mahogany, walnut and gold-leaf decoration . . .

Determined to be calm and fair, Pierce rode out to the cemetery in a driving snowstorm. She was there before him, and he stood facing her on the opposite side of the grave. The headstone bore a simple inscription – Samuel Radcliffe 1830–1891 – but its granite was no harder than the expression on Pierce's face as he stared at the woman who had destroyed his family. Tears and snow were glistening on her face, as she raised her eyes and looked at him.

'I loved him very much, you know,' Gwen said.

Chapter Nineteen

The wind whipped away the words and, realising that they could not talk here, Pierce led Gwen back to his carriage. She asked him to take her to Gunther's soda parlour at the McVicker's Theatre in Madison Street, because she had worked at this theatre for many years and had sat in this parlour with Sam on countless occasions. She was composed now, her face slightly flushed as she thawed out after the extreme cold outside, her fine eyes and patrician features giving a glimpse of the girl Samuel Radcliffe had admired. Gwendoline Hughes was not what Pierce had expected but, then, how was Jezebel supposed to look?

'You blame me for everything, don't you?' she said.

'Yes.'

'He said you would.' She sighed, and drew a deep breath. 'I met him at a party given by James McVicker in '73, when I was twenty-five,' she began.

'And I was ten,' Pierce said flatly. 'Didn't it occur to you that he was married?'

'Not to start with, no. Why should it? There were lots of single men in Chicago, of all sizes, ages and nationalities and, with most of them, dollars took precedence over dalliance! Only after a while did I begin to suspect, so I asked him.'

'And he lied.'

'Oh no,' Gwen said immediately. 'He told me all about you – he was terribly proud of you – and your mother.' She hesitated. This was where it became difficult.

'But you didn't stop seeing him.'

'By that time, I was too deeply in love with him, and he with me . . .' By that time, Gwen reflected, I had allowed him to seduce me. 'Part of the problem was that your mother would not move to Chicago . . . Look, I ought not to go on. It isn't my place to discuss your mother behind her back, and I only know what Sam told me.'

She could almost feel his hurt, and the rawness of the emotions within him, and begin to understand a bewildered young boy who had been wrenched away from his home and his father more than twenty years ago.

'I would like to know what he told you,' Pierce said steadily.

'Catherine loved Philadelphia and hated Chicago, and with Sam it was the exact opposite. "I was born to be in Chicago," he used to say. He grew to think of himself and the city as contemporaries – Chicago having been established as a town in the 1830s – and empathised with the way that Chicago grew so rapidly from nothing but a desolate strip of marsh and prairie grass. He felt a real bond, and a real pride, in the fact that the railroad was the single most important reason for that phenomenal growth, because railroads had made him what he was, too.' Gwen smiled affectionately. 'To put it very simply, Samuel loved trains. He had a passion for trains in the same way that some men have a passion for food, or . . .' She stopped.

'Women,' Pierce said conversationally, but with the slightest hint of sarcasm.

'He even loved the names of the railroad lines: Chicago and Rock Island; Illinois Central; Baltimore and Ohio; the Atchison, Topeka and Santa Fe . . . They were poetry to Samuel, and the sound of a steam engine was music to his ears.'

'I remember.' And the memory hurt, because Pierce was still hurt that this woman had known his father so much better than he had.

'Chicago has always been vigorous and uninhibited, and comes down heavily on the side of having a good time, just like Sam! He was a man who worked hard and played hard, and after doing his share of rebuilding the city after the Fire, in '75 he began building the Prairie Avenue house, but still Catherine refused to move. And then she found out about me.'

Pierce knew that bit. His mother had told him that his father was having an affair with an actress, and that he did not love them any more.

'Samuel always said that she used it as an excuse to go back to England, and to take you with her,' Gwen said apologetically, 'but I do not expect you to believe that. What I do want you to believe is that he adored you. He would have given me up sooner than lose you, but he wasn't given a choice. Catherine's departure was very sudden – in fact she had sailed before Sam knew anything about it.'

Pierce's heart was banging uncomfortably in his chest. This meeting was a mistake. He had been better off thinking badly of his father, rather than having doubt cast on the integrity of his mother. He could hear his mother's voice now: 'Your father doesn't love you any more . . . doesn't love you any more . . . doesn't love you any more . . .' When it is your mother who tells you these things, you believe it.

'So you moved into the Prairie Avenue house instead,' he said grimly.

'I have never set foot in the place.'

He looked at her, his face registering sheer disbelief.

'It's true,' Gwen insisted. 'I have never seen the outside, let alone the inside.'

'Why not?'

'Because I was never asked.' Gwen met his eyes frankly.

'That house was intended to be a family home. That house, and the social and business life that went with it, were never intended for me.'

'And you accepted that? You were content to be his . . .' He had hated her for as long as he could remember, but was too well brought up to insult her to her face by saying the word.

'His mistress.' Content? She had been many things in those years with Samuel, but content was not one of them. She had loved him to distraction, but had never quite managed to lose sight of what she had sacrificed for that love. It had not been easy to stay on in a little rented house, working at McVicker's in second-rate roles because Samuel did not want her to leave Chicago. Giving him the 'best years of her life' might be a cliché, but it was true nonetheless. Here in Chicago, in this theatre and that modest house, her youth and beauty had bloomed and faded until at last Samuel, having sold out to Pullman, agreed that she could tour with Adelaide Neilson for a couple of seasons. 'He went to see you at Oxford in the summer of '84, didn't he?' she said suddenly.

The shock had been considerable, Pierce remembered. He had been completing his degree at Oxford University when his father walked in, without warning, and triggered an excruciatingly painful interview. His hatred of his father was so deeply entrenched that he had refused to listen to anything Samuel had to say, and had walked out, shouting that he never wished to see his father again. Well, that was one wish that had been granted. And a terrible sense of loss gripped him and twisted at his heart.

'You were in England, too, at the time,' he remarked, 'because that was when I found out who you were.'

'I was with Daly's company, and we were appearing in London,' Gwen agreed. 'Samuel was very upset by your attitude,' she said delicately, 'but at least he persuaded you to go to Harvard to complete your education.'

'He did nothing of the kind,' Pierce exclaimed indignantly. 'I accepted no help from him, then or at any other time! Harvard was Mother's idea.'

Gwen shook her head. 'Samuel persuaded her to let you go back to America by the simple means of doubling her allowance.'

Pierce stared at her in horror. It couldn't be true and yet, when he thought about it, money had flowed very freely in his mother's mansion after Samuel's visit that summer. It was horrible, and he wished that he had never started this. Why, oh why, had he booked a passage on the bloody *Campania* and so come across the Smith-Sinclair company, and Gwendoline Hughes!

'You continued to act, then?' he commented.

She looked surprised. 'Acting was, and is, how I earn my living. What else should I do?' She saw his expression, and smiled wryly. 'You thought I was a kept woman all those years – oh no, my boy, not my style; not my style at all!'

Gwen tilted her head slightly to one side, and surveyed him shrewdly. 'You are so like him! In appearance – although you are a little taller, a bit more handsome, and much more educated – but also in your outlook. If Samuel had a fault, it was that he believed everything and everyone could be bought. He never could understand that I had inherited not only a Puritan work ethic from my New England ancestors, but also a propensity to carry a heavy burden of guilt. He never did comprehend that I, like Hawthorne's Hester Prynne, had a scarlet letter emblazoned on my breast – A for adulteress – even though mine was invisible.'

God, she was good! It was only by reminding himself forcefully that she was an actress that Pierce prevented himself from believing her. He almost began to feel sorry for his father, who had not stood a chance against this lovely, silver-tongued enchantress. All actresses were witches and spellbinders, he thought, remembering Amadine.

'How did you justify adding the money to that Puritan load of guilt?' he asked sarcastically.

'What money?'

'Samuel's money, of course, what else?'

'I haven't taken any of his money.'

'Oh, come on, what sort of fool do you take me for! He must have left you millions!'

'He wanted to leave me well provided for,' Gwen said quietly. 'He wanted to give me a house, here in Chicago, and a generous income. I refused to take a single cent.' She smiled at his incredulity. 'Yes, Samuel didn't believe me either. He thought I was holding out for a larger sum. You see,' and she leaned towards him, 'refusing the money was the one bit of control I had. You will discover one day that one cannot choose whom one falls in love with,' and she noticed the startled knowingness in his eyes. 'Ah, apparently that is a lesson you have already learned! I felt guilt about the break-up of your parents' marriage, even though I could not, and still cannot, be sure that it would not have happened anyway. But I knew that I would not, could not, take Samuel's money – the money that belonged rightfully to his wife and son. It was within my power to say no, and I did. Ask the lawyers if you don't believe me.'

Pierce recognised that he ought to have done so long ago, but his stubbornness had prevented him from enquiring into the details of his father's estate. If she was telling the truth, it would explain the unexpected size of that estate. If she wasn't telling the truth – oh, what the hell, what real difference did it make! Suddenly he was terribly, terribly tired.

'I don't understand why the lawyers didn't tell you,' Gwen was saying.

'I don't discuss the matter with anyone. And that is because I haven't taken a single cent either.'

'But that's dreadful – Samuel wanted you to have it!' She looked shocked. 'You mean that your mother is the only person enjoying the fruits of his labour? Oh, he wouldn't like that, he wouldn't like that at all!'

Fatigue was overwhelming Pierce. He had not said all he wanted to say, not by a long chalk – there remained the matter of Samuel's suicide to discuss – but he simply could not take any more. Murmuring his excuses, he blundered out into the snow and made his way home. At East Bellevue Place, just off Lake Shore Drive and close to the Potter Palmer mansion, Pierce's house was about as far away from his father's Prairie Avenue address as he could decently go. *En route* he found a telephone and left a message at the Auditorium for Amadine, saying that he could not see her that night. Then he took a bottle of bourbon to his room and drank himself into a deep sleep, which was illumined by vivid dreams in which his father courted Amadine while he, his mother and Gwen looked on.

Amadine went to Rector's – a highly suitable restaurant for her, everyone teased – for dinner with the theatre crowd after the show, and put on a cheerful enough performance of her own. Nat Goodwin and Maxine Elliott were there, after appearing at Hooley's in *An American Citizen*, and Wilton Lackaye, who was at the Grand Opera House in *The Royal Secret*.

'There will be wedding bells at any moment,' whispered Gwen, looking at Nat and Maxine. 'Nat's divorce was in the paper yesterday.'

'You see,' hissed Jay to Amadine, rolling his eyes meaningfully in Hal's direction.

Amadine gave him a withering glance, but was particularly nice to Hal that night. Hope burned again in Hal's breast, but Amadine knew that she was only getting back at Pierce for letting her down this evening, which was a pretty silly thing to do when he was not there to see it.

At Henrici's the next morning she ordered coffee and a pastry, and ate it slowly. Then she ordered more coffee and

drank it even more slowly. The Chicago *Daily News* began
to look somewhat dog-eared as she grimly read and re-read
an account of the country home Henry James had just purchased at Rye in Sussex, and of the interest being shown in
Peter the Great in London, since Henry Irving had put on
a play about the Russian Tsar. Considering that yesterday
the paper had included a paragraph about the death of
Irving's pet dog, Fussie, and a few days earlier had covered
the engagement of Lawrence Irving and Ethel Barrymore,
Amadine reflected that one could keep up to date here with
the London stage as well as, if not better than, in London.

But still Pierce Radcliffe did not join her.

She retraced her steps, and exchanged another smile with
the newsboy. 'Still here,' she teased. 'Haven't you a home to
go to!'

'No, miss.'

Amadine stopped, and turned to face him. He was small
and thin, dressed in an ill-fitting coat with the collar turned
up, a cloth cap that covered his ears, and trousers tucked
into battered boots. His hands were stuck into his coat
pockets, and he carried a large sheaf of newspapers under
one arm. She had assumed that he was about ten years old
but, looking at him more carefully, she saw that his small
size might be due to malnourishment, because his face
looked older.

'How old are you?' she asked.

'I think I'm about fourteen,' he replied doubtfully.

'And you really don't have a home?' When he shook his
head, Amadine went on, 'But where do you go – where do
you sleep at night?'

'Here and there,' and he gestured at the surrounding
streets.

'In this weather!' she exclaimed in dismay.

He did not answer, but instead grinned cheekily. 'You all
alone today, then?'

It was sweet of the boy to have noticed Pierce's absence,

but a bit embarrassing. 'My friend didn't turn up,' she said, 'so I had to breakfast on my own.'

'I wouldn't leave you on your own,' the boy declared stoutly, 'if I was your friend.'

Amadine laughed. 'You are my friend. Here, give me another newspaper for some people at the hotel, and have breakfast on me,' and she pressed five dollars into his hand.

The boy's jaw dropped, and he looked from the money back to Amadine's face as if he could not decide which was the most beautiful.

'Someone'll think I stole it,' he said uncertainly.

'Then refer them to me – Amadine Sinclair at the Auditorium Theatre. Can you remember that?'

'Easy.' The dollars vanished into his capacious coat pocket.

'Try to find a room for the night,' she said quietly. 'It's so cold . . .'

'Yes, miss. Thank you, miss.'

'I'll see you tomorrow. Same time, same place.' And, after briefly touching his cheek, she walked on down State Street.

There must be lots of boys like him here, she thought, and in Boston and New York, and in London and Manchester . . . At home, in Father's parish, there had been scores of needy children but they all had families, they all had *someone*, and they all had a roof over their heads, even though that roof leaked. In big cities the situation was very different, and she castigated herself for not noticing it before. Either I have been walking round with my eyes shut, she decided, or I drive too often.

She found Gwen, Constance and Blanche in the second-floor reception room of the hotel, sitting near the enclosed balcony overlooking the lake. It was an odd thing that no one commented on Blanche's presence at such an expensive establishment as the Auditorium, and a sign that her companionship was taken increasingly for granted. Of course this was exactly the effect Blanche was trying to achieve, and why she had taken a few risks in order to be here.

Money, and particularly the bargain with her stepfather, remained an overriding concern. She still owed Gwen fifty dollars and, although she had accumulated several weeks' wages, the usual allowance had to be wired to her mother from Chicago. Also, in Chicago Blanche was faced with finding boarding-house fees and paying for her food. However, it wasn't only money that made her wish that the train journey could go on for ever, but the fact that the social and geographical gap between the principals' hotel and her humble lodgings would leave her out of things. She was not automatically included in their gatherings and excursions, although she did her best to ingratiate herself into their company as unobtrusively and as often as possible. Then it occurred to her that an hotel of the size of the Auditorium must have smaller and cheaper rooms than those that the principals would be occupying, even if such accommodation was mainly intended for servants. If this was so, and the rate for such a room did not include food, she might be able to afford it. With luck her colleagues wouldn't query her presence at their dinner table and, if she did not get away with that, she could always resort to using a stage-door Johnnie or two as a meal ticket. It would not be the first time, and neither would it be the first time that such a man went away disappointed at the end of the evening. Blanche was a virgin, and she fully intended to stay that way until she met a prize who was worth the price.

Blanche decided to give it a try and, as she had hoped, Gwen and Amadine had given her a ride from the station in their cab. 'I just can't face another dingy boarding house, with a cracked mirror and chipped handbasin,' she had said – a bit embarrassing when one owed fifty dollars, but never mind – 'and thought that Chicago was the place to treat myself, the hotel and the theatre being under the same roof an' all. They'll let me have an iron and an ironing board, won't they?' And right on cue Gwen had said, 'You can share mine,' and sure enough they had been ironing their shirtwaists, washing their handkerchiefs and gloves, and steaming the creases out of their skirts over Gwen's bath. Blanche had expected Frank to voice an objection, but even he had said nothing, and indeed hardly seemed to notice her or to notice anyone or anything else these days.

So Blanche was able to sit close beside Gwen in the hotel and greet Amadine, along with the others, as Gwen seized the newspaper Amadine was carrying.

'Anything exciting happened? Oh, only a hold-up at a Chicago and Alton railroad station. Tell me, girls, what do you think have been the most newsworthy items in the papers this week?'

'The Chris Merry murder trial,' Blanche asserted with relish. 'They'll hang him, won't they?'

'I was very disturbed to read that *only* seventeen people had died from impure-water diseases last week,' Constance remarked, 'including three from typhoid. I thought seventeen was rather a lot.'

'Amadine?'

Amadine was considering her answer. 'There was that chap who jumped to his death from the Masonic Building, and that fire at the corner of Market and Quincy, but, no, it has to be the battleship *Maine* sailing to Havana.'

'You all get ten out of ten for current affairs,' Gwen declared, 'but I don't agree with any of your choices.'

'Why not?' Blanche wanted to know.

'None of them affect us directly, whereas my choice does. Have you noticed how many traffic accidents there are in this town? The headlines are there nearly every day: "Crushed under Grip Car"; "Death after fall from a North Clark Street cable car"; "Shock from Amputation kills, after man run over by Chicago and Eastern Illinois train"; "Switchman killed in fall from freight train"; "Struck by street car at Clark and Polk" . . . This town is a death trap!'

'Not for me,' Constance declared with a smile. 'I don't go out often enough – it's too cold and snowy out there.'

'You went out this morning,' Blanche pointed out.

'I needed some gloves from Marshall Field's,' Constance explained, flushing.

'And yesterday morning, at the same time.'

'Someone is interested in putting on one of my husband's plays,' Constance lied, with infinite dignity.

'There are a lot of suicides, too,' Amadine remarked, apropos Chicago's news coverage.

Gwen went very still. In Washington, Pierce Radcliffe had referred to Sam's death as suicide, but she still did not understand what he meant by that. Sam's death had been an accident, surely? She wondered if she ought to tell Amadine about her connection with Pierce. It seemed fairly obvious that she, Gwen, was one of the chief reasons he had been tracking the tour round the country, while in addition he harboured a grudge against actresses, and certainly it was no coincidence that suddenly Amadine had been free to join the Rector's party last night. Gwen was afraid that Amadine really liked the man and she couldn't blame her – Pierce Radcliffe was so like his father that she knew exactly what Amadine saw in him. She was less sure about the nature of Pierce's feelings for Amadine, but as the worst that could happen was that he broke the girl's heart, and that was a risk one took in any romantic relationship, Gwen decided to say nothing.

For several days Pierce found it difficult to concentrate on anything but his personal affairs. Oddly, he found himself thinking of his mother, rather than of Samuel or Gwen. With extreme reluctance and a sense of the ground moving beneath his feet, as if a seismic shift was occurring in the very foundations of his life, he admitted that there could be a grain of truth in Gwen's version of events. Catherine ought to have moved to Chicago, added to which her departure for England had been so precipitate that even Pierce had not realised the move was permanent. And – even if it was true, and that was looking doubtful – she ought not to have told him that his father did not love him.

Gwen had remarked that Catherine was the only person enjoying Samuel's money. Pierce now reflected that she was also the only person who was happy. He had always been faintly amused by his mother's way of life. She had purchased an imposing mansion on the outskirts of her home village in Oxfordshire, where she flaunted her new wealth and status in the face of the gentry who had not acknowledged her in her youth, and in the face of her old friends whom now she did not deign to acknowledge. She played the lady of the manor to the manner born and, although she had few friends, her status seemed to bring her real pleasure.

She remained possessive of her only son. In every letter she asked when he was 'coming home', refusing to accept that Pierce considered his home to be America. How many times hadn't Pierce urged her to visit America during the summer months, or in the fall perhaps, instead of him trailing across the Atlantic yet again? Catherine declined decisively. There was no way, she asserted, that she would ever set foot in that dreadful place again. Pierce began to see that, for Catherine, all Samuel's millions would have no meaning in America. Possessing such wealth in Chicago, and particularly the Chicago of the early 1870s, would have been pointless because it could not buy the lifestyle she wanted. A rueful grimace twisted the corners of Pierce's mouth as he reflected that for Catherine, like Fanny Kemble, this really was 'that dreadful America'.

He began to experience a lightening of the spirit as he comprehended that even if he could not change the past, he could come to terms with it. But before taking that vital step, there was one more thing he had to do. Pierce went to Illinois Central's Randolph Street Depot and spoke to several of the staff. Then he got in touch with Gwen and – and perhaps this was a mark of increased respect for her – invited her to lunch.

Gwen sat uneasily in the Palmer House, enveloped in an all-too-familiar cloak of guilt, because she had not told Amadine about this meeting and was worried in case the other woman found out and took offence. It was totally ridiculous; on the other hand, perhaps it was a natural reaction to a Radcliffe. Old habits die hard and so, apparently, do old emotions.

He was asking her about the work she did after that Daly tour to London.

'Sam didn't like it if I left Chicago, so I went back to McVicker's. But eventually I persuaded him that I could not stay for ever, and that I must take an opportunity to tour with Booth.'

'But he didn't want you to go.'

'Of course not. He wanted his own way. Don't all men?'

Deciding to treat that as a rhetorical question, Pierce went on, 'Did you come back to Chicago to live?'

Gwen shook her head. 'When I finished touring, I went to New York.'

'You were in New York when he died?'

'At Daly's again – well, Samuel died just before the season started. Look, why do you want to know all this?'

'It seems relevant to my father's state of mind at the time of his death.'

'Samuel's death was an accident,' she insisted.

'I don't think so.'

There was a long pause. 'You are suggesting,' Gwen said at last, 'that Samuel committed suicide, and that I was the reason?'

'One of the reasons.'

Being in a public place, Gwen kept a tight rein on her emotions. 'This is nonsense,' she hissed in a low voice. 'For one thing, by that time Samuel and I were only friends.

There was nothing physical between us any more, and for all I knew he could have had another mistress. He wasn't lonely, if that is what you are implying – we still saw a lot of each other and he had a full social life.'

'So why did he do it?'

'He *didn't* . . .'

'In October 1891 my father was run down and killed by a train at the Randolph Street Depot. There were several witnesses to his death, and one man in particular is adamant that it was not an accident.' Pierce leaned forward, his intensely blue eyes hard and cold. 'This railroadman was only a few yards away from the incident. He saw Samuel walking across the track and then he saw the approaching train. Seeing the danger, he shouted to Samuel to watch out, but Samuel took no notice and calmly – this is what the man remembered most, my father's complete calm and determination – walked in front of the train.'

The colour was draining from Gwen's face, but she was shaking her head vehemently. 'No,' she said. 'I saw him only a few days earlier. He was well, and he was cheerful. He talked non-stop about the 1893 Exposition, and how it would put Chicago on the world map. You know how he loved this town – mind you, I had the distinct impression that he thought the Expo would be one in the eye for Catherine! No, Pierce, your father would not have missed that exhibition by choice, believe me.'

'He would if the balance of his mind was disturbed.'

'Samuel Radcliffe was the sanest man I ever met!' Gwen pushed back her chair from the table and stood up. 'And come to that, where were you when he died? You don't like to think about that, do you! It's so much easier to blame me.'

Pierce remained at the table after she had gone, refusing food but finishing the wine. Where had he been in the fall of 1891? Here in Chicago much of the time, building up his bicycle manufacturing business and avoiding his father, as if

Samuel were afflicted with a particularly nasty infectious
disease. It had not been difficult to ensure that their paths
never crossed. Pierce's home was in the north of the city,
while his father lived in the south. Pierce's factory was
nowhere near the Pullman works, and he never went to the
theatre. His preferred restaurants and bars were in keeping
with his youth and were far removed, geographically,
socially and aesthetically, from those patronised by his
father.

Sitting in the Palmer House hotel, Pierce drained his
wine glass but continued to linger, alone and absorbed, in
the rapidly emptying restaurant. What else had he been
doing that fall? Oh yes, he had still been interested in steel
railway cars, and in fact he'd had a hand in one that was
exhibited at the Chicago Expo. There was a future in metal
railroad cars, he was convinced of it. Wooden cars were
flaming death traps, literally. He ought to pursue it, just as
he ought to get a stranglehold on the automobile industry
here in America. If only he had the money . . .

He did have the money. Millions of dollars were lying
fallow, unused and unappreciated, waiting to be picked up
and transformed into billions of dollars.

But still he could not do it. A frown marred those lean,
finely boned features as Pierce contemplated the obstacles
that continued to bar his path to his father's fortune. He
could, after these discussions with Gwen, overcome his disgust at his father's affair with an actress. He might be able
to suppress his instinctive resolve to make his own fortune –
an attitude based on the fact that Samuel had started with
nothing, and therefore whatever his father had done, he
could also do – on the grounds that Samuel had accepted
financial backing from a wealthy Philadelphian businessman. However, the obstacle confronting Pierce now was
one that was the most difficult to negotiate. He really did
believe that his father had committed suicide. If he could
not lay the fault at Gwen's door, then he was left with only

himself to blame. And how the hell did he reconcile himself to that?

During the week Frank hired three new members for the company: a married couple, and an extremely pretty young man whose dark, Italianate good looks would show to excellent advantage in *Romeo and Juliet* and *Much Ado*, which was now in rehearsal. He eyed the boy speculatively but, even if Frank's heart had not belonged to Theo, the youth was not his type, Frank preferring a more mature man. Then Ida Norris sidled up to him and put in a plea for an itinerant Englishman. Frank listened with some cynicism; he knew the type – he had been one himself. However, he was not completely heartless, and he could do with an extra pair of legs in the Shakespeare and an extra pair of hands behind the scenes.

'There are no speaking parts available,' Frank warned without preamble, 'only helping out backstage, and a bit of walking-on.'

'Suits me,' shrugged George White, who had expected nothing else. 'You don't remember me, do you?'

'Ought I to remember you?'

'We were at the Lyceum together – '83, '84, thereabouts. Lawrence Barrett and *Richelieu*. Ring a bell?'

'I remember *Richelieu* all right. How could one forget?'

'Ghastly, wasn't it,' George said reminiscently. 'I've never quite worked out what went wrong. Barrett was considered a great tragedian here in America, second only to Booth, but London never warmed to him.'

'Do you remember the last night of the season when Irving, who had just come back from his first tour of the States, presented Barrett with the Order of the Garter that Kean wore in *Richard III*? I think about it every time I see the Kean scenes in *Trelawny*.'

'Very moving,' agreed George. 'No one can make a speech, or a presentation, more stirring than Sir Henry.'

Frank was not unduly impressed by the man's appearance and wondered what on earth Ida saw in him, but for all his reservations he knew that he would offer him the job. There, he thought, but for the grace of my big brother, and the position he gave me, go I. He was still trying to place the fellow at the Lyceum in '83. Suddenly he snapped his fingers.

'Did you have very fair hair in those days?'

'Yes,' George confessed. 'It still is very fair but tends to look grey in some lights, so I dyed it.'

And with a satisfied nod, Frank gave him the job.

George did not rush to give the good news to Ida, but paused to savour the moment. He was not afraid that Amadine might recognise him. A leading lady of her rank was unlikely to notice the stagehands, even if they occasionally walked-on while she was performing, and it was even less likely that she would place as much as a toe over the threshold of the men's car on the train. He was surprised at how calm he felt. No surge of euphoria, no exultation, just a steady sense of everything coming right.

It was Ida who exulted, so far forgetting herself as to fling her arms around his neck in her excitement. To think that now he would always be here, that at the theatre or on the train he would be only a few steps away!

By Friday, Frank knew that he could postpone the evil moment no longer. Removing his hoard of stolen cash from the hotel safe, he pushed the canvas bag into his coat pocket and set off for the notorious Chicago Levee.

Chapter Twenty

From the Auditorium it was a comparatively short walk to the corner of Harrison and Dearborn and then into the alley called Custom House Place, but Frank was venturing into a world far removed from the theatres, hotels and restaurants that were his customary milieu. The Levee was Chicago's vice district, crammed with brothels, saloons, pawnshops and peep shows, its streets crawling with whores, pimps and thieves. It was also the centre of organised crime, where corrupt politicians and police were paid a percentage to look the other way, and where these politicians controlled the whisky, cab and clothing concessions. Here were Chicago's extremes of good and bad taste, where girls could be had for twenty-five cents if a man was prepared to risk a mugging, and where luxurious bordellos provided the finest champagne.

Frank had been here before, but never in daylight. However, he felt that his strategy was a sound psychological move: not only did he feel safer on these streets during the day than at night, but he wanted to meet these men on his own terms, as a sober, suited businessman. Finding the door he sought, he knocked and was admitted by a man with the build and face of an ex-boxer, who told him to sit down and wait. They would keep him waiting, Frank thought wryly, for some considerable time as part of *their* psychological strategy.

This saloon was where it had happened, but it looked different in the daytime and, strangely, it seemed more sinister. Frank began to think he had made a mistake; he had felt safer outside at this hour, but he might have been better off inside when there were more people about. Two years, he thought, two years almost to the day since he had walked in here for the first time and his entire life had changed.

He had been in Chicago on tour – of course, what else? – and had been feeling depressed. It was just another dead-end job, and he was beginning to see that all his life would ever be was a series of dead-end jobs, and that he might be lucky to stay in work at all. It was in that frame of mind that he glanced at the newspaper one day and read a report of Hal's production of *Romeo and Juliet* at the Lyceum, which Hal was renting in Irving's absence on tour. As Frank had not known that his brother had formed his own company, the shock was considerable. The contrast between Hal's success and his own painful inadequacy was even worse.

By nature a loner, mainly for fear of revealing his homosexual tendencies, Frank wandered into the Levee on his own that night. All he wanted to do was drink himself into a stupor so that he did not have to remember, let alone face up to, his overwhelming sense of failure. He had come into this saloon. At this distance in time he could not recall what had made him choose this bar over all the others but, by God, he wished he had gone someplace else.

He was already extremely drunk by the time he got into conversation with a friendly stranger who insisted that Frank share his bottle of excellent whisky. Instead of becoming maudlin as he had expected, Frank began to feel more cheerful. The stranger was so friendly that he even wondered if the fellow shared his homosexuality and whether this might be his lucky night. When, after a quiet word in the barman's ear, the stranger beckoned Frank through to a private room beyond the saloon, his hopes had soared.

So the gambling salon had come as a disappointment, but Frank was very drunk, as well as enjoying himself with his newfound friend, and readily agreed to a game of cards. Although he was not a companionable man, he played cards from time to time with the other actors on the train, and was passably proficient at poker. Later he could remember absolutely nothing about the game, probably because of his excessive intake of alcohol, and did not even notice that the room was empty except for those at his table. Then suddenly his 'friend' threw his cards on the table, stood up, and accused Frank of cheating. Frank indignantly protested his innocence, but the allegation was supported by the other players.

'There's only one way to settle this,' the other man announced grimly. He seemed much more sober than Frank, despite apparently having done full justice to the whisky bottle. 'You'll not refuse to fight, I hope?'

With the room swimming around him, Frank struggled to his feet. 'A duel? Certainly.' And he slashed at the air with an imaginary rapier, because at that moment he was drunk enough to believe that an old-fashioned sword duel was scheduled and, with his stage experience, he fancied he was rather good at that sort of thing.

But the other man pulled out a gun.

'Sorry,' said Frank, 'but I don't shoot. Never fired a gun in my life.'

Something hard and cold was being pressed into his hand. He stared at it stupidly. It was a gun. He had no idea what sort of gun, but definitely a firearm of the handgun variety. He fiddled with it nervously, and the assembled group dived for cover.

'You want a fight,' Frank announced grandly, 'you got a fight.'

By this time the drinking saloon had closed so they repaired there, it providing a larger space for the proceedings. The two combatants were told to stand back to back, then start walking, stop on command, turn and fire. Frank seemed to have tottered only a few steps, in a very erratic line, before he heard the command to turn, but he did as he had been told and pulled the trigger. The pistol jerked in his hand and he looked up at the ceiling, convinced that he had fired into the air.

Then he saw the other man lying face down on the ground. Face down, facing the other way. Funny, thought Frank. If he turned round when he was told, he should be facing towards me. His legs gave way under him and he heard the words 'He's dead', before slumping to the floor and passing out.

When he came round, he was alone in the room except for two men whom he did not remember seeing before. In a few blunt words they informed Frank that he had killed his opponent. What's more, he had fired before the command was given and had shot the other man in the back. Frank was appalled. To be accused of cheating at cards was bad enough, but this . . . In vain he protested that he had heard the command, and that he was innocent of the cheating charge in the first place. He was hauled to his feet, pushed into the back room for a quick, and stomach-churning, glimpse of the corpse, then propelled back to a seat in the saloon.

'We can go to the police,' one of the men said, 'or we can fix it.'

'How would you fix it?' Frank asked.

'We know where this guy lives. We could take the body home, and have him listed as a suicide.'

'But how could it be suicide if I shot him in the back?'

'On the Levee, anything is possible. It's all part of the service – the service for which you will pay, Mr Smith.'

How did they know his name? He supposed that he must

have told someone during the course of the evening, but did not remember doing so, and certainly did not remember the names of any of the men here. Slowly Frank's brain was assimilating the situation, and the cover-up that was being suggested.

'How much?' he asked.

'It'll be expensive,' the man said thoughtfully. 'This kind of operation involves so many people, you see. At least the guy wasn't married, so there ain't a grieving widder or starving orphans, but we'll have to square everyone who was here, along with the police and the other authorities.'

'I don't have much money. I'm only an actor.'

'Which is why we'll give you plenty of time. We even understand that you have to leave Chicago to earn your living, but you must bring, or wire, payments at regular intervals. Or we'll find you – wherever you are . . .'

Frank's head was aching, and he felt very sick. No, he was thinking to himself, I don't like this. I cannot pay blackmail money all my life. It was an accident, and haven't they been cracking down on gambling in the Levee? This place could be illegal. 'I think I'll take my chances with the police.'

The man leaned forward, and said very quietly, 'You thought you were being invited into the bedroom, didn't you!'

Frank started retching, and was violently sick into a bucket, which the second man grabbed from behind the bar and thrust at him just in time. He stared at that implacable face in front of him. This was January 1896, and the fate of Oscar Wilde was still fresh in everyone's mind. Even if he managed to extricate himself from this appalling situation – because there was something very odd about it – Frank knew that revelations about his homosexuality could follow him back to London and do untold harm to himself and to his family. He had no choice but to pay.

'How much?' he asked again.

'I don't think we need set a final figure, do you?' the man said easily. 'Let's say a hundred dollars a week, and see how it goes.'

'But I don't earn anything like a hundred dollars a week!'

'Oh, dear.' The man shook his head. 'We'll have to open an account for you, Mr Smith. You pay us as much as you can, as often as you can, and we will enter those payments in the credit column of your account. But a hundred dollars will be entered in the debit column every week, along with the interest.'

He had done his best but, as usual, his best had not been nearly good enough. He was well in arrears, but now he was older and wiser, and he had a plan.

At last Frank was summoned to the inner sanctum and to the same two men, wearing what seemed to be the same clothes and what were certainly the same expressions. Frank still did not know their names – he wired money to a Chicago account, but suspected that it was in a false name – or their exact positions. They were fences, or agents, or bagmen for the big boys who ran the Levee. Seeing them again after all this time made Frank's fists clench, but give them their due: he had never heard a word about the man he was accused of killing.

'This is very good, Frank,' the first man enthused after he had counted the thousand dollars Frank handed to him, 'very good indeed. I knew we were right to trust you, and let you go to London.'

'I would like to see my account.'

That took them by surprise. He was aware that they were inspecting him sharply, but he stood firm and returned their stare. After a moment's hesitation, an account book was produced from the depths of a desk drawer.

Frank pulled out a pocketbook and sat down to compare their entries with the meticulous record he had kept of his payments. Rather to his surprise, they tallied. Even so, the outstanding balance was terrifying. He owed ten thousand dollars. 'I have a proposition for you, gentlemen.' Taking their silence as permission to elaborate, he continued, 'You must be convinced by now that I am not a wealthy man . . .'

'No, but your brother is,' the first man interrupted.

'I *wish*! We have been having a disastrous tour, and the expenses have been enormous. Did you know that the great Irving himself only made a profit of six thousand pounds on his last tour here? This figure,' and he tapped the accounts book, 'represents a virtually impossible task for me but I am prepared to try, on condition that it stops there. Is that a deal? If I pay you ten thousand dollars when I next visit Chicago, will you consider the matter closed?'

There was another pause, longer than the previous silence, as the two men glanced at each other and then at Frank. He hoped and prayed that they would conclude they had milked him enough.

'Yeah, it's a deal.'

Frank stood up and held out his hand, which was taken, gingerly, by the chief spokesman. He had no idea how much store was put on a handshake in the Levee, but it meant something to him and he was sure they knew that.

'How do you intend to raise the money?' the man asked.

'I imagine I'll have to steal it,' Frank said drily, 'don't you?'

Frank had not been back at the Auditorium for long before Amadine came to him, asking for a hundred dollars in cash. He counted it out for her, in small bills as she requested, and watched as she signed the receipt. The idea of the company being paid in gold coin had never been fully developed, and anyway had been suggested by Frank only in order to ensure that they were paid in cash, which he could control.

'Have you ever wondered what it must be like to be homeless?' she asked.

'I've known what it is to worry about where the next job

is coming from, and how to pay the rent,' he returned. 'In our profession, who hasn't!'

Amadine nodded. 'Yes, I've worried about the rent, too. But, looking back on that period, I don't think I ever doubted that something would turn up, that somehow I would survive.'

'The confidence of youth,' Frank suggested. 'Not that you are a wizened old crone now!'

She smiled, but clearly her mind was elsewhere. 'This boy is only fourteen years old,' she murmured. 'Frank, I don't know why I asked you such a silly question – with your family property in Sussex, even if the profession did let you down, you would never be without a roof over your head.'

So Hal had told her about Sussex. Interesting. Evidently Hal's intentions towards Amadine were just as serious as Frank suspected. However, today of all days, the family home was not the most reassuring topic of conversation. Frank could imagine, all too easily, a set of circumstances that would result in his family throwing him out of the house and refusing to speak to him again.

'I'm a younger son,' he said carefully, 'and under the primogeniture system everything goes to Hal.' But you must be aware of that, he thought, watching Amadine's reaction and wondering if she would marry Hal for his money.

She certainly seemed very thoughtful and preoccupied. 'During the past few days I have realised just how transitory this life is, and just how fleeting are its moments of success,' she said soberly. 'One minute I'm being cheered by thousands, and the next I'm being ignored by – well, never mind that . . . What I am trying to say is that I do hope this tour is a financial success because I really need the money.'

Frank's heart sank. Oh, great . . .

'I don't have a home of my own. When we sail for London in June, I need enough money to rent a decent house or flat, and tide me over until the next job comes along.'

'But Hal . . .'

Amadine looked at him steadily, and then simply shook her head. 'But don't tell him, not just yet.'

'Don't worry, I won't,' Frank assured her with alacrity. 'But, Amadine, surely you are being inundated with offers from other producers?'

'Not one so far.'

'Then they believe that you are being inundated with offers. It's like the beautiful girl who sits at home alone – men are scared to ask her out because they assume she has more invitations than she knows what to do with.'

'Kind of you to say so.' Amadine turned to go. 'But look after my nest egg for me, Frank, because right now it looks like the only thing between me and the streets!'

After she had gone, Frank leaned back in his chair and stared at the ceiling. It was one of those moments that came upon him from time to time when he tried to imagine murdering Amadine. He tried to visualise circumstances and situations that would make it possible to kill her and get away with it, and so secure ten thousand dollars. He wondered if he could bring himself to do it, or would he fail at that, just like he failed at everything else?

No sooner had Frank managed to push aside this terrifying, but strangely fascinating scenario than Hal appeared and he, too, had money on his mind.

'Constance has asked me to finance some legal proceedings in London,' he announced in a worried tone. 'There is a dispute over the authorship of one of Everett Grey's plays, and Constance is receiving lawyer's letters, demanding large sums in compensation.'

'Nothing to do with us,' Frank said unsympathetically.

'I know, but it isn't easy to tell her so to her face, not when her eyes are swimming in tears and she is wearing that stricken look, which makes me feel a complete heel.'

'Blame me – I'm quite prepared to be the villain who is not willing to dip into the company coffers in order to fund personal problems,' Frank declared without a flicker of hypocrisy. 'What did you tell her?'

'I tried to persuade her to negotiate a deal whereby she gives the other party the income from the new production if he drops his claim to the old. But she suddenly said no, she wasn't offering anything to anyone, or negotiating anything with anyone, because that would be admitting that the other party is in the right. That was when she asked me to lend her the money for a lawyer. She said that I could dock it from her wages next season,' and Hal groaned.

'One can see the logic behind that remark,' Frank said cautiously.

'Not from where I'm standing! I don't want to work with Constance next season. I don't want to work with her ever again. If I did, I would lend her the money out of my own pocket, but the prospect of watching her struggle to pay it back – of having her on *my* back for another season, out of sheer pity – and of her sinking deeper and deeper into the financial mire through a misconceived court case is too terrible to contemplate.'

'Tell her that it would be money down the drain,' Frank insisted. 'She hasn't a snowball's hope in hell of winning the case. Everyone knows that Everett Grey never had an original idea in his life, and stole plots right, left and centre.'

'Correction – everyone but Constance knows that.'

'I seem to remember hearing talk about several disputes concerning Grey,' Frank said thoughtfully. 'If Constance fights this case, there will be a queue of people waiting to try their luck in court.'

And he watched impassively as Hal grimaced, nodded and went to give Constance the bad news. At least, Frank reflected, his advice had not been influenced by his own personal position. He genuinely believed that Constance should not waste money on a lost cause.

Negotiation, not litigation, was Hal's final word of advice.

Constance returned to her hotel room, and knelt beside the trunk containing Everett's manuscripts. She had only gone to Hal because she was at the end of her tether. For one thing, it was her son's birthday, and she found herself making all sorts of bargains with God: if He would only make Charlie well, she would never miss his birthday again, or tour again, or grumble again. But the night before her confrontation with Hal, she had played Juliet – and had heard the sigh of disappointment from the audience when it was announced that she, not Amadine, was playing that night. Then she had received the lawyer's letter, and been badly frightened by its tone and the amount of compensation demanded. She had gone to Hal out of sheer desperation, but came away feeling lonely and let down.

She looked at Everett's manuscripts. Each one was as familiar as an old friend. She knew every word and stage direction, every nuance of every plot. They had been her husband's only bequest, and she had always believed that one day they would be appreciated for their true worth and would bring in a respectable income for her and the children. Yet, if Hal was to be believed, they were worthless trash.

Closing the lid of the trunk, Constance rose to her feet, picked up Everett's photograph and hurled it to the floor. Seven years' bad luck, she thought, staring at the shattered glass. But then, there had been little in her life but bad luck ever since she met and married the man.

During the second week of her stay in Chicago, Amadine continued to buy her newspaper outside Marshall Field's every morning – from Ben, as she had learned the boy was called – and to breakfast at Henrici's, even though Pierce Radcliffe did not join her. If she were honest, she might admit that the hope of seeing him again was the reason she still came to the bakery and lingered over her coffee, but Amadine was not honest about it. She was too deeply mortified by the events in the elevator to examine her feelings for Pierce in any way whatsoever. When, on Thursday and after an absence of eight days, he did sit down beside her, Amadine achieved masterly control over her emotions.

'I thought you had gone to New York,' she said without enthusiasm, and without lowering the newspaper.

'No, you hoped I had gone to hell.'

'You went there a long time ago, and I can only assume that Satan allows you some sort of dispensation to come back here and annoy people.'

'As the only person I annoy is you, you must have done something really dreadful to warrant my release from hell-fire and damnation.'

Amadine laid down the newspaper and shot him a sharp, suspicious glance, recalling that 'hellfire and damnation' had been the first, and highly unfortunate, words she had spoken to him, in the Waldorf-Astoria roof garden in New York. It seemed years ago. 'On the contrary,' she said sweetly, 'if you are the devil's little helper, I must have done something really good and virtuous to warrant your attention.'

Pierce gave a mocking sigh. 'I should know better than to exchange religious epithets with a rector's daughter. But I wouldn't mind pursuing the subject of your virtue – that could lead us into some interesting territory.'

'Not over breakfast.'

'But first thing in the morning is one of the best times . . . or so I've been told.'

Hastily Amadine hid her blush behind the newspaper, and said in a faintly muffled voice, 'Go away.'

'I'm sorry to have neglected you, but I've been busy.'

'You don't owe me an apology, or an explanation.'

'You didn't miss me, then?'

'There are two ways of missing people,' said Amadine with asperity, 'and I do not intend to prolong this conversation by spelling out which of them applies to you.'

Pierce watched as she started gathering her things together, and doing mysterious things with gloves and dollar bills.

'I saw *Trelawny* last night,' he remarked, 'and liked the new frocks. Much more becoming than the originals, particularly the one you wear in the second act, which displayed your charms to great advantage.'

He had a way of saying things, and of flicking a lazy glance over her body while he said them, that made Amadine feel he could see straight through her clothes to the naked flesh beneath. She felt that even in the pitch darkness of the elevator he had been able to see . . . Growing hot under the collar in more ways than one, Amadine headed for the door, and flinched.

'Is winter always this cold in Chicago?' she gasped, leaning into the wind as the icy blast knifed into her cheek.

'Yes, but don't let it put you off the place.'

'There's only one thing likely to put me off this, or any other, place,' she retorted, with a grimace in his direction.

He grinned and tried to guide her down State Street, but she insisted on crossing the road at her usual corner. Outside Marshall Field's Ben was looking out for her, his cheeky grin turning to a glower when he saw Pierce.

'My other newspaper, please,' Amadine said, 'and there's a tip for you, if you can guess which hand is holding it.'

She held out both gloved hands and, after a moment's consideration, Ben chose the left.

'Here you are,' Amadine sighed, pretending huge disappointment and resignation as she took off the glove and gave him the dollar bill concealed within it. 'You'll beggar me yet. We'll be changing places, and I'll be selling the newspapers.'

Ben smiled happily, but then his face clouded. 'When are you leaving, miss?'

'Sunday, but I'll be back again very soon.'

Pierce shook his head as they walked on. 'Another

admirer! I knew I had competition from Haldane-Smith, but I didn't realise how wide you had cast your net. I can see that I'll have to look to my laurels.'

'Hal looks wonderful in a laurel wreath, but I don't think it's quite your style. It needs the toga.'

'I rather fancy a toga, and America has enough classical buildings to form a suitable backdrop. It's the influence of ancient democracies on our architecture . . .' Suddenly he pushed her into the shelter of a shop doorway. 'Right hand, please,' he demanded.

Reluctantly Amadine held out her right hand and Pierce pulled off the glove to reveal another dollar bill.

'Now that is the sort of behaviour that will get you noticed by the devil,' he remarked, 'not to mention the men in white coats at the lunatic asylum.'

'Ben is my friend.'

'I'll bet he's your friend, if you give him that kind of money.'

'You employ boys at your bicycle factory, don't you?'

'Yes, but . . .' He glanced at her eager expression. 'Oh no, Amadine, definitely *no*. I am not giving a job to every waif and stray who appeals to your sympathetic heart.'

'But Ben deserves better than standing, and sleeping, on draughty street corners every day and every night. He is bright and intelligent . . .'

'. . . and a skilled manipulator of female sensibilities,' Pierce said drily. 'In addition, he is probably a thieving rascal.'

'You don't know that. You don't know anything about him, and I really do wish that you would give him a chance!'

'If you take Ben off the streets tonight, there will be another boy in his place tomorrow.'

'Just because you cannot help them all doesn't mean that you shouldn't help one.'

Pierce groaned, partly at her perseverance and partly at his inability to win an argument with her. 'The answer is still no,' he said firmly.

'Well, at least buy your newspaper from Ben every day. Although, knowing you, you'll probably go out of your way to avoid buying it from him out of sheer cussedness.' And Amadine, who was dreading leaving the boy, stamped the snow off her boots on the doormat of the Auditorium Hotel as if she was wiping Pierce off her feet and out of her system at the same time.

Next morning the snow was so heavy that she was tempted to breakfast at the hotel, and it was only the thought of Ben on his arctic street corner that drove her out. Battling up Michigan Avenue in the blizzard, she thought Pierce was right: she must be mad. However, she wasn't the only one because the sidewalks were thronged with heavily shrouded figures, and the streets – busy with traffic – were being swept, the snow piled in high banks at the side of the road.

She bought her newspaper but, with the snow so heavy and another customer waiting to be served, did not linger. Telling Ben that she would talk to him after breakfast, she stood on the edge of the sidewalk and waited to cross the road.

The blizzard obscured her vision and she started forward, only to see the approaching streetcar at the last moment and step back again. But then she was aware of pressure on her back and she was staggering forward into the path of the car, into the whiteness of the snow and then the blackness of oblivion.

Chapter Twenty-One

Outside the blizzard was raging but, inside, a warm glow permeated the Auditorium Theatre. Not only was the company basking in its Chicago success, but rehearsals for *Much Ado*, held in the late mornings and on non-matinée afternoons, were proving pure joy.

Hal's familiarity with the play, after his years at the Lyceum, had enabled him to put it into production with the minimum of delay. While admiring Henry Irving's interpretation of the role of Benedick, he had not always agreed with the great man's adaptation of the original text and had therefore enjoyed shaping the play to his own preferences and present circumstances. In particular, he had gone out of his way to be fair to Constance. While ensuring that the mockery and humour of Amadine's Beatrice and the romantic gallantry and caustic wit of Benedick occupied centre stage, Hal never lost sight of Shakespeare's central theme of the defamation of Hero. He had seen versions in which Hero's part was so mangled that the poor girl was left looking vacuous and silly. Hal was determined that this should not happen to Constance, and sought cuts elsewhere.

He was concentrating on only three complete sets – the interior of Leonato's house, the garden and the church – with other scenes played at the front using simple, painted

cloths. The end result would not be as sumptuous as Hal
would have wished – the church scene, for instance, was
unlikely to approach Irving's miracle of illusion – but a
team of Chicago scene-painters had embarked on a series of
perspectives that should be ready when the company
returned to the city at the end of February.

This morning Claudio and Don Pedro were among the
actors called for the rehearsal. Telling them to go through
the scene at Hero's tomb, Hal settled in for the morning's
work with a sense of real enjoyment. Claudio began:

> 'Done to death by slanderous tongues
> Was the Hero that here lies;
> Death, in guerdon of her wrongs,
> Gives her fame which never dies.'

Death gives her fame, Hal heard dreamily, and for some
reason his thoughts slipped to Amadine. He still shuddered
at the memory of the fire in Baltimore, and how near he
had come to losing her. If she had died . . . Well, death
would have given her fame, no doubt about it. She would
have become a legend, not merely the popular performer
she already was.

Hal wrenched his mind back to the present, and ordered
the two actors to start the scene again. Where was Amadine
anyway? It was unlike her to be late for rehearsal. She had
not been seen since she went out for breakfast, Gwen
informed him, in reply to his enquiry. Believing her to be
with Pierce Radcliffe, Hal allowed his irritation to show.
Why couldn't Amadine have breakfast in bed like any other
self-respecting leading lady? Preferably his bed. But no,
she had to go traipsing through the streets and the snow
like . . . like . . . Unable to find an analogy, Hal continued
with the rehearsal, skipping Beatrice's lines, but the effect
was so unsatisfactory that he changed his schedule and
switched his attention to a scene between Hero and Ursula.

The passage, in which Hero pretended to speak ill of Beatrice, was one that Constance played well – for obvious reasons, Hal thought wryly. In the rest of the play she was adequate, but no better than many others. Indeed, he rather liked young Blanche, and wouldn't mind trying her out in a few of Constance's roles. Not only did the girl bring a sparkle of personality to the stage, but she managed to smile off it, which made a pleasant change from Connie's downcast countenance.

When they broke for lunch, Amadine had still not appeared. Ida was running back and forth between the hotel and the stage area, her expression increasingly worried and, surfacing from the morning's work, others began to share her anxiety.

'Perhaps we ought to ask Radcliffe if he knows where she is,' Theo said tentatively, remembering that he had kept the man's card.

'Certainly not,' Hal snapped. 'There isn't the slightest need to involve him. Come on, Theo, you're an American – tell me where to start looking.'

'This is my first visit to Chicago,' Theo protested. 'You probably know the place better than I do!'

'Then we need Jay to . . .' Hal paused. Jay had said something about attending to a bit of business, and he had been lost from sight for several days. 'Oh, there you are,' he said with relief as, at that moment, Jay walked into the theatre.

Jay had made a cross-country dash to Philadelphia. He regretted leaving the warmth and comfort of the Auditorium for a seat in a day car, but go to Philly he must, and he wasn't shelling out for a sleeper when the cost came out of his own pocket.

The Gayety Theatre had given off a satisfying hum of activity. The scenery painters were producing a series of mighty pretty pictures of modern Philadelphia as backdrops for the opening scenes; a piano player was belting out a catchy little number; and two chorus girls were being drilled by the dance director. The place was freezing and Jay imagined that the girls were glad to keep on the move, but he sat in the stalls wrapped in a rosy glow. He was glad he had come; out there in the sticks this seemed like fantasy-land, but being here brought home that it was actually happening.

However, as soon as he saw his partner, the rosy glow cooled to a chill of concern. Bill had a wild-eyed look, his face haggard, his hair unkempt and his necktie awry. He looked more like a heavy gambler after a long night that ended on a losing streak than a theatrical entrepreneur.

'What happened to you?' Jay asked in alarm.

'It's what's *going* to happen to me,' Bill replied, slumping into a chair beside him. 'I'm starting to see gaol staring me in the face.'

'O ye of little faith!'

'You may mock, but it ain't you who's trying to keep the cheques circulating.'

'You've done this sort of thing before.'

'Not on this scale. Jay, last week I was so close to the wire that I had to take a late train up-country, carrying a wad of cash for deposit when the bank opened the next morning. It was too close for comfort, I'm telling you.'

'But it's early days yet.' Jay looked at his friend, perplexed and worried.

'Ten weeks,' Bill said wearily. 'We're aiming to open April 4.'

'Then I don't understand why expenses are out of control.' Jay indicated the group on the stage. 'How many people are we paying?'

'That's why I had to speak to you. We've settled with the writer and the musician until we open, but everything else is ongoing.' Bill began ticking items off on his fingers. 'The theatre rent has to be met, and we can't leave off the heat indefinitely. We're paying them,' and he indicated the people on the stage, 'but they're complaining that they can't manage for much longer without a full chorus line – *and* we'll need boys as well as girls. The principals will arrive at the beginning of March, and the orchestra a little later.'

Jay conceded that he had chosen an expensive way of launching his career as a producer, but 'Might as well be hung for a sheep as a lamb,' he murmured philosophically, if illogically.

'We're paying for the scenery, and the artists' wages,' Bill continued, having progressed to his second set of four fingers and thumb, 'and I had to say that they could start on costume design and props. I'm delaying payment of outstanding accounts for as long as possible but . . . It's a nightmare, Jay, a bloody nightmare, and it's only just begun!'

'All you have to do is spread our business about a bit,' Jay said soothingly. 'If an account is outstanding, shop somewhere else until you can pay it. And distribute the cheque-cashing as widely as you can, otherwise it will become obvious what we are doing.'

'What do you mean, *will* . . .? It's as plain as daylight to the whole of Philadelphia now.'

'If that's so, it could be seriously awkward.'

'When the manager of the Bellevue cashed a cheque the other day, he remarked, "I suppose this must be the cheque that makes good the last one".'

Jay groaned.

'It's not people like him I'm worried about,' Bill went on, 'but the bank. People here will carry us along, if only because they'll have as much to lose as us, but the bank'll have our guts for garters without a qualm.' He glanced at his watch. 'As you're here, you may as well spend some of the money. I'm due at Marks to choose materials for costumes.'

Despite his concerns over finance and Bill's state of

mind, Jay enjoyed browsing in Marks Brothers store among the colourful and luxurious bales of fabric. It was fun selecting the shades of colour, to match the list given to Bill by the designer, and impossible to resist the temptation to order the very best quality. Hang it all, only the best would do for *The Philadelphia Girl*! In fact it was old man Marks himself who applied a brake to their enthusiasm, gently pointing out on several occasions that the cheaper stuff would look just as good on the stage, and that in the theatre illusion is everything.

Before they left the store, Bill handed over a cheque covering purchases made on a previous visit. Marks beckoned them into his private office, and whispered, 'Take an old-timer's advice, my boys, and get yourselves a bank in Texas or Oregon or all points west. Give you more time, and more room for manoeuvre, if you get my drift.'

Jay and Bill smiled weakly and, over lunch, agreed that the whole of Philadelphia knew what they were doing, but that they were in too deep to back out now.

At the Gayety, Jay's yo-yo-like spirits rose again. The chorus girls were still battling away and Jay's imagination took wing, filling the stage with their beautiful friends and relatives, executing the complicated steps of this snappy little routine wearing costumes in the gorgeous materials he had just chosen. This show was going to work, it was going to 'go' – it really deserved to 'go' – and if anyone knew a winner when he saw one, it was Jay Johnson, yes, sir! And those girls were charming, very charming indeed. When *The Philadelphia Girl* was launched on an unsuspecting world, he might give himself a bit of a holiday, and give himself a bit of a treat at the same time . . .

Only on the journey back to Chicago, sitting up in the day car trying to sleep, did he start to worry again. That the kites could be kept flying he did not doubt – it had been done before, for larger sums and in a more hostile environment than this – but it was looking more and more as if Bill was not the right man for the job.

'Keep me posted on how things are going,' he had instructed his partner, 'and wire me in an emergency.'

The flat, frozen landscape of the Midwest flashed by the train window, but Jay did not see it. He was visualising a Western Union telegraph form, bearing news of doom and disaster, and he knew that, from now on, the sight of any telegram would fill him with dread.

Tracing Amadine was just the job to take his mind off his own troubles and, disdaining Hal's suggestion that the police should be contacted, Jay hurried off to his best source of information – the newspaper offices. In the meantime Frank had ascertained that one of the front-of-house staff had been accosted by a ragamuffin boy earlier in the day.

'The lad was spinning some yarn about Amadine having had an accident,' Frank reported to Hal.

'And our man did nothing about it?'

'Oh, he did something,' Frank said grimly. 'He sent the boy packing, with a flea in his ear, on the grounds that such an urchin could not possibly know of Miss Sinclair's existence, let alone her current whereabouts.'

Hal, already grey-faced with worry, went a shade paler. 'Of course he could be right, but I'm sufficiently desperate to start searching the hospitals. Where do you think we should start – Cook County?'

Frank nodded. 'I'll call a cab.'

'Do so, but I want you to stay here and stand by to change tonight's bill. Even if we find Amadine alive and well, she might not be able to play.'

It was still snowing heavily when Hal, in his long, black overcoat with astrakhan collar and pulling his hat low over his eyes, emerged into the street. He was climbing into the cab when Jay dashed up and jumped in beside him. He had struck pay dirt at his first port of call. Confirming that they should drive to Cook County Hospital, he told Hal about an accident report concerning an unknown woman run over by a streetcar that morning.

'But if it was Amadine, someone would have recognised her,' Hal objected.

Jay gestured at the swirling snow. 'In this weather? And the corner where the accident happened is on Amadine's regular route to Henrici's.'

Leaning back in the cab, Hal closed his eyes at the horror of it all and so, even if the sight had held any significance for him, he did not see the lonely little figure of a 14-year-old boy battling through the blizzard along the road to the hospital.

When he saw her, lying in bed in a general ward at Cook County, Hal was sure Amadine was dead. She was so white – except for a livid bruise on her forehead – and so still, that it seemed impossible she could ever walk or talk again. But she was alive. Hal's legs wobbled and he sat down suddenly. Made of strong stuff was our Amadine, he thought confusedly; it must be all that Yorkshire grit. He tried to concentrate on what the doctor was saying.

Amadine was unconscious, and lucky to be alive. The car had caught her a glancing blow on the head and knocked her into the snowbank at the side of the road, the height and depth of which had undoubtedly saved her from more serious injury.

'There do not seem to be any broken bones,' the doctor went on, 'but we cannot assess the extent of the head injury until she wakes up. We must hope that she suffers nothing worse than a bad headache.'

They must hope that there was no brain damage, Hal interpreted. He made a conscious effort to pull himself together, and to take charge of the situation.

'Go back to the theatre,' he instructed Jay, 'and give

Frank the news. Warn Constance that she will be playing Juliet this evening, and tell Ida to come here with night-clothes and anything else Amadine might need when she wakes up.'

If she wakes up . . .

At the theatre the news was received with quiet despair and prayer in some quarters, and an excited babble in others. Theo fell into the first category but, when the initial shock was over, he fumbled in his pocket for Pierce Radcliffe's card. Hal would not like this, but the man must be told. Amadine would want him to know.

Death gives her fame, Hal was thinking again, and it seemed like a premonition.

The medical staff had refused to move Amadine from the ward until she regained consciousness, but had placed screens around her bed to afford some privacy. Sitting beside her, holding her limp hand in his, Hal was reminded vividly of their vigil at Laurie's bedside in Boston, and found himself wondering, with stricken heart, who would be next. There was some reassurance in the steadiness of Amadine's pulse, but his patience was not rewarded with any other movement, not even the flutter of an eyelash.

When Ida arrived, she sat down on the other side of the bed. Of course she was worried sick about Miss Amadine, but her mind was leaping ahead. It was already late on Friday afternoon, and the company was due to leave Chicago on Sunday. Looking at Miss Amadine, it was as plain as the nose on your face that – even if she woke up in the next five minutes, which didn't seem likely – she wasn't going to be on no train thirty-six hours from now. She'd have to be left behind, like Mr Laurie had been left in Boston, and that meant only one thing: Ida would be expected to stay with her. But I can't, thought Ida in a panic, not now that George is settled. There's all those pretty actresses in the company; if I'm not there to fight my corner, I'll lose him.

Hal pulled out his pocket watch, and Ida guessed that he was calculating how much longer he could stay.

'Mrs Grey asked me to do her hair this evening, and dress her,' Ida said hesitantly.

'Your place is here with Miss Amadine,' Hal said curtly.

'Yes, sir.' There it was then. No doubt about it: she'd be waving George goodbye on Sunday.

Hal's personal feelings for Amadine were interwoven with his concern for the company and the tour as a whole. As it was impossible to calculate how many days or weeks might elapse before Amadine could work again, all he could do was make short-term plans. Connie would do Juliet – oh God, there were times when he thought he'd go mad if he had to play Romeo with her one more time! Certainly he was not prepared to do so night after night, indefinitely. If Amadine could not perform, he'd use an understudy for the Pinero. It wouldn't be the same without Amadine, but what else could he do?

He looked at Ida's worried face. 'It's important that Amadine sees a familiar face when she wakes,' he explained, 'so that is why you must stay.'

'I'll be here,' said a deep voice behind him.

Radcliffe. Hal cursed silently, but stood up and shook hands.

'Doubtless you cannot disappoint your public,' Pierce said politely, 'so I'll sit with her tonight. I suggest that you come back in the morning.'

Hal could feel his hackles rising, but had to accept that he had no choice but to go to the theatre.

Pierce was looking at Ida, who was on her feet, hope blazing in her eyes and evidently eager to be off. He assessed the significance of the bag she was clutching.

'You can leave that with me if you have to go to the theatre, Ida.'

'But it's her nightclothes . . .'

'I think that, should Amadine wake and need anything, calling a nurse is well within my capabilities. Look,' he added more kindly, glancing at Hal, 'I'll send a message to the Auditorium if there are any developments.'

At that Hal and Ida left, and Pierce sat down in the chair Hal had vacated. He had put on a cool front with Haldane-Smith, but it was very far from what he was actually feeling. He had hurried here the moment he heard about the accident, and had to pour on every ounce of charm with the hospital staff in order to be allowed in. Now, sitting here alone with her, the seriousness of the situation was beginning to sink in. He knew very little about brain injuries, and had no idea whether or not she could hear him, but, in a low voice, he began to talk.

'Amadine Sinclair, you are the most stubborn, stupid woman I have ever met! What on earth did you think you were doing, blundering about in a blinding blizzard, when you could have been tucked up warm and safe in your bed. There was not the slightest need to put a toe outside the door of the Auditorium Hotel but, oh no, you must go wandering off, and tempting fate as usual. Falling under streetcars, indeed – whatever next! Look at you! That bruise is a real beauty, and it'll be even more colourful tomorrow. You are extremely lucky that the damage isn't any worse. Your head could have been . . .'

His voice tailed off, and he swallowed hard as he visualised the smashed, broken body that might have been left lying in the snow on State Street.

'So, once the swelling goes down, your beauty will be restored in all its glory. And it is glorious, isn't it . . .' Pierce leaned forward and stroked her cheek. 'I don't think I've ever told you just how beautiful you are, but then, you don't need to be told – you see it in the mirror, and in the eyes of everyone around you every day. On the *Campania* I tried to pretend that I was immune to it, but I'm not. No matter how hard I try, I can't forget you. I see your lovely face wherever I go, and whatever I do.'

His long fingers were smoothing away the tumbling dark hair from around her face, tracing the outline of her eyebrows and caressing the softness of her skin.

'I'll tell you what I wish would happen. I wish that you would make a miraculous recovery, but that there would be just one little, tiny thing wrong with you that would mean you had to give up the theatre. And then you could stay here with me. I'd like to show you Chicago in the summer. We could go to the beach, and sail on the lake. We could sail across to Mackinac Island and stay at the Grand Hotel – it has the longest front porch in the world . . .'

Amadine's eyelashes fluttered. For a fraction of a second, the gleam of green eyes flickered in Pierce's direction, but it was gone before he noticed. He was playing with Amadine's fingers and warming to his theme, launching into a long list of American attractions he wanted her to see.

'I suppose that I'd best not take you up into the mountains,' he murmured regretfully, 'because you'd only . . .'

'Oh, go on, force yourself.'

Her voice was very faint but Amadine's eyes were open, and she was watching him with just the suggestion of a smile.

'How long have you been awake?' Pierce demanded.

'Only a moment,' she lied. 'Where am I?'

'Hospital.'

'No, really? You amaze me,' she said sarcastically. 'Which hospital, idiot?'

'Cook County, Chicago. Do you remember anything about the accident?'

Amadine shook her head, and winced. 'Lord, but my head hurts. I remember Chicago, but not an accident. Where are you going?'

'To fetch the doctor.'

When Pierce saw her again, about an hour later, she was wearing her own nightgown, had been given medication for the headache and, at his instigation and expense, was occupying a private room. The doctors were not committing themselves, but they seemed pleased with her progress. The fact that she could not remember the accident did not seem to alarm them, but more would be known after tests were carried out in the morning.

'Lift me up so that I can see into the mirror,' Amadine pleaded.

'Just as I had decided that you are not a vain woman, you must prove me wrong,' he remarked, with a crooked smile, as he complied

'Vanity has nothing to do with it.' After she had satisfied herself that the facial damage was comparatively superficial, her eyes closed with pain and exhaustion. 'My looks are how I make my living. You don't seriously imagine that audiences come to marvel at my acting talent, do you? Believe me, I only wish they did.'

She drifted into sleep and, after a moment's hesitation, Pierce left the room. The cold hit hard as he walked out of the hospital, and he was turning up his coat collar when the small figure detached itself from the shadows.

'Hey, mister.'

In the darkness it took Pierce a few moments to register that the pinched little face looked faintly familiar, and then to place the boy out of his usual context.

'Ben, isn't it? What are you doing here?'

'Is she all right, mister?'

'How long have you been here?' It was two o'clock in the morning, for God's sake!

'Since this afternoon. They wouldn't let me in to see her.'

Remembering the hassle he had had to gain admittance to Amadine's bedside, Pierce could understand that it was highly unlikely this scruffy ragamuffin would be allowed anywhere near. But the cold was intense, and the child could have had nothing to eat. Pierce could feel his heart softening.

'I saw you go in, mister, so I waited.'

'Amadine is sleeping now, and it seems that she is not seriously hurt,' Pierce said kindly. 'We will know more later this morning, but I think she has been very lucky. By all accounts, it was a nasty fall.'

'She didn't fall. She was pushed.'

Pierce's face tautened and, in the brightness reflected off the snow by the hospital lights, he examined Ben's open, earnest countenance. He placed an arm around the boy's shoulders.

'You'd better come with me,' he said.

Chapter Twenty-Two

The doctors were satisfied that Amadine had suffered nothing more than concussion, and that there would be no lasting damage. However, to be on the safe side, they wished to keep her under observation at the hospital for several days, this to be followed by a period of rest and recuperation. She looked more ill than she had the previous day. Her face was whiter, the bruising and swelling more pronounced, a patch of dark hair had been shaved around the wound at her temple, and her finely boned features were drawn with pain. She listened to what Hal and Pierce had to say, but with a listlessness that was disconcerting.

'You will need somewhere to stay while you convalesce,' Pierce said eventually. 'My family has a house in Prairie Avenue, which I will be glad to place at your disposal.'

At this Amadine's eyebrows rose, but her surprise was nothing compared to the *frisson* this announcement engendered in Hal and Ida.

'I do not live there myself,' Pierce said, rather irritably. 'The house has not been occupied since my father died, but I can have it made ready in a day or so.'

'Wouldn't an hotel be easier?' Hal enquired coldly. He would be grateful to leave Amadine in Chicago in a safe pair of hands, but wished heartily that those hands were not Radcliffe's.

'Possibly, but surely it would be less pleasant?' Pierce rejoined. 'And there may be a nurse to accommodate, as well as Ida.'

'Amadine?' Hal asked, hoping to appeal to her better nature.

The headache had subsided to a continuous throbbing, but she was finding it impossible to think clearly. However, through the fog, she groped for the practical aspects of the problem. Suites at the Auditorium, or any other hotel, were expensive, and her absence from the tour would be reflected in the box-office takings.

'Thank you, Mr Radcliffe,' she said formally. 'I would like to stay at your father's house, although I will not be filling it with as many helpers as you imagine.'

'Look, if they say you need a nurse, then a nurse you . . .'

'Ida will not be staying in Chicago.'

The girl, who had been sitting in the corner of the room, looked up in astonishment, the abject misery on her face transfigured into a blaze of hope.

'I feel that the least I can do is lend you to Constance,' Amadine told her. 'It will make things much easier for everyone at the theatre, and that is much more important than providing me with clean nightgowns.'

'But how will you manage?' Ida cried.

'I can do my own hair – I'm not completely helpless! And I dare say that the staff at Mr Radcliffe's house will help with the laundry. Now, go back to the hotel and . . .'

She began instructing Ida to send her theatre clothes on the train with the other costumes and props, but to pack her personal wardrobe separately and leave it at the hotel for collection.

'I must make a few arrangements about the house, but I'll be back later,' Pierce said, after Ida had gone. 'I have a surprise for you.'

'Pierce, there's nothing I need.'

'Oh, he'll think of something,' muttered Hal.

'This isn't a something, it's a someone,' Pierce said enigmatically.

'Can you cope with a business problem?' Hal asked tentatively.

'The repertoire,' Amadine said slowly. 'Again.'

'How would you feel about us doing the Pinero without you?'

'I feel that you should do anything that will boost the box office. But,' and Amadine frowned slightly, 'I'm not sure that I see Constance as Paula Tanqueray or Rose Trelawny.'

'Not Constance,' Hal said quickly. 'I was thinking of trying Blanche in your roles.'

Amadine's eyes widened, and for several minutes she considered the matter in silence. 'Good thinking,' she said at last. 'Yes, give it a go.' She paused again, and then added, 'You might find that Constance is more difficult to convince than I am.'

He had not thought of that. Oh *God* . . .

'There is one sure-fire way of appeasing her,' Amadine went on. 'Offer her the use of my stateroom while I'm away.'

'Would that do the trick? Really? But suppose she doesn't want to move out when you come back!'

Amadine found the energy for a slight shrug. 'I'll sleep in her room. Honestly, it wouldn't bother me.'

'It would bother me – a lot! Your stateroom is right next to mine, and I'm fussy about who I sleep with.'

Amadine laughed. 'I'm not suggesting that you take the cohabitation that far. Not unless you want to, of course.'

'You know what, and who, I want.'

'The answer is no, Hal.'

It came so suddenly, and was voiced so quietly, that for a moment his mind went blank. Then the import of those four words sank in and he began an immediate, and instinctive, counter-attack.

'I know that I said you ought to think about my proposal, and give me an answer later on, but not now! You are in no fit state to reflect seriously on such an important matter. We'll talk about this again when . . .'

'No, I don't want to talk about it again after today. I cannot marry you, Hal. I am very fond of you, but I do not love you. And no,' and she laid a finger softly against his lips, 'don't say that I might learn to love you, because I won't.'

There was this enormous emptiness inside him, as if the bottom had dropped out of his world and taken everything else with it.

'I do realise that it's all my fault,' Amadine went on apologetically. 'Quite clearly the obvious thing to do – the sensible thing to do – was for us to have an affair and enjoy working together, even if we didn't get married. I'm afraid that doing the obvious and sensible thing isn't my strong point.'

'Is it Radcliffe?' he asked harshly.

She considered the question. 'I'm not sure,' she admitted eventually. 'I think that he may be a factor, but I can assure you that, even if he didn't exist, I still would not marry you. Whether – if I had not met him – I would have gone to bed with you, I don't know.'

That made no sense to Hal, but he could not be bothered with the finer nuances of the situation. He was still convinced that Amadine was suffering from the effects of the accident, and that she ought not to be making such crucial decisions.

'I won't give up hope,' he insisted, 'and I won't take no for an answer. Not here. Not now. Not while you are in a hospital bed, only twenty-four hours after a serious accident.'

'Get on with your life, Hal, and don't waste any more time and effort on me. I'm not worth it.'

'Not worth it! Good Lord, you really are concussed!'

'Perhaps that streetcar merely knocked some sense into me. You don't know me, Hal. You don't know anything about me. If you did, you'd probably run a mile . . . a thousand miles . . .' With an immense effort, Amadine raised herself in the bed and leaned across to kiss him lightly on the mouth. 'Sorry I'm making such a mess of your tour. I'll get better and get back to work as quickly as I can. But I don't intend to make the same mess of your private life as I have made of my own.'

Even though it was Saturday, Pierce found his father's lawyer at the office downtown. He approached the meeting with a rueful sense of putting his pride in his pocket and eating humble pie. All those fine sentiments about never taking anything from Samuel's estate, which he had voiced so often and so adamantly to this man, and to his son in New York, and yet now . . .

Rather stiffly, he explained that he needed the use of the Prairie Avenue house for a few weeks – not for himself, but for a friend – and would therefore be grateful if the house could be prepared to receive guests. Being too tactful to reveal any reaction to this unexpected turn of events, Howard Morton merely produced a set of keys and informed Pierce that a resident housekeeper had cared for the property since Samuel's death, and that she would make the necessary arrangements. Was the friend male or female, he enquired, young or old, and were there any special requirements?

Morton listened incredulously to Pierce's explanation. He and his wife had been to the opening night of *Tanqueray* and had adored Amadine Sinclair; and, of course, news of the accident was all over the papers. That lucky son of a bitch, he thought, looking at Pierce with new respect. But the irony of the son installing an actress in Sam's house was not lost on him, and it was this aspect of the matter that lingered in his mind after Pierce had gone. He did hope there was not some deep, devious element of revenge behind Pierce's philanthropy but, no, why should there be? And Morton decided that he preferred to stay with the positive aspects of this development: that using the house would be just the first step, and that it would lead to Pierce's acceptance of his rightful inheritance.

Driving down State Street after collecting his 'surprise', Pierce noticed that another boy was selling newspapers outside Marshall Field's. He did not comment, but read the situation perfectly and conceded that it was up to him to put matters right.

'Remember,' he instructed outside Amadine's door, 'not a word about what you saw yesterday, and not a word about our little arrangement.'

He opened the door and went in, pushing the boy in front of him so that Amadine saw Ben first. Giving a shriek of delight, she flung wide her arms to hug him, then smiled as the boy hung back. She shook hands with him gravely, and asked him to sit down.

'You can hug me,' Pierce said optimistically. 'I'm not easily embarrassed.' But Amadine continued to gaze at Ben and, with a mock sigh of disappointment, Pierce perched on the end of the bed.

'Ben, you look different,' Amadine declared. 'Perhaps it's because I have never seen you without a hat before.'

'No, it's because he's had a bath,' Pierce informed her.

'At his house,' Ben said, jerking his head in Pierce's direction, 'and the servant there found these clothes for me while mine are being washed.'

'You are keeping those clothes,' Pierce remarked. 'Your own disintegrated at the mere mention of water.'

'Would you mind starting at the beginning?' Amadine begged, feeling concussed all over again by this tangled tale of domesticity.

She was given an edited account of Ben's movements after he witnessed the accident: how he went to the Auditorium but was turned away, then made his way to the hospital where he waited for Pierce, who took him home and gave him a meal and a bed for the night.

'You did all that for me?' Amadine's eyes misted with tears as she gazed at the boy, and the glance she gave Pierce indicated that he wasn't doing badly either.

'Unfortunately I think that this young man's impulsive nature may be his downfall,' Pierce announced. 'Tell me, Ben, what did you do with your bundle of newspapers after the accident?'

'Dumped them on the sidewalk, so that I could run to the theatre.'

'And today there is another boy on your patch.'

'You noticed.' Ben grimaced, but then shrugged his shoulders. 'Can't be helped,' he said bravely.

'You've lost your job? Because of me?' Horrified, Amadine sat up in bed.

'Calm down,' Pierce soothed. 'Everything is under control. Do you like bicycles, Ben? Hm, I thought you might, most boys do. So, would you like to come and work for me, making bicycles at my factory? Hey . . .'

A tornado in ivory silk, with raven hair and warm, scented flesh, launched itself across the bed and wrapped her arms around him.

'You deserve that hug,' Amadine whispered against his ear.

Pierce closed his eyes and buried his face in her hair so that Ben should not see his expression. The sensation of her slender body against his, the feel and the scent of her soft skin, left him dizzy with desire. He wanted to hold her for ever, but knew that only seconds were vouchsafed to him.

'I am beginning to see that you are one of those women who always get their own way,' he remarked as Amadine subsided back into bed. 'From the start you decided that

Ben ought to work for me, but I do think that your methods are a trifle extreme – there was no need to throw yourself under a streetcar in order to make your point!'

Ben was gazing at Pierce with nearly as much hero-worship as he usually reserved for Amadine. Bicycles had come as a complete surprise. 'When do I start?' he asked eagerly.

'In a week or two. In the meantime, I suggest that you stay at Prairie Avenue with Amadine.'

Amadine agreed emphatically, and Pierce and Ben exchanged a conspiratorial look. That move had been arranged in advance. Pierce wanted Ben to keep an eye on her, and Ben was enchanted both by the responsibility and by the idea of being a spy.

Situated two miles to the south of the downtown area, Prairie Avenue – or at least the six blocks from 16th to 22nd Streets – was Chicago's equivalent of Fifth Avenue in New York. Here were the opulent mansions of the very rich, with spacious gardens and leafy elms, the wealthy world of closed carriages and shining horses, of exclusive clubs and smart parties, of private schools, reserved church pews and boxes at the Auditorium. Known as the Prairie Avenue set, the residents included the Pullmans, Marshall Field, Philip Armour, John Glessner, William Kimball and John Doane.

It utterly astonished Amadine that they had also included Pierce Radcliffe's father.

Staring at the immense Second Empire-style château, she was certain that this must be the wrong address. When she first met Pierce, she had classed him as a wealthy man, only to revise this opinion when she learned of his need for financial backing, and since then she had not given the matter much thought. Pierce was not here to be interrogated – with Amadine's reputation in mind, they had decided that he should not be seen installing her in the house – but Ben appeared in the doorway, and so Amadine slowly made her way up the granite steps to the heavy oak door of the four-storey red-brick and sandstone mansion.

The entrance hall set the style, and established the mood of the house. Modelled in finest mahogany, its plinths and deep lintels, carved columns and capitals, and high pan-elled ceiling reflected Samuel's great love of wood, and were a testimony to his ability to find and employ the very best German and Czech cabinetmakers. A shaft of colour streamed from a stained-glass window, highlighting the beauty of the wood and enhancing the glowing shades of the Oriental carpets, illuminating what might otherwise have been a dark and overpowering vestibule. On the left of this hall was the white-and-gold drawing room, decorated like a seventeenth-century French salon, and behind it the library. To the right were a reception room, the dining room, and behind them a glassed-in conservatory.

After ascending the graceful wooden staircase, Amadine was ushered into a vast, oak-panelled room, boasting a huge English four-poster bed, and with a fire blazing in the hearth. She kept to this room for three or four days, under the watchful eye of a nurse, and, when she did venture downstairs on a regular basis, soon established the library as her favourite place. It was of more manageable proportions than the main reception rooms in the house and it was here that Pierce, who visited in the early evenings, would find her sitting with Ben.

Samuel Radcliffe's books were in pristine condition, the number of volumes with uncut pages indicating that he had not been much of a reader. The shelves of books seemed to have been as much for decoration and show as were the Old Masters on the walls. Or, Pierce wondered, had the books been intended for Catherine, Samuel's more educated wife, the daughter of the village schoolmaster? And it gave him a strange sensation to watch and listen as the rector's daugh-ter helped Ben with his reading, correcting him gently as he stumbled through a passage of Dickens.

By the second week of Amadine's stay, the nurse had been dismissed, Ben's entertainment and education had been extended to card games, and Pierce stayed for dinner.

'Hal and the others are in St Paul and Minneapolis this week,' Amadine said after Ben had gone reluctantly to bed.

Pierce detected a wistful note in her voice. 'You need another week's convalescence,' he warned, 'preferably more.'

Amadine was torn between her enjoyment of his company and her duty to the tour. If only she could have combined the two . . . If only she could have felt about Hal as she felt about Pierce . . . 'I do enjoy my work, you know. I don't want to give it up.'

'Tell me again how you came to be an actress.'

She glanced at him suspiciously, wondering if he was trying to catch her out. 'I was alone in London and needed to earn a living. I had nothing to trade but my looks.'

'I had not thought of beauty as a commodity.'

'It is an asset from which one extracts as much advantage as one can, while it lasts. For instance,' she went on in a lighter tone, 'I doubt if I would be sitting here with you now if you didn't find me moderately pleasant to look at! But there is another side to beauty: it is all anyone sees. No one looks any further, or deeper, than the surface. And it doesn't last.'

Pierce laughed. 'You will still be gorgeous at ninety,' he assured her.

'No, I'll be old and, if I'm not a good enough actress, no one will pay to see me after I'm forty. And if I'm not careful, I'll end up like Gwen.'

'What about Gwen?' he asked sharply.

'I don't know the details but, reading between the lines, she sacrificed her youth to a man who let her down and she missed her best chances on the stage. Now she must take what parts she can find, while she struggles to maintain her invalid mother. She is looking old age in the face, and she doesn't even have a home of her own.'

An invalid mother, and no home of her own. For Pierce the pieces of Gwen's jigsaw shifted into place, and the picture it made was not pretty. His own attitude seemed even less attractive, and he made an abrupt and early departure for his own home.

The next day Amadine felt well enough to go out, and decided that she ought to show her appreciation of Pierce's hospitality.

'We'll buy him a present,' she announced, 'although he probably won't thank us for it.'

'You can always say that it's a belated birthday present,' suggested the housekeeper, informing her that Pierce's birthday had been a fortnight ago – the day before the accident, in fact.

'Then we will have a special dinner as well.' Amadine eyed Ben sternly. 'The dinner will be for two, but you can have a glass of champagne if you behave yourself.'

'I always behave myself,' he said indignantly. 'What shall we buy him?'

'Nothing too expensive, because I am a bit short of ready cash.'

It took all morning but eventually, at Spaulding's, a jewellery and artwares establishment at the corner of Jackson and State, she found a miniature automobile in solid silver. According to the shop assistant, the model represented a Duryea car that had won America's first automobile race, held in Chicago on 27 November 1895, and Amadine knew that she absolutely had to buy it, even though it cost more than she could really afford.

She was resting during the afternoon, planning what to wear for that special dinner, when the neighbour came to call. Amadine had found Chicago society to be warm-hearted, generous and unstuffy, but there was always the exception to the rule. This woman had come to stare, to poke her inquisitive nose into Amadine's affairs, and to show that not everyone in the city considered an actress to be respectable company.

'No one has been inside this house for years,' the visitor remarked, 'but at one time Samuel Radcliffe used to entertain frequently, even though neither his wife nor his mistress was in residence.'

'He had a mistress?' a startled Amadine enquired.

'An actress.' A pair of bright eyes fixed on Amadine meaningfully. 'At least Samuel had sufficient sense of what is right and proper not to install her here.'

Meaning that Pierce *had* installed his actress lover here. Amadine poured another cup of tea, and said nothing.

'There was a family quarrel,' the woman went on, disappointed at Amadine's lack of reaction, 'over the actress, presumably. It is believed that Pierce Radcliffe took his mother's part – well, he would, wouldn't he! My,' and she gave a little tinkling laugh, 'but Samuel must be spinning in his grave to think of Pierce bringing you here, as bold as brass.'

'You know,' and Amadine leaned forward with a confidential air, 'you can always tell a gentleman by the way he treats his mistress.'

'Really?' the visitor said faintly.

'And by the manner in which they treat their illegitimate children,' Amadine went on sunnily, pausing to ring the bell and ask the maid to summon Ben. 'Ah, there you are,' she beamed as Ben entered the room, and she kissed him enthusiastically on both well-scrubbed cheeks. 'Ben and I met for the first time a few weeks ago but now he is living with Mr Radcliffe, and we are all one big, happy family!'

As the visitor departed hastily, Amadine made a very rude gesture behind her back. 'You didn't see that,' she informed Ben, 'and I really must remember to set you a better example.'

However, as soon as Amadine was alone, her mood changed. Mr Radcliffe had some explaining to do when he arrived.

But he didn't arrive and when it became clear that supper would spoil, Amadine told the housekeeper to serve the meal. Even Ben was subdued and disappointed, and went off to bed after dinner without demur. Amadine did not know whether to be angry or worried. He could have had an accident – in fact, that was almost a probability given her own track record in recent months – or he could have found something better to do, or he could have had a hidden agenda of his own when he invited her to stay at this house. And now she had served her purpose.

The housekeeper went to bed, but Amadine sat on at the dining table, sipping champagne by candlelight. Then suddenly she heard a noise, and tensed. Was it the front door closing? She listened for footsteps and, yes, surely that was Pierce crossing the hall. Hurriedly she composed herself, adopting a relaxed pose and an expression of indifference.

Pierce paused in the doorway and looked at her. She was sitting in a high-backed chair at the end of the long refectory table, which had been cleared of food but on which the crystal and silverware gleamed in the glow of the candles. Framed by deep-red velvet curtains at the window, her black hair was combed back from her face in a severely simple style, softened only by a smooth wave at one side concealing the wound at her temple, emphasising the purity of her finely sculpted features. Her gown was of dark green velvet, cut low and square at the neck with short, cap sleeves, and emerald-and-diamond jewels sparkled against her creamy skin. He wanted to tell her how amazingly beautiful she looked, but could not find the words.

'I didn't expect to find you up, but thought I would call on the off chance,' he said casually, closing the door behind him and walking across the room.

'Don't flatter yourself that I waited up on your account,'

Amadine drawled. 'I merely thought it a pity to waste the wine.'

Pierce poured himself a glass of champagne, noted the second, unopened bottle in the cooler, and sat down. 'Your health.'

Amadine did not reply and, sensing a chill in the room despite the blazing fire, Pierce surveyed the elaborate table setting, and Amadine's gown and jewels, with fresh eyes. 'Was this evening a special occasion?' he hazarded.

'Depends what you mean by special. Only a surprise birthday party for you. Evidently it wasn't special enough for you to grace it with your presence.'

'I didn't say that I would come for dinner tonight, but,' he added hastily, 'I didn't say that I wouldn't and I really am very sorry. You should have told me.'

'Then it wouldn't have been a surprise.' Amadine leaned back in her chair and stared at him impassively. 'But there is not the slightest need to apologise. It isn't as if Ben and I are proper house guests who might deserve some simple courtesy from their host.'

Pierce grimaced. 'Ben was disappointed, too?'

'I hope you don't think that I was disappointed. It is merely rather irritating when one goes to a lot of trouble for nothing. The housekeeper was also somewhat vexed. Why are you looking at me like that?'

'Because you care that I missed the party.'

'Only for Ben's sake. It is immaterial to me what you do.'

'I had a business meeting tonight, and I didn't realise how late it was.'

'Time flies when you're having fun,' Amadine said sarcastically, 'and doubtless that meeting was much more fun than enduring an evening with an invalid and an orphan!'

Pierce looked at her. 'Some invalid!'

'I hope the meeting was a success. Perhaps you found the finance for your automobiles?'

In the light of the fresh revelations about Gwen, Pierce had spent the evening with Howard Morton. 'Yes,' he murmured, 'the money is there if I want it.'

'In that case, you'd better have this,' and she picked up the birthday gift and threw it at him.

Some instinctive response enabled him to catch the parcel, but he made no immediate move to open it. 'I'm not used to receiving birthday presents,' he said slowly. 'Only my mother remembers, and I'm usually in America at this time of year.'

'Your father must have remembered, or his housekeeper would not have known the date.'

Pierce undid the wrapping paper, and revealed the tiny silver car. 'It's perfect,' he exclaimed, 'and perhaps it's a sign that I should take the money!'

He placed the little automobile on the white tablecloth and for a moment they both looked at it, the silver gleaming in the candlelight.

'This theatrical tour of yours has been very good for me,' Pierce said thoughtfully.

'Oh, I *am* glad,' Amadine retorted sarcastically. 'It has been an unmitigated disaster for everyone else.'

'Try telling that to Ben.'

'Ben lost his job because of me and, after tonight, I think that his faith in his new benefactor might be a trifle dented. By the way, one of the neighbours believes that he is your illegitimate son.'

'What on earth gave them that idea?'

'I did.' And, for the first time that evening, Amadine smiled. 'She told me about your father's domestic arrangements, and indicated that he might be less than pleased that you had flouted propriety by bringing your actress-mistress here. I thought that a bastard, by another mistress, might add to the general delectation.'

Pierce stared at her, speechless, his face darkening.

'With that little piece of fiction, I achieved two things,'

Amadine continued. 'I rid myself of an extremely unpleasant visitor, and I inflicted – or so I hope – permanent damage on your reputation. How dare you use me for your little games!' She stood up and glared at him. 'Pretending to be so kind and considerate, and all the time you were sticking up two fingers at your father's memory, reminding everyone what an s-h-i-t he had been. And, to you, the icing on the cake is that the whole thing is a charade, because I am not your mistress, and . . .'

'That can be changed,' Pierce grated, gripping her by the shoulders, 'and not before time.'

Amadine struggled to free herself but his grip tightened, and she was reminded of the superior physical strength of a man. As that tormenting mouth came closer, he transferred one hand to her chin and held her head steady, while his lips applied a hard and bruising pressure to hers. She did not want to want him, not now when both of them were so angry, but as she sensed his strength of purpose and knew that this time he would not be denied, the treacherous tug of desire rose within her. With a gesture of compliance, she wound her arms around his neck and returned his kiss.

Dimly aware of his fingers fumbling with the buttons at the back of her dress and knowing the intricacies of these fastenings, she turned round so that he could see what he was doing. Even so, he cursed softly under his breath as his haste made the task more difficult, but then Amadine felt his hands on her bare skin as he peeled open the bodice of her gown and slipped it off her shoulders, so that it fell in a shimmering mass at her feet. Naked to the waist, she leaned back against him and closed her eyes as his hands cupped her breasts and supported their soft weight. Her breasts had been bared for him before, but only in the darkness of the elevator, and now she knew by the sharp intake of his breath, and the shudder that ran through him, that their beauty pleased him. She knew, too, that with the pads of his thumbs stroking her nipples to hard, rosy peaks, her own desire was as obvious as his own.

She opened her eyes and glanced at the profile next to hers. Pierce was a tall man but, in her high-heeled green satin shoes, Amadine was nearly six feet in height and easily able to reach his lips from this awkward angle. As he stabbed her mouth with a series of short, sweet kisses, she caught sight of their reflection in the mirror on the wall. It was a blurry vision, for her glazed eyes were only half open, but she watched, fascinated by the erotic image, as Pierce's hands smoothed down her body, to burrow beneath her underwear and across the flatness of her stomach. She waited in an agony of suspense for him to touch her between the legs, arching back against him with a smothered gasp as his hand crept closer and the heat of desire spread swiftly through her body.

Then the fingers of his right hand slid into the moist, slippery crevice and instinctively she started to swivel to face him, but his left hand clamped firmly on her stomach and held her tight against him, his breathing heavy and ragged as the fingers explored with devastating intimacy. But suddenly she stiffened, and he paused.

'I hope that you aren't going to ask me to stop,' he said harshly, and he moved his body against hers in a way that left no doubt about the size and hardness of his erection.

Amadine had remembered the image in the mirror, and what an unexpected visitor would see. 'The door . . . someone might come in . . .'

Without a word Pierce released her and walked swiftly to the door, shedding clothes as he went, and locked it. He looked exactly as she had expected, Amadine thought as, naked herself now, she watched him undress. His chest was broad and deep, the wiry black curls of hair tapering in a triangle to his trousers, the soft light lending an oily sheen to his skin. And she watched with dry throat and thumping heart as he tossed aside his trousers and underwear to reveal long, powerful legs and so much more besides. In a swift, fluid movement, he put out the candles and came towards her, pulling her by the hand to the hearthrug in front of the fire. Then their arms went round each other and they clung together, aware of nothing but the beauty of their bodies, of the softness of Amadine's breasts crushed against his chest, and of the hardness of his erection against her groin. Mouths welded together, they sank down on to the rug and, as Pierce's expert fingers began to work their magic again, Amadine was consumed with an aching fire of need that licked and curled within her with more intensity than that fuelling the logs in the hearth. She had never known such wanting, such desire – so overwhelming and all-consuming that it verged on the edge of pain. How marvellous it was, she thought as she looked at their bodies in the flickering firelight, that this was all the act needed – no scenery or costumes or props, but just the two of them, joining their flesh with exquisite pleasure.

Pierce's lips were trailing kisses down her neck as his hand slid across the silken skin of her inner thigh and crept between her legs again. This time his touch lingered on a place that sent a shaft of desire spiralling through her so fiercely that Amadine cried out and writhed against him, and when his kisses reached the dark triangle of hair, she knew that he intended his mouth to complete what his hand had started.

'No,' she said suddenly, and reached down urgently to grip him by the shoulders, because there was only one thing that could fill the emptiness, this craving void, that yawned within her. 'I want *you* . . .'

Pushing her back on the rug, Pierce positioned himself between her outspread legs, his face contorting as Amadine reached down to touch his arousal and guide him into her. He bent his head to kiss her as the tip of his flesh touched hers, and then he entered her . . .

*

Afterwards Amadine lay against his shoulder, and then raised herself on one elbow to look at his expressionless face in the flickering firelight.

I love him, she thought with dread in her heart. I love him, and that is why I did not hear that inner voice telling me that this lovemaking was wrong; indeed why I did not think about the voice at all until now. I love him, and now what am I going to do?

He felt her move and when she subsided against his shoulder again, his arm tightened around her. It seemed impossible that he had possessed such perfect loveliness, such a dizzying richness of black hair and green eyes, of rosy lips and rosier nipples, of full breasts, creamy skin and long, long legs. Looking at her now, so calm and still, it was equally impossible that she had looked and behaved as she had done a few moments ago. Pierce remembered everything. He remembered her eyes looking up at him with pupils dark and dilated with desire; the wild, wanton look on her face; and the way she tossed her head and writhed beneath him. Most of all, he remembered how she had held him, and helped him inside her, and how her inner muscles had squeezed tight on his throbbing flesh, gripping and then releasing him in a relentless rhythm that wanted to draw him into the very heart of her being. And, when his passion was spent, one thing became extremely, and uncomfortably, clear.

The rector's daughter had not been a virgin.

It ought not to matter, but it did.

Pierce understood perfectly the hypocrisy of his position. He had not been a virgin either, and he doubted very much that Amadine had expected, or wanted, him to be. He admitted that her compliance and expertise had increased his physical enjoyment of the act. He recognised the unfairness of his doubts, and of the analogy with the theme of *Tanqueray*. Therefore, surely he was man enough to rise above this and accept Amadine for what she was.

But he did not know what, or who, she was – her sexual experience had turned her into a stranger. He had expected something else. Someone else. He tried to tell himself that he did not think less of her – if he did that, he must think less of himself as well, because he had made love to her 'without benefit of clergy' as he believed the saying went, and therefore why shouldn't some other man have done the same? Did he wish that she had refused to make love with him? Well, no, he didn't . . . At least he didn't think that he did.

It was just that he had not thought Amadine was the sort of woman who slept around. So was it jealousy that disturbed him – had he wanted her virginity for himself? Perhaps there was an element of that, perhaps hell was the vision of Amadine lying with another man, with a succession of other men, with Haldane-Smith in particular. But no, it wasn't that. He wanted Amadine to be true to herself; and *his* Amadine, the Amadine in his heart and mind, was not promiscuous.

It ought not to matter but, even after careful reflection, it still did.

Chapter Twenty-Three

It was the night that the tour left Madison for Oshkosh that events began to quicken towards tragedy.

That day Jay had received the telegram he had been dreading: Bill needed money urgently. He needed a great deal of money – one thousand dollars, to be exact – and he needed it yesterday. Lying in his berth on the train, Jay contemplated the inescapable fact that he did not possess a thousand dollars; having remitted to the upstate bank every cent he had earned on this tour, he now possessed nothing at all. The only funds to which he had access belonged to his employer, Charles Frohman.

Every time he closed his eyes, the image of the safe was imprinted on his eyelids. He could almost feel the coldness of the handle, and the weight of the door as it swung open. He could see the cash bag inside, holding Frohman's share of the box-office receipts for the last few performances. There would be just enough . . .

But he couldn't take Frohman's money. How would he pay it back?

Yet what else could he do? If those cheques were not met and this whole scam came to light, he and Bill faced ruin. They faced *gaol*.

He must borrow the money from Frohman on an unofficial basis. He could work out how to pay it back later. Something would turn up – it always did.

Having decided to take the money, the next consideration was the time factor. The money must be wired from
Oshkosh in the morning, or the cheques might reach the
bank first. Come on, he urged the train: start, damn you!
And only when he felt a jerk of movement and a rumble of
wheels did he sink into an uneasy sleep.

When he woke, he knew something was wrong but could
not immediately tell what it was. Then he realised that the
train was not moving. Jay climbed out of his berth, went to
the door and peered outside. The far horizon was beginning to brighten, but only shed a pale light over the
desolate landscape, the frozen wasteland in which the train
had stopped. Oh no, Jay groaned, not a breakdown, not
today of all days, *please* . . .

When the train had pulled out of Madison, Constance had
opened her door and walked into the parlour of the Palace
Car. This was the sixth night out of Chicago, the sixth
night she had occupied Amadine's stateroom, and the
sixth night she had waited in vain for Hal to call. She had
decided that the time had come to give destiny a nudge in
the right direction.

Leaving the parlour in darkness, Constance groped her
way to the sideboard, picked up a glass and deliberately
dropped it on the hard oak surface. It made a satisfyingly
loud crash but, to be on the safe side, she let out a shrill, and
apparently involuntary, shriek. As she had hoped and
planned, Hal's door opened.

'Oh, curse it,' she muttered aloud, pretending not to
notice him, 'and I can't see a thing . . .'

'Allow me,' and Hal lit a lamp.

'I'm sorry if I woke you, but I couldn't sleep and thought
I'd have a glass of water and then I dropped . . . Do be careful where you put your feet – there might be glass on the
floor.' She crouched down and began picking shards from
the carpet.

Hal watched the ripple of her silky blonde hair hanging loose around her bare shoulders, and the movement of her slender body beneath the almost transparent white silk of her nightgown. He stood very still, but one part of him did move, stirring into life beneath his robe. Amazing how it seemed to have a life of its own. You'd think that a man ought to be able to control it, that it would respond to sheer brainpower but, no, it was more like a reflex action. He wanted Amadine, not Constance, but his anatomy was saying: 'You've not had a woman since this tour started and, if Amadine isn't available, Constance will do.' Probably, at this moment, virtually any woman would do.

Hal poured a glass of Scotch, and tossed it back in a single draught. The liquor hit his stomach, and he felt better. Amadine would be at Radcliffe's house, and he wondered if Radcliffe was there, too. Replacing the glass on the counter, his hand brushed against Constance's bare arm and he felt her tremble. She was much smaller than Amadine, the top of her head barely reaching his shoulder and, considering that she was the mother of two, she had a touching innocence.

Almost lazily, Hal trailed his fingers over her bare back and, as she turned to face him, he saw the acquiescence in her eyes. He kissed her, coolly at first but then, as Constance opened his robe and pressed her body against his, with increasing enthusiasm. Hal lifted her, and carried her into the bedroom.

Constance awoke from a shallow sleep at about the same time as Jay, and also realised that the train had stopped. She slipped out of bed and locked the door, so that there should be no awkward interruptions at crucial moments, and when she snuggled back against him in the bed, Hal was stirring – in more ways than one.

'Why have we stopped?' he muttered, evidently referring

to the train, and he began to get out of bed. 'I'd better find out what's happening.'

'You don't need to go,' Constance said, restraining him. 'Let someone else deal with it, for a change. Frank and Jay are perfectly capable, and you need some rest after all the burdens you've had to bear recently. Besides,' and her hand slid down to caress his already aroused body, 'obviously you don't really want to leave now . . .'

He did not need much persuasion. With any luck, Constance thought, I'll become pregnant.

Investigating the cause of the delay, Frank noticed that his brother was missing from his bed. This was the first time this had happened on the tour and obviously he must have slept with Constance, a development about which Frank had slightly mixed feelings. He did not care whom Hal slept with, but he did hope that this particular liaison would not lead to a permanent relationship. As the tour progressed, Frank had joined the chorus of critics who claimed that Constance was a bad influence on Hal's performances, and what was bad for Hal's career was also bad for Frank's future.

Jay had already rooted out the driver, and ascertained that there was nothing wrong with the train itself, but it had been signalled to stop.

'The river up ahead is in flood, after a thaw, and the bridge is unsafe.'

Frank nodded. He had encountered this kind of problem before on other tours. 'How do we reach Oshkosh?'

'We'll have to cross the river further upstream,' the driver said. 'It'll mean backing up a-ways along this line, and switching to another track.'

'How long will that take?'

The driver shrugged. 'Depends on the weather, and the amount of traffic. A large number of trains use these lines, and there's only one bridge that's passable.'

Jay glanced out of the window. It was beginning to snow. Oh, great! Thaws enough to flood the river, then freezes again. Today of all days. Every snowflake seemed to reduce the chances of his reaching the bank in Oshkosh in time.

'If we pass through any towns – the sort and size that might have a bank – could we stop for a few minutes?' he asked optimistically.

'No,' said Frank firmly.

'But the boys and girls,' and Jay gestured in the direction of the company cars, 'will need to eat.'

'We have enough food in the kitchen to provide everyone with a basic meal, and that will have to do. I do not intend to lose a minute more than necessary in reaching Oshkosh because, come hell or high water, we are putting on a performance there this evening.'

Jay walked along to the observation room and threw himself into a chair, from where he surveyed the situation with increasing frustration and despair. The snowflakes seemed to fall in a series of straight lines, forming an image of prison bars at the window.

As the train jerked backwards and began to reverse along the line, Blanche finished dressing and made her way to the Palace Car for breakfast. To her consternation, she found the kitchen staff preparing coffee and rolls for the entire company and only Frank sitting at the table. She hesitated, her dislike of Frank making her reluctant to join him, and then saw the steward carrying a tray into Constance's room – coffee and rolls . . . for two . . .

Blanche flinched, as though she had been slapped in the face, and was sure that Frank smiled at her discomfiture – indeed, it did cross Frank's mind that although a liaison between his brother and Constance was bad enough, a relationship with Blanche Villard would be even worse. For a moment she stood, staring in shocked horror at that closed door. She had been really enjoying playing Amadine's roles and, having made a success as Rose Trelawny, the longer Amadine stayed away, the better as far as she was concerned. If only the girls in New York could see me now, she thought every time she took a curtain call, and every time she played opposite Hal. Blanche had been given a glimpse of the life she wanted, and she would not give it up without a struggle.

Yet she did not resent Amadine, or have any jealousy of her personal or professional position. Amadine seemed so fine, and so far above her, that Blanche could only admire and try to emulate her. Constance, however, was another matter entirely and at this moment Blanche's jealousy of Constance, for sharing Hal's bed, was the fiercest emotion she had ever experienced – winning, by a short head, over her hatred for her stepfather. She was no nearer settling *that* situation either, having neither accumulated the money she needed nor come up with an alternative solution. Too late, she thought grimly, as she realised that Hal would have presented the perfect answer to her problem: if she could have married Hal, she would not have needed to fear her stepfather snitching to Grandmama about the theatre, because Blanche would have been shouting it from the rooftops herself.

She became aware that Frank was still watching her.

'I'm glad of the opportunity for a private word,' he said.

Blanche looked at him suspiciously, and did not sit down.

'I know that Hal appreciates your help with the Pinero, but I do hope that you are not allowing your new, and very temporary, status to go to your head. The rules still apply, and you are still expected to obey them.'

'Oh, I don't believe this!' Blanche exclaimed. 'Just because I went out for a breath of fresh air yesterday . . .'

'You left the theatre without permission. Again. And if you break the rules just one more time, I shall fine you five dollars.'

'I'll bet Amadine is allowed to come and go as she pleases,' said Blanche bitterly.

'You didn't sign the register either, and before you bring Amadine into the argument again, I would remind you that she is meticulous about doing so. In Baltimore the habit probably saved her life. Without her signature in the register, we would not have known that she was on the premises.'

Blanche felt that she was getting the worst of the argument, and accordingly she aimed a low blow. 'I'll leave you to breakfast alone,' she said nastily, 'or is Theo coming to hold your hand?'

She had the satisfaction of seeing Frank flush bright red and then turn deathly white. Blanche conceded that rules could have a useful purpose, but she resented not being treated like a star even though she had assumed Amadine's responsibilities. Well, one day she would be a star and if she came across Frank Smith, oh boy, would she get even!

Theo had no objection to being marooned in the wilderness if it meant that he could forge ahead with *Barbara Frietchie*. Rain, hail, snow or blow – as he phrased it in his letters to Susannah – he rose at dawn and put in a couple of hours' work on the play before breakfast. To date, the Southern belle had met, and accepted the attentions of, her Yankee captain and been roundly condemned by her friends and neighbours for so doing. She had quarrelled with the 'boy next door', whom many people had expected her to marry, and had accused him of cowardice for refusing to fight on either side. Her brother, wounded at Gettysburg in the Confederate Army, had asked Barbara to hide him from Yankee search parties; and the Yankee captain had seen him, but sent the search party away.

At this juncture Theo was working on the wedding of Barbara and the Yankee, which was to be interrupted by the arrival of Confederate troops and the attempted murder of the Yankee by a Southern sharpshooter. It was all good, stirring stuff and Theo scribbled away happily before stopping for a smoke. He laid down his pen, and sighed. He would have liked to smoke while he worked, but the little room would soon fog up and there was the danger of ruining the paintwork and upholstery. No, he had better do the decent thing and trot along to the smoking room.

The combined smoking room and men's washroom was located at the other end of the men's car and, most of the men still being asleep, Theo negotiated the narrow passageway between the berths without difficulty. At this hour the washroom was empty, neat and clean, the wash basins, urinals and white ceramic toilet bowls gleaming, the panelled washstand with white marble top and nickel-plated fixtures uncluttered, the spittoons sparkling and the towels fresh. A bench ran along one wall and Theo sat down on it, lit a small cigar and closed his eyes. The dialogue for the wedding scene was taking shape, and he concentrated on a crucial speech. He heard the door open, and bare feet pad across the slate floor.

'Morning,' said a youthful voice.

'Good morning,' Theo replied politely. Not being in the mood for conversation, he hoped that someone else would come in and the two newcomers could talk among themselves. The dialogue was coming good, and he fumbled in his pocket with his free hand for the small notebook and pencil he always carried.

'Do you know what's happening with the train, sir?'

A touch irritably, Theo opened his eyes, and his life changed for ever.

The most beautiful youth he had ever seen was standing in front of the wash basin, his back towards Theo but his face reflected in the mirror. He was watching Theo in the glass, and smiling as he lathered shaving soap on to that lovely face. Of medium height but wonderfully well shaped, he was clothed only in a pair of white undershorts, which showed off his smooth, slightly olive, skin. Italian, Theo thought dazedly, dragging his gaze from taut buttocks and muscled thighs to tumbling dark curls and dancing brown eyes.

'I'm afraid not,' he managed to say.

'Most of the guys are betting on a wash-out up the line. There's been a bit of a thaw.'

'Very possibly,' Theo agreed, taking a puff at his cigar and locating the notebook. Rather ostentatiously he made a few notes and tried to look occupied and important. But, his head bent over the book, his gaze kept sliding across the slate floor to the bare feet by the washstand. He wrenched his attention back to the book, very conscious of being watched in the mirror, but then he saw the feet, first the right foot and then the left, step out of the undershorts. Raising his eyes – he simply could not help himself – he watched as the beautiful, and now naked, youth soaped himself all over. Absolutely *all* over. And Theo experienced the fiercest, most gut-wrenching stab of sexual desire that he had ever known.

For a few moments he sat there, transfixed. Then, terrified that his reaction had been noticed, he stubbed out the cigar and replaced the notebook in his pocket. Somehow he galvanised his frozen limbs into action and walked to the door and, his breeding coming to his rescue, managed a polite, social smile as he made his exit.

Back in his room, he sat down and clasped his hands tight together to keep them from trembling. The young man must be new, he thought. He must have joined us in Chicago, otherwise surely I would have noticed him before. Still in a state of shock, still experiencing a strange combination of numbness and intense arousal, Theo wondered dazedly what had happened to him. What did this mean?

But part of him did not want to know what it meant. And one thing was definite – he was never setting foot in that washroom again.

*

Gwen was writing to Amadine, passing on Miss P's latest bulletin on Laurie's progress, and was finding it strange to think of Amadine living at Prairie Avenue, being visited – or more – by Sam's son. Pierce seemed very sure that Sam had killed himself. Gwen did not believe it, but then she did not want to believe it. Had she neglected Sam? Had he been lonely and unhappy, and felt that there was nothing to live for? If so, was it her fault? The possibility, however remote, was beginning to weigh on her conscience and perhaps, when she returned to Chicago, she ought to find out more.

Her next letter was to Nicholas Lang who, to her surprise, was continuing the correspondence. At least there was never any difficulty in finding something amusing or interesting to report – on this tour there was more drama off the stage than on! After the news of Amadine's accident, she brought him up-to-date with the progress of *Much Ado*.

'One of my greatest regrets is that I never played Beatrice. I did Hero, of course, just as I was Celia but not Rosalind, and the Queen in *Hamlet* but not Ophelia. Sometimes I blame the choices I made in my life, which led to a lack of opportunity, but at other times I'm certain that I was never pretty or talented enough . . .' Gwen stopped. Talk about fishing for compliments – this was more like holding out a begging bowl! She tore up that bit. 'However, I'm certain that what will be will be, and there is no use repining. At least I'm still here, working with people I like and admire, and I have my health.'

But for how much longer did she have her health? These days she often found herself dwelling on her mother's illness, calculating that her mother had been about sixty when the first symptoms appeared. Gwen would be fifty years old on 8 March so she might have only ten years left – ten years in which to accumulate some savings and acquire a home. It was an impossible task. She might have longer, because obviously there was no certainty that she would develop dementia. On the other hand, she might have less.

Either way, there was no use worrying. She could only do her best. That was all anyone could do.

She picked up Nicholas's last letter and re-read the closing paragraph.

'Now, my dear Gwen, I know we agreed not to meet, but I did not promise that I would never try to change your mind on the matter! I shall be in St Louis during your engagement. Please, do agree to meet me there! As the precise time of your arrival will be uncertain, I cannot welcome you off the train, but perhaps afternoon tea at the Planters Hotel would suit? Shall we say four o'clock?'

It was foolish to think that she could go on just writing to this man indefinitely, so why not give it a try? All she had to lose was that last little bit of self-respect and self-confidence, if and when she saw the disappointment in his eyes, and surely she was mature enough to take the risk?

'I will probably regret this,' Gwen wrote, 'but, very well, four o'clock at the Planters on 22 February.'

Stop, start; stop, start; darkness fell, and still they had not reached their destination. The company was becoming tetchy as food rations ran low and Hal, emerging exhausted from Constance's bed, was worried about letting down an audience.

'I wonder if people will wait,' he commented to Frank. 'If they do, I'm prepared to go on at any hour of the day or night.'

'A milkman's matinée,' Frank agreed. 'Yes, I've done a few of those in my time. Look, some people will wait. We must just hope that there will be enough of them to make the show worthwhile, and justify the effort.'

Of course Frank had his own reasons for not wanting to lose the Oshkosh takings. He had calculated that he could 'cook the books' by three thousand dollars during the next two weeks, as the first portion of the amount he owed in Chicago. To acquire the remaining seven thousand dollars, he intended to stage a 'robbery' of the third and fourth weeks' receipts.

He glanced at his brother's handsome, honest face. He would pay back the money, every last penny. If it took him the rest of his life, he would pay it back.

'Frank, if it doesn't put you out, I think I'll travel on to St Paul as soon as possible,' Jay announced. He had realised that whatever happened tonight, performance or no performance, the company train would be very late leaving Oshkosh for St Paul the next day. He dared not risk it, not with the weather as it was. His problems were compounded by the next day being Sunday, but if he wired the money at crack of dawn on Monday, there might be a remote chance of it beating the cheques to Bill's account. 'I've some stuff to do first thing, and need an early start.'

'Back to being an advance man, eh?' Frank quipped.

'I'll take my cash with me, if you don't mind.'

'Why should I mind? It's your money.' And Frank led the way into his room, opened the safe with the key he always kept in his coat pocket, and stood back while Jay removed the cash bag.

When the train did crawl into Oshkosh at last, only Jay did not rush to the theatre. Clutching his overnight bag, containing a clean shirt and the cash, he hurried through the swirling snow to find out the time of the next train to St Paul.

Constance had summoned Ida to her stateroom to help with her hair and make-up, in order to save time when they reached the theatre, and was too enveloped in her own glow of happiness to notice that the girl was utterly miserable.

Ida had sat in the women's car all day, but George had not come to speak to her. He could easily have done so, and without anyone taking particular notice, because there was plenty of mixing between the men and women on train days. Several times she had gone to the ladies' bathroom at the front of the car and, on her way in and out, had peeped through into the other car. George was there all right, playing cards and having a fine old time. There had to be a reason why he was avoiding her. He had been behaving strangely since Saturday.

She had rushed from the hospital to give him the good news.

'Miss Amadine is too ill to leave Chicago, but she says that I needn't stay. So I can go on the train with you!'

George had stared at her and, slowly, his expression grew darker and darker. 'Are you telling me that Amadine is staying in Chicago – for how long?' And he had gripped Ida's arm tightly.

'I don't know.' Ida winced, for the pressure on her arm was painful. 'Until she's better – a few weeks, I suppose.'

'A few *weeks*!'

George had walked away and although later on he had been more polite, it was clear that the courtesy was an effort for him. Since then, instead of their new-found proximity cementing their relationship, he had barely acknowledged her existence. Ida was convinced that she was losing him, if he had ever been hers to lose. But why? What have I done, she wondered, or what *haven't* I done?

'I am very grateful for your help at the theatre, Ida,' Constance was saying, in her most gracious tone of voice, 'but in future I am unlikely to need your assistance here on the train unless the circumstances are exceptional. Kindly do not come to my room unless specifically asked to do so.'

Having disposed of the most likely source of an embarrassing intrusion on her privacy, Constance dismissed the girl and began gathering together a few items she needed for the theatre – her perfume, gloves and a particular scarf that she wanted to tie lightly over her freshly arranged hair instead of wearing a hat. She found the perfume and the gloves soon enough, but the scarf was more difficult to locate. Drat Ida, where had she put it! Constance was on the point of summoning the girl again when she found it in one of the drawers beside the bed.

And the scarf was not all she found. Nestling at the back of the drawer, wrapped in a silk handkerchief, was Amadine's pearl-handled gun. Amadine must have omitted to take it from the train when they disembarked in Chicago, and had since forgotten about it.

Constance handled the pistol gingerly. Having watched Amadine with the weapon, she knew how it worked, but had not changed her view that she could never actually fire it. After a moment's hesitation, she replaced the gun in the drawer, but took care to place it conveniently at the front where it could be found easily.

Chapter Twenty-Four

Amadine rejoined the tour in St Louis, radiant with health and high spirits. In Hal's opinion, she had the indefinable glow of a woman who had been well satisfied in bed, and who was anticipating being pleasured again in the very near future. 'Are you staying at the Planters?' he asked.

'Yes, we are.' She looked at him steadily, emphasising that her use of the plural was not accidental.

Hal turned away, his lips set in a bitter line. It ought to have been him who took her to bed, and he knew that on several occasions he had come close. The final confirmation that he had lost Amadine was so devastating that he did not know how to face a lifetime without her.

'Will you be staying at the hotel during our engagement here?' Constance enquired.

Amadine was surprised by the sudden interest in her sleeping arrangements. 'I will rejoin the train when we leave St Louis,' she agreed, and then she understood. 'But you can stay in my stateroom, Constance. With only three one-night stands between St Louis and Chicago, it isn't worth your moving out. I'll use your old room.'

The relief and pleasure on Constance's face were easily interpreted. Good, thought Amadine; Hal hasn't been pining away, then.

'Do you need a rehearsal for *Tanqueray* tonight?' Hal asked abruptly.

'I could do it in my sleep,' Amadine assured him. 'In fact, after some of my less brilliant performances, people have assumed that I did! No, as we have plenty of time today, why don't we tackle *Much Ado*? I'm word perfect – I think – but badly in need of a bit of match practice, as you might say.'

Only Gwen demurred, saying that she was tired and asking to be excused. She was very pale, with dark shadows under her eyes betraying a sleepless night. Hal readily agreed that she should meet them at the theatre in time for the evening performance.

Gwen and Blanche had been thrown together a good deal of late and the previous day, in Jefferson City, Blanche had decided to confide in her friend.

'We return to Baltimore the first week in April,' she concluded, 'and I haven't a snowball's hope in hell of raising the entire four hundred and fifty dollars by then.'

'You mustn't pay the man anything,' Gwen said sensibly, 'because he will only be back for more.'

'If I don't give him the money, he will tell my grandmother everything.'

'Let him!'

'I would, if I had only myself to consider, but there is my mother's allowance to take into account.'

'Wouldn't your mother stand by you?'

'No,' Blanche said flatly. 'She is the type who will stand by her man, even when he's rotten through and through, and by her allowance.'

At least, Gwen reflected, my mother supported me through thick and thin, even when she disapproved of the choices I was making. 'If you asked him nicely, Hal might speak to your grandmother. He can charm the birds out of the trees, you know.'

Blanche did know. However, if Hal did not bother to use his charm on her, he was hardly likely to want to use it on her grandmother, was he? Anyway: 'She wouldn't be impressed. Of course, if it was Sir Henry Irving, that would be different.'

'Oh, Hal will be Sir Edward one of these fine days, you mark my words.'

Blanche stared at her. She would have said that it was impossible for Hal to become more desirable than he already was but, amazingly and horrifyingly, he just had. All the signs were that he was still sleeping with Constance, and all Blanche could do was hope that Amadine's return would put a stop to it. If Amadine did not resume her rightful place in the Palace Car, Blanche really felt that she would not be responsible for her actions.

'You have a few weeks in which to decide what to do,' Gwen consoled.

'I know what I'd like to do,' Blanche exclaimed. 'I'd like to subject my stepfather to a long, and very painful, death.'

'Don't be silly, dear. That's no way to talk. You know perfectly well that you could never hurt anyone.'

Couldn't I? Blanche thought about it. If it wasn't too messy, if it was done at a remove – like pushing someone off a cliff, for instance – and if it was really and truly a matter of her own survival or theirs, then Blanche rather thought that she might be able to do it. However . . .

'No,' she said with a smile, 'of course you are right.'

They left the theatre together after the performance, pausing at the stage door briefly to sign a few autographs. Blanche being in greater demand, after a few moments Gwen stood aside and glanced along the well-lit street. A man was standing about ten yards away, and Gwen's heart gave such a peculiar lurch that she pressed a hand to her breast.

It was Nicholas. She was sure it was him. He was exactly as she had imagined him to be: tall, spare and elegant, with a mane of silver hair beneath his top hat, and holding a silver-headed cane. He was watching her as intently as she was watching him and then, without a sign or gesture, he turned and walked away.

At first Gwen was numb, and then distraught. She was sure it was Nicholas – after all, it was entirely possible that he would be in Jefferson City tonight, as he was due in St Louis tomorrow, and that he would decide to have a sneak preview. And she had been standing directly under a light, so he must have seen every wrinkle and grey hair! No wonder he walked away! All night she tried to convince herself that she was mistaken, and that a different man would turn up for tea the next day, but she could not shake off the belief that she had been seen to be old, and had been rejected.

The following afternoon, with a heavy heart, she dressed in a favourite gown that matched the blue of her eyes, and pinned a flattering hat on her carefully combed hair. However, nothing would disguise the crow's feet at her eyes, or the lines that gouged ravines from the side of her nose to her mouth. Sitting in front of the mirror, Gwen lifted the sagging flesh of her cheeks so that these deep valleys were smoothed away, and she looked ten, even fifteen, years younger. But she had to let the loose folds of skin sag back into place, and then she was old again. The upper part of her body was moderately well preserved, she decided; her arms were still slender and her breasts, which had never been large, were maintaining their shape and sufficient uplift. But she could weep for the tiny waist, flat stomach and slim legs that once had been hers. She was not fat but, despite the fact that she watched her diet, she carried unsightly rolls of excess flesh and, as the day wore on, her feet and ankles swelled.

She timed her arrival at the hotel carefully, not wanting to be too early or too late. Entering the tearoom, she

glanced round nervously but, there being no lone gentleman at any of the tables, she found an empty place and sat
down. After telling the waiter that she was waiting for a
friend, ten minutes passed with agonising slowness. The
next ten minutes dragged by even more slowly. The waiter
hovered and, from sheer embarrassment, Gwen ordered
tea for two and again covertly inspected the other occupants of the lounge. Seeing no likely candidate, she
enquired at the desk if Mr Lang had left a message for her.
No, there was no message. Gwen returned to her table and
poured a cup of tea, thankful that her acting experience
enabled her to maintain a certain sang-froid.

At five o'clock a huge hollowness opened up, and ached,
within her, and she fought the sting of tears at the back of
her eyes. He wasn't coming. It had been him at Jefferson
City last night, and he had taken one look at an old woman,
well past her prime, and bolted. Discourteous of him not to
leave a message – from the tone of his letters, she would
have expected him to do that – but presumably he had left
town as quickly as he could.

At six o'clock Gwen rose and made a dignified exit. She
recalled a passage from Mark Twain's *Life on the Mississippi*
about sending a fool to St Louis, which said that if you did
not tell the people there that he was a fool, they would
never find out. 'There's one thing sure – if I had a damned
fool I should know what to do with him: ship him to St
Louis – it's the noblest market in the world for that kind of
property.'

There's one thing sure, Gwen cried to herself, and that's
that there was a damned fool in St Louis today, and no
mistake.

Jay was existing in a permanent state of confusion and crisis.
He had cleared that first hurdle: the money wired from St
Paul had reached Bill in time. When he received Bill's
laconic, and absurdly casual, acknowledgement of the

funds, Jay went out and spent money he could ill afford on several stiff drinks. He felt as if he had lost stones in weight, gained a million grey hairs and aged ten years. He could not go through that again.

However, in order to avoid a recurrence of the problem, he needed a financial cushion in case Bill allowed another crisis to develop. And this was where Jay made his mistake. Had he confined his activities to 'rolling over' one payment, it might have worked. Barring accidents, he could have remained one payment in arrears until the end of the tour, by which time the profits from *The Philadelphia Girl* would be pouring in and he could make good the shortfall. But, unable to bear the strain, he fell into temptation and 'borrowed' another thousand dollars.

From then on, his fear of receiving a cable from Bill was replaced by dread of a query from Charles Frohman. Jay's accounts were in a hopeless muddle, complicated by the fact that box-office takings varied from place to place. For example, the receipts from St Joe and Kansas City together did not equal those from Minneapolis, which they were supposed to cover, and Jay had to wait over the weekend and supplement the cash with that taken in Jefferson City. It had reached a stage where Jay looked at the figures and his eyes glazed over.

Ironically, the situation was exacerbated by his former efficiency. He had forwarded funds to Frohman's office with such metronomic regularity that the now spasmodic nature of the remittances must be ringing alarm bells all over New York. While he was on the road, they might make allowances, but they would certainly expect him to catch up with his paperwork during the imminent two-week stay in Chicago.

When the tour pulled out of St Louis, only three one-night stands – at Springfield (Illinois), Peoria and Davenport – remained before the company returned to the capital of the Midwest. Jay sat alone in the observation car and pored over his accounts. The figures offered no comfort. He needed to talk to someone, and there wasn't a whole lot of choice about who that someone could be. With a certain amount of feeling that 'Bill got me into this mess, so he can bloody well get me out', Jay sent a cable from Springfield on Thursday, telling Bill to meet him in Chicago on Sunday.

'You're looking very cheerful, Ida,' Amadine teased, as the train rolled out of Peoria. 'Anyone would think that you were glad to have me back, even though I'm more trouble than Constance!'

'She doesn't want me around in the Palace Car, and we all know why, don't we!'

They were in the room that Amadine was using at the front of the women's car, and Ida was plaiting Amadine's hair in readiness for bed. There was less room here than in the Palace Car stateroom, and Ida felt cramped and uncomfortable as she worked.

'You should've taken your old room,' she complained. 'Too generous by half, you are.'

'Don't be such a spoilsport, Ida. Just because the rest of us are sleeping alone tonight, doesn't mean that Hal and Constance must, too.' Amadine watched the maid's face in the mirror. 'Or perhaps you aren't sleeping alone,' she suggested, 'which is why you are so cheerful.'

'I'm sleeping alone until someone names the day,' Ida said darkly. 'No weddin', no nuthin', that's my motto.'

'Which puts the rest of us in our place,' Amadine grimaced wryly. 'We are a wicked, immoral lot, and living up to the public perception of us!'

'I thought you was different,' and Ida's lips pursed in disapproval. 'So, are you going to marry Mr Radcliffe, or what?'

'I don't want to think about the future,' Amadine said emphatically, 'and I certainly haven't made any wedding plans.'

Must be nice to be able to pick and choose, thought Ida as she climbed into her own berth a little later. Still, mustn't grumble, not now that George was showing a bit of interest again.

He had approached her yesterday in Springfield and been as nice as pie. Said how much he had missed her, but he was sure she understood that he had been giving all his attention to his work – couldn't risk being sacked, could he, especially out here in the back of beyond. Ida knew that she ought to send him packing. She had her pride and was perfectly well aware that he was treating her badly, but he was the only bit of romance and interest in life that she had. So she smiled, and said that she had missed him, too. Then this morning, when everyone was busy at the theatre in Peoria and she was organising Miss Amadine's things on the train, George had nipped back to catch her alone.

'Come on,' he said, 'show me what it is you do. Honestly, I'm really interested.'

Furtively, and feeling guilty because she was sure Miss Amadine wouldn't like it, Ida let him sit down on Amadine's bed while she tidied up and sorted the laundry. Then she allowed him to persuade her to show him the Palace Car.

'I've never seen it,' he explained. 'Most of the others have been in to rehearse, or are invited to dinner, but I haven't been asked.'

'They'll get round to you eventually.'

'I'm not holding my breath.' And he examined, in minute detail, the stateroom currently occupied by Constance, before going next door to inspect Hal and Frank's accommodation. 'How the other half lives,' he remarked jocularly, 'and to think that, after all this luxury, they have to slum it in a suite at the Auditorium or the Parker House.'

He was affability itself, but the way he handled Amadine's things, and rifled through the drawers in the staterooms, was unpleasant and intrusive. Ida sensed that something was wrong, but was so nervous about being discovered here with him that she told herself she was imagining it. All the same, she hurried him out of the Palace Car and off the train as quickly as she could.

Hal was making love to Constance although that was hardly the most apt description of the act. Hal was a very angry man; a disappointed and frustrated man. He used Constance to assuage these feelings, while at the same time fantasising that she was Amadine. The difference in his attitude since St Louis was obvious, but Constance did not care. She was almost certain that she was pregnant.

She had slept with Hal every night since Oshkosh, and the really interesting thing was that, for very personal reasons, she ought to have been unable to do so. Constance's body was obligingly regular in its habits, and only twice before had her 'time of the month' not appeared on cue, and that had resulted in Katie and Charlie. Of course, it was important to continue sleeping with Hal as often as possible, so that if she was not pregnant now she soon would be, because this was the only way she could force him to marry her.

The room was in darkness – Constance disliked making love with the light on – and Hal was lying on his back, hands folded behind his head, staring at the ceiling.

'I think I'm expecting a baby.'

Hal grunted morosely in response. Then suddenly he sat bolt upright. '*Baby!*'

His bellow penetrated the thin partition between this room and that next door where Frank, taking advantage of his brother's absence, was counting the cash he had accumulated. His resources being in a much healthier state than Jay's, he was calmly and methodically checking the contents of several large cash bags when he heard Hal's voice. A baby! Not exactly welcome tidings, he imagined, but only to be expected. There were some advantages in loving men,

Frank decided; not many, not in this day and age, but definitely some . . .

Hal jumped up and turned on the light, before sitting down on the edge of the bed and staring at Constance in consternation.

'You cannot possibly say that – it's much too soon . . .'

'It is too soon to be absolutely sure,' she agreed, 'but there are certain signs . . . Well, let's say that a woman knows about these things.'

'I thought that a woman also knew how to stop these things happening.'

Constance's eyes widened ingenuously. 'No methods are foolproof, and if a man wants to ensure that he doesn't become a father, there are some precautions that *he* can take.'

Touché, Hal admitted. Of course, considering the number of relationships he'd had in his time, it was a miracle that this had not happened before. It was just a pity that it was Constance – and even more of a pity that it wasn't Amadine.

'If you are right, what do you intend to do?'

'You mean, what do *we* intend to do,' Constance said sharply.

'I mean exactly what I said.'

'This is as much your child, and your responsibility, as mine.'

He had always thought that she looked young and innocent when her silky fair hair streamed loose on her shoulders, but at this moment there was a cold and calculating gleam in those big blue eyes.

'You planned this, didn't you!' he exclaimed. 'This is what you wanted right from the start, and that is why you are telling me about a child now, even though you cannot know for sure. Your pregnancy is wishful thinking, not the truth.'

'I admit that I have loved you from the start, and that I

have always believed we were right for each other. But as for the rest . . . Hal, those are very hurtful things to say.'

'I still want to know what you intend to do if you are pregnant.'

'Chicago would be a good place for our wedding, don't you think?' she asked eagerly. 'We have two weeks there, so don't need to rush the arrangements, but it gives enough immediacy for the baby's eventual arrival not to seem too premature.'

'*Wedding!*' Another bellow reached Frank's ears. 'I'm not marrying you.'

'But you must.' She looked genuinely shocked.

'I dare say that I ought, but I'm still not going to.'

'Why not?'

'Because I don't love you, and because it would be a personal disaster for both of us. Damn it, Connie, I don't even want to go on working with you, let alone spend the rest of my life with you!'

'Then why did you sleep with me?'

'I should have thought that was obvious.' He passed a hand wearily over his eyes, and paused for a moment. 'It was a mistake, and I'm sorry. I should not have done it. Believe me, I won't do it again.'

Constance winced. She had expected him to be surprised at her announcement, and go a bit quiet for a while, but after that she thought he would grow accustomed to the idea and even be excited by it. She really had thought Hal would marry her. She had believed he was a gentleman.

'I'll make you marry me,' she said shrilly. 'I'll shame you into it if I have to.'

'That would be a first-rate start to our married life,' he observed cuttingly, moving to the door and opening it. 'I will take financial responsibility for the child, but that's as far as I am prepared to go. No wedding, Constance. Not in Chicago, or anywhere else.'

Frank heard the door bang, but he was already kneeling in

front of the safe, concealing the cash bags at the very back of the bottom shelf behind Amadine's jewellery boxes. He was locking the safe door as Hal entered the adjoining room.

'I wasn't expecting to see you,' Frank remarked cautiously.

'Constance can't keep her mouth shut tonight, and I need my sleep.'

So he doesn't want to talk about it. Frank gave a mental shrug, and went to bed. He lay awake for a long time. He had enough money to pay his dues in Chicago, but needed to perfect his plan for stealing it from the safe without suspicion. Tomorrow night they were in Davenport, and after that he would make his move.

Unable to sleep, and knowing that Theo would be working on his play, Frank rose early and slipped quietly through the cars to Theo's room. Sure enough, Theo's papers and a coffee pot were on the table, but there was no sign of the man himself. After a moment's thought, Frank walked along to the smoking room, and went in. And froze . . .

Theo's resolve never to enter that washroom again had lasted all of two days – forty-eight hours of turmoil, in which terror had warred with the most extraordinary excitement. Although pulled by an invisible magnet, he put up a stout resistance each morning over his daily quota of *Barbara Frietchie* until he could bear it no longer, and went to the washroom at precisely the same time as he had done that first day.

Lighting a cigar, he justified his presence here. For one thing, he genuinely needed a smoke; for another, there was nothing unnatural about admiring a man's body – he had not felt guilty in the Accademia in Florence, gazing at Michelangelo's *David*, had he? A work of art, that was all the young man was, and no harm could come of appreciating the symmetry of his form.

Theo felt much better after this piece of sound reasoning, even managing to make a few notes in his little book, before he heard the door open and nearly jumped out of his skin with nervousness and hope. The disappointment when the new arrival proved to be another member of the company was piercing, but this rollercoaster of emotion rose again when the beautiful boy was next to arrive. As Theo's mouth went dry, the young man, who was addressed as Carlo by his colleague, proceeded unselfconsciously with his ablutions.

This suited Theo better than being on his own with him. The presence of others made him less conspicuous and enabled him to watch without being watched himself. At one point his eyes did meet Carlo's in the mirror, and he felt himself flush with embarrassment as he quickly looked away again, but afterwards he succeeded in convincing himself that no one else could have noticed anything untoward. However, when he returned to his room, he was shaking and in a state of intense physical arousal. He tried to ignore the fact that this reaction had not occurred during his appreciation of the *David* and attempted, with the same lack of success, to concentrate on his work.

After that he went to the washroom every day, looking forward to it and dreading it in equal measure. He lived for those few brief moments, but despised himself for it, loathing the lack of control over his own actions and the fear that he was helpless in the grip of powerful emotions.

One thing he did not do: he did not put a name to those emotions.

The company began to comment on his regular appearances among them.

'I am smoking too much,' Theo explained truthfully.

'You work too hard,' Carlo observed, pausing, razor in hand, to eye him sympathetically.

Theo was absurdly pleased that his movements had been

noticed, but only made a non-committal gesture and muttered something about working no harder than anyone else. However, he chose that morning to loiter on the bench in the washroom for longer than usual, and was rewarded by a sudden exodus that left him alone with his quarry.

'What is it you do exactly?' Carlo asked.

Theo explained the clerical work and general organisation he undertook for the Chief.

'You're writing letters this early in the morning?' Carlo indicated the notebook in Theo's hand.

'Oh Lord, no, this is my own work.' And, with self-conscious pride: 'I'm a playwright.'

Eyes wide, Carlo padded across the floor and sat down beside Theo. Thank God he had replaced his undershorts or Theo, breathing in the scent of freshly soaped skin, might not have been answerable for the consequences. Carlo gazed at Theo with an admiration most people reserved for Shakespeare.

'You must be so clever!'

'Not really,' Theo replied modestly. 'Not clever enough to have had any of my plays produced, anyway.'

'Huh,' his companion snorted, 'some producers don't know quality when they see it.'

At one time Theo would have agreed with that view wholeheartedly, but he had learned enough recently to realise that producers were not always wrong in their assessment of material, and that the quality of his previous work had not been up to the required standard.

'Luck has a lot to do with it,' Theo replied neutrally, 'and I am optimistic that I'm on the right track with my latest piece.'

'What is it about?'

'I can't tell you, I'm afraid. It's a secret until Hal and Amadine have read it.'

'Aren't they wonderful? Isn't Amadine the most beautiful thing you ever saw?'

'No,' murmured Theo, not daring to look at the supple young body only inches away from his. He forced a laugh. 'I'm a married man, so you must not expect me to admit to finding another woman more beautiful than my wife.'

'It must be great to be able to write,' Carlo said wistfully, 'and have an education.'

'You have other advantages,' Theo assured him drily. 'Oh, and don't say anything about my work – our secret, eh?'

Since then Carlo had scrupulously avoided mentioning the subject in the presence of a third party, but eagerly enquired after the playwright's progress when they were alone, the shared secret forming a bond between them. On the morning of Frank's visit, Carlo and Theo were alone in the washroom.

'Will there be a part for me in this play of yours?' Carlo enquired.

Theo was very tempted to try and oblige, but in all honesty the boy was too young and inexperienced for anything except walking-on, looking exceptionally pretty in a blue or grey uniform. 'It's too soon to say,' he said apologetically. 'At the moment I'm fully occupied with the principal roles, which I am hoping Hal and Amadine will play.'

'I'm sorry, I didn't mean . . .' Carlo backed off with profuse apologies, conscious of having overstepped the mark and pushed himself too far forward. He was naked, standing about two feet from Theo, towelling himself dry.

It was at that moment that Frank entered the room, and this was the little tableau that froze him in his tracks. Carlo heard the door open and turned his head slightly, but Theo did not notice.

'Here,' said Theo huskily, 'you've missed a bit,' and he took a corner of the towel and very carefully wiped a trickle of water from the boy's back. Then he saw Frank, and went scarlet. As horror and guilt warred on his face, he looked like a man whose wife has just discovered him in bed with the parlour maid.

'Sorry,' Frank managed to say after what seemed an eternity. 'I just wanted . . . It doesn't matter, I'll see you later.' And before Theo could speak, Frank turned and ran. He ran, or at least walked extremely quickly, back to the Palace Car where, thankfully, Hal was still sleeping, so Frank could grieve unobserved and uninterrupted.

Such a development had never crossed his mind. It ought to have done – of course it ought to have done – but his whole focus had been on wondering whether Theo had any homosexual tendencies, not on analysing what type might attract him. He should have thought . . . That lad wasn't *his* type – absolutely gorgeous, but just not an avenue he wished to explore – and he was amazed that Theo wanted him. One would imagine that Theo would look for rather more in the way of intellectual stimulation, as well as sexual attraction, but there was no accounting for taste.

It would have been easier if Theo had preferred women. Anything was better than this! The irony was that he had been bracing himself to make a move. After the pay-off in Chicago he would be free in mind and spirit, free to devote his energies to other things, free to enjoy himself. And now what did it matter? What did anything matter! Every time he closed his eyes he could see Theo's face against the background of that beautiful young body, and whenever he opened his eyes the image was still there. He must get a grip. He had a day's work to do and no one, absolutely no one, must suspect that anything was wrong.

He heard Hal running water into the wash basin, and joined his brother at the shaving mirror.

'Rehearsal of *Much Ado* this morning?' Frank enquired.

Hal nodded. There was a long pause.

'Coming into breakfast?' Frank ventured.

'Is Constance up yet?'

Frank wiped shaving soap from his face, and peered cautiously into the parlour. 'No.'

'In that case I'm coming into breakfast.'

Hal bolted his food, but his haste was unnecessary because Constance did not appear, and she was still missing when Hal, Frank, Amadine, Gwen, Blanche and Theo assembled prior to making their way to the theatre in Davenport.

'We ought to find out if she's all right,' Amadine suggested.

'You ask her. Better coming from a woman,' Hal said hastily.

The look Amadine gave him clearly conveyed her opinion that this was a pretty weird statement from a man who had been sharing Constance's bed for the past month or so. However, she knocked on Constance's door and went in.

'She is not feeling well,' Amadine reported a few minutes later, 'and I must say that she looks distinctly pale and wan. I do hope that it isn't catching.'

'I don't think we need worry on that score,' Hal remarked drily.

It was Saturday, and Frank was carrying the cash box containing the company wages. Opening the box, he extracted the envelope enclosing Constance's money and gave it to Amadine, who returned briefly to the sickroom in order to hand it to the patient.

'Can we cope without Constance today?' Frank asked.

'Brother dear, we may have started this tour without a proper system of understudies, but we have learned from our mistakes. Covering for Constance is the least of our worries.'

'Right,' said Frank, eyeing his brother warily. 'That's all right, then.'

During the day Frank managed to avoid any meaningful contact with Theo. There was a moment in the early afternoon when Theo approached him, but Frank brushed him aside with a curt 'Not now, Theo, I'm busy', and hurried away. Fortunately there was a great deal to do. In view of Constance's indisposition, Hal ordered a run-through for understudies in readiness for *Trelawny* that night. When he was satisfied with those performances, he rehearsed several scenes from *Much Ado*, and therefore work on the stage was continuous until it was time to set the scenes for the evening performance. Evidently Hal was determined not to return to the train! Frank could understand why, but the company were muttering among themselves and he could see their point of view, too.

For his own part, Frank worked hard all day, in his shirt sleeves because the theatre was hot and stuffy; or perhaps, he reflected, he was simply working up his own head of steam. Hot and bothered, that was him today; perspiring and preoccupied; a state of mind and body that was not improved when a piece of stage machinery jammed during the interval in the evening performance. Fixing it, and setting the new scene, took Frank, George and the rest of the team more than half an hour, and the theatre manager had to apologise to the audience for the delay.

All in all it was an absolutely rotten day, and Frank was more than thankful when the curtain came down. Collecting his jacket from the chair in the prompt-corner where it had been hanging all day, he automatically felt in the pockets to check that his wallet and keys were intact, and then went to the manager's office – where Jay was already waiting – to cash up.

The entire company was exhausted, and went straight back to the train and bed. The Palace Car was in darkness and Hal, after a whispered warning to Frank, tiptoed past Constance's door to the sanctuary of his own room. Explaining that he did not want a light from his window to attract Constance's attention, he lit only one dim lamp and undressed as quickly as he could.

In the adjacent cubicle, the low lamp allowed Frank enough light to open the safe and place his cash box and Jay's cash bag on the upper shelf, then put the box containing Amadine's pearls, which she had worn onstage that night, on the lower shelf. Then he locked the safe, left the car and walked along the track to check on the loading of the scenery and props, before returning to bed. The last thing he did, as usual, was place the key to the safe under his pillow.

After such an exhausting day, nearly everyone slept long and late that Sunday morning. The train had rolled into Chicago and been shunted into the siding where it would stand for the next fortnight, while many of its occupants still languished in their berths or lolled around in various stages of undress.

Eventually a trickle of people, chiefly from the lower echelons, left the train and began to trudge through the snow into the city, in search of lodgings and a meal. George White was among the first to go, closely followed by Carlo, whose departure was watched by Theo with mingled sensations of regret and relief. A whole two weeks without those encounters in the washroom was a dreadful prospect, but the enforced change in routine might break the spell.

Quickly Theo scribbled a note to Hal to the effect that he would meet him later at the hotel and then, with his bag in one hand and struggling with the typewriter under the other arm, he levered himself down from the train.

'Need a hand?' asked a genial voice behind him. 'I can carry your bag if you can manage the typewriter.'

'Thanks, Jay.' Theo relinquished part of his burden with relief. 'You're another early bird, then.'

'It isn't early,' Jay asserted. 'It's damned late for someone who has as much to do as I have. By the way, I've a cab waiting – I take it you would like a lift to the hotel?'

In the Palace Car, Amadine was breakfasting alone. She glanced at her watch impatiently. Where was everyone? She had not seen Pierce since St Louis, and in addition she wanted to hear the story of Ben's first week at work. Pierce had found the boy lodgings with one of his factory foremen, but Amadine was worried that they would not be looking after him properly.

'At last,' she exclaimed as Frank appeared. 'I was beginning to think that everyone was dead!'

'Just dead tired.'

'Yesterday was gruesome, wasn't it! Never mind, it's lovely to be back in Chicago.'

'If you say so.'

'No need to ask if you slept well, apparently, but I hope that Constance had a good night after her indisposition yesterday?'

'How should I know?'

'But presumably Hal knows?' When Frank merely shrugged, Amadine's eyes widened. 'How was she feeling last night?'

Frank had the grace to look sheepish. 'We didn't ask. Her door was closed, and the light was out, so we assumed she was sleeping.'

'But surely Hal . . .'

Frank hesitated. 'I take it that you know Hal and Constance were . . . Quite. Well, they had a slight disagreement on Friday, and I think he was steering clear.'

'You mean to tell me that, because of a lovers' tiff, neither of you spoke to her last night?' Amadine jumped to her feet and glared at him, outraged. Muttering '*Men!*' under her breath, she strode to Constance's door, rapped on it sharply and went in.

And screamed.

Chapter Twenty-Five

Constance was lying on the bed, the pearl-handled gun by her right hand, her head and pillow soaked in blood. She had been shot in the right temple and, in the opinion of the police, had been dead for some time.

When the police began questioning her ashen-faced colleagues, it was soon established that Amadine had been the last of the company to see her alive, when she visited Constance in her room before leaving for the theatre the previous morning. However, the staff had seen her during the day: she had not left her room, but they had taken several meals in to her, and had last seen her at about seven o'clock in the evening. The cook said that she seemed sad rather than ill, and had taken some light refreshment, but the porter insisted that he had heard her 'throwin' up', a piece of news that drained what little colour remained in Hal's cheeks, and caused Frank to cast him a sharp glance. The cook had gone into town at half-past seven but the porter remained on duty, preparing the berths in the sleeping cars. He had not heard a shot.

'So we know that she died between seven o'clock last night and nine o'clock this morning, when Miss Sinclair discovered the body,' murmured the police officer.

'I was wondering if she killed herself,' Hal said. 'I know

that she had money worries. Of course I told her that we – the company, that is – would help, but . . .'

Again Frank glanced at his brother, but he said nothing.

'No,' Amadine announced emphatically. 'No matter how many worries Constance had, she would never commit suicide. She had two children who depended on her. The idea of her killing herself in that bed, with photographs of those children staring at her, is absolutely ridiculous. Anyway, I don't believe that she would have fired the gun.'

The policeman had been coming to the gun. Amadine admitted that it was hers.

'Where was it kept?'

'When I occupied that room, I kept it in a bedside drawer. I am very much afraid,' Amadine went on slowly, 'that I left it there during my absence from the tour.'

'Did everyone know about it, and know where it was kept?' The officer glanced round the Palace Car. All the principals were present, along with Theo and Jay, who had been summoned from the hotel, and Pierce Radcliffe. One by one they all said that they knew Amadine had a gun, but that they had not known it was no longer in her possession and in fact had forgotten about it, as apparently Amadine herself had done.

One look at Amadine's stricken face confirmed that a lecture on the responsibilities that accompanied ownership of a firearm was unnecessary, as well as being too late. The policeman glanced round the room again. Had one of them done it?

'It is possible that Mrs Grey was killed by an intruder unconnected with your theatrical group,' he said. 'Has anyone seen any suspicious characters hanging around the train?' No one had seen any such person, although several of those present recalled unexplained incidents concerning Amadine and glanced at her anxiously. 'I assume the doors of the train are locked in your absence?'

Frank confirmed that this was so. The train was never

left unattended but, the staff being unable to guard all the cars simultaneously, the doors were locked. The porter knew roughly what time the company would drift back from the theatre, and opened one door in each car in readiness for the influx.

'What happens if anyone returns, unexpectedly, to the train during the day?'

'We bang on the rear door of the men's car until the porter hears us,' said Theo. 'Primitive, but effective. As a matter of fact, I came back myself yesterday . . .'

He was interrupted by the arrival of another police officer who had been examining the train for any signs of damage or forced entry, but who had found no such evidence. Then a third officer, who had been inspecting Constance's room, beckoned from the doorway. After a whispered consultation, the senior officer returned.

'We are nearly finished here for the time being, but we do not want anyone to go into Mrs Grey's room. It will be best if we bag the valuables and take them with us for safekeeping, but perhaps one of you would like a receipt?'

'If you feel it is necessary,' Hal agreed, with a puzzled frown, 'but I wouldn't have thought any of Constance's trinkets warranted such a fuss.'

'Obviously we have a different definition of trinket.' And the first item he showed them brought a gasp of surprise from all the company.

'That is my diamond necklace,' Amadine exclaimed, 'And it ought to be in the safe. Frank?'

Frank was staring at the necklace blankly, but when the emeralds and the sapphires were spread out on the table, his expression changed from puzzlement to extreme alarm. Pulling the key from his pocket, he ran to the safe and opened the door.

'It's gone,' he said hoarsely, strewing the contents of the safe over the floor. 'It's all gone – we've been robbed.' He knelt there, his face grey and beads of perspiration gleaming on his forehead.

'Calm down,' Hal soothed, 'and let's find out exactly what is missing.'

Frank stood up, but then sat down suddenly on the bed as his knees gave way. 'What am I going to do?' he murmured dazedly. 'What the hell am I going to do?'

Jay was trying to push into the small cubicle. 'What do you mean, we've been robbed?' he demanded. 'Has anything of mine been taken?'

'It depends on what you had in there,' Frank said dully. 'There appears to be only last night's takings left.'

'And my pearls.' Amadine was kneeling on the floor, opening jewellery boxes, most of which were empty.

'Come on, Frank, buck up,' Hal said bracingly. 'We have only lost a few nights' takings.'

'I'm sorry, Hal, but I was behind with the banking.'

'How far behind?'

'Too far. They've got away with more than ten thousand dollars.'

Hal gaped at him, his mouth open but no sound emerging. 'But, Frank,' he managed to say at last, '*why* . . .'

'Don't ask,' Frank said wearily, 'just don't ask.'

But it was obvious that questions would be asked. Jay started panicking as soon as they regrouped in the parlour.

'I was behind with the banking, too, and Mr Frohman ain't gonna like this, not one little bit. Frank, how come you didn't notice anything wrong when you put the Davenport takings in the safe last night?'

Frank explained that the light had been faint, and that he had been tired. The extra money had been hidden behind – screened by, he corrected hastily – the jewellery boxes, and all the boxes were there. He was not in the habit of opening them to check the contents. 'As for your cash, Jay, I have no idea how much you keep in the safe at any one time. That is your responsibility.'

'But, Frank, there is only one key, which you insisted on keeping,' Jay pointed out in a dangerously quiet voice. 'And that safe does not appear to have been forced.'

'And how, and why, did my jewellery end up in Constance's room?' Amadine wondered.

To most people, it was beginning to look as though Constance had become involved in a robbery that went wrong.

'I'm interested in this key,' said the police officer, rising to his feet. 'Mr Smith, you will come with us to headquarters, and I trust that no one will object to a thorough search of their belongings?'

'The men and women of the company have dispersed all over town,' Hal said in dismay. 'Anyone who had the money would have disposed of it by now.'

'I am aware of that, sir,' the policeman agreed, a trifle wearily, 'but a search of the people, the baggage and the train must be done. The chances are that whoever took the money also murdered Mrs Grey.'

The others watched in silence as the police ushered Frank out of the car.

'My God,' Hal said faintly, when his brother had gone, 'they think Frank robbed the safe and killed Constance!'

However, the police were not sufficiently convinced of Frank's guilt to keep him downtown for long. Perhaps they believed his story, or perhaps the influence of Pierce Radcliffe counted for something in Chicago but, whatever the reason, Pierce brought Frank to the Auditorium shortly after the others arrived there. To no one's surprise, the search of the baggage and the train had revealed nothing so far.

'Do you believe Frank is innocent?' Pierce asked Amadine later.

'I don't know what to believe – my head is spinning with ifs and buts and maybes. But I do know that Constance's death is my fault.'

'How do you work that out?'

'If I hadn't forgotten that blasted gun, she could not have been shot with it!' Amadine rested her aching head on the back of the chair, and closed her eyes. 'Do you realise that Hal is dealing with death for a second time on this tour – another cable to send to a grieving family at home, another set of formalities, another funeral . . .'

'My lawyer will take care of everything, as I have just told Haldane-Smith.'

'The awful thing is that no one liked Constance very much. I don't think anyone actively disliked her, but she was not a person of whom one grew fond. After we found the body, we didn't weep and wail and grieve for a friend. We just sat in stunned silence, thinking: Oh, my God, not another disaster! and: How did it happen? Oh, Pierce, those poor children! We – the company – must do something for them, even if we only send them some money.'

'What money?' Pierce asked grimly.

Amadine did not answer for some time. 'The police might find the money,' she said eventually, but not with any great conviction.

'In Chicago ten thousand dollars doesn't amount to much. The death of Constance is another matter, of course. It is a high-profile case, and the police will be quite excited about it for a day or two. However, both crimes are complicated by the fact that it is possible they were committed in Davenport, Iowa – not only another town from here, but a different state. If little progress is made, both police forces have an ideal excuse for passing the buck.'

'And when we leave here, we'll be forgotten? Bloody hell,' Amadine exclaimed, 'in that case *I'll* find out who did it, if it's the last thing I do!'

'It just might be . . .' Pierce was watching her, frowning slightly.

'You mean that I might be next on the murderer's list?'

Pierce did not reply.

'No,' said Amadine slowly, 'that isn't what you meant. Constance was using my room, sleeping in my bed . . . You think that she was murdered in mistake for me.'

'It is one of several possibilities,' Pierce agreed neutrally.

'That would exonerate everyone in the company, because the world and his wife knew that Hal and Constance were sleeping together, and that I used her old room when I rejoined the train in St Louis. Oh, hold on a minute, you're back to the phantom gunman and stalker again, aren't you!'

'It was no phantom who shot Constance.'

Amadine sobered immediately. 'We must find out the truth for her sake, not merely to save my skin and my guilty conscience. But where do we start?'

'With each other,' said Pierce promptly. 'I want you to look me in the eye and tell me that you are sure I did not take the money or kill Constance.'

'Don't be silly, of course I don't think . . .' Amadine paused and considered the matter. There could have been a time when she might have suspected him of taking the money, to finance his automobile venture, but obviously she did not suspect him now. 'I am sure you had nothing to do with it,' she said with complete conviction.

'And I am equally sure that you didn't, so . . .'

'Hold on, why are you so sure?'

'Oh, come on, Amadine, you are the most transparently honest person I have ever met! I don't think you are capable of telling a lie, let alone committing murder. And as for money, if you picked up a quarter in the street, you wouldn't rest until you had found its rightful owner or given it to a worthy cause!'

'You make me sound like a freak,' Amadine protested.

'A freak of nature – yes, that's one way of putting it!' He smiled for the first time that day, and pulled her to her feet and into his arms. 'I'm sorry about Constance, but so relieved that you are safe.' He kissed her, and then put her from him with a visible effort. 'We have established that we can trust each other, but we must trust no one else.'

'Not even Hal?'

'You must admit that if Constance was murdered deliberately, for personal reasons, Hal is a prime candidate.'

'Oh God . . . I don't think that I'll make much of a sleuth. I'm too involved with all these people.'

'Which is why they might open up to you more than to the police. Very well, the next step is to treat both incidents as separate crimes, although I must say that I believe they are connected – too much of a coincidence otherwise.'

'They must be connected – my jewellery was found in Constance's room.' Amadine frowned. 'Isn't it odd that my jewellery wasn't taken!'

But Pierce's mind was on another aspect of the case. 'The clues to Constance's murder – because I agree that she did not commit suicide – are motive and access to the train. The clues to the robbery are the key to the safe, and access to the train.'

'I think that, like the police, we should start by talking to Frank,' Amadine said.

'You don't have to talk to us if you do not wish to do so,' Pierce told Frank when he joined them in Amadine's room.

'It would be a relief to speak to someone, and you two are about the only people I can trust. I'm very grateful for your assistance at the police station, Radcliffe.'

'I didn't do much. You fought your own corner very effectively.'

'Even so, I was glad of the support. Chicago hasn't been a lucky place for me, and having a local man on my side was a big help.'

'You managed to convince them of your innocence?' Amadine asked.

'I wouldn't go so far as to say that, but I think I persuaded them that I had no motive for either crime. I had no personal relationship with Constance, and bore her no ill will. I pointed out that the most likely cause of Constance's death was that she disturbed the robber while the theft was in progress. If she had seen me taking money from the safe, she wouldn't have thought anything of it – if anyone was entitled to take money from the safe, it was me.'

'Did you take the money?' Pierce asked quietly.

'No, I didn't.'

'Suppose,' Amadine suggested, 'that someone disturbed Constance while *she* was robbing the safe?'

'Haldane-Smith was right when he said she had money worries,' Pierce confirmed. 'I gather that the police found letters contesting the rights to one of her husband's plays, and demanding compensation.'

'Not ten thousand dollars' worth of compensation, surely?' Amadine exclaimed.

'No, but . . . Who would have known how much money was in the safe, Frank?'

'Only me.'

'Not even Jay? He used the safe as well as you.'

Frank shook his head. 'He didn't know how much I banked, or how much I kept back.'

'So whoever robbed the safe got lucky? They may have wanted, and expected to find, only a few hundred dollars – say, four or five hundred?'

'I suppose so.'

'The robbery hinges on the key to the safe,' Pierce said again, 'which is why the police hauled you off downtown, and why we are talking to you before we talk to the others. You are certain that there was only one key?'

'Of course I'm certain,' Frank said, a touch impatiently.

'Is the key unique, or do several safes have the same type of lock?'

'I have not the remotest idea, but if you are suggesting that someone went round America purloining keys in the hope of finding one that fitted, I think it highly unlikely.'

'Could a duplicate have been cut from the original?' Amadine asked.

'Possibly.' Frank considered this suggestion for a moment. 'But I cannot believe that the original has been out of my possession. I even sleep with the damned thing under my pillow.'

'And you sleep alone?' Pierce enquired delicately.

'On this tour – definitely!'

'Where do you keep the key during the day?'

'Here,' and Frank patted his jacket pocket, 'with the keys to the freight and baggage cars.'

'But you remove your jacket from time to time?'

'Not often – being in a state of undress undermines one's authority,' Frank said stiffly. 'However, I do leave my jacket in the prompt-corner occasionally. I did so yesterday.'

'So someone could have taken the key from your pocket without you noticing?'

'Yes, but it would be a very risky thing to do. No one would know – not even I would know – how long I would leave it there before putting it on again. And I always check the pockets for my wallet and keys when I do put it on.'

Pierce sighed. 'What about your movements on Saturday – you checked the safe before you left the train?'

'The night before I counted all the cash I had in the safe, after I added the Peoria takings. I had already made up the wages, and I placed the envelopes in the box. On Saturday morning I took the cash box to the theatre . . .'

'Wait a minute,' Pierce interrupted. 'Anyone who knew anything about your routine would realise that the Peoria takings would be in the safe?'

'And the Springfield takings, and probably St Louis.'

'And the float,' Amadine contributed. 'Everyone knew you kept a float.'

Frank looked at her. 'You are being very forbearing, Amadine. You didn't like us carrying so much cash, and warned against it most strenuously. Yet not once have you said: "I told you so"!'

'Not a very constructive comment to make,' she shrugged.

'And Jay's share of the takings was there as well.' Pierce's mind was set firmly on the contents of the safe. 'But an outsider wouldn't know that. An outsider would see you leaving the train with a cash box in the morning, and returning with a cash box at night. They wouldn't know that there was a safe. Even if they did know, they couldn't be certain that you were not carting the entire contents back and forth to the theatre every day. Anyway, go on.'

Frank described how he had walked to the theatre with the others, and worked in the theatre all day without a break. Some of the company had been allowed out for refreshments, but he and Hal had food sent in.

'It was one hell of a day,' he said with feeling.

'Because Hal was in one hell of a mood,' Amadine responded.

'That was because he and Constance . . . well, never mind.' The evening performance had ended late, he went on, due to a problem with stage machinery. He left the stage staff to dismantle the scenery and went to the theatre manager's office to cash up. 'That was when I put on my jacket.'

'Did you notice anything odd, or out of place, that day?'

'Not a thing.' Frank turned to Amadine for confirmation. 'Did you? Everything was normal as far as I was concerned, except for Hal's foul mood, and the blasted machinery breaking down.' And the fact that I wouldn't speak to Theo, he thought, and that I was so upset I didn't keep my mind properly on the job . . .

Amadine agreed. 'And Constance being absent was unusual. She hadn't missed an hour's rehearsal all tour, let alone a performance. She always looked pale and vulnerable, but she had the constitution of an ox.'

'You and Jay sorted out the Davenport takings with the manager, and then what did you do?'

'Checked that the stage staff had the scenery and props under control, and returned to the train with Hal. The rest you know – I put the cash box, and Jay's cash bag, into the safe and did not notice that anything was amiss. But the robbery must have taken place between my leaving in the morning and returning at night.'

Pierce nodded. 'Because the Davenport receipts, and the pearls Amadine wore during that performance, were not taken. Yes, I agree. Can we be so certain about the time of the murder?'

'No,' Amadine said sharply, 'because these dolts – Hal and Frank, that is – did not have the common courtesy to look in on Constance before they went to bed.'

'Neither did you,' Frank retorted.

Amadine winced. 'The thought did cross my mind, but I felt that neither Constance nor Hal would welcome my arrival at that juncture, and Ida had been told not to go to Constance's room unless specifically summoned. Still, it's no excuse really.'

She noticed that Frank was looking completely exhausted, and indicated to Pierce that they ought to leave the discussion there for the day, but Pierce had one last question.

'Why were you so far behind with the banking?'

Frank stood up and gave them the answer he had given the police. 'I am hopelessly inefficient, I'm afraid. You know us theatrical types – not really cut out for administration and finance. And I had such a lot to do, after Tom's death.'

Pierce and Amadine let it go at that, but after Frank had gone they exchanged a worried look.

'I believed nearly everything he said,' Amadine said slowly, 'but not the last point. Frank does have too much work to do, I grant you that, but he is not inefficient. Quite the contrary.'

'You think he fell behind with the banking intention-ally?'

'Yes,' said Amadine. 'Don't you?'

It was not easy, but eventually Pierce persuaded Amadine that he ought to speak to Hal alone, convincing her that Hal would talk more freely about Constance in her absence.

In the suite shared by the two brothers, Frank had fallen into a deep, almost drugged sleep, and Hal closed the bed-room door so that he should not be disturbed. To begin with, the two men talked about the formalities connected with Constance's death, with which Pierce's lawyer would assist, but it was immediately apparent that this was a very different Hal from the man Pierce had encountered at earlier meetings. On those occasions, Hal's love for Amadine had been but thinly veiled, along with his jealousy of her association with Pierce. This new Hal was haggard with grief, seemingly heartbroken at the death of his one true love.

'I can't take it in,' he said brokenly, passing a weary hand over his eyes. 'This time yesterday everything was fine – wonderful, in fact – and now my very reason for living has gone.'

'I had not realised that you and Constance were so close.'

'We were to be married, here in Chicago. But instead of a wedding, there is to be a funeral.' Hal's voice shook, and he paused in order to regain his equilibrium and British stiff upper lip.

Pierce did not know whether to believe him or not. That was the trouble with dealing with actors, particularly one of Hal's calibre; it was virtually impossible to tell what was artifice and what was sincere.

'I have sent a message to the family,' Hal went on when he had regained control, 'but I can hardly bear to think of the effect on those poor little children. And I have sent a score of cables to members of the profession – they'll rally round, bless their hearts, and make sure that the children are not left without food or shelter.'

'Amadine was suggesting that the company should send some financial assistance to the children.'

'She would do that – she has a kind and generous heart.'

Even Hal's conversation sounded vaguely artificial, Pierce thought, as if the dialogue had been lifted from a 50-year-old melodrama.

'And we will do so,' Hal continued, 'as soon as our financial problems are sorted out.' He glanced at the bedroom door and then looked away quickly, as if anxious not to draw attention to Frank. 'By the way, Radcliffe,' and his tone was exquisitely casual, 'will there be a postmortem, do you think?'

'Yes, bound to be.'

'But it's obvious why she died – she was shot. So there isn't any point in investigating further, surely?'

'I'm no expert on these matters, but I understand that the usual procedure is to examine the entire body and report on anything, even the general state of health, that might be relevant.'

'Oh.' With consummate skill, Hal managed to alter his expression to one of intense distaste at the prospect of a surgeon's scalpel defiling the body of his beloved.

'While on the subject of Constance's health, why did she stay in bed on Saturday?'

Hal shrugged. 'You'd better ask Amadine that question. She spoke to Constance before we went to the theatre.'

'Constance merely told Amadine that she was not feeling well, and did not elaborate on the exact nature of her symptoms. Also, according to Amadine, Constance had seemed perfectly well the previous day.'

'Well, I don't know what was wrong with her. Probably a woman's problem of some kind.'

'So you don't know if she really was ill, or just shamming? Or perhaps sulking, after some sort of quarrel?'

'Quarrel – what quarrel?' Hal demanded. 'Look, if you are implying that Constance and I had a fight on Friday night, you couldn't be further from the mark. And it's the fight she had with someone on Saturday night that you should be worrying about – although, come to think of it, I don't know what the hell it has to do with you!'

'Amadine and I are only trying to help Frank,' Pierce assured him. 'The law seems to be treating him as a prime suspect, and we want to assemble the widest possible picture of the whole affair. I'm interested in Constance's health because one of the mysteries of the case is how the murderer – and the robber, if they are one and the same person – gained access to the train. It seems to me perfectly possible that Constance let him, or her, in. Either she was expecting a visitor, and that is why she didn't go to the theatre, or someone – presumably someone she knew – attracted her attention through the window. Either way, she could have opened the door of the Palace Car and let them in, without the staff knowing.'

'I hadn't thought of that.' Hal leaned forward eagerly, but then shook his head. 'But who could it have been? She didn't know anyone in America outside the company.'

'This is embarrassing in view of your personal relationship, but could Constance have planned to rob the safe? We know that she needed money.'

'I suppose there could have been a side to her character that I did not know,' Hal replied cautiously.

'And was there a time when Constance was jealous of Amadine?'

Hal went red with embarrassment and spluttered a bit before saying, 'It is possible – not that she had any reason to be jealous, of course.'

'Of course,' Pierce agreed smoothly, thinking that if Hal lied about that, he had probably lied about everything else. 'Again I must apologise if this gives you pain, but there is something I must tell you.' He told Hal about Amadine's befriending of Ben, the newspaper boy, and how the lad had witnessed Amadine's accident. 'Ben is positive that Amadine was pushed.'

'Then you were right about the incidents in Boston and Philadelphia!'

'That was my first reaction, but the boy is certain that Amadine's assailant in Chicago was a woman.'

'Oh God, you think it was Constance!' Hal closed his eyes, as if fate had dealt him one blow too many.

'Ben did not see the woman's face. She was wearing a cloak, with a hood pulled forward over her hair, and he only saw her from behind. She gave Amadine a sharp shove, and then hurried away without waiting to see what happened next – in that blinding snowstorm, she disappeared in seconds.'

'We'll never know if it was Constance, will we!'

'We might, if you would allow Ben to look at Constance's clothes. We could ask Ida to mix in some other coats and cloaks, then see if Ben picks out the correct garment. You see, Hal,' and it was the first time Pierce used the name, 'I think we have to work on the theory that whoever pushed Amadine in Chicago also set the fire in Baltimore. And the Baltimore incident was always likely to be an "inside job".'

'You reach a stage where you feel that things cannot get any worse. But they do . . . they do . . .'

After Pierce had gone, Hal sat alone, drinking, far into the night. In his mind's eye, he visualised the newspaper headlines, and the pictures of Constance that would dominate the news for the foreseeable future. Death gives her fame . . . Yes, now Constance would receive all the publicity and attention she had always craved.

'I wish that you could have been a fly on the wall,' Pierce admitted to Amadine, 'because you know him better than I do. I couldn't tell when he was lying and when he was telling the truth.'

Amadine listened carefully to his account of the proceedings but only once, when Pierce relayed Hal's marriage plans, did her expression change from absorbed attentiveness to wide-eyed scepticism.

'That doesn't ring true, but why should he lie?'

'And why was he in a bad mood on Saturday? Regrettably, there didn't seem to be much point in asking him outright, any more than it was worthwhile asking whether he went into Constance's room last night and shot her while everyone else was asleep.'

'Which he could easily have done, but he would only deny it,' Amadine agreed, and then she frowned in an effort to remember. 'This morning Frank said something about Hal and Constance having an argument on Friday night.'

'Something Hal specifically denied.'

'Interestingly, Frank mentioned it *before* I discovered Constance was dead, and he has not said a word about it since. It's almost as if he thinks Hal murdered Constance, but doesn't want to point the finger.'

'If Hal did kill Constance, he could have taken the money to make it look like a robbery,' suggested Pierce.

'He had easy access to the safe key. He bolted his breakfast that morning, and rushed back to his room – the key could still have been under Frank's pillow.'

'We only have Frank's word for the fact that the cash was stolen before he returned to the train on Saturday night,' Pierce agreed.

'This is ghastly,' Amadine groaned. 'I really am beginning to suspect that one of my friends is a thief and a murderer. But which one, Pierce, which one?'

Chapter Twenty-Six

It came as a shock to Amadine to discover that, in the eyes of the police, she was as much a suspect as anyone else. Of course, when she looked at the facts, she could see their point of view. Apparently she had been the last of the company to see Constance alive; she had discovered the body; and the indications were that Constance had been killed with Amadine's gun. She even gained the impression that they would like her to be the guilty party. The death of Constance was already a *cause célèbre*, but Amadine Sinclair's direct involvement would transform it into the most glamorous crime of the century.

When they questioned her, three areas received particular attention. First, Amadine's financial position: she was forced to concede that an injection of cash would not be unwelcome. Second, her movements and those of the company on that Saturday in Davenport: she had not left the theatre all day, but was unable to say with certainty whether all her colleagues had been present all the time. Third, and most important, the gun. The police wanted to know every detail of where she had purchased it, where she had kept it at each stage of the tour and who had seen it. Then they asked her why she had bought it.

Reluctantly, because somehow she was sure it was a red herring, Amadine told them about the incidents in Boston and Philadelphia, and about the fire in Baltimore. Now the police officer was really interested, noting down every detail, however trivial, and asking again whether any strangers had been seen loitering in the vicinity of the train. It was only after an extensive grilling that Amadine was released, and she joined Gwen in her dressing room.

'Could I do with some extra cash?' she seethed. 'Oh no, officer. What, *me*, officer? I'm an actress – didn't you know that we are all millionaires!'

'They asked me the same question,' Gwen said in a tired voice.

'What did you tell them?' Amadine tried to sound as if the answer was not important.

'I felt bound to admit that I have an invalid mother to support and that, despite my advanced years, I have no home of my own and nothing put by for my imminent old age.'

'Oh, dear.'

'The young – the *very* young – policeman wasn't quite so tactful. His expression and tone of voice conveyed quite clearly his opinion that I am a failure.'

'How can such a respected member of the profession be a failure!'

'I am penniless and, in America, that makes me a failure.'

'You aren't someone who uses money as a yardstick.'

'Even by other standards, I haven't been a raging success,' Gwen said sadly. She seemed to be sagging slightly in the chair, suddenly old and tired. 'This is the land of opportunity. If you don't take that opportunity, and make something of yourself, then more fool you.'

'You have made a living out of the theatre and that is no mean achievement,' Amadine insisted. 'I hope that I'll be able to say as much one day, but I'm not counting on it. And as for brash young policemen with no manners, your only concern is to keep your name off the list of suspects.'

'They'll have me down as a likely candidate for robbing

the safe.' Gwen levered herself out of the chair. 'I didn't take the money, or kill Constance. I have hurt enough people in the past without hurting more now. Oh, and if you're discussing this with your precious Pierce, give him this message from me: tell him that if I couldn't take Sam's money because it was not rightfully mine, I'm certainly not likely to take Hal's.'

It was a message that made no sense to Amadine, but clearly rang a bell with Pierce when she relayed it later in the day.

'It is a long story,' was all he would say in reply to Amadine's demand for an explanation, 'but I am inclined to cross Gwen off the list of suspects. The really interesting news is that, by devious means, not entirely excluding bribery and corruption, I have managed to obtain a copy of the postmortem report. Almost certainly Constance died between 7 p.m. and midnight on Saturday.'

'How do they know?'

'Physicians have been studying rigor mortis for many years,' Pierce explained, 'along with the rate at which the body cools after death. It is still an inexact science, with many inconsistencies in the findings, but they are getting better at it all the time.'

'So Constance could have died after we returned from the theatre,' Amadine said thoughtfully. 'We were late-ish that night, due to the delay while the machinery was fixed, but we were back before midnight.'

'The next finding is that she was killed by a bullet fired from your gun.'

Amadine was silent for a few moments. 'Are they sure?' she asked heavily. 'I would give anything for it not to be true!'

'A gun barrel has grooves cut, in spirals, into the inner surface; when the gun is fired, these grooves cause the bullet to rotate for reasons of flight and accuracy. In a case like this, the scientists can compare the grooves on the

bullet taken from Constance's body with those in the barrel
of the gun. The technique has been known for quite some
time – I believe this kind of examination was pioneered by
the Bow Street Runners in London.' Pierce watched the
expressions chasing across that mobile, expressive face. 'You
mustn't blame yourself,' he said gently. 'You might just as
well say that it is my fault, for suggesting that you acquired
a gun.'

'There's that, too,' Amadine agreed, but she did not
smile. 'Does the report say anything else?'

'It confirms that it is extremely unlikely that Constance
committed suicide. For one thing, it is a very odd fact that
women hardly ever shoot themselves. For another,
although Constance was right-handed, and she was shot in
the right side of the head, the gun would have had to be
held at a very awkward angle.'

'It wasn't an accident, either. By no stretch of the imagination can I envisage Constance playing with a gun
because she had nothing better to do.'

'No, it is murder. Definitely.' Pierce paused before playing his trump card. 'The last finding could be our best lead
so far: Constance was pregnant. Only just – a matter of a
few weeks – but still pregnant.'

Hal . . . Amadine could think of nothing to say.

'I'll bring Ben to the theatre this week,' Pierce went on,
his mind going back to his conversation with Hal, 'but I
thought *Tanqueray* was not entirely suitable for such a
young and impressionable mind.'

At that description of Ben, Amadine did smile, but only
briefly. 'I don't think that doing *Tanqueray* tonight is in
terribly good taste. I have to kill myself in the last act.'

No doubt about it: Blanche Villard was amazing. Amadine
watched in stunned admiration as the young American
slipped seamlessly into Constance's roles, starting with the
part of Ellean in *Tanqueray*. In the past she had played the

vulgar little Lady Orreyed, and played her rather well, but the transformation into the saintly stepdaughter was effortless and word-perfect.

'I really do believe,' Amadine gasped to Gwen, 'that if Hal was taken ill tomorrow, Blanche could step into his shoes as Aubrey Tanqueray, and pull it off!'

'I wouldn't go so far as to say that – she isn't Charlotte Cushman – but I agree that she can take over any female part, from you or the humblest super, at the drop of a hat. Remarkable,' and Gwen shook her head. 'Of course it remains to be seen whether or not she can create an original role of her own.'

'With Hal to guide her, she could.'

Amadine had heard the old saying that, in a murder case, it was essential to examine the *cui bono* factor: who benefits? It occurred to Amadine for the first time that Blanche had benefited from Constance's death: she had inherited Constance's roles, which were a step up from her previous position on the professional ladder, and, unless Hal really had intended to marry Constance and was heartbroken by her death, she had acquired a clear path to becoming his mistress. A position which, if Blanche continued to play her cards with such subtlety and acuteness, could lead to a more elevated status.

'I keep wondering if the murder and the robbery were two separate crimes,' Amadine mused, 'or whether the murder was a result of the robbery, or whether the robbery was staged to conceal the real motive for the murder.'

'If you are wondering whether Blanche needed money, she did,' Gwen said, 'and I think the time has come for her to tell you about her reasons.'

Even Amadine's friendly and informal invitation to give an account of herself made Blanche very ill at ease and defensive.

'I must say, Gwen, that you're a big help! I wouldn't 've

told you if I'd known you'd sneak on me.' With heightened colour and an air of righteous indignation, Blanche supplied an abbreviated but truthful account of her family circumstances and her stepfather's demands for money. 'And, no,' she concluded defiantly, 'I did not tell the police about him – I'm not stupid! I gave them a sob story about my mother, and left it at that.'

'Did the police ask for your mother's name and address?' Amadine asked.

Blanche nodded. 'I suppose they'll rush out and check if I wired her ten thousand dollars recently.'

'But you didn't volunteer any information about your grandmother?'

'And have them tell her that I'm an actress, and mixed up in a murder? For land's sakes, Amadine, that is exactly what I am trying to avoid!'

Gwen was trying to remember the names Blanche had mentioned during their original discussion: Dora Hamilton, and old Mrs Hamilton of Mount Vernon Place; yes, that was it. She made a mental note to pass on the information to Amadine.

'Did you leave the theatre during the day on Saturday?'

'Why don't you look in Frank's register?' Blanche retorted.

'Because the register is useless in these circumstances,' Amadine said evenly. 'Obviously anyone leaving the theatre with nefarious, or murderous, intent, is unlikely to advertise the fact by signing the register. Anyway, since when has that book been any indicator of your movements?'

Rather sulkily, Blanche conceded that point. 'If you must know,' she went on with a bravura display of nonchalance, 'I did pop out for a few minutes. Hal was being beastly to everyone, and I felt that if I didn't escape into the fresh air for a few minutes, I'd scream.'

Fresh air? The temperature in Davenport had been below freezing.

'However,' Blanche continued truculently, 'I did not go back to the train. I went into a tearoom for a snack.'

Not having the time or the resources to check this state- ment, Amadine was forced to accept it. 'How much have you saved towards the five hundred dollars for your step- father?' she asked.

'Two hundred – so I can repay the fifty I borrowed, if that's what is worrying you! Oh, sorry,' and Blanche looked shamefaced. 'I didn't mean it to sound like that. It's just that . . .' Her voice trailed away.

It's just that you are frightened, Amadine thought. We all are, whether innocent or guilty.

'I have done my best to save,' Blanche went on, 'but after sending my mother's allowance, and paying for board and lodging . . .' Again she broke off, reddening.

'You aren't paying for board and lodging now,' Gwen remarked quietly.

It dawned on Amadine that Blanche was currently occu- pying the room reserved for Constance at the Auditorium Hotel, and she wondered if Hal or Frank had agreed to the arrangement.

'It seemed a pity to waste it,' Blanche said, her head tilt- ing with a slight show of defiance.

Indeed. And free board and lodging were another bene- fit of Constance's demise.

'I'm not cancelling next week's première of *Much Ado*,' Hal announced on Tuesday.

Amadine knew that he had received a visit from the police the previous evening, and guessed that it concerned Constance's pregnancy. Whatever the case, Hal wasn't telling. Like all of them, he had gone straight to bed after last night's performance – no convivial suppers upstairs in the Auditorium dining room, or across town at Rector's or Henrici's, not this week.

'You're mad,' she declared. 'In our present circumstances,

the Hero plot is fine, but the clowns? And as for you and me trying to lift ourselves sufficiently for the repartee of Benedick and Beatrice . . .'

'We are actors, Amadine,' he reminded her coldly. 'Our personal feelings don't come into it, and our personal lives should not affect our work.'

'Your future wife has just been murdered! Let's stick with *Tanqueray* and *Romeo* – at least those pieces are supposed to be tense and tragic.' She took in the taut lines of his handsome face, the set of his thin lips and the haunted look in his eyes. 'A pity that *Hamlet* isn't in the repertoire. The Prince that you would give now would be the definitive version, and ought to be preserved in amber for future generations to enjoy and marvel at.'

A reluctant smile twisted the corners of his mouth, but the slight relaxation of expression only made him look even more exhausted.

'We proceed with *Much Ado* as planned,' he repeated. 'It will be no bad thing for everyone to keep busy this week. Take our minds off . . .' He swallowed, and then went on: 'Blanche will take over as Hero.'

Now there's a surprise, thought Amadine.

She went in search of Jay, locating him at the same moment that Theo appeared with the morning mail. Jay stared at the letters in Theo's hand with a hunted look on his face.

'I hope there isn't anything for me,' he said apprehensively.

'Why, what are you expecting?' Theo demanded.

'The sack,' Jay said miserably. 'Notification that the great Charles Frohman has dispensed with my services.'

'Not today he hasn't,' Theo assured him. 'Not by this post, at any rate.'

Jay took out a handkerchief and mopped his forehead. 'A respite, albeit temporary. What is the old saying? "The condemned man ate a hearty meal." I haven't been able to touch a morsel of food since Sunday morning.'

Amadine took him by the arm and steered him firmly in the direction of her dressing room, sat him down and closed the door.

'Frohman can't fire you, just because the safe was robbed.'

'Oh yes, he can, and I have very little doubt that he will. But you are right about one thing,' and Jay groaned, 'it won't be just because the safe was robbed. It will be partly because of the fearful mess I made of everything *before* the safe was robbed.'

'You fell behind with the banking.' Amadine nodded. 'It does seem rather a coincidence that Frank did the same thing at the same time.'

'But that's the point,' Jay said eagerly. 'It wasn't coincidence at all. It was because Frank fell behind that I did, too.'

Amadine lifted both eyebrows in a gesture of exaggerated enquiry.

'I don't know why Frank stopped going to the bank regularly,' Jay said. 'He maintains that he is inefficient, but that simply isn't true – he is one of the most organised tour managers I've come across, and I've come across a few, yes, sir! Now me, I'm your original scatterbrain when it comes to money – which probably explains why I don't have any of my own. I relied on Frank to keep my banking habits regular. Frank went to the bank – I went to the bank. Easy. And regular as clockwork. But as soon as Frank slackened off . . . Well, you get the picture.'

Amadine did, and conceded that Jay fitted this picture of inefficiency far more snugly than did Frank.

'Your Mr Frohman is not a very understanding employer?'

'He's entitled to be angry. My accounts are in such a muddle that I'm struggling to calculate how much money Frohman is owed, and how much was taken from the safe. If I ever do manage to work it out, I'm afraid that he will hold me personally liable for the sum that would not

have been in the safe if I had remitted it properly.' Jay
was rumpling his sandy hair with one hand, his body limp
and defeated, as if he was a puppet which had been cut
open so that the sawdust was spilling out, taking all his
old cockiness and self-confidence with it. 'I do realise,' he
said in a low voice, 'that it seems very wrong to be so
worried about losing a job when Constance has lost her
life.'

'We are all worried about something. Look, you'll get
another job. Easily.'

'You reckon? After this?' Jay shook his head. 'Frohman
ain't gonna give me a recommendation. I doubt I'll even
make it back to advance man. Oh God, Amadine, I don't
want to go back to being an advance man! You know
what terrifies me? That he'll throw me out, here in
Chicago, when I'm absolutely broke and haven't even the
fare to New York. That blasted bandit took my salary
along with everything else, and I need it. I have commitments . . .'

'There's the Davenport receipts.'

'Oh, yeah. I can really see Frohman giving his blessing to
the idea of my taking a hundred bucks out of the one little
payment that's been salvaged.'

Amadine sighed. She would have liked to reassure him
with an offer of financial help, if the worst did happen, but
was in no position to do so. Her own finances were in a par-
lous state after the robbery and, if they improved,
Constance's children were a more deserving cause than Jay,
or Blanche, or even Gwen.

'You mentioned that you had commitments,' she said
tentatively.

Jay hesitated slightly. 'I've been helping out a friend,
sending cash when I can, and I'm afraid he has come to rely
on it.'

'Does he know the bad news yet?'

'Funnily enough he was due in Chicago on Sunday, but

never turned up. I wired him the glad tidings, and right now he is one very unhappy man.'

'Of course you and Theo had left the train before we knew anything was wrong.'

Jay nodded. 'We shared a cab to the hotel, and the way the police reacted, you'd think it was the "getaway vehicle"! If they've gone through my luggage once, they've done it a thousand times. They even examined the bag itself, as if they thought it might have a secret compartment. I have no idea what ten thousand dollars in cash looks like, but I would have thought it was rather a bulky item – too bulky for secret compartments, anyway. *And*, if I had stolen the money, I would have acted differently.'

'What would you have done?'

'Nipped off the train the instant it arrived in Chicago, stashed the loot somewhere safe, then raced back to the train and waited, with my other luggage, for the crime to be discovered.'

Amadine thought for a few minutes, and could not fault that reasoning. 'Did you go back to the train on Saturday?'

'Yes,' Jay said frankly, 'In fact, I spent some time there, because I didn't go to the theatre during the day. No offence, Amadine, but I could recite those plays off by heart by now. Saturday was one of those boring days when I had nothing much to do, so I wandered round town for a while, felt cold and came back to the train mid-morning. Ironically, I worked on my accounts for a while before dozing off.'

'Where were you sitting?'

'In the men's car. Sometimes I go into the Palace Car, but that day I didn't want to disturb Constance. I woke in the early afternoon and, at about two o'clock or thereabouts, walked back into town for a bite to eat and a drink.' He hesitated. 'I'm afraid that I had several drinks,' he said apologetically, 'and played some pool. Like I said, I was bored.'

'What time did you come to the theatre?'

'Oh, I was in and out all evening as usual. The saloon was across the street from the theatre, so it was easy to keep an eye on things. The delay when the machinery broke down meant not only that Frank and I cashed up late, but also that I'd had a few drinks too many. I asked Frank to put my cash bag in the safe, and crashed into bed. I slept like a log and woke rather late on Sunday morning.'

'I still think that it was a miracle my jewellery wasn't stolen – a miracle, but also a mystery. Perhaps I should be wishing that it had been taken instead of the money, because the jewellery was insured and the money wasn't!'

'Yes, it seems an odd thing,' Jay said thoughtfully. 'Perhaps the robber intended to take the jewels, but heard someone coming and had to leave in a hurry.'

'Could be, but it doesn't explain why it was in Constance's room.' Unless, Amadine reflected, Constance was the person who was heard coming.

'The only other reason I can think of is that the jewellery would be too difficult to dispose of, particularly if the thief was an amateur.'

'Now that is a good point. Thanks, Jay.'

The jewellery was returned to Amadine by the police that afternoon, and Constance's personal belongings were also released. Blanche's appropriation of Constance's space not yet having extended to her dressing room, Ida stored them there. The task upset the usually resilient Londoner, as Amadine noticed, but it transpired that other aspects of the situation were adding to Ida's distress.

'The police think I did it,' she wailed. 'They questioned me, and Walter, and the Pullman staff for ages, much longer than they kept anyone else.'

'Because you have access to the Palace Car,' Amadine explained patiently, 'and you were close to Constance. Were you able to give the police any useful information?'

'Lord knows. I just told the truth. I told them that I didn't neglect Mrs Grey – she ordered me not to go to her room unless I was sent for. I didn't even know she was ill on Saturday, not at first. I was in your room, Miss Amadine, seeing to your things as usual, and then I went to the theatre where I helped the wardrobe mistress with the *Much Ado* costumes until you needed me. I only found out that Mrs Grey was sick when she was wanted for a fitting.'

'Did you leave the theatre later on?'

Ida shook her head.

'Not even when the performance ground to a halt when the machinery broke down?'

A blush tinged Ida's city-pale face. 'I watched them mending it.'

Amadine thought that she saw the light. 'Do you have a friend in the company?'

'Sort of,' was the cautious reply, and then it all came out in a torrent. 'And it wasn't him that did it, neither! That Walter can tell his lies until he's blue in the face, but just because I let George have a little look round the Palace Car doesn't mean . . .'

'Hold on,' Amadine said sharply. 'You let who do what?'

'George had never been in the Palace Car, so I let him have one little look. I'm sorry if I did wrong, but I didn't see the harm and I still don't.'

'And Hal's valet saw him there, and told the police?'

'He's jealous, and out to make trouble. Now the police believe George and I was in it together but we wasn't, honest to God. I wasn't in nuthin' with no one!'

'Of course you weren't, Ida, but, to be on the safe side, wouldn't it be a good idea if someone – Mr Radcliffe, for instance – had a word with George? Then we could help you to iron out any little problems with the police.'

'I suppose so,' but Ida looked unconvinced and, if anything, more worried than before.

*

His impatience to discover the truth overcoming other considerations, Pierce brought Ben to the theatre that night. Unbeknown to Amadine, Ida was instructed to collect coats and cloaks from the other women and to arrange them, with Constance's clothes, in the dead woman's former dressing room. Hal, Pierce, Ida and an excited Ben gathered there after the performance.

Ben was barely recognisable as the street-child whom Amadine had befriended. Scrubbed to a shine and neatly dressed in a new suit, he was on his best behaviour in this unfamiliar environment. Yet the rough edges had not been smoothed away, and his innate assertiveness – which might easily turn into aggression if his life took a wrong turn – had not been squashed. Only Pierce had any confidence in this exercise. Hal and Ida looked Ben up and down, and then watched his every move, with cynical scepticism.

Ben took his time, subjecting each garment to a detailed inspection before moving on to the next. In complete silence and in the stillness of the small room, he took centre stage without a flicker of embarrassment or the slightest dent in his self-confidence.

'That one,' and he pointed to Constance's distinctive fur-trimmed cloak.

'You are certain that the woman who pushed Amadine under the car was wearing that cloak?' Hal said slowly.

''Course I'm certain.'

'It doesn't mean that the woman was Constance,' said a quiet voice behind them. Unnoticed in the tension of the moment, Amadine had entered the room and quickly understood what was happening. 'Someone else could have been wearing the cloak.'

A brief flare of hope lightened Hal's face. 'Who would have had the opportunity to take it?'

'Apart from the hotel staff – and I think we can discount them – Ida, Gwen and Blanche.' Amadine had creamed off her stage make-up and her face was white with shock.

Ben stared critically at Ida. 'It wasn't her,' he asserted. 'She's much too big.'

Ida could be kindly described as a strapping wench, and her relief at being exonerated from the crime was tinged with indignation.

'That probably clears Gwen as well,' Amadine remarked, 'but ask her and Blanche to come here, Ida.'

As Amadine had anticipated, Ben immediately pronounced Gwen too tall, but when he looked at Blanche, he nodded. 'Could be.'

Hal handed the cloak to Blanche. 'Please put it on.'

She did so, glancing nervously from person to person. 'What am I supposed to have done?'

After the situation had been explained, Ben nodded again. 'She's the right size.'

'It wasn't me. I wouldn't do a thing like that.' Blanche, panic-stricken, pulled off the cloak and thrust it at Hal as if it was red-hot. 'I was with Gwen all the time we were here. Gwen, tell them!'

'We were together most of the time,' Gwen admitted, 'but . . .'

'Gwen, I never went out. I was paying more than I could really afford for a room at the Auditorium Hotel and I intended to make the most of every moment. It was such a thrill for me to be able to sit in the reception room and look out over the lake – if we could see the lake, because it snowed nearly every day! We were there together, every morning, until we went to the theatre.'

'She's right,' Gwen announced to the room in general. 'Yes, Blanche was definitely with me at the time of Amadine's accident.'

'And Constance?' It seemed that Hal was still hoping that she was not the culprit.

Gwen and Blanche exchanged a look, and Gwen shook her head. 'Constance went out every morning, round about the time Amadine left. She always said she had an errand –

gloves at Marshall Field's, a scarf from Schlesinger and Mayer – but, come to think of it, she never showed us her purchases.'

'She followed me.' Amadine's voice was steady, and her expression was composed as she turned to Pierce. 'Did she set the fire in Baltimore, too?'

'I think so. I had a word with Theo, and he confirms that Constance used his typewriter on a number of occasions. Not only would it have been easy for her to write the letter that lured you to the theatre and leave it surreptitiously at the hotel desk, but she knew you well enough to be sure that you would respond to such a cry for help.'

'I vaguely recall a conversation with her on the subject, but surely you don't suspect her of shooting at me in Boston!'

'No, and it certainly wasn't Constance who followed you in Philadelphia. However, those incidents may have given her the idea: there was a mysterious assailant about, who would probably be blamed if anything did happen to you.'

'He wasn't in Chicago, not while I was watching,' Ben announced cheerfully.

Amadine had been about to leave the room, but she paused and stared at him. 'What do you know about this?' she demanded.

'He,' and Ben jerked his head at Pierce, 'told me to be his eyes and ears, and never let you out of my sight. But there wasn't anything to see or hear, and then I went and missed the best bit.' He was seriously put out that Constance had been murdered while he was occupied elsewhere.

'So that's why you let him stay at Prairie Avenue,' Amadine said grimly to Pierce. 'To spy on me. I should have known that you weren't a natural philanthropist.'

'He's all right,' Ben protested.

'Constance hated me enough to try to kill me,' Amadine said slowly. 'Twice.'

'She may not have intended to kill, but merely to incapacitate you, and to ensure that you left the tour,' Pierce consoled. 'And jealousy isn't the same as hate.'

But nothing anyone said could alleviate the horror of what Constance had done.

'I suggest that we summarise our findings so far,' Pierce said when he arrived for breakfast with Amadine the next morning.

'We know that Constance was shot, with my gun, between 7 p.m. and midnight.'

'We *think* – because we have only Frank's word for this – that the robbery took place between approximately nine in the morning and half-past eleven at night.'

'Constance was pregnant, which might give Hal a motive if he did not wish to marry her. And Hal did have the best opportunity for the murder and the robbery.'

'No,' Pierce insisted. 'Frank had the best opportunity for the robbery, and we don't buy his inefficiency excuse for falling behind with the banking. Also, he was the only person who knew that the safe was stuffed with cash and, as the safe was not forced, a key had to be used – the key that was kept in Frank's pocket or under his pillow.'

'We decided to exclude Gwen, but Blanche had a motive for robbery and for murder. The fact that Jay's financial transactions are in a muddle is suspicious, and we know that he could have smuggled the stolen cash off the train.'

'We know that Constance had a motive for robbery, and your jewellery was in her room. Also, nothing but the cash from the safe was stolen.'

At that, Amadine frowned. 'There's something nagging at the back of my mind. Never mind, it'll come to me later if it's important. Go on.'

'We don't know what Constance did all day, except that a few light refreshments were served to her at lunchtime and in the early evening, but she was last seen alive at seven.'

There was a moment's silence as both Pierce and
Amadine tried to think of anything else they could add.

'More questions than answers, I'm afraid,' Pierce said
ruefully.

'I still have to talk to Theo, and we agreed that you
would interview Ida's George.'

'I thought I would put a detective agency on to Blanche's
family in Baltimore, and I could ask them to take a look at
Theo while I'm about it.'

'Surely that isn't necessary,' Amadine protested. 'I'm
inclined to rule out Theo entirely.'

'So am I, but there's no harm in confirming that he is
who he says he is.'

'I concede that we didn't meet his family when we were
in Philadelphia, but nothing will persuade me that Theo is
anything but an upright citizen.'

'Then perhaps I ought to speak to him, while you take on
the awful George.'

'We don't know that George is awful, but I would prefer
to stick to our original plan. It wouldn't do for me to be too
friendly with stage staff and supers. Besides, if anything
came of it, Ida would never forgive me. Oh Lord,' and she
sighed, 'I do hope that we're wasting our time. It isn't that
I don't want to know who killed Constance – I just don't
want it to be one of my friends.'

'Don't pin your hopes on some random intruder,' Pierce
warned. 'The facts regarding the key indicate that the
robber, at any rate, had access to either Frank's jacket or his
bed. However, the time of Constance's murder does make
it more difficult for her killer to be one of the company.
Everyone would have been at the theatre between seven
and at least eleven o'clock. There are a very limited number
of people who could have done it after the performance, yet
before midnight.'

'You are forgetting the delay while the machinery was
fixed. Any one of us – except Frank, who was doing the

fixing – could have hurried back to the train and still returned to the theatre in time for the next act.'

'Be taking a bit of a chance though, wouldn't it?'

'Not for seasoned performers. It was obvious from the start that the machinery job would be a long one.'

'Therefore everyone would have been aware of the situation?'

'With the possible exception of Theo, yes. And if Theo wasn't at the theatre all evening, he wouldn't have been missed.'

'What about Jay? Like Theo, he wasn't essential to the performance.'

Amadine thought for a moment. 'Jay wouldn't have been missed either,' she said at last, 'and I should think he knows enough about theatrical matters to have assessed the implications of the machinery breakdown.'

'Which puts us back to square one,' Pierce said ruefully. 'Back to one of the company, and probably one who was thoroughly familiar with the Palace Car.'

'But everyone in the company knew that Constance was ill, and that she would be in her room in that car. Surely that was the one evening that a prospective robber would avoid?'

'Unless that robber had a particular reason for needing the money at that juncture, and was prepared to take the risk. And unless a murderer saw a golden opportunity to confront Constance on her own.'

Ever since the idea was mooted, Pierce had not relished the prospect of speaking to George White. He could not say why this should be, but the moment he set eyes on the man his apprehension was justified. Pierce was well acquainted with English manners and mores and he knew instantly that, from the dyed hair to the fake accent, George was a fraud. Added to which, he possessed an extremely unpleasant attitude. Most people were over-eager in their anxiety to be seen to assist with enquiries, but not this one. He had smiled, and shaken hands, politely when Ida brought him into the office that Pierce had commandeered at the theatre but, as soon as Ida left, animosity spread over his face like a sneer. He did not sit down.

'Who are you, anyway?' he demanded. 'And what is your relationship with Amadine?'

'What the hell has that to do with you?' Pierce asked in astonishment.

'That's for me to know and you to find out.' George leaned forward, resting his hands on the desk. 'Ida only drops hints and smiles knowingly, but if I find out that you are sleeping with Amadine, I'll swing for you.'

'Now, look here . . .'

'No, you look here. I don't have to answer any more questions about the murder. I have already spoken to the police.'

'Ida thinks that the two of you are the chief suspects.'

'Ida is a fool.'

'So why did you agree to meet me?'

'Ida said that it was Amadine's idea, and I want to appear co-operative. Mustn't ruffle Hal's or Frank's feathers.'

'You call them by their first names?' Pierce asked in surprise.

'I worked with them years ago, when they were just starting out and were no better than me. What do you expect me to call them: "sir"?'

Pierce, fighting an urge to punch this obnoxious person on the nose, was also puzzled. He associated an 'I'm as good as you' attitude with Americans, not a down-at-heel Englishman. Of course it was perfectly possible that George had seen better days, but the discourtesy and belligerence seemed aimed at him, Pierce, personally.

'Of course,' and George's smile held a hint of menace, 'if you send for Amadine, I'll answer all the questions she cares to ask. In fact, it would be a pleasure.'

'And I'll tell the police to question you and Ida again, because the only rational explanation for your attitude is that you have something to hide.'

'Be my guest.' George shrugged. 'They can't pin anything on me, and neither can you.'

Which denoted either complete confidence in his own innocence, or a belief that not only was he as good as anyone else, but a damned sight more clever.

Pierce decided not to waste any more time on the man. Abruptly he left the room and went in search of Frank. To his considerable disappointment, Frank informed him that, in his opinion, the one person who definitely could not have committed either crime was George White.

'I am positive that he could not have left the theatre all day, for the simple reason that I gave him too much work to do.'

'Where was he when the machinery was being fixed?'

Frank laughed. 'Right under my nose, helping me to fix it!'

'And after the performance?'

'George is one of the crew who dismantles the scenery, takes it back to the train and loads it on the freight car. The rest of the company is in bed before he even climbs aboard.'

'Pity. I was really hoping it would be him.'

'Why? What has poor old George done to rattle your cage?'

'I find him thoroughly objectionable. Don't you?'

'No.' Frank looked surprised. 'Polite sort of chap, and a very willing worker. He has fitted in rather well.'

So the antagonism had been personal, Pierce reflected as he walked away, but he was more worried about the man's unhealthy interest in Amadine. Suddenly he stopped short. George White might not be Constance's killer, but he certainly fitted the profile of the gunman, the stalker, and the writer of the filthy anonymous letters intercepted from Amadine's mail by Theo. Later the same day Pierce found an excuse to have another word with Frank.

'I'm still interested in those incidents involving Amadine. Can you remember where you were when that shot was fired, for instance?'

'That was months ago.' Frank looked at him incredulously. 'Oh, very well, let's try. Give me the time and the date of both occurrences.'

Pierce did so, and Frank consulted a well-worn sheaf of papers that apparently comprised the tour schedule and a note of which play had been performed on each day at every venue.

'They were matinée days. Amadine was on for the Boston performance, but in Philadelphia she wasn't needed and went off on her own. I was at the theatre all day on both occasions. All the stage staff were with me and can vouch for my whereabouts in Boston, and the entire company was at the theatre that afternoon in Philadelphia.'

Thanking him, Pierce walked away. Frank seemed to have supplied his stage staff, and therefore George White, with an alibi.

Chapter Twenty-Seven

Amadine had put off talking to Theo, because she considered him to be the least likely suspect, but then Pierce told her something that raised a doubt. Apparently Theo had told the police that he had returned to the train on Saturday afternoon, but although the porter remembered opening the door for him, he did not recall seeing Theo thereafter. Which was odd, Pierce reported, because Theo was in the habit of ordering coffee when he worked on the train. On the other hand, it could be that the staff were unreliable witnesses because, according to them, Jay had disappeared from view, too.

'How is the play coming along?' Amadine asked casually. 'Can I read it yet?'

'Good Lord, no! I'm sorry, but I couldn't possibly . . .'

'Hey, relax. I only thought that if you spent part of Saturday on the train, you might have been taking an opportunity to work on it.'

'That was the idea,' Theo agreed, 'but I'm afraid that it was one of those days when I stared for hours at a blank sheet of paper and couldn't write a word.'

'If the work was going badly, did you notice anything unusual going on around you?' Amadine asked optimistically.

'I didn't leave my room. Even though I wasn't making

much progress, I felt I must keep trying. I arrived at about three in the afternoon, and left at seven.'

'You didn't see Jay?' And when Theo shook his head, Amadine reflected that it fitted with Jay's account, because he had left the train again by three. 'And on Sunday morning you and Jay went to the hotel together.'

Theo groaned. 'Worst move we ever made. The police are convinced that one of us smuggled the cash off the train, and they have been searching us, our luggage and our hotel rooms inch by inch.'

'Presumably they asked for the names of anyone you know in Chicago, to whom you could have passed the cash.'

'I don't know anyone here – I had never been here before our previous visit. Hal and Frank are better acquainted with Chicago and its people than I am. Or Gwen. Or Jay – you should have seen the sheaf of messages waiting for him when we checked in.'

'Jay usually does receive a lot of messages. It's in the nature of his work. But did you see him speaking to anyone?'

'No. I left him at the desk, going through the messages, while I went up to my room. We met in the lobby again to take a cab back to the station a little later.'

'You are friendly with Frank, aren't you?' The question brought the blood rushing to Theo's face but he nodded, and Amadine went on: 'So do you have a theory about why he accumulated so much cash in the safe?'

It was a while before Theo answered. 'Frank is not inefficient,' he said slowly, 'but he has had too much work to do. He took on too many of Tom's responsibilities after the old man died, and yet refused to relinquish other duties. I was hired to take care of the correspondence and I could easily do the accounts as well, but Frank wouldn't hear of it.'

'You actually offered to do the accounts, the banking, everything?'

'Several times. And according to Hal, Constance did too, but Frank always refused.'

It looked more and more as if there was method in Frank's madness or, put another way, a very good cause for his carelessness.

'I am sorry to press the point, Frank,' Amadine said, 'but the conclusion is inescapable: if you omitted to bank the money, you did so for a reason. I find it very difficult to believe that you would steal from Hal, so won't you tell us what is going on?'

Frank looked at her, and then at Pierce, before staring out of the window with troubled eyes.

'Would it be easier to speak to just one of us?' Pierce suggested. 'If so, either Amadine or I will leave.'

'No,' said Frank. 'No, it isn't that . . .' He looked at them again, and clearly it was a huge effort for him to go on. 'I didn't steal the money, but I was intending to . . .'

And Pierce and Amadine realised that, all along, this was the only explanation that made any sense.

Haltingly Frank told them about the incident in the Levee. His description of the moment when he was accused of cheating, and of the fight that ensued, was fairly rudimentary, because to this day he had little recollection of the sequence of events and the aftermath, too, was somewhat blurred. However, the facts spoke, or seemed to speak, for themselves and Frank's deadpan delivery was, if anything, more effective than a dramatic account. Amadine was riveted to his every word, but Pierce's face bore an expression of sheer incredulity.

'Frank, Frank,' he groaned, 'you didn't fall for that old chestnut!'

'I'm afraid that I did,' Frank murmured, 'to start with, anyway.'

'What do you mean?' Amadine demanded. 'What old chestnut?'

'There wasn't a murder,' Pierce explained. 'The Levee operators saw Frank coming, and set him up. He would be an easy target: obviously from out of town – the English accent is a dead giveaway – and he probably chattered about the theatre and the touring company. So they got him drunk, lured him into a game of cards and accused him of cheating. Then they faked the fight. I'm not saying that people are never killed on the Levee, because they are, but this set-up stinks and I cannot believe that you, Frank, didn't see straight through it!'

Frank said nothing, and Amadine sprang to his defence. 'I expect that it looked very different at the time, especially if onc has had a lot to drink.'

'Yes, but afterwards . . .?' Pierce was watching Frank closely. 'You are an intelligent man, Frank. When you sobered up, you must have realised that their hold over you was tenuous, to say the least. It was their word against yours, and a story like that would never hold up outside this city or this state. The idea of it holding up in London is ridiculous.'

'You mean that Frank ought to have paid a small sum of money, enough to keep the Levee men happy while he was in this area, but stopped paying as soon as he left the state?' Amadine asked.

'Something like that. Unless,' and Pierce's eyes narrowed, 'he isn't telling us the whole story.'

'You are quite right, of course,' Frank said wearily. 'I had my doubts about being blackmailed over the incident right at the start, and certainly saw through the episode later on. But there was something else . . .'

'Was a woman involved?' And Amadine saw the despair in Frank's eyes, and she watched as he walked to the window where he stood with his back turned towards them. 'It wasn't a woman,' she said softly. 'It was a man. Oh, Frank . . .!'

Frank closed his eyes and leaned his forehead against the window pane. Pierce was startled and, to be honest, rather embarrassed, but Amadine rose and swiftly crossed the room. Gently she took hold of Frank's shoulders and swivelled him round to face her, and then she put her arms around him and held him close. He was very tense, but after a moment he gave a deep sigh and seemed to relax slightly.

'Thank you,' he said quietly, and sat down again. He still avoided Pierce's eye.

'You must remember,' Amadine told Pierce, 'that this happened only months after Oscar Wilde was gaoled. Of course Frank would be worried about an accusation against him, and he would believe that rumours about his sexuality, fed into the theatre system here, could pursue him across the Atlantic. It is always a sensitive subject, but that was a particularly sensitive time.'

Pierce was trying valiantly to adjust his thinking and outlook to fit the new circumstances. Apart from one or two obvious examples at school and university, which he had managed to ignore, homosexuality had not impinged on his consciousness and accordingly he neither approved nor disapproved. However, he did find it totally bizarre to be discussing the matter with a couple of actors, one of whom was the rector's daughter, over breakfast on a snowy February morning in Chicago.

'A bad business,' he said weakly, for want of anything more constructive to say.

'In my position, you get used to it,' Frank returned stiffly.

'This was to be the final payment, but the cash was stolen before you could take it yourself?' Amadine looked for confirmation from Frank and, having received it, asked, 'So what do you do now?'

'I was hoping that you could tell me.'

'I'll give you the money,' Amadine offered briskly.

'You . . .?' Frank gaped at her 'But I couldn't take money from you – after all, a lot of the stolen cash should have been yours.'

'Got any better ideas?' she demanded.

'Where do you intend to find this money?' Pierce enquired delicately.

'I thought that perhaps I could borrow it from you.'

'Oh God, this is so embarrassing.' Frank walked back to the window.

'I don't see why either of you think it necessary to pay anything to anyone,' Pierce exclaimed. 'Surely it wouldn't matter now if the truth about Frank's sexual preferences did come out? I presume he hasn't had a relationship with anyone like Lord Alfred whatsisname, so where's the harm?'

Amadine hesitated, but Frank swung round in horror. 'It would matter dreadfully,' he insisted. 'It is a criminal offence, for one thing. For another, although most of the profession wouldn't turn a hair, society would have a collective fit.'

'Do you care about society?' Pierce was surprised.

'No, but Hal does. In his position, he has to care. He wants to be accepted as one of London's leading actor-managers and, in order to succeed, he needs the support of that society. Anyway, I gave my word that I would pay. We shook hands on it.'

'That settles it then,' Amadine said, with a note of finality in her voice.

'You really think that sort of rubbish matters down on the Levee?' Pierce looked from one to the other, and shook his head. The English – he'd never understand them. 'I'll collect the cash first thing in the morning, and go with you to the saloon, Frank.'

'I'm going, too,' Amadine declared immediately, 'and don't try to stop me. I can be useful. If they see that I'm not shocked by these revelations, they will be less likely to renege on any agreement.'

'Do you believe that Frank didn't steal the cash?' Pierce asked later.

'Yes, but it doesn't matter whether I do or I don't. I must still lend, or give, him the money.'

'Why?'

'I owe him. Frank saved my life, in the fire in Baltimore. Surely my life is worth ten thousand dollars? It is to me, even if it isn't to anyone else.'

'I had forgotten about that,' Pierce apologised contritely. 'Of course we will give him the money, even though . . . Never mind . . .'

'Go on.'

'It occurred to me that if he did steal the money, and now he has persuaded you to pay off the Levee, he is ten thousand dollars better off.'

'I don't see Frank stealing from his brother for his personal benefit.'

'Have you considered another important point – how did he intend to conceal his misappropriation of company funds at the end of the tour? The day of reckoning would come. You and Hal would expect to be paid.'

'I expect he would promise to pay us back as soon as possible.'

'There would be a damned sight less to pay back if you weren't around.'

'Oh, I don't believe this! You think that *Frank* . . .'

'A very short time ago you wouldn't have believed that *Constance* . . .'

'Point taken, but even so. Frank saves my life in Baltimore and then kills me – where? Boston, I suppose, for the sake of alliteration!'

'He wouldn't have wanted you to die that day in Baltimore,' Pierce said seriously. 'Much too soon – you were needed to boost the box office.'

'Go and lie down in a darkened room,' Amadine advised, 'and with luck you will feel better in the morning. What do you think this is – a company of homicidal maniacs? Sure, Constance pushed me under a streetcar, but no one, and I repeat no one, is going to make another attempt on my life.'

'Half,' Pierce said firmly the next morning. 'We offer the Levee half the agreed amount. It isn't that I begrudge you the money, but they don't deserve one red cent and, to be honest, your English sense of fair play sticks in my craw.'

Frank and Amadine looked at each other. 'I don't begrudge the money either,' Amadine said, 'but in the circumstances, taking into account what has been paid already, perhaps half would be fair.'

An Englishman's word is his bond, and Frank hesitated. He would have preferred to pay the lot and feel that he had struck an honourable bargain in dishonourable circumstances, but the money was not his and therefore he could not quibble. Reluctantly he nodded.

In sharp contrast to Frank's former, furtive visits to the Levee, the trio swept downtown in style, Amadine dressed to impress in velvet and furs. Although it was Frank who knocked at the saloon door and did the initial talking, he was made to look insignificant in comparison with the imposing height, extraordinary good looks and expensive clothes of his companions. As soon as the two Levee men appeared, it was obvious that they were taken aback by the appearance and confident, almost arrogant bearing of the couple who flanked him, one on either side.

'You will have heard that our safe was robbed,' Frank said without preamble. 'My money was stolen. I have brought half of what we agreed, and that will have to do.'

The men laughed. 'We'll take the rest next time you're in Chicago,' one of them said easily. 'As a special favour. Otherwise . . .'

Amadine elbowed Frank aside. 'Don't think that you can threaten us,' she exclaimed in her most cut-glass English accent. 'We know that there wasn't a murder here that night, and as for the other matter . . . Times have changed, gentlemen, and no one cares about these things any . . .' But she was cut off in midstream as Pierce stepped forward.

'You don't know me,' Pierce began pleasantly, 'but I know you. Believe me, I have pinpointed your exact location, and understand every twist and turn of your filthy operation. My name is Radcliffe, by the way and, yes, I am the son of Samuel Radcliffe, which means that I own a considerable slice of Pullman. And that means that I am one of the biggest employers in this town, and that I have clout at City Hall. Clout such as you can only dream about, *gentlemen.*'

He took another step closer.

'They're English,' and he jerked his head in the direction of his companions, 'and they do things differently over there. But me, I'm American, and I'm more than prepared to play this your way. Much against my will and better judgement, you are being given half the sum Frank Smith agreed to pay you. Take it and be grateful. If there are any repercussions, and I do mean any, then be prepared for the consequences. I can promise you that not only will your friends at City Hall suddenly find that they can dispense with your services, but you will also discover just how inflammable this sort of situation can be – I do hope that you have a fire escape . . .'

Pierce placed the bag containing five thousand dollars in cash on the table, but did not release his hold on it. 'Agreed?' he said menacingly.

Amadine's eyes were huge emerald pools of astonishment but, for once, no one was looking at her. The Levee men knew when a scam had run its course.

'Agreed,' the spokesman said, with as much ease and confidence as he could muster. 'No need for any unpleasantness. We all understand each other.'

I'm glad that someone understands, Amadine thought, still looking at Pierce as if he were a complete stranger.

Pierce let go of the bag, and watched as the man made as

if to grab it, but then hesitated and let it lie in no-man's-land on the table.

'I don't like descending into the gutter,' Pierce said softly, 'but if I have to come this way again, rest assured that I will bring a few street sweepers with me, and the Levee will be a much cleaner place when we leave than it was when we arrived.'

He turned on his heel and propelled Amadine and Frank out of the saloon ahead of him.

'That went okay,' he said in the cab. 'They won't be any more trouble.'

'You were bluffing, weren't you?' Amadine said to him later.

All she received in reply was a hooded, enigmatic glance from those cold blue eyes before he smoothly changed the subject.

No, she thought with a shiver, he was not bluffing. He would do whatever was necessary, to keep his word, to fight his corner and to keep one step ahead of the rest. Doubtless he was an excellent and very successful businessman, but a greater contrast with her gentle, unworldly father she could not imagine. However, Pierce had been able to lay his hands on a large sum of money at a moment's notice, and had done so without demur.

Amadine found it astonishing to look back to the beginning of the tour, and recall those carefully laid plans for 'two sets of two', enabling the principals to enjoy the occasional day of rest. Her 'pair', Laurie, was still in hospital in Boston fighting an infection in his right leg, and Hal's partner, Constance, was dead. God help them all if either she or Hal were indisposed, because they were running out of substitutes. Doubtless, Amadine thought with a wry smile, Blanche would substitute for her, but who would substitute for Blanche?

'If you have no objection,' she said to Hal, 'I would like to look at Constance's personal belongings, in case I notice something that the police missed.'

'By all means,' Hal agreed courteously.

Courtesy was the only emotion he displayed towards her these days, except on the stage, and indeed he was aloof with everyone, even Frank. Amadine thought she knew why.

'She was pregnant, wasn't she?' she said sympathetically. 'I'm really sorry, and if you want to talk about it . . .'

'I don't want to even *think* about it,' he replied violently. 'And I don't know how the hell you found out, but I hope you aren't blabbing it all over the Auditorium.'

'You might credit me with some discretion! Incidentally, does Frank know?'

'I haven't told him.'

'Some time soon, you and I really must talk about money. At the risk of sounding defeatist, I doubt we'll see the stolen cash again and we need to discuss the implications of that.'

'I've asked Theo to verify the missing sum, and he will probably do the accounts and banking from now on.'

Hal does think that Frank took the money, Amadine thought, which means that Hal didn't take it.

'Could the première of *Much Ado* be a benefit for Constance's children?' she suggested. 'I'm sure the company would donate a day's pay.'

Hal nodded. 'Good idea. I'll ask Jay to find out if the theatre management and Frohman will contribute.'

But he still seemed lacklustre and preoccupied and therefore, when Frank walked into Constance's dressing room that afternoon, Amadine dared a little subterfuge.

'You know that she was pregnant, don't you?' she asked guilelessly, as she bent over Constance's trunk.

'Has Hal told someone at last? Thank God for that!'

'So he did tell you, too?'

'Yes and no.' Frank paused and sought the right words. 'I overheard them talking about it. The partition is rather thin.'

'When I occupied that room, I could hear the murmur of voices, but not what you and Hal were saying,' Amadine remarked, 'so they must have been talking fairly loudly. More like an argument, was it? You did hint as much at breakfast on Sunday.'

'If I tell you, please don't pass on the information to the police.'

'Of course I won't. They argued about the baby, I suppose?'

'Yes, and I had the impression that Hal was none too pleased,' Frank said carefully, 'and that Constance was talking marriage. Hal didn't seem too pleased about that, either.'

'I'm not surprised. They weren't a bit suited, on or off the stage.'

'No,' Frank agreed, 'but Hal must have changed his mind, because he seems genuinely upset at losing her. And the pregnancy means that he could not possibly have harmed her himself.'

Wrong, thought Amadine. The joint threat of marriage to Constance and impending fatherhood is the best motive so far for her murder. Frank knows that as well as I do. Just as Hal thinks that Frank took the money, so Frank thinks that Hal murdered Constance.

'Are you looking for anything in particular?' Frank asked, watching her sift through the contents of the trunk.

'Inspiration, chiefly, but I'm not finding it here.' Amadine closed the lid of the trunk, and transferred her attention to a smaller portmanteau.

'In your position, I don't think I would want to touch anything of Constance's with the proverbial barge pole.'

'I think we have to accept that she was a very sad person. Look at this, for instance.' She held up a cheap brooch and a paste necklace. 'I'd say that her whole life was a struggle, and that she never had anything nice of her own. I cannot imagine her stealing my jewellery, but I can easily envisage her taking it into her room to try on. And standing in front of the mirror, telling herself that it looked just as good on her as it did on me.'

'You give her more understanding than she deserves.'

Amadine smiled. 'I'm very unlikely to qualify for sainthood, Frank. For one thing, saints don't go to bed with attractive Americans without a marriage certificate. Actually, saints probably have to be celibate, so I'm doubly damned, along with most people I know. Including you, I trust.'

'I'm headed straight for hell in the eyes of the church, but perhaps the fact that I have been celibate for simply ages might reduce the sentence. Come on, you're the rector's daughter – you should know!'

'My dear Frank, the longer I live, the less I know! But I must admit that since I found out about you, I have wondered . . . *Theo* . . . Perhaps you . . .?'

'Hoped? Yes, but happily I said nothing and did nothing before I found out that he was married.'

'Oh, poor you! You must have been devastated.'

Not as devastated as he had been in the washroom, but Frank managed a casual shrug. 'Anyone can be unlucky in love.'

'He doesn't know about you?'

'Lord, no. He's the very last person I would want to know.'

Amadine had abandoned her search of the portmanteau, and picked up Constance's handbag. She rooted through it systematically until she came to a small notebook. She glanced at it and was about to stuff it back into the bag when she paused, and took another look at one page.

'Frank, just confirm something for me. You did give me Constance's wage packet that morning, didn't you, and I took it into her room?'

'That's right,' Frank agreed, 'and then we left for the theatre. Why, have you found something interesting?'

'Yes,' Amadine said in a peculiar voice, 'I rather think I have.'

'Do you remember,' she asked Pierce, 'that I hesitated when you said that the cash from the safe was the only thing missing? Well, now I realise what was nagging at my mind. Constance's wage packet was also missing – at least it wasn't on the chest where I left it.'

'No mystery there. Either she put it in a drawer or her bag for safekeeping, or the robber took it.'

Amadine shook her head. 'She remitted it to London.'

'She *what*? But she was ill in bed.'

'Not as ill as she made out. Look at this.' Amadine showed him the notebook. 'Evidently Constance was a lady of meticulous and regular habits. She sent the lion's share of her salary to London, presumably for the children, every pay day, and that particular day was no exception. Here is the entry in her notebook, and here is the cashier's receipt.'

'Constance went out,' Pierce said slowly, 'unless someone else sent the money on her behalf.'

'It looks like her signature on the form.'

'So her illness was tactical rather than physical, although I suppose the pregnancy could have been a factor?'

'Don't ask me,' Amadine said in alarm. 'I know absolutely nothing about such matters. From the evidence of the post-mortem report, I would have thought it was too early in the pregnancy for morning sickness, but I'm only guessing. The point is, she appears to have left the train during the day without anyone knowing. What does that tell us?'

'She must have kept the door of her room closed. The staff would assume that she was asleep, or resting, and would not disturb her unless she called for them.'

'And then she slipped away quietly because she didn't want any of the company to realise that she was faking her illness, or to think that if she was well enough to go to the bank, she was well enough to perform.'

'But the train doors were locked. How did she get on and off?'

'Getting off is easy enough,' Amadine said. 'The keys are left in the doors – the company cannot be locked in, they're not in prison! And the fire hazard is even more important: the doors must be opened quickly in an emergency.'

'If the doors can be opened from the inside but not from the outside, someone must have let her back in.' Pierce thought for a moment. 'The staff would have mentioned opening the door for her, so who else was there?'

'Of our group, only Jay and Theo. Of course one never knows about Blanche – she slips in and out of theatres with practised ease.'

'Is there a time on that receipt?'

'No, just the date.'

'She would have gone fairly early,' Pierce decided, 'to make sure the office was open. She would have wanted the expedition over and safely accomplished.'

'In that case, it's more likely to have been Jay who opened the door for her, because Theo only arrived in the afternoon.'

'Are you sure that you didn't see Constance that day?' Amadine asked Jay.

'I've told you, and the police, a thousand times.' Jay was beginning to sound rattled. 'I wasn't likely to go barging into her room – I'm a single man, what would she have thought?'

'We think that she may have dressed and gone out, but that theory leaves us with the problem of how she re-entered the train without anyone seeing her.'

'I can assure you that she didn't hammer on the door for admittance while I was there – not while I was awake, anyway.' Jay thought for a few minutes. 'Unless someone opened the door for her and doesn't want to admit it, I can think of only one explanation: she didn't lock the door behind her when she got off.'

'Turned the key so that the door could be pushed to, but not properly closed. Good Lord, Jay, you're a genius. I never thought of that.'

'Don't get too excited,' he advised cautiously. 'It's something of a long shot. I'm trying to remember what the weather was like that day – for instance, was a gale blowing? – because there wouldn't be any guarantee that the door would stay in that position.'

'And if it blew open, someone would close it properly.' Amadine nodded. 'Still, it's the best idea we've had so far.'

Because, if that was what happened, it was possible that the murderer simply pulled open the door and climbed in. The downside to that theory was that it meant the murderer could be virtually anyone.

Chapter Twenty-Eight

The première of *Much Ado About Nothing* took place on the Monday of the company's second week in Chicago, and should have been the pinnacle to which Amadine had been striving. Attempting her own interpretation of a classic role in a new production felt quite different from simply slotting into an established version, as she had done with Juliet. She had been studying the part for months, rehearsing for weeks, risking comparison with the greats of past and present when, at the outset of the tour, the merest suggestion that she might try Shakespeare had petrified her.

She had expected to spend the day rushing to the bathroom as usual on opening nights, but did not do so even once. Amadine's heart was thudding and her throat was dry, but she felt an almost calm acceptance of the inevitable: if she had not got it right by now, it was too late to fix it and she must try harder tomorrow. Standing in the wings, she glanced at Hal's mask of composure and smiled at him. When he smiled back, it was the first real communication they had shared since Constance died.

And they were wonderful, their achievement surpassed only by the warmth and appreciation of the audience. Chicago laughed in the right places, tensed in the right places, and had a lump in its throat over the supposed death

of Hero, because it knew that Constance had been due to
play the role. Perhaps some of the cheers were for the pluck
of the company in sticking to the schedule and battling on
in adversity; doubtless there were those who watched and
wondered if a murderer strode the stage; but none of these
considerations belittled the triumph of the reception given
to *Much Ado* that night.

Yet Amadine suffered a slight sense of anti-climax. She
had been good – she knew that for herself, as well as by
Hal's reaction and the way they had played together – but
there was no feeling of euphoria or of having achieved what
she set out to do. She had expected that, as she grew more
experienced, the highs would be higher and the lows would
be lower, but the opposite seemed to be the case. Perhaps it
was a result of this tour, on which there had been so many
fresh starts and opening nights, and so many distractions.
Perhaps – and here she did feel a glow of hope in her
heart – she was, by some mysterious metamorphosis, being
transformed into a professional.

For Gwen, *Much Ado* was routine, and although she
rejoiced in the fine performances of Amadine and Hal, she
found herself harking back nostalgically to all the Beatrices
and Benedicks she had known. Stop it, she admonished
herself, it's your generation showing; but that was hardly
surprising because the day after the première, Tuesday 8
March, was Gwen's fiftieth birthday.

She kept the news to herself, wishing neither to celebrate a birthday of any kind so soon after Constance's
death, nor to advertise her age. The only people who had
ever marked the day were her mother and Samuel
Radcliffe, so circumstances prescribed that the morning
mail brought no anniversary greetings, only a cheerful
letter from Miss P with good news regarding the health of
Gwen's mother, adding an optimistic note to the effect
that Laurie might be allowed out of hospital shortly.

However, soon after handing her this letter, Theo slipped a second envelope into her hand. Mailed from New York and addressed in familiar handwriting, Gwen guessed that it contained an explanation, or rather an excuse, for Nicholas Lang's failure to keep the rendezvous in St Louis. Well, she was not interested in his excuses. She had been made to feel a fool. In fact she had been made to feel so unhappy that the hollow ache inside her was worse than a physical pain, and accordingly she was not leaving herself open to any more disappointments. From now on, she would take no more risks.

She pushed his letter into her bag, intending to throw it away when she reached her room, and returned her attention to the newspaper. Suddenly she began to shake. The 'On the stage' column of the Chicago *Daily News* reported that Sir Henry Irving was celebrating his sixtieth birthday, but went on to say: 'Ellen Terry is the main trouble which confronts Irving. Despite the fact that she is growing old and stout and that the public wants young heroines, she refuses to allow Irving to get a younger leading lady. The result has been disastrous to the baronet, and now he has been forced to abandon the Lyceum . . .'

Gwen was so upset that she had to hurry to the privacy of her room. Tears poured down her face. Darling Ellen, wonderful, magical Ellen who, Gwen was only too aware, had celebrated her forty-ninth birthday nine days ago. How dared they describe her in those terms, and how dared they blame her for the financial problems of Henry Irving – who, Gwen choked furiously, was a knight, not a baronet. In Gwen's opinion, Irving's difficulties were of his own making and he had used Ellen badly for years, often choosing plays for his repertoire that showed him to advantage but gave insufficient scope for her unique talent.

Oh, what it was to be an actress, and to be growing old! Irving's sixtieth birthday was an occasion for national celebration but, a decade younger, his leading lady was being consigned to the scrapheap, and Gwen wondered how a woman was supposed to combat the inevitable ravages of time. Middle-age spread was not a mere phrase, but a sad and immensely painful fact of life. Apparently some women did fight it, occasionally with disastrous results. Only last Tuesday the press had reported the case of the wife of a 'prominent Oak Park citizen' who was asphyxiated, accidentally, by gas in her bathroom. Apparently the woman died because she was trying to lose weight, by means of hot-air and steam baths. First, she took a hot-air bath, sitting on a chair beside a little gas stove that had a rubber hose attached, and then she plunged into the hot water. On the day of the fatal accident, the rubber hose slipped from the gas fixture without her noticing. It isn't fair, Gwen thought indignantly. Why should a man's old age be more dignified than a woman's?

Of course she appreciated that her pain was more acute because this had happened today of all days, and unfortunately it wasn't over yet. She had agreed to meet Pierce Radcliffe at his lawyer's office, in order to discuss the facts surrounding Samuel's death.

Howard Morton was a tall, well-built man in his late sixties, with thick silver hair and a twinkle in his eye. Greeting Gwen, he gave her such a curious, old-fashioned look that she flushed, imagining what he must have heard about her from Sam and comparing that with the raddled old crone he now confronted. He would think that Sam had no taste in women at all.

'It is a great honour to meet you, Miss Hughes,' Morton said courteously. 'I have seen you perform at McVicker's on countless occasions, and now I see that you are just as charming off the stage as on.'

How polite he was, and how practised at saying the right thing. In her present mood Gwen did not fall for the flattery, but she did find comfort, and gain some confidence, from the fact that he had seen her in her heyday. Yet it was sobering, too, to realise that all that remained of her life, apart from a few faded photographs, were the memories that lived on in the minds of men like this who had witnessed her brief hour upon the stage. Artists painted pictures, authors wrote books and composers created symphonies but, at the end of the nineteenth century, actors left only a blurred footprint in the sand.

Having decided to speak openly, Pierce outlined the case for his father's suicide, which relied chiefly on the testimony of staff at the railroad depot who had witnessed the incident, even though the inquest had delivered a verdict of accidental death. In her turn Gwen declared that Samuel was not the suicidal type, but conceded that Pierce had sown the seed of doubt in her mind. Howard Morton listened in silence, and with a distinctive air of utter attentiveness. Then he smiled.

'Feeling guilty, huh? You, Miss Hughes, because you parted from Sam in later years and, if I recollect correctly, were in New York when he died. You, Pierce, because you had been estranged from your father, and rejected his efforts at reconciliation.'

Pierce started to protest at that interpretation, but then leaned back in his chair and nodded, just as Gwen was nodding.

'Something like that,' he agreed.

'Neither of you has anything to feel guilty about,' Morton said cheerfully. 'Miss Hughes, Sam thought the world of you to his dying day, and he looked back on your years together with the utmost affection and gratitude. Pierce, he was deeply disappointed that you remained estranged, but he never held it against you. He laid the blame fairly and squarely at your mother's door.'

'But was he depressed, or disappointed about something else?' Gwen asked. 'In retrospect he became such a contradiction in those later years. When we met face to face, he would chatter away happily and be really enthusiastic about things – the Expo, for example – but when we were separated geographically, it was as if he withdrew into himself. Sam was never a letter writer, of course – he admitted that he wasn't well educated – but he wouldn't even have a telephone, which was odd for someone who welcomed the latest inventions as eagerly as Samuel did.'

'Of course he wasn't depressed,' Morton scoffed. 'And he didn't kill himself. Young Pierce here has been letting his imagination run away with him.'

'You cannot discount the evidence of the eyewitness,' Pierce insisted. 'My father walked in front of the train, with a look on his face of calm acceptance of his fate and utter determination, ignoring the warning shout.'

'The only expression on Sam's face as he crossed the tracks was likely to be the calm certainty that he would reach the other side. Doubtless he was on his way to see a new engine or a new passenger car – he still hung around railroad depots like a small boy. And he ignored the warning for a very obvious reason: he didn't hear it. Deaf as a post.'

'Deaf!' Pierce felt very foolish.

'As a man of your intelligence would have realised soon enough, if the incident had involved anyone but your own father.'

Gwen was engulfed in relief. 'So that was why he wouldn't use a telephone!'

'And why he did all the talking – much easier to keep up his own end of the conversation than struggle to make out what you were saying. No, Sam's death was an accident, pure and simple. At sixty-one, he was comparatively young, but at least he went the way he would have wanted – with his beloved trains. Also, he was gone in an instant.' Morton snapped his fingers. 'Sam literally did not know what hit him, and he did not linger on in pain and discomfort.'

So that appeared to be that. And even if Gwen was

uncomfortable in the present, and faced the future with apprehension, she could be easy about the past and that was more than a lot of people could say.

'Dare I hope,' Morton went on, 'that this means I can finally hand over Sam's assets?'

'Gwen, please accept the bequest he wanted you to have,' Pierce said earnestly. 'My father was a wealthy man, so there is plenty for everyone, and I would like you to have it.'

She laid a gloved hand gently on his arm. 'Thank you, but my answer remains no. Taking Sam's money still doesn't feel right. No good could come of it, and I could never be happy about it.' And with that she left the two men to their deliberations.

'A woman of principle,' Morton remarked when the door had closed behind her. 'Sam said as much. But I trust that you will be good enough to take this fortune off my hands?'

Pierce sighed. 'Yes,' he said at last. 'Having met Gwen, I think I can make my peace with my father, and only wish that I could have done so to his face.'

'Water under the bridge,' the lawyer said briskly. 'Good, good, so the Duryea brothers and Henry Ford can expect some competition in the automobile business, eh? Does the lovely Miss Sinclair approve?'

'What has Amadine to do with it?'

'You first parted with your so-called principles in order to house her in Prairie Avenue. Then, last week, you requested five thousand dollars which, from the little you said, I assumed was destined for her.'

'Only indirectly. Amadine would not take money for herself, but she is an inveterate collector of lame ducks and good causes, while at the same time she labours under an immense burden of obligation to everyone in the entire universe.'

'She sounds an expensive proposition but, after today, you can afford her.'

*

'The police have released Constance's body for burial,' Hal said heavily, 'so we can hold the funeral tomorrow.'

Amadine glanced out of the hotel window. It was snowing. As usual. 'Oh,' she said without enthusiasm. 'Well, it will be a relief when it's over.'

'And they say that, as things stand at the moment, there is no reason why we shouldn't be able to leave as planned on Sunday.'

'Good,' she responded mechanically. But was it? Could she bear to leave this magical city, perhaps never to see it again? 'I assume that means the police are not making much progress with their enquiries.'

'They tend towards the theory of a random intruder. Your suggestion that Constance left a door unlocked, when she went to the bank, is very popular.'

'I thought it might be! Still, I don't blame them for not having a clue who did it. I haven't a clue myself.'

'On the plus side, we have the success of *Much Ado*. Great reception last night, and glowing notices today. Well done!'

'It was entirely thanks to you that we pulled it off.'

They were being stiffly polite to each other, and Amadine knew that Constance's death had changed everything for ever. Hal was not the same person any more. He seemed older, more contained within himself, more responsible. He would never make another pass at her, that was for sure. Indeed, she wondered if he would ever make another pass at any woman.

'We don't need to panic completely about the financial situation,' he was saying. 'Frank banked the takings during the first part of the tour, so the account in New York is comparatively healthy, although obviously not as healthy as we would wish.'

'We can still make a financial success of this,' Amadine agreed stoutly. 'There are twelve weeks to go, including return visits to Washington, Baltimore, Philadelphia,

Boston and New York. With *Much Ado* in the repertoire, we can expect full houses.'

'I should warn you that Theo is worried about the number of personal chitties for cash that you and I, and Frank himself, appear to have signed.' Hal paused, and sighed. 'I'm afraid that your signature might have been forged.'

'Really?' Amadine grimaced, but then shrugged. 'We can sort it out in New York when we see the final figures. I'm not going to make a fuss over a few dollars.'

'A few thousand dollars.'

'Oh. Well, I expect these things happen in the best regulated families.'

'They don't happen in my family. Not until now, that is.'

It was the nearest he had come to pointing the finger at Frank, and Amadine, not knowing how much Frank had confided in his brother, did not wish to comment.

'The company has been paid, which is one good thing, and all the hotel and restaurant bills have been settled,' Hal went on, 'so we aren't leaving a trail of debts behind us. Basically the situation boils down to the fact that you and I are out of pocket.'

'And Frank, presumably.'

'And Frank.' Hal's tone was grim. 'However, I wish to make it clear that you will not suffer. I will make good your shortfall out of my own share of the profits.'

'You will do no such thing!' Amadine exclaimed indignantly. 'It is a very gallant gesture, Hal, but I'm a partner in this enterprise. If I share the profits, I share the risks as well. Anyway, you need the money more than I do – you have to finance your own season in London in the autumn.'

'What are your plans for the autumn?'

'I haven't any. Like the murder of Constance and the theft of the money, my future is an area about which I haven't a clue.'

*

At Hal's request, Theo arranged a funeral tea at the hotel, and the prospect of warmth and free food cheered the lower ranks, although they remained subdued. Watching them, Theo was reminded of the words of Edward Everett – former governor of Massachusetts and president of Harvard, politician, preacher, poet and orator – words that had an eerie aptness, considering the place where Constance was murdered and the company's reaction to her death:

> When I am dead, no pageant train
>> Shall waste their sorrows at my bier,
> Nor worthless pomp of homage vain
>> Stain it with hypocritic tear.

Certainly they had laid Constance to rest with the bare minimum of ceremony, and no one had wept a hypocritical tear – or any other kind of tear. Now there was an inexorable sense of things moving on as if, having observed the ritual of burial, Constance's colleagues took a step away from her and back on the path of their own lives. So much remained unresolved, yet Theo could feel Constance slipping away into a mere memory, and into the myths that were such a part of the warp and weft of theatrical life.

Not since Christmas had the entire company gathered together, and Amadine went out of her way to mingle. She saw Ida standing alone, looking disconsolate, which probably meant that George had left if, indeed, he had attended the funeral in the first place. As George's duties kept him at a remove from Amadine in the theatre, and he used only the men's car on the train, she had never met him. Then she saw the hotel bellboy hand a cable to Jay. The publicity man's face tautened and he stared at the message for such a long time that the bellboy, waiting for his tip, gave up and walked off in disgust.

'I knew Frohman would fire me,' Jay said bitterly, show-ing the cable to Amadine. 'Evidently he considered it proper to wait for the funeral before delivering the blow.'

'At least he isn't suggesting that you should be responsi-ble for replacing the cash that should have been banked before Davenport.'

'Not yet, but he will.'

'He isn't offering to pay you, either. What will you do?'

'Beg, borrow or steal, I suppose.' And then Jay looked appalled. 'Sorry, shouldn't have said stolen – poor taste in the circumstances. Actually, I'd like to reach Philly in the not too distant future, but I don't know how.'

'Is Frohman sending someone to replace you?'

Jay shrugged, and gestured at the cable. 'You know as much as I do, but surely he has been in touch with Hal?'

'I'll ask.' After a brief exchange with Hal, she hurried back. 'Theo will be doing Frohman's banking as well as ours, but I said, and Hal agrees with me, that we can give you a ride to Philadelphia if you want one.'

'Could you? Gee, that would be great.' Relief flooded Jay's face and brought back a vestige of colour.

'We could still use your help in dealing with the press, particularly in the aftermath of all that has happened. Would you be prepared to handle that side of things for us, in exchange for free board and lodging as far as Philly?'

'Sure I would,' he said fervently. 'I'll do anything you ask, anything at all. Honestly, Amadine, I'm skint, cleaned-out, stony-broke . . .'

'All right,' she broke in with a laugh, 'I get the picture! The trouble is that the rest of us are stony-broke as well.'

After Amadine had left, Jay examined the loose change in his pocket and decided that he could treat himself to a beer. He was both relieved and disappointed by Amadine's offer. While he was grateful for food and transport, *The Philadelphia Girl* was due to open on 4 April and he wanted desperately to be there for that great, triumphant,

star-studded occasion. The tour was only due in Philly
on Easter Sunday, 10 April, but without the means of
acquiring the fare, he could see no possibility of reaching
the city sooner. He could only hope that, as the tour
would be in Baltimore the previous week, Bill would come
to the rescue. Jay groaned. Explaining his current financial
position to Bill was going to be one of the most difficult
things he had ever had to do.

Throughout this stay in Chicago, Amadine's encounters
with Pierce had been hurried, had often included a third
party and invariably concerned the murder inquiry. The
intimacy had gone, and there had been no opportunity to
rekindle it. In her hotel suite, over a nightcap after the
show on Friday night, Pierce looked remote and stern, an
uncompromising man whom it was difficult to connect with
the passionate lover of a few short weeks ago. But these had
not been short weeks; they had been a seemingly endless
and traumatic sequence of days and events, which had
driven a wedge between everyone involved.

Amadine was very aware that the next day was her last in
Chicago, and that the future was crowding in on her. When
she left here, there were no guarantees: she might never see
Chicago again; or see Ben again; or, and her heart twisted in
her chest, she might not see Pierce again. But that relationship would end in tears sooner or later, so why not sooner?

'According to the detective agency, Theodore Wingfield
Davis is exactly who he says he is,' Pierce informed her.
'The family is one of the oldest and most respected in
Philadelphia, as well as being one of the wealthiest, to
whom ten thousand dollars is small change.'

'So Theo doesn't have a motive for murder or robbery,
and can be crossed off the list of suspects.' Amadine gave a
sigh of pleasure. 'What a relief!'

'Also, Blanche's story checks out so far. There is certainly a considerable disparity in the social standing of the

mother and grandmother. However, Dora shows no signs of having achieved sudden wealth so, unless they are boxing very clever, Blanche did not pass the money to her.'

'Is there any chance that Dora could have met Blanche here?'

'Not unless she had a magic carpet to whisk her to Chicago and back in a night – the neighbours confirm that she has been around as usual.'

'Any sign of Dora's husband?'

'He has not been located yet, but the agency has a name for him now, so he should be tracked down before long. He doesn't appear to be hanging around Dora, which is good news for Blanche.'

'I cannot believe that Blanche would commit murder for a man like that,' Amadine said with a frown.

'Killing Constance might have had nothing to do with the stepfather,' Pierce pointed out. 'It could have had everything to do with Hal, who would be a husband made in heaven for an ambitious young actress like Blanche.'

'I still wonder if Jay could have passed the money to someone in Chicago. He certainly appears to be penniless, but that could be a bluff, and we only have his word that his friend did not turn up as arranged.'

'And he told you that he had been sending money to this friend?' Pierce thought for a few moments. 'I saw him with a chap in Philadelphia,' he said slowly, 'and I was sure they were up to something.' He told Amadine how he had followed Jay and the two men from the hotel to the Bellevue Restaurant, and that he had suspected that a bit of kite-flying was going on. 'I cannot imagine why I didn't think of it before,' he concluded ruefully.

'It certainly sounds as if Jay has some sort of business venture in Philadelphia,' Amadine agreed. 'Could you ask the detective agency to look into it?'

Pierce shook his head. 'I don't have a name or address for

either of the other men, and the kite-flying is pure guess-work on my part.'

'I don't suppose . . . No, forget it. I couldn't ask you to do that.'

'Couldn't ask me to go to Philadelphia, and investigate the matter myself?' He smiled crookedly. 'My dear Amadine, you could ask me to go to the ends of the earth, or even to hell and back, and I would do my utmost to oblige.'

She chose to ignore the implications of that remark. 'Then would you go? Oh dear, I seem to be getting deeper and deeper into your debt.'

'We are getting deeper and deeper into something,' he said, with one of his enigmatic looks.

'I wonder if these mysteries will be solved before we go home.'

'Are you looking forward to going home?'

'One of the things I wanted from this tour was to be recognised as a serious actress,' she said evasively. 'I believe I achieved that on Monday night, but now I find that it isn't enough. It's like climbing a mountain and thinking that you have reached the summit when suddenly another rise confronts you, and you don't know if that slope and that challenge will bring you to the top, any more than the last one did.'

'You don't have to go home.'

Her heart began to thud uncomfortably in the base of her throat.

'England does not have to be your home.'

Still Amadine did not respond.

'You could stay here, and marry me.'

The silence went on for ever. There was a picture on the wall above the fireplace, a landscape of trees and water. Did it depict Chicago, or was it another American scene? Strange how she could focus on that inconsequential question in the eternity that followed Pierce Radcliffe's proposal.

'Please, Amadine, marry me and stay here,' he said softly.

It could be anywhere, the place in that picture. It could be in America, or in England, and there was a message there somewhere if she cared to delve a bit deeper, but this was less about what she cared to do than what she could do.

'No,' she said expressionlessly. 'Thank you, but I can't do that.'

'Can't, or won't?' he exclaimed bitterly. 'Damn it, I refuse to take no for an answer!'

'Which is the reaction of a spoiled child, who should learn that he cannot have everything he wants,' Amadine retorted. 'Incidentally, why do you want to marry me?'

'I love you, of course.'

'Nice of you to mention it.'

'I thought you loved me.'

Oh, I do, she thought. I really do. But *it* wouldn't do, don't you see? And then she realised that of course he couldn't see, that no one could see or understand, and suddenly the world was a very lonely place.

'I'm with Dr Johnson on this one,' she said lightly. '"I am willing to love all mankind, except an American."'

'You are impossible. What sort of answer is that?'

'Your father had an actress for a mistress, so why not simply let history repeat itself? You can call on me in London, and I will visit Chicago as often as I can.'

'I don't want a mistress.'

'You must be the only man in the world who doesn't!'

'I ought to have said nothing,' he said tightly. 'I should have realised that such a beautiful woman as you has marriage proposals every day of the week. I cannot imagine why I thought mine might have any more success than any of the others.'

'I wish I could explain.'

'Don't bother.' He rose, and walked towards the door.

'Shall I see you again?'

'There isn't much point, is there!'

'I owe you all that money.'

'I don't need the bloody money.'

'Of course you need it, if you want to manufacture automobiles.'

'Amadine, I have approximately four million dollars. What you owe me is chicken feed.'

'You do?' Her eyes widened, but then she went on the defensive. 'You needn't think that will make any difference to my answer.'

'Oh, do me a favour! You may have gone down in my estimation, but not so low that I think you can be bought. And I think you might do me the courtesy of conceding that I would not want a woman who could be bought.'

She was so ashamed that she turned away her face, fixing her unseeing gaze on that picture again. Why did everything she say or touch come out wrong?

'I was hoping you would bring Ben to say goodbye tomorrow,' she said in a stifled voice.

'To hell with Ben,' he said violently.

'But you must look after him for me!' she cried.

'Must I? Give me one good reason why I should do anything for you!' But instead of waiting for an answer, he slammed the door behind him.

Somehow, after a sleepless night, Amadine dragged herself through the next morning, and then through a matinée. On this, her final day in Chicago, there seemed to be more flowers and notes than usual, but none from the one person who mattered. However, in the late afternoon she did raise a spark of interest in a discussion between Hal and Frank. As the new *Much Ado* scenery, props and costumes were to be taken on tour, the two men were debating whether or not to abandon some of the old items that were no longer being used.

'You haven't done *Julius Caesar* for months,' Frank remarked. 'Unless you want it for next season in London, that could go.'

Hal nodded. 'And *Romeo and Juliet*.'

'Surely that is a useful standby,' objected Amadine.

'I never want to play Romeo again,' Hal said with suppressed intensity. 'We will be playing *Tanqueray*, *Trelawny* and *Much Ado* for the rest of the tour, and as far as I'm concerned, you can burn the rest.'

'You'll have only *Much Ado* to start next season,' Frank protested.

'Did you say burn?' Amadine queried.

'That is the only way to dispose of the superfluous stuff.'

'Can't we sell it, even for a small sum?'

Hal shook his head. 'Customs regulations mean that we are not even allowed to give it away. No, we'll burn it, but we must do so on the lake shore – they tend to be a bit sensitive about fires in Chicago.'

'Won't the police suspect that we are destroying evidence?'

'They have had plenty of time and opportunity to go through everything with the finest-toothed combs,' Hal said shortly, 'but I'll let them know our plans.'

'I'll go to the station and start loading the wagon,' Frank remarked. 'We can light the bonfire immediately after the curtain comes down tonight.'

Out of respect for Constance, no farewell parties could be held, so the bonfire was something to look forward to. On a clear, cold night, most of the company made their way down to the lake shore where Frank and his staff built a pyramid of wooden flats and canvas hangings, of 'marble' steps and pillars, which looked too heavy to lift but were handled easily by two men, and of drapes and costumes whose offstage tawdriness was disguised by the darkness. After carefully testing the strength of the wind, and cautiously not heaping too much on the pile to start with, Frank set it alight and a weak cheer went up as the fire took hold.

For a brief moment, Amadine went rigid. Watching the

flames lick through the mound of scenery, she was vividly transported back to Baltimore and starting to suffocate in her dressing room. But then, taking a deep breath of fresh air, she could see beauty in the red and gold of the fire, and in the bright showers of sparks that shot up into the night sky. It was satisfying to burn the excess baggage in order to travel lighter, but there was also a sense of the fitness of the occasion. The fire, here on the lake shore in the blackness, was like a funeral pyre, a final farewell to Constance.

Most people were standing well back, their faces illuminated only occasionally when the fire flared up with sudden ferocity. But when Frank was organising another batch of fodder for the fire, Amadine caught a glimpse of a man's face as he heaved another flat into the flames. Nausea welled within her, bile trickling into her mouth and momentarily she swayed, nearly falling with faintness. But when she looked again, the face had gone.

Unsteadily she backed away towards the water's edge. For an awful moment she had thought . . . But no, of course, she had been mistaken. It was only the light, or lack of it, playing tricks.

Chapter Twenty-Nine

As Amadine expected, the police were out in force at the railroad station on Sunday morning. She had given considerable thought to the means by which a member of the company could have concealed the money, from passing it to an accomplice, to opening a bank account in a false name, to hiding it in the vastness of the Auditorium Theatre. She had come to no firm conclusion, but was certain of one thing: if *she* had stolen the money and then hidden it, she would not want to leave Chicago without it. Evidently the police were of the same mind, and were searching all the personal baggage again, as well as undertaking a final inspection of the baskets and boxes containing props and costumes.

During this lengthy process, Amadine wandered back into the station building in the hope that one of them – or, even better, both – might come to say goodbye. And then, suddenly, a small figure was running across the concourse towards her.

'Ben, I was so afraid that you weren't coming!'

'He said he couldn't come.' Ben, she noticed, rarely referred to Pierce as anything but 'he'. 'But I said that I wanted to see you, even if he didn't. Have you two quarrelled?'

'It doesn't matter about him – it's you I really wanted to

see.' Amadine located an empty bench where they could sit down. 'Are you happy at the factory?'

'Sure, it's fine. Beats standing on a street corner any day.'

'And the people with whom you are lodging, do they treat you well? They give you enough to eat, and a warm bed . . .?'

'Miss Amadine, it's fine, honest. Why all the questions?'

'I want to make sure that I did the right thing by interfering in your life. You see, there are those who believe I am not an influence for good – they call me a jinx. Do you know what that is? It's someone or something that brings bad luck, and I couldn't bear to leave you here in a worse state than I found you.'

'That's silly,' Ben declared scornfully. 'The only bad thing you're doing is going away. He says he asked you to stay, but you wouldn't.'

'Not wouldn't, Ben, *couldn't*. There is an important difference.'

'Don't you like us enough to stay?' and for the first time a wistful note entered the boy's voice.

'I like you a lot, but it isn't as simple as that. Life very rarely is that simple.'

Ben nodded, having learned early on, in the school of hard knocks, that life was a peculiar, and often cruel, business.

'I guess I'll be going,' he said, standing up and thrusting out his hand stiffly. 'I hope I'll see you again one day.'

'So do I, but I bet that when I visit Chicago again, you will have forgotten all about me,' she teased, trying to swallow the lump in her throat.

'No, I'll never forget you.'

He began to turn away, but Amadine kept hold of his hand.

'Take care of yourself, Ben – and take care of him for me.'

'Okay, but I'd rather take care of you.'

Eyes swimming in tears, Amadine watched the straight-backed little figure as he strode bravely across the concourse and was lost from view.

Outside the station, Ben made straight for a waiting cab and climbed in. He sat down beside Pierce, who glanced at him but said nothing as the vehicle moved off. After a few minutes Pierce produced a large white handkerchief, which he pressed into the boy's hand.

'Here,' he said, 'you seem to have caught a cold. Just as well we've got you off the streets, or it could have turned into double pneumonia.'

Blanche could not believe it. Amadine was settling back into her former stateroom in the Palace Car.

'But that's where Constance . . .' Blanche gasped. 'Aren't you frightened?'

'Of what – ghosts?'

'Among other things,' Blanche said, with a shiver.

'My dear Blanche, I am accustomed to living in a rectory that is centuries old, and which must have witnessed many deaths over the years. As long as the room has been thoroughly cleaned and aired, and the sheets on the bed have been changed, I don't have a problem.'

No, it was Blanche who had the problem. Promoted to Constance's old room in the women's car, she sat and seethed. She had counted on Amadine's sensibilities being too delicate to contemplate sleeping in the bed where Constance died, at which juncture Blanche had planned to step forward and bravely offer to occupy the room. Like Constance before her, Blanche had studied the advantages of such close proximity to Hal's sleeping quarters and, unlike Constance, she now had a role model. Blanche was almost positive that Hal had not slept with Constance before she moved into that room, and what had happened once could happen again.

In different circumstances she would have gloried in the prestige of having her own stateroom, but as the train left Chicago *en route* for Kalamazoo, all Blanche could think about was the length of the women's car that separated her from Hal, and of Amadine's proximity to him. It had not escaped Blanche's notice that Amadine had been out of sorts for the past couple of days, and that Pierce Radcliffe had been conspicuously absent from the theatre last night, and from the depot this morning.

Blanche groaned. Had it all been for nothing? After everything that had happened, and everything that she, Blanche, had achieved, was it possible that Amadine would change her mind and have Hal after all?

For Theo, resumption of the train journey brought old terrors and fresh fears. On Sunday he had been flooded by a tide of conflicting emotions at the sight of Carlo on the train, part of him having hoped that the young man would stay in Chicago, and the rest of him dreading such a development. The next morning he tried to work on the play, before rising and virtually sleepwalking his way to the washroom. However, the instant he opened the door, he was jolted into full consciousness. Carlo was already there.

'Hi,' the youth said, his face lighting up in a smile. 'I got here early so that I wouldn't miss you.'

Oh God, panicked Theo, he likes me. Now what do I do?

'How nice,' he said non-committally, sitting down and lighting a small cigar.

'Have you been working on your play since the crack of dawn?'

'I have been trying, but with very little success. Too many other things to think about, I'm afraid.'

'Oh, I *know*.' He swung round to face Theo, razor suspended in one hand. 'Isn't it simply awful! My folks couldn't believe I was involved in a murder inquiry. Mama tried to stop me leaving home yesterday – she thinks I might be next.'

'Your family live in Chicago?'

Carlo nodded. 'They run a restaurant downtown. I'm surprised you haven't smelled the pasta!'

'We only meet when you're washing,' and Theo's gaze travelled over the slim, olive-skinned body, and he wished that his hands could do the same.

'The pasta is the reason I'm always washing! I swear the smell of cooking gets into every hair and every pore.' He finished shaving, stripped off his shorts and began, with the utmost fastidiousness, to soap himself.

Did Carlo know what he was doing, Theo wondered? Did he have any idea of the effect he was having on his audience? Was he doing it on purpose, or was he innocently unconscious of what Theo was thinking and feeling?

'I hope your mother won't worry about you,' Theo said.

'There were tears when I left but, then, there always are. She'll be over it by now, and back to the plans for my sister's wedding. You're married, aren't you?'

He turned to face Theo and moved a few steps towards him, his genital area more or less on a level with Theo's face. Involuntarily Theo leaned back a little and groped hurriedly in his pocket for a photograph of his daughter, which he held up in front of him, rather like a shield or a devout Christian brandishing a cross to ward off evil.

'I love kids,' Carlo exclaimed, gazing at little Emily. 'My eldest sister has three already, and another on the way, and my . . .'

By the time the youth had washed off the soap, dried himself and dressed, Theo had heard his entire family history – and been bored out of his skull by it. But he sat and listened because he wanted to watch and, even as he did so, part of his mind remained detached and analysed the situation. He had nothing in common with this boy; their families and backgrounds were poles apart, while Theo's education and intellect were far superior. The conversation, if the exchange deserved such a name, was stilted and, to Theo, distinctly hard going. He found himself struggling for something to say, for he did not want to *talk*; he only wanted to *touch* . . .

'Same time tomorrow?' Carlo asked.

No, I can't, I mustn't . . . 'Sure,' said Theo.

That the youth sought him out both thrilled and terrified him: thrilled him to a high point of sexual arousal, and terrified him if he tried to work out what that meant and where it was leading. The boy liked him, but how much and in what way? Theo was afraid that he was playing with fire, venturing into an area that was physically and morally dangerous and from which no good could come, and yet which he was powerless to resist.

The urge to touch was becoming stronger and stronger. Taking into account his singular lack of success in his other struggles, how long would it take for him to succumb to this temptation?

It took a week – seven days that saw the company travel from Kalamazoo to Grand Rapids, Detroit, Toledo, Cleveland and on to Pittsburgh. And it happened, of course, in the washroom.

Everything was normal at first. The now customary stilted conversation took place, with Theo noticing that this simple, uneducated boy was much more adept at maintaining the flow of small talk than he was. Then the subject of *Barbara Frietchie* came up. Carlo was clearly fascinated by Theo's creative talents and, flattered by this interest and appreciation, Theo became more expansive than usual, and began to elaborate on the intricacies of the plot and on the difficulties a playwright had to overcome.

The beautiful boy padded across the slate floor on his bare feet and sat down beside Theo, listening intently to every word. The worshipful gaze of those big brown eyes, and the slight flutter of those long lashes, was too much. Theo lost concentration, his voice tailing away into silence, and then he bent his head and pressed his mouth to the soft, smooth skin of the boy's shoulder. His lips lingered on silky velvet before he raised his head and gazed into the eyes only inches from his. Afterwards, when he relived the incident – as he did, over and over again – Theo had no idea how long that moment lasted and how many hours passed while he drowned in those brown depths, but neither did he receive any message or reaction from the interchange. Frozen in that split second, for in truth that was all it was, Theo had no comprehension whatsoever of what the other man was thinking or feeling. In retrospect he was convinced that the youth did not recoil, but neither did he respond. Perhaps he was taken by surprise, as Theo himself was. Perhaps he could not adjust to this development or make his feelings clear. Theo did not wait to find out. Theo ran – out of the washroom, down the aisle of the men's car and into his room, where he sank into a chair and buried his face in his hands.

He was terrified. He was in the grip of something that he could not control and which threatened his entire existence. What was the boy thinking? Would he say anything to anyone else? Did he feel the same, or was he repelled by the gesture and the physical contact? Would he confront Theo and demand an explanation – or an apology – or more . . .? If he talked about the incident, would it be among his friends in the company, or to Hal and Frank?

In his room, Theo sat and shivered.

Somehow he got through the rest of the day, but in the evening life dealt one of those blows in which destiny specialises.

Theo sat down to dinner in the Palace Car as usual, with Amadine, Hal, Frank, Gwen, Jay and Blanche, and someone raised the topic of Oscar Wilde. It might have been Blanche, but on the other hand it might not. He did think, as he reviewed the situation in the small hours of the morning, that it was Blanche who picked up the subject and ran with it, and kept it alive and in the air, but he could not be absolutely sure.

It began with a discussion about Wilde's plays in which Theo, ever eager to learn, took a genuine interest. Amadine had appeared in *An Ideal Husband* in London, and Blanche had played in both *A Woman of No Importance* and *The Importance of Being Earnest* in New York, but no one else had any first-hand experience of Wilde's work. Amadine was outspoken in her praise of the wit and comedy of his plays, and said that she thought it a shame that they were not produced any more.

'The sooner the fuss dies down, the better,' she insisted.

'A fuss,' choked Blanche. 'You call the Wilde affair a *fuss*!'

'What would you call it?' Amadine enquired.

'A disgrace,' Blanche replied heatedly, 'and that is one of the more polite descriptions.'

'I would call it a tragedy,' Hal remarked thoughtfully, 'particularly as it was so unnecessary. I mean, why did he do it? He ought to have ignored the Marquess of Queensberry and his insults, instead of instituting legal proceedings and denying what was patently true.'

'Is that your opinion, Amadine?' Blanche asked, in a more moderate tone as she tailored her response to Hal's. 'What do you think about men who . . . who do what Oscar Wilde does?'

'Oh, I'm with Mrs Pat on this one,' Amadine said, somewhat flippantly – although none the less sincerely – because she was acutely aware of the silent presence of Frank. 'I don't care what people do in their private lives, as long as they don't do it in the street and frighten the horses.'

'But, in a way, Oscar Wilde did frighten the horses,' Blanche said.

'Yes,' Amadine agreed reluctantly. 'The court case was a

grave misjudgement, but I suppose he felt he had no alternative.'

'Nonsense.' Surprisingly, it was Gwen who now spoke out against the poet and playwright. 'Like Amadine, I have no personal prejudice in this respect, but the most important aspect of the case is being overlooked. Oscar Wilde is married, and the father of two sons. He had no right to indulge in sexual romps with anyone, male or female.' Her mouth twisted into a wry grimace as she contemplated the irony of this statement being made by her, of all people.

'Had he been a single man, the general condemnation might have been less virulent,' Hal commented. 'As it is . . . well, it's very hard on his wife and children.'

'They had to go abroad, didn't they,' Blanche asked, 'and change their name? Can you imagine what it will be like for those poor little boys, growing up with a shadow like that hanging over them!'

Theo did not want to imagine it. He wanted to get up from the table, go to the privacy of his room and be violently sick. But, struggling to control his feelings and his churning stomach, he stayed where he was for fear that a sudden exit might arouse suspicion.

Blanche's suspicions about Frank were already aroused, but she was less sure about Theo. However, the case of Wilde proved that marriage and fatherhood were no barriers to such proclivities, and no proof of 'innocence'. Her gaze settled on Theo in an 'is he or isn't he?' sort of way and, unfortunately for Theo, her contemplation coincided with a furtive, worried glance from Frank.

They know, Theo thought desperately. Probably everyone knows.

Thank God for Amadine who, subtly and diplomatically, changed the subject to Charles Wyndham and his courtesy and generosity to Wilde, then launched into several fresh anecdotes about her time in his Criterion company. Blanche could still be heard muttering to Gwen, wondering whether Wilde was sorry for the disgrace and misery he had brought on his family, and whether 'The Ballad of Reading Gaol', recently published in London, contained a properly abject apology. However, under cover of Amadine's increasingly vivacious reminiscences, Theo was able to escape without attracting undue attention.

If his family had been so shocked by his interest in the theatre, and by his joining the tour, how much more horrified would they be by the revelation that he was a homosexual?

The prospect of his family, and of Philadelphia society, discovering his dreadful secret was appalling. With the example of the Wildes fresh in his mind, he contemplated Susannah and Emily in exile, changing their names and identities in order to avoid the disgrace of being associated with him. But he hadn't actually done anything. Nothing much, anyway. Only a kiss, that was all. There was no reason why anyone should ever know, because he certainly would not share the information. The only person who knew was Carlo, and he wouldn't tell . . . would he? He wasn't in the least likely to be a blackmailer . . . was he?

'I can't think why the police didn't arrest your precious George on the spot,' Walter, Hal's valet, had said to Ida while they were working in the Palace Car on the first day out of Chicago. 'I watched while they searched his bag, and I saw it with my own eyes.'

'Saw what?' Ida had replied loftily.

'His gun.'

Gun! Ida nearly jumped out of her skin. Firearms were not common currency among the citizens of London, and, being unaware of the tests on Amadine's weapon, as far as Ida was concerned any gun could have been used to kill Constance. Walter was of the same opinion, which was why he was grinning at her with such satisfaction.

'Drunk again, were you?' Ida snapped waspishly.

'I saw it all right, and so did the police. What I don't understand is why they didn't take more interest in it. Great big thing, it was, and could have killed Mrs Grey easy.'

Ida decided not to lower herself by granting this allegation the favour of a reply, and walked out of the car with an indignant toss of her head. But, much against her will and greatly to her distress, the possibility that George had been involved in one or both crimes could not be dismissed as easily as Walter. She had remembered something else: that George had opened several drawers in Constance's room that day she had allowed him into the Palace Car, and he might well have seen the pearl-handled pistol. Knowledge of, and access to, two guns could not be ignored.

'People are saying that you have a gun,' she said tentatively, half-expecting him to flare up as he sometimes did.

Instead George laughed, and looked rather pleased with himself. 'Good. Perhaps these "people" will grant me more respect in future.'

Ida could not understand the connection between respect and possession of a firearm, but did not wish to show her ignorance. 'Have you ever used it?'

'Why? Are you worried that I might use it again?'

'I'm not worried,' Ida said quickly. 'I was just curious about why you wanted a gun.'

'You are worried. You think I might have killed Constance, and that you might be next. Or Amadine . . .'

If there was one thing Ida disliked about George, it was his tone of disrespectful familiarity when referring to the principals. To him, it ought to be Miss Amadine, or preferably Miss Sinclair. However, she remained too besotted to remonstrate. The trouble with George was that occasionally he could be horrid, but when he was good, he was very, very good. Utterly charming, in fact, and in a strange way he seemed to be growing younger and better looking.

The truth was that George was losing weight. Since joining the tour his workload had been such that his drinking opportunities were reduced, while at the same time sobriety was essential. Inebriated stage staff were a safety hazard that Frank Smith was unlikely to tolerate, and George had no intention of losing his position. This job was too important. Amadine was too important . . . He was beginning to look much more like his old self. His face was thinner, the skin less mottled and discoloured, and some of the blemishes seemed less noticeable. If he got rid of the hair dye, he would be easily recognisable as the handsome man who had once walked the London stage.

However, the downside to this development was that Amadine might recognise him. So far she had not noticed him – at least he did not think that she had – even though he had passed within a few feet of her on several occasions at the theatre. He was determined that their initial confrontation should be on his terms, when he possessed the invaluable element of surprise and could extract the most advantage from it. He could not risk waiting much longer for this encounter, but had not yet found a way of speaking to her in circumstances where they could be alone with no fear of interruption.

As the train pulled out of Pittsburgh, *en route* for Washington, George decided that it was time to give fate a helping hand: if opportunity would not knock of its own free will, it must be created. Yes, he had been right not to discard Ida, because the girl might still have her uses. She had been easily assured that he had no intention of shooting Amadine and had ended up laughing with him at the mere idea, and at the time his denial of any such intention had been genuine. The only person he had itched to eradicate was Pierce Radcliffe. But now his obsession took a different turn as, not for the first time, his precise goal shifted and assumed a new shape. Suddenly he was consumed with the conviction that if he couldn't have Amadine, no one would . . .

Therefore he was more than usually receptive to Ida's

complaints about how difficult Amadine was being, and to Ida's opinion that Pierce Radcliffe was the cause of her mistress's moodiness and uncharacteristically sharp tongue.

'So the big romance is off,' George commented.

'Looks like it. Of course, I never liked him, not from the moment I clapped eyes on him,' Ida declared. 'I don't understand what she saw in him. She could have had Mr Hal – she only had to snap her fingers and he would've come running. What more did she want, I'd like to know! Still, there's no accounting for taste.'

'If Amadine had encouraged Hal, Constance might still be alive.'

This suggestion was under constant discussion among the company. No one cared to point the finger at Hal, but the possibility that Constance had been murdered by mistake for Amadine was dissected at length and with the utmost relish.

'It wasn't me who killed Constance. You do believe me, don't you?' George said earnestly.

''Course I do, silly. But someone did. And someone took the money, too.'

'Funny how no one ever suspects Amadine.'

Ida may have been suffering under the lash of Amadine's tongue, but she was loyal to the last. 'I should think not indeed! But that Radcliffe feller is a different kettle of fish - you can see he's got a ruthless streak.'

'And you think Amadine hasn't?' George smiled. 'I reckon Miss Amadine is more than capable of clawing her way to the top, and of getting her own way, no matter who gets hurt in the process. Oh yes, she's the type who will pick people up and then put them down as the fancy takes her.'

This sounded so unlike the Miss Amadine whom Ida knew and loved that, had anyone but George voiced this opinion, she would have flown at them, spitting fire. 'It isn't strange that no one suspects Miss Amadine,' she maintained steadfastly. 'Everyone likes her.'

'Correction – everyone, particularly every man, *loves* her.'

'Including you, I suppose.' Ida was goaded into sarcasm.

'Yes.'

'You?' Ida laughed. 'That's a waste of time and effort if ever I saw one. She'd never look at you.'

'You think not?' George leaned forward, and smiled. 'That's where you are wrong, Ida, very wrong. More wrong than you can ever know.'

There was such a strange note in his voice that for a moment Ida was worried, even frightened. Then she laughed.

'You had me going there, for a minute. Of course all the men are in love with Miss Amadine. It's something the rest of us women have to live with. We learn not to take it seriously, and to pick up her rejects – like Miss Blanche is working on Mr Hal.'

George's face tautened. 'Don't call me one of Amadine's rejects,' he said slowly. 'I don't like it. And it isn't true.'

The thundercloud that darkened his face frightened Ida again. 'I didn't mean anything by it,' she said hastily.

He let it go at that but Ida's wariness remained so that, when he arrived unexpectedly at the door of Amadine's hotel suite after the performance in Washington that night, she let him in rather than argue on the doorstep.

'You can't stay – she'll be back soon,' Ida hissed. 'It's a miracle she ain't here this minute.'

'No, it isn't. She's gone to a party with Hal, as you well know. Some sort of official reception that will keep her occupied for some while yet.'

'What do you want?' Ida asked, glancing round nervously as if she expected Amadine to materialise suddenly from the depths of one of the armchairs, or to appear in the bedroom doorway.

'To see you, of course. It isn't often I'm free after the theatre – usually I'm lugging great chunks of scenery back to that damned train.' He walked past Ida into the parlour and, to her horror, sat down on the sofa. 'Aren't you going to offer me a drink?'

Ida began to protest, but changed her mind. 'Only if you promise to drink it quickly.' She sloshed Scotch into a glass, hating doing so because it felt like stealing.

George took the glass and deliberately sipped the Scotch slowly in order to annoy and worry her. He patted the sofa cushion beside him. 'Come and sit with me. There, isn't this nice. We ought to meet in places like this more often.' He slipped his arm around her.

She should have been in seventh heaven, and would have been, if she hadn't been terrified of Amadine walking in at any moment. 'This isn't right,' she said anxiously.

'I'll tell you what isn't right – Amadine keeping you up until all hours while she goes off to parties.'

'It's my job.'

'How long have you had this job?'

'Three years.'

'Does Amadine ever talk about the days when she started out in the profession?'

'Not to me, but I've heard her talking about Mr Wyndham and people like that, to the other principals. Oh, do hurry up. She'll be back in a minute, honest, and then I won't have a job.'

'You're trying to get rid of me,' George said in mock indignation. 'You are expecting someone else!'

'Don't be daft. I'm . . .' Ida was unable to complete her sentence because at that moment George's mouth descended on her, and he kissed her firmly, albeit briefly. 'Oh, George,' she said weakly.

Then came the sound George had been waiting for – a loud rap on the door, and the bellboy was telling Ida that someone in the lobby wanted to see her urgently.

'There,' George exclaimed. 'I said you were expecting someone.'

'It must be a mistake,' Ida said uncertainly, 'but I suppose

I'll have to go and see. George, please come down with me.'

'I haven't finished my drink.'

'You mustn't be here when Miss Amadine comes back!'

'I won't even be here when you come back,' he promised with a smile, raising his glass in mock salute as Ida hovered in the doorway.

'Be sure to close the door after you,' she said, picking up the key.

'Has anyone ever told you that you worry too much?'

George leaned back in his seat and languidly blew her a kiss, but the instant the door closed behind her, he was on his feet. Tossing back the Scotch in a single gulp, he placed the glass on the tray with the decanters and walked swiftly into the bedroom. The covers were turned down, and Ida had laid out Amadine's fine silk nightgown on one side of the big double bed. Hairbrushes, combs, hand-mirrors and perfumes littered the dressing table, but George went straight to the big walk-in wardrobe where Amadine's clothes were hanging. Taking hold of one of the soft silks, he raised it to his nostrils and inhaled the very special smell of her; not just her perfume, but the very scent of her skin, so that as he pressed the silk against his cheek, it was almost as if he caressed her cheek, her shoulder or breast.

Then he stepped into the wardrobe, cautiously positioning the door so that it allowed in just a chink of light and a breath of air. There was a chance that Ida might see him if she hung up the dress Amadine was wearing tonight, but she would not give him away – she would be too nervous of getting into trouble. And after he had confronted Amadine, it would not matter what Ida said or did, not any more.

Concealing himself as best he could among Amadine's silks, satins and furs, George stood quietly in the darkness and waited.

Chapter Thirty

Ida looked round the lobby with a puzzled frown on her face. The bellboy having vanished, she went to the desk to enquire who had been asking for her. At that moment, and quite coincidentally, Pierce Radcliffe entered the hotel.

'Ida,' he exclaimed, 'the very person . . .'

Jumping to the conclusion that he was the person who had sent for her, she eyed Pierce defensively. 'Miss Amadine isn't here.'

'I'll wait for her – upstairs, preferably.'

'I can't let you into her room, sir, not without her permission,' Ida said virtuously, adding pointedly, 'she might not want to see you.'

Pierce stared at her for a moment, with raised eyebrows. 'You are quite right, Ida,' he said at last. 'I only hope that you guard Amadine this efficiently against any other uninvited visitors.'

'I do my best, sir.' And, leaving Pierce to take a seat in the lobby, Ida rushed back to the suite to ensure that George had gone. After breathing a sigh of relief at the sight of the empty parlour, she clucked with exasperation at the dirty glass and hurried into the bathroom to rinse and dry it. Then, perched on an upright chair by the door, she settled down to wait and to dream of that kiss.

Pierce passed the time going over in his mind what he

wanted to say, and the reason for his visit. He had been in Philadelphia, and he wanted to pass on to Amadine the results of his investigations there.

As usual, he had checked into the Stenton, and devoted himself to his own business affairs for the first few days of his stay. He had kept a weather eye open for Jay Johnson's friend in the lobby of the hotel, and in the bar, but saw no one who answered that vague description he was carrying in his head. When there was no sign of the man at the Bellevue Restaurant either, Pierce began to feel concerned. He had no other leads to follow, and realised that there was every possibility that his quarry had been a visitor to Philadelphia that day in early December. But then, on his fourth visit to the Bellevue, he struck lucky. A rustle and a stir among the other diners drew his attention to a table where a woman and two men were being seated. The woman was attractive in a showy, flamboyant way and one of the men was a stranger to Pierce, but the second was definitely the same fellow who had dined here with Jay that night. However, he had blossomed in the interim: he was better dressed, more confident and greeted the *maître* like an old friend.

Pierce continued with his dinner at a leisurely pace until he saw a suitable opportunity to invite the Bellevue manager, Larry McCormick, over for a drink.

'Ought I to know who she is?' he asked, indicating the showily pretty woman.

'She isn't the toast of the town yet, but she will be. That's Nancy Loring, and she's the leading lady in a show that's due to open here shortly.'

'Her escorts are connected with the show, I suppose?'

McCormick nodded. 'Beside her is Bill Stewart, the producer, and sitting opposite is the stage manager.'

Jay's friend, Bill, was the producer? Pierce was beginning to see light at the end of a very long tunnel.

'I've seen Bill before,' he said casually. 'Always seemed to have a cheque book in his hand. I thought that perhaps . . . But no, evidently I was mistaken.'

McCormick chuckled. 'You were spot on. But the kites aren't the only things that have taken off, because that show looks like being a success. I might even be proud of my contribution, and at least I won't be regretting it because, so far, all the cheques have been honoured. Mind you, it was nip and tuck at one point and I was afraid Bill was going to blow it.'

'When was that?'

'Let me think.' McCormick frowned in an effort to remember. 'Beginning of February, I guess. The crisis lasted a couple of weeks, more or less. I thought Bill would bust a gut dashing round town with that cheque book, and flitting up-country to the bank, still hoping no one noticed what he was doing. Funniest thing you ever saw.'

'Hysterical,' Pierce agreed drily. 'But apparently he sorted something out, and he isn't dashing round any more?'

'He must have had an injection of cash from somewhere but, if he has, he isn't saying from where.'

'Pity,' drawled Pierce with a smile. 'I wouldn't mind tapping the same source to help my new venture off the ground. Perhaps Bill could give me a few tips!'

'I doubt it,' said McCormick shrewdly. 'He's an amateur compared to you. And the day you start flying kites is the day I believe *men* can fly, and I buy shares in a wing-making factory.'

'It will come,' Pierce assured him gravely. 'Yesterday it was railroads, today it's automobiles, and tomorrow we fly. Trust me. I intend to be there.'

'It's supposed to be the road to hell that's paved with good intentions, not the flight path to heaven.' McCormick finished his wine and stood up.

'What is the show called, by the way?' Pierce asked.

'*The Philadelphia Girl*, of course. What else!'

After tracing the show to the Gayety Theatre, Pierce strolled round next day and inspected the publicity notices outside. Miss Nancy Loring looked very fetching in the photographs, and the chorus line certainly had its attractions – unless one was hooked on Amadine Sinclair. Prominent among the notices was an announcement to the effect that the show was opening on 11 April, not 4 April as originally planned. That made sense: a cash shortage back in February could have delayed the production in all sorts of ways. However, none of the notices mentioned Jay Johnson, and there was still no confirmation that he was in any way involved in the enterprise.

Pierce had reviewed the situation thus far when Amadine entered the lobby of the Washington hotel. She saw him immediately but, although he was a man who could read a business situation expertly, he could not fathom the enigma of the expressions that flickered across her face.

'I've been in Philly,' he said shortly, 'and I thought you would want to know what happened.'

Her expression changed again, a faint light dying from her face and eyes. 'You'd better come up,' and she preceded him into the elevator.

After a sleepy Ida let them into the suite, Amadine walked towards the bedroom. 'I don't want to delay Ida any longer, so I'll change out of these things. Help yourself to a drink while you're waiting.'

Inside the cupboard, George tensed as Amadine and Ida entered the bedroom. He was uncomfortable and hot, but came alert again at the realisation that his meeting with Amadine was only moments away. His heart was banging so loudly that he was sure she must be able to hear it.

But as the conversation between the two women progressed, he liked what he heard less and less. Radcliffe was here. Oh my God, now what did he do? Ida had assured him that the affair was over. Couldn't the stupid cow get anything right?

Ida was asking Amadine if Mr Radcliffe would be stopping long, and Amadine snapped back that it was none of Ida's business.

Perhaps Radcliffe would not spend the night in Amadine's bed, in which case matters could proceed as planned. Anyway, for the moment, George had no option but to stay where he was and find out.

'So,' said Amadine in a chilly voice, 'is Jay our culprit?'

'It is a distinct possibility,' and Pierce brought her up to date. 'I have no proof that Jay is connected with that show but, if he is, a lot of things start to make sense.'

'Short of asking him or this Bill person outright, how can we find that proof?'

'Follow Jay from the moment he sets foot in Philly.'

'He told me that he wanted to reach Philadelphia quickly,' Amadine recalled, 'and we are in Baltimore next week, which is only a hop, skip and jump away. No suspicions would be aroused if I gave him the fare and released him from his obligations to us.'

'I'll tell the detective agency to follow him – he knows me too well for me to risk it.'

'Even if Jay is connected with that show, he might have nothing to hide. The likelihood is that he kept quiet about it because it clashed with his position *vis-à-vis* Frohman.'

'There are several other points to consider. For instance, Bill's cash problems occurred at the beginning of February, and were solved within a couple of weeks.'

'And we believe that our safe was robbed on 26 February, so Jay did not use that money to help Bill out of his difficulties.'

'No, but I'll bet that he used Frohman's money. He did a rollover – after kite-flying, it's one of the oldest tricks in the book.' He explained how a rollover worked. 'We tended to accept that Jay had been led into bad banking habits by Frank, but in fact, like Frank, he knew exactly what he was doing.'

'Frank admitted that he intended to stage a robbery in order to cover up his own thefts. Could Jay have done the same?'

Pierce shrugged. 'Again, it would make sense, but at this juncture it's another imponderable. The police might be able to check it out, but I would prefer to leave them out of this for the time being. Let's not spoil Bill's fun unnecessarily.'

'The main point in Jay's favour is surely that the show's financial crisis was over when the safe-robbery occurred. Even if he did plan to stage such a robbery, he did not need to do it that night. He did not need the cash so desperately that he would risk being seen by Constance.'

'I know.' Pierce rubbed his eyes wearily. 'We come back to that every time, don't we – the connection, if any, between the two crimes and the timing of same. But I'm sorry, Amadine, I'm too tired to sort it out now.'

'Where are you staying tonight?'

'I have no idea – I came straight here from the station – but with luck this place will have an empty room.'

Amadine hesitated. She did not want to send out the wrong signals, but she owed him hospitality and did not like to think of him walking the streets of Washington in search of a bed at this hour of night.

'If the hotel cannot accommodate you, you can sleep here. And I do mean here,' and she gestured at where he was sitting, 'on the sofa.'

'Thank you. If I'm not back in ten minutes, you'll know I've been fixed up elsewhere.'

He left immediately, and Amadine walked slowly into the bedroom.

George edged closer to the slight gap in the door. Placing

one eye to the aperture, he could see Amadine's profile, the long plait of dark hair down her back and the curve of her breasts beneath the silk robe. She had been in such a hurry to dismiss Ida – or, more likely, to see Radcliffe – that she had not finished undressing, and under the robe she was still wearing petticoats, chemise, knickers, a light corset and stockings. George's throat was dry as, in a state of throbbing arousal, he watched Amadine remove all her clothes and stand naked before him. She was more beautiful than ever, and at that moment George wanted her more than he had ever wanted anyone or anything in his life: not to woo or caress, but to violate and possess.

However, he remained motionless, his hands clenched into tight fists. This was the ideal moment to confront her, while she was naked and alone and at a disadvantage, and ought to have been the culmination of his long and patient campaign. But he did not know if she was alone, or if Radcliffe was still in the other room.

Amadine slipped into her nightgown and, in case Pierce returned to claim the sofa, put on the robe again. In her earlier haste, she had told Ida to leave her coat and evening gown on the chair, but she might as well hang them in the cupboard while she was waiting. Picking up the dress, she turned towards the wardrobe, but then heard a knock at the door. Dropping the dress on the chair, she returned to the other room and admitted an apologetic Pierce.

For a while there was much toing and froing between bedroom, bathroom and parlour as Amadine transferred spare bedding from a chest at the foot of her bed to the sofa, and she and Pierce prepared for bed. Then darkness, and silence.

George was devious but not resourceful and, like many men with a tendency to violence, he was a coward. Ida was right to be frightened of him when he turned nasty because

George could, and in the past had been known to, assault women when the mood and the drink took him, but he would never have the courage to take on the Pierce Radcliffes of this world. He cowered in the closet in a turmoil of fear and fury, afraid of what Radcliffe would do to him if he were discovered, of the effect this would have on his long-term plans for Amadine, and blaming everyone but himself for the position he was in.

Ida: given the opportunity, he would throttle her with his bare hands. She was unreliable, ugly and stupid, and he had kissed her, for God's sake, overcoming his repugnance and finer feelings for the good of the cause. And because she had convinced him that Amadine would be alone tonight, he had tipped the bellboy to deliver that message, so that was good money down the drain.

Radcliffe: if he'd had his gun with him, George really believed that he could have shot the bastard right between the eyes and enjoyed every second of it.

Amadine: was a slut who needed bringing to heel by a strong man, and George knew just the chap to teach her the lesson she deserved.

Hal . . . Frank . . . even Laurie Knight. George hated them all. He hated their status, their lifestyles, their success. Why should he be a humble stagehand while they swanned around in their finery and their Palace Car? He was just as good as them. He'd had bad luck, that's all – one piece of bad luck in particular, although he intended to turn it to his advantage. What's more, he'd done something none of them had done and before long they would know it. Then he would get the respect he deserved. Then he could tell them to stuff their job where the sun don't shine.

In the meantime he was stuck in a cupboard with Amadine fast asleep only inches away, and Radcliffe between him and the door.

Cautiously George emerged from the closet and, as

Amadine made no sound or movement, he padded softly across the room. The bedroom door was closed and he had to move the knob a fraction of an inch at a time, braced for the slightest squeak, before he could creep into the adjacent parlour. His eyes were adjusting to the darkness. He could see the outer door and, hearing steady breathing, ascertained that Radcliffe was asleep on the sofa and not barring the path between George and freedom. All he had to hope now was that the outer door was unlocked. George moved forward slowly, a step at a time, one eye on the door and the other on the bulk of Pierce Radcliffe, covered by a quilt, on the sofa. He had sat in this room a few hours earlier, and could picture the route perfectly.

Unfortunately for George, he did not know that Pierce had placed his bag, open and spilling some of its contents, on the floor beside the upright chair on which Ida had maintained her vigil. The said chair lay directly between George and the outer door, and within a few paces his foot collided with the bag. He tripped and fell, sprawling his length on the floor and knocking over a vase of flowers. In the quiet of the night, the noise sounded like the battles of Gettysburg and Waterloo combined. As Pierce grunted and then jerked into life, George picked himself up and lunged for the door. It would not open. Fumbling in the dark, his fingers found the key in the lock, and thankfully he lurched into the corridor and ran for the stairs as if the hounds of hell pursued him.

Pierce groped for the light switch as Amadine stumbled into the room.

'What on earth . . .?' she began sleepily.

The outer door was open. Clad only in his undershorts, Pierce peered into the corridor. Nothing. Thoughtfully, he closed the door, picked up the vase and flowers, and surveyed the wet floor.

'We had a visitor,' he said, 'although I don't understand how anyone got in.'

Amadine looked at him sceptically, before switching on the bedroom light. The closet door was open. It had not been open when she went to bed, had it? No, she was sure that it had not.

'I think someone might have been hiding in the bedroom cupboard,' she said in a strangled voice.

Pierce began to dress.

'Where are you going?' Amadine asked in alarm.

'To report this to the hotel management, of course.'

'Don't leave me on my own! We'll tell them in the morning. Just help me to make sure that no one else is here, and that nothing has been taken.'

After a thorough search of the suite, and ascertaining that Amadine's pearls were still on the dressing table, they made sure that the outer door was securely locked and went back to bed. But Amadine could not sleep. For the first time, in all the alarums and excursions of this dreadful tour, she was frightened.

In the end they did not mention the incident to the hotel management, being too concerned for Amadine's reputation if Pierce's presence in her room should become known, but Amadine did tell Ida. The girl went white and began stammering her innocence of any involvement, and ignorance of what could have occurred, but when she calmed down she agreed that they would inspect every inch of the hotel suite every night. Which they did, but Amadine still did not sleep well and was glad when the tour progressed to Baltimore.

Baltimore brought decision time for Blanche. However, this visit to her home town was unusual in another respect in that, instead of staying with her mother, she occupied the hotel room intended for Constance. Given the choice, there really was no contest. The accommodation and the food at the hotel were infinitely superior, and the company was a darned sight better, too. Looking out of her window at the Baltimore skyline, Blanche settled on a course of action.

If only Hal did not share a suite with Frank! Her room was on the same corridor and, opening the door a crack, Blanche peered out. The passage was empty and everything was quiet. Leaving the door ajar, she withdrew into her room again, but then – thank you, God – she heard a door close and, glancing out hurriedly, saw Frank entering the elevator. Hal's valet answered her knock but admitted her without demur and, to Blanche's relief, Hal himself did not seem displeased to see her.

'I am so sorry to bother you,' she said with studied timidity, 'but I wanted to ask your advice. I hate to be a nuisance.'

'You, a nuisance?' Hal smiled reassuringly. 'My dear Blanche, have you been ill on this tour? No. Have you been temperamental or uncooperative? No. Have you landed yourself into scrapes or upset your colleagues? No. Or, have you been a tower of strength, a model of reliability and adaptability, and in fact made it possible for the tour to continue? Yes, you have. So you see, my dear, no one on this tour has been less of a nuisance than you.'

'You might not think so after what I have to say.' Visibly plucking up courage, she told him about her relationship with her grandmother and how she had concealed her connection with the theatre. 'But I cannot keep the secret from her any longer. I don't mind for myself – Mother is always harping on about the possibility of an inheritance, but that's hogwash, and who needs an inheritance when one has one's work – but Grandmama will take it out on my mother, and I couldn't bear that.'

'Do you really and truly want to continue with your theatrical career?'

'Yes,' Blanche said with total sincerity. 'I love it. There's nothing else in the world I want to do.'

'I'm very glad to hear it. You are very talented, and it would be a shame to waste it. Right, so somehow you have to convince your grandmother that a career in the theatre is a Good Thing.'

She smiled at his gentle emphasis, and nodded. 'But how?'

'Would it help if I had a word with her?' Hal suggested diffidently.

'Would you, really? But no, I couldn't ask you to do that. You have done so much for me already.'

'You have done a lot for me, too,' he reminded her, 'stepping into the breach, and into new roles, at a moment's notice. I am very grateful, and would welcome an opportunity to redress the balance.'

'She doesn't live far away,' Blanche said, with apparent shyness. 'Just across the street, so it needn't take long. Oh, I'm sure she would listen to you. Anyone would!'

Surprisingly, for one for whom flattery was an everyday occurrence, Hal preened slightly. Blanche was a dear little thing. She made him feel cool, capable and in control.

They called on Mrs Hamilton in Mount Vernon Place the following morning, arriving unannounced because Blanche decided to risk the element of surprise. She was inordinately proud to be seen with Hal. He was so handsome and well dressed, and she could tell that her grandmother was instantly impressed by his beautiful English accent and his double-barrelled name. However, eyebrows were raised when Mr Haldane-Smith's professional status was explained.

'The *theatre*!' intoned Grandmama in a most Lady Bracknellish way.

'Mr Haldane-Smith is a classical actor,' Blanche hastened to assure her, 'a Shakespearian actor, and he manages his own company.'

This seemed to restore Hal's status in Mrs Hamilton's eyes, to some extent anyway, but her mollified air did not last long. Coached by Blanche in advance, Hal proceeded to indicate subtly that Blanche's interest in the theatrical profession was very recent and that it had not been altogether by choice. Fame, he intimated, had been thrust upon her.

'She was spotted in New York, and recognised instantly as having the potential to be a very fine actress,' Hal said with his most winning smile.

'Dorothea has been performing on a *stage – in public*?'

'She has been working with me on my current Shakespearian production for the past month or so.' Hal chose his words with care, trying to tell the truth as far as possible, if not the whole truth. 'Due to a tragedy in my company, she has been elevated to one of the leading roles and is doing so well that she would like to continue with the tour. With your permission, of course. I do hope that you will agree, Mrs Hamilton, because we would hate to lose her.'

Mrs Hamilton's expression did not bode well and, as she struggled for words, it was clear that something on the lines of 'over my dead body' would ensue.

'In fact,' Hal added thoughtfully before she could speak, 'if Bla . . . Dorothea has nothing else planned, I would be glad if she would accompany me back to London and work with me next season. I feel sure she would be as great an asset to the English stage as she would to the American.'

Blanche turned bright pink and her eyes sparkled as she swung round towards him. This piece of news had definitely not been rehearsed in advance, and she had never been happier, or looked prettier, than when she gasped, 'Oh, Hal, that would be marvellous!'

Mrs Hamilton looked at her granddaughter critically, and saw that she was very attractive and vivacious indeed. Yes, it was entirely possible that Dorothea could be a success at this sort of thing and, after all, what else was the girl to do? Working as a governess or a shop girl would not enable her to meet the right kind of man and make a good marriage. The London *stage* still sent a *frisson* of horror down Mrs Hamilton's spine, but *London* would remove the girl from Dora's influence and that would do no harm. Quite the contrary, in fact.

'I would like to see this play,' she announced, 'before I decide whether or not this scheme has my approval.'

A box was arranged for the following evening and, escorted by her unmarried son, Mrs Hamilton made her first visit to the theatre. Blanche had assessed the situation perfectly. *Much Ado* was ideally suited to make a good impression, and the contrast between Amadine's dark vivacity and the sweet, blonde innocence of Blanche's Hero worked to the advantage of both actresses. Venturing backstage after the performance, with the air of an intrepid explorer in uncharted territory, Mrs Hamilton looked at her granddaughter in a new light.

'Very nice,' she said in a neutral tone. 'Yes, not bad at all. I didn't know you had it in you. But I'm not sure about this Sinclair woman – she's the one who keeps coming to our church.'

'Amadine goes to church every Sunday,' Blanche explained. 'Her father was a clergyman, and so is her brother. Her other brother is a lawyer, I believe.'

That put a different complexion on things, and again Mrs Hamilton was aware of the subsidence of some of her prejudices. 'You can continue with this business if you want,' she said abruptly, 'but don't come running to me if it all goes wrong.'

'Thank you, Grandmama,' and Blanche so far forgot herself as to throw her arms around her grandmother's neck and kiss her. 'That means I can tell Mother about it tomorrow.' She paused, hoping that her grandmother would assume Dora had been unaware of the situation until now. 'It isn't her fault I'm doing this. You won't let it affect her allowance, will you, please?'

'No, no.' Mrs Hamilton waved a hand impatiently. 'Although I still think you must get it from her side of the

family. And while on the subject,' she flourished her programme under Blanche's nose, 'I see that you are calling
yourself by some fancy name. Ashamed of the Hamiltons,
are you?'

'Of course not, but I thought you might be ashamed of
me.' Blanche met her eyes steadily. 'I have always thought
you were ashamed of me.'

'I cannot imagine what gave you that idea,' Mrs
Hamilton said gruffly.

'Does that mean that if a newspaper interviews me, I can
tell them who I am?'

A rather wild expression appeared in Mrs Hamilton's
eyes at this unexpected sally. 'I suppose so,' she replied,
and retreated before any more defences were breached.

Blanche smiled. By now, everyone knew that Jay was
leaving the tour, but he might have time to arrange an
interview with *The Sun*.

Next day Blanche went to see her mother and told her the
whole story, including the threat from her stepfather.

'If you want to live with him again, that's your affair,' she
told Dora bluntly, 'but he isn't going to blackmail me and
get away with it. And remember, all you have to do in order
to retain your allowance is forget everything about my
theatrical career except Edward Haldane-Smith. As far as
you know, I started acting with him, and not before.'

She did not tell Dora about the proposed visit to
London, and she did not invite her to the theatre – Blanche
was extremely anxious that Dora and Hal should not meet.

As anticipated, her stepfather was looking out for her.
She met him outside the theatre on her way to a matinée.
'I'll see you tomorrow,' she said haughtily, 'same place as
before.' But when she arrived at the saloon, instead of the
bundle of dollar bills he was greedily anticipating, she was
carrying a copy of *The Sun*. With a flourish she opened it at
the page containing her interview, featuring a drawing of

her in her Hero costume. With a delicious sense of accomplishment, she pointed to the paragraph that described her family connections with the city of Baltimore, and her Hamilton relatives in particular.

'As you see, you will receive nothing else from me,' she said, 'except this.' And, picking up his glass of beer in one hand, and his hat in the other, she poured the beer slowly over his head before stalking out into the street, where she was tempted to let out a most unladylike shriek of satisfaction.

She had a sense of a chapter closing on her life and, for the few days that were left of her stay, walked the streets of the city with the feeling that it could be for the last time. However, before leaving Baltimore, there was one more thing she wanted to do. The ubiquitous presence of Frank Smith meant that she was forced to spend more time loitering on hotel landings than was seemly, but again fate seemed to be on her side, because she contrived to bump into Hal in the corridor and coax him into her room for a private word.

'I haven't thanked you properly for all your help,' she said. 'You were wonderful, and I don't know what I would have done without you.'

'My pleasure.'

'Were you serious about me going to London next season, or did you say it merely to impress my grandmother?'

'Of course I was serious.' Hal was standing just inside the door, which Blanche had closed firmly, but he showed no sign of wanting to sit down – or do anything else. 'I think we work very well together, and our compatibility could form a sound basis for my new company.'

'Will Amadine be coming, too?'

'I doubt it.'

'So you and she aren't . . .?' For all her pre-planning, Blanche could not think of a polite way of saying it, but she really had to know.

Hal smiled faintly. 'No, we aren't.'

Blanche moved a step closer, looking up at him appealingly. 'Thank you again for everything you have done for me,' she said softly. 'I really am so grateful.' She stood on tiptoe and kissed his cheek. 'You have no idea how grateful I could be,' she murmured.

The invitation was unmistakable and might have been anticipated by a man of Hal's experience, but he stood motionless, as if frozen in shock. Blanche pressed a little closer.

'No,' Hal said abruptly, 'truly, there's no need . . .' And he opened the door and fled.

Blanche's knees gave way and she sat down suddenly on the bed. She was so upset that she wanted to cry, but she couldn't. She was so humiliated that she wanted to die, but she couldn't do that either. Instead she had to face Hal again tomorrow, and the next day, and the day after that . . . She had offered that man her virginity, and been refused. He did not want her, not in that way, and where did that leave her? Not even back where she was before, because he might decide that such a forward hussy had no place in his London company. She had gained her grandmother's approval but, without Hal, that triumph turned to dust. And yet, after such an embarrassing rejection, she did not see how she could offer herself again.

Hal bolted to his room, and indeed would have bolted the door, had Frank been in. However, as Frank was out, he poured himself a large whisky and sat down, eyeing the door apprehensively as if marauding women might come bursting through the mahogany.

He tried to remember if he had ever refused such a tempting offer before and decided that, no, he hadn't, so it all went to show that there was a first time for everything. So, why had he done it? Partly, he thought, because it was simply too soon after Constance. To sleep with another woman only a few weeks after Constance's death seemed in poor taste, even though he had ended up loathing the woman. But, if he were honest, there was more to it than that, and by the time he was on his third Scotch, he had found the courage to admit that he was terrified – if that wasn't a complete contradiction in terms.

Constance's pregnancy was what terrified him. All his professional life he had sown his wild oats among the leading ladies of the theatre world, and it was surprising that none of that seed had taken such determined root before. Perhaps it had, and the wise, and compassionate, lady had not held him to account. But with Constance there would have been no escape. Despite his wriggling and his vehement protestations, he would have been forced to marry her. She would have told the story all over London and his status, career and ambitions could not have withstood the onslaught of public opinion. Her death had saved him from an awful fate because he had not wanted her, on either a personal or professional basis, and in retrospect Hal knew he had been a fool to take her to bed in the first place.

He did not intend to make the same mistake, or take the same risk, again. His playboy days were over. From now on he kept both his trousers and his lips buttoned. The next woman he slept with would be Mrs Edward Haldane-Smith, and she would be chosen firmly with his professional future in mind. She would be selected purely on the basis of being a suitable *Lady* Haldane-Smith.

Jay duly left the tour in Baltimore, with sincere protestations of gratitude for Amadine's generosity in providing the fare to Philadelphia, plus a small bonus to boot. However, barely forty-eight hours later, Amadine was wishing that she had not dismissed him so summarily. Preparing to go to the theatre, she picked up her pearls, only for the string to break and the pearls to cascade over the floor.

'Hellfire and damnation,' Amadine muttered, crawling

round the room on her hands and knees, frantically trying to pick up the stones. When she had finished, she sat back on her heels and stared at the pile of pearls, hoping that she had not lost any. Then she thought of the insurance policy, and hoped that it covered such eventualities as repairs and the loss of individual stones. And then she realised that Jay had been in charge of the insurance policy, and that he was not here to ask.

Theo. He was in charge of Frohman's finances, and with any luck Jay had handed over all the paperwork, including the policy. Amadine hurried to Theo's room, and met with instant success. Returning to her suite with the document, she sat down and began scanning the various clauses. Then something caught her eye, and she stopped, and she stared at it for a long time.

The words and figures in front of her solved one mystery, and probably provided the key to all the others.

Chapter Thirty-One

It was as if her explanation of certain events opened up new avenues because, on the short journey between Baltimore and Philadelphia, Amadine made another discovery. Sitting alone in the observation car, thinking that the spring thaw would enable her to sit on the platform and enjoy the countryside, she saw something so blindingly obvious that she could not imagine why she had not seen it before. She understood how the culprit had entered and left the Palace Car without being noticed.

'The key to the observation room door is left in the lock, like all the other door keys,' she told Pierce. 'It being winter, we have not opened that door all tour, but if someone left it unlocked, no one would notice.'

'Because the observation room is screened from the rest of the Palace Car by the staterooms.'

'That's right. To reach it, you have to walk through the parlour and down the narrow passage past the two staterooms. The staff rarely go in there, and cannot see into it from the kitchen or parlour area.'

'So the culprit unlocks the door in Davenport, and returns to the train later. He or she exits the same way, and locks the door again at their leisure.'

Amadine nodded. 'It would have to be done before the

train moved off, in case the motion caused the door to swing open.'

'If you are right, it has to be an insider who was involved.'

'A Palace Car regular, because I cannot recall an occasion when an ordinary member of the company went further than the parlour. And before you ask who uses that room frequently, I do.'

'And who else?'

'Jay.' Amadine paused. 'And that isn't all. Look at this.' She showed him the insurance policy and pointed at the date on which the cover had been taken out.

'The week *after* the robbery,' he exclaimed. 'So your jewellery was not insured at the time!'

'A fact that was known only to Jay. He must have forgotten to do it originally and, if he did rob the safe, didn't want to leave me with a personal debt of that magnitude.'

'He was off the train and round to the Gayety Theatre like a homing pigeon,' Pierce said grimly. 'Right, let's think this thing through on the basis that it was him.'

'He did not join us for breakfast that day, and went into town later. He said that he was bored and cold, and returned to the train, where he fell asleep in the men's car; but in fact he was in the observation room.'

'Where he, of all people, would be acutely conscious of the safe in Frank's room, only a few feet away, and of how it would provide the answer to all his problems.' Pierce thought for a moment. 'He did not know how much money Frank had accumulated in the safe, but thought that there would be enough cash to cover what he had taken from Frohman. He must have planned to bring his remittances to Frohman up to date as far as, say, St Louis, and then admit to having a week's receipts stolen.'

'He unlocked the observation-room door, but left the train by a normal exit, and went back into town, where he spent the rest of the day in and out of the saloon near the theatre. Rather like John Wilkes Booth. Oh God,' and Amadine shuddered, 'did Jay really kill Constance?'

'He still had to obtain the safe key, and his best opportunity would be the period when the stage machinery broke down, and he would be able to estimate that Frank would not need his jacket for some time.'

Amadine nodded. 'He took the key from Frank's pocket, and hurried back to the train, entered through the observation door and opened the safe. He must have been flabbergasted by the amount of money.'

'He left by the same door, before or after hiding the money, and ran back to the theatre to return the key to Frank's pocket. Then he hung around for the rest of the performance, and cashed up with Frank and the theatre manager as usual. Then what?'

'That evening Jay did not return to the train with Frank, and put his money in the safe,' Amadine said slowly. 'He asked Frank to do it. Jay was back on board long before Frank, or any of us.'

'So that he could lock the door from the inside. And the next day he smuggled the cash into Chicago and handed it to Bill, who almost certainly did keep their appointment.'

'There is still Constance to consider,' Amadine maintained stubbornly. 'I will accept, reluctantly, that Jay took the money, but I still cannot see him as a killer. And I still say that he would not plan a robbery for the one night that Constance was ill and . . .' Her voice trailed away. 'What a fool I've been!' she said suddenly.

'You think that Jay did not know Constance was in her room.'

'He probably thought that she was at the theatre as usual.' Amadine's mind was whirling as she tried to sift the details. 'He didn't come in to breakfast, and could easily have left the train without knowing that Constance was unwell – she had not been ill before on the tour. His sojourn in the observation car later might have coincided with Constance's trip to the bank; anyway, if he was dozing, he wouldn't have noticed the odd noise here and there.'

'At that point, Jay had nothing to hide,' Pierce pointed out. 'He wasn't trying to conceal his actions, or his presence in the Palace Car.'

'He only went into the theatre much later in the day, so he missed the understudies' rehearsal, and he is so blasé about our productions now that he wouldn't have noticed who was onstage during his brief, intermittent visits during the evening.'

'And while the machinery was being fixed, he would have believed she was in her dressing room.'

'If he thought about it at all, which I doubt. He just assumed . . . Oh God, what are we going to do?'

'Ask Jay for an explanation,' Pierce replied calmly.

'Just like that? You think he will co-operate and give us the answers to our questions? Actually, it's a funny thing, but Jay was the one person who did have answers to the questions – he came up with some really plausible and convincing solutions.'

'Because he knew the sort of questions that would be asked, and had the time to dream up a few red herrings. And I have no idea whether he will co-operate or not but, having come this far, I'm in the mood to see this thing through to the bitter end.'

'Let them have their first night,' Amadine begged. 'Not just for Jay, but for all the people who have worked so hard on that show, and aren't to blame for this awful business.'

Pierce grimaced slightly in exasperation, but agreed.

'If you collect me from the theatre on Monday evening, we could go straight round to the Gayety,' Amadine suggested.

He looked at her doubtfully. 'I was not intending that you . . .'

'You aren't excluding me from the dénouement,' she said

indignantly. 'And it will be perfectly safe – Jay would never hurt me.'

'I'm sure that Constance felt exactly the same way,' Pierce said grimly.

The Monday night audience for *Tanqueray* was short-changed, Amadine thought guiltily, because her performance was well below her best. Her mind was not in Broad Street but at 237 Eighth Street, between Race and Vine, at the Gayety Theatre and the première of *The Philadelphia Girl*. She had warned Ida that she wanted to leave quickly, but in the event there was not even time to change. Pierce was waiting in the wings and bundled her into a cab, still in her *Tanqueray* dress and diamonds.

'You might just catch the last few turns,' Pierce said, explaining the rush. 'There is a full house but, as it's you, they said we could stand at the back.'

'How is it going?'

Pierce, who had been watching *The Philadelphia Girl* from a seat in the stalls, gave a wry smile. 'The irony is that Jay has a hit on his hands. Not my line of country, but everyone else is loving it, and even I must admit that the song-and-dance routines are clever and attractive.'

Amadine could not decide whether the success of the show made matters better or worse but, watching from her vantage point, agreed that a success it undoubtedly was. There was an excitement, an electricity, in the air that made her flesh tingle and the hairs on the back of her neck prickle. The response of the audience was signalling that this show was not only good, it was special. At the final ovation, her eyes sought Jay and found him in one of the proscenium boxes; a Jay she had never seen before, wearing evening clothes, with hair slicked back and face beaming with confidence. He and Bill were applauding enthusiastically and then, the cast on the stage turning to acknowledge them, took a bow themselves.

Threading their way through a throng of well-wishers behind the lowered curtain on the stage, Amadine and Pierce found Jay taking the plaudits of the cast and visitors. He saw them and walked towards them, his hand outstretched . . . And then he saw the expressions on their faces. He stopped and stared at them, his smile fading and his hand slowly falling back to his side.

'So this is why you wanted the money,' Amadine whispered.

Jay did not reply but, very slowly, his hand went to his pocket and – and afterwards witnesses said that they thought it was part of the publicity for the show, the gesture was so melodramatic – he pulled out a gun and levelled it at Amadine.

'I'm sorry, Amadine, but I'm going to have to ask you to come with me.'

Pierce moved towards her, but Jay was quicker off the mark, grabbing Amadine with his free hand and holding her in front of him like a shield. He pressed the gun to her right temple, propelling her off the stage, into the wings and out towards the stage door. A line of carriages and cabs was waiting in the street and, with the gun, Jay beckoned to the first driver in the queue.

'Go down Race to the river,' he said harshly, pushing Amadine inside.

Amadine had not tried to struggle or cry out, believing that she could calm him as soon as they were alone.

'Put away the gun, Jay. I know that you won't hurt me.'

'Trusting soul, aren't you! Always prepared to think the best of everyone, but even you must realise that I'm in a tight spot and that you are the only trump card I've got.' He did move the gun from her temple, but kept it levelled at her.

The carriage was moving rapidly down Race Street into an area of old warehouses, salthouses and sailmaking premises, interspersed with a few shabby residences and tradesmen's shops, as they crossed Front Street and went on down to the city's principal waterfront thoroughfare. Pushed out of the vehicle into Delaware Avenue and the chilly night, Amadine could just make out the dark shapes of the piers that jutted into the Delaware River. She knew that, out of sight, to the south were the ferry buildings and the horsecar turn-around at Market Street, but here, at this time of night, the waterfront was quiet and deserted. Keeping a tight hold on her elbow, Jay pulled her up the street and on to one of the piers, walking to the far end, where he looked down at the river and drew a shuddering breath.

'The cab driver will tell them where we are, and Pierce won't be far behind,' Amadine remarked, matter-of-factly.

'We'll have to be quick then, won't we?'

His voice sounded flat and dead. Amadine had no idea what his intentions were, but in a strange way she did not feel threatened. She was not nearly as afraid of Jay and his gun as she had been of that faceless, nameless intruder in her hotel room.

'You didn't know that Constance was there, did you?' she asked.

Jay shook his head. 'I opened the safe, and couldn't believe my eyes when I saw how much cash it contained. I hadn't brought a bag to put it in – I thought that it would go in my pockets – and, fumbling around in the dark, I must have made a noise, because the next thing I know the light goes on and Constance is waving a gun at me. I tried to pretend that I was there officially, that Frank knew about it, but she didn't buy that.'

'And then *she* saw all the money.'

'She wanted a share, and it was so much more than I had reckoned on that I wasn't arguing. Plenty for both of us, I said.'

'So what went wrong?'

'Constance saw your jewellery, and wanted to take that,

too. No, I said. For one thing, it's too easy to trace and too difficult to get rid of. For another it isn't insured, and Amadine will have to pay for it out of her own pocket.'

'Which made her want it all the more.'

'We argued, but she took it to her room to try on, while I closed the safe and followed her with the cash. She gave me a bag and agreed that I should hide all the money until the fuss died down, but she wouldn't hand back the diamonds.'

Amadine's hand went to her necklace. 'Damn the diamonds . . . Oh Jay, and the jewellery was your idea . . .'

'Hoist with my own petard,' and briefly there was a touch of his old bravado. 'I was panicky because I had to take the key back to the theatre, and when I tried to make her see sense, she turned nasty. Started waving the gun at me again, and saying that she wanted all the money or she would tell Hal that I was a thief, and that I couldn't accuse her of anything without incriminating myself. I tried to take the gun from her, and in the struggle it went off . . .' Jay fell silent and stood, staring into the swiftly flowing river. He was still holding his own gun but, standing beside him on the pier, Amadine had forgotten about it. 'Such flimsy, fragile creatures we are,' he said in a wondering voice. 'She died instantly. One moment she was there, and the next she had gone, snuffed out like a candle flame.'

'But you didn't mean to kill her,' Amadine said, in what she hoped was a comforting, calming way. 'It was an accident. All you have to do is tell the police what you have told me – there will be a prison sentence, I expect, but after a few years you will be out, and you can stage another *Philadelphia Girl*.'

He laughed harshly. 'And tell them how I nipped out of the observation room and hid the bag under the car, retrieving it after the show and locking the door from the inside. I didn't sleep a wink in case someone raised the alarm that night, but as soon as we reached Chicago, I knew

I was home free. Of course, my journey to the hotel with
Theo was my second trip. I'd already given the cash to Bill,
along with a cock-and-bull story about how I came by it,
and was sufficiently panic-stricken to hand over every cent
and keep nothing for myself. Oh, sure, the police will be
very understanding! Still,' and as he turned towards her
there was just enough light for Amadine to see the eager,
almost boyish pleasure on his face, 'my *Philadelphia Girl*
was great, wasn't she? I know how to pick 'em, yes, sir!'

The sound of footsteps and voices carried from the
street, and lights bobbed rapidly towards them.

'Looks like this is it,' Jay said. 'Here,' and he handed
Amadine his gun. 'I don't suppose you would do me a
favour, and shoot me with it?'

'No.'

'Then it's lucky that I can't swim.' And, as his pursuers
poured along the pier, Jay jumped.

Amadine cried out, and turned away, blindly thrusting
the gun into Pierce's hand as he reached her side. She did
not want to look at the river, to see if Jay's head broke the
surface again. She wanted to remember him by his boyish
enthusiasm and eternal optimism, which could have taken
him to the top of the tree if only things had not gone so
tragically wrong.

'Why did he do it?' Amadine asked Pierce later. They were
in her hotel room, with Hal and Frank. 'Why go to such
lengths? *The Philadelphia Girl* is a good show, but in the end
it is only a piece of tawdry make-believe. Yet it cost two
lives!'

'Things got out of hand,' Pierce said soberly. 'They
snowballed and multiplied, as bad deeds tend to do, and he
was carried along by events until he was in too deep to get
out. But also, I think he was a victim of time and place.
America is the land of opportunity, but there is tremendous
pressure on people here to succeed. A man like Jay sees

success all around him – he sees men starting out with nothing and making a fortune. He not only *wants* to do the same but feels that he *must* do it, because wealth is America's only measure of success, so he seizes every opportunity for fear of ending up a failure, and takes chances along the way. Jay was not alone in his methods, or in his gambling instincts, but some people get away with it and others don't. Some people end up on Fifth Avenue in New York and, I'm very sorry to say, others end up in the river.'

'If only Constance had not been greedy,' Hal murmured, watching Amadine's fingers toying feverishly with her necklace.

'Do you think that Bill knew what Jay had done?' Frank asked Pierce.

'From what Jay told Amadine, and judging by Bill's expression and behaviour at the theatre, I would say no, he didn't. But doubtless we will find out more tomorrow.'

'I would like to come with you if you intend speaking to him,' Frank said. 'I still consider myself responsible for the money.' And it was noticeable that he did not look at Hal when he spoke. The two brothers now knew that neither of them was guilty of either crime, but their suspicions of each other had left a permanent scar on their relationship.

'I don't want *The Philadelphia Girl* to close,' Amadine said, as she accompanied Pierce and Frank to the Gayety the next morning.

'Now there's a surprise,' Pierce remarked sarcastically. 'Are you suggesting that they should keep their ill-gotten gains?'

'If no one knew that the show was being financed with stolen money, it seems a shame to penalise them. And, from a strictly financial standpoint, if the show continues and makes a profit, Bill can pay us back.'

Pierce nodded reluctantly. 'I think a lot depends on what Bill has to say.'

Bill was ashen-faced and trembling. 'I didn't know. Please believe me, I didn't know!' He stubbed out a cigarette, and immediately lit another. 'They fished Jay out of the river early this morning, and only this time yesterday . . .'

'He gave you the money in Chicago,' Pierce prompted.

'Yeah, but, as I've spent the whole night telling the cops, he told me he'd struck lucky at cards in St Louis. The original stake for this show came from Jay's gambling, so why shouldn't I believe that he'd done it again?'

'But, afterwards, didn't you connect this sudden wealth with Mrs Grey's murder and our robbery?' Frank enquired.

'I haven't read a newspaper in months. I've been living in a vacuum, thinking of nothing but this show.'

'Has all the money been spent?' Frank went on.

Guiltily Bill glanced at his evening suit, crumpled now but obviously brand-new. 'More than I would wish, but not quite all of it.'

'Do the police believe that you were not involved?' Amadine asked.

'Lady, I only wish I knew. They haven't accused me of murder, so I suppose that's something to be grateful for. In the meantime, what do I tell the boys and girls when they turn up for the performance?'

They were interrupted by the arrival of the police, who wanted to interview Amadine and interrogate Bill again. Pierce and Frank wandered into the auditorium while they waited, and sat looking at the stage.

'Amadine is right: it would be a pity to put all those people out of work,' Frank said tentatively. 'And, if you and I could dream up a rescue plan, everyone could recoup their losses.'

'I have been resigned to the idea from the start,' Pierce assured him. 'Once Amadine starts on one of her worthy causes, she is irresistible – in the worst possible way. I have already said a silent farewell to another chunk of my father's fortune, although I take your point that I might get it back.'

'First Ben, the waif and stray; then my debts on the Levee; and now a musical revue. I should think that you really bless the day we crossed your path!'

Pierce shrugged. 'Easy come, easy go. Jay's shenanigans have made me wonder about some of the ploys my father might have used to conjure up his millions out of the comparative pittance he made as a carpenter. Once you've got started in America, a sort of momentum takes over and either you multiply your millions or you multiply your problems. But getting started, that's the thing.'

'Not a problem you have, apparently.'

'Ah, but that is one reason why I understand Jay's point of view. For years I turned my back on my father, and one of the reasons I did so was because he had started with nothing and made a fortune, and I felt that I had to do the same. I had to prove myself. If he could do it, so could I. I find it a very sobering thought that, despite my superior education and start in life, I didn't do as well as he did.'

'Perhaps your ploys were different.'

Pierce smiled. 'We'll never know, I suppose, but at least I'm fairly certain that my father would thoroughly approve of *The Philadelphia Girl*, although Gwen would be a better judge of that than I am.'

'Gwen?' Frank shot him a puzzled look. 'Look, if friend Bill can convince us of his innocence, I suggest he repays whatever he has left in the kitty. If this show is as good as you and Amadine think it is, he can finance his running costs out of the box office and repay us gradually out of the profits.'

Pierce shook his head. 'There are Frohman's losses to consider, too. No, the best thing is to calculate what you are owed and what Frohman is owed, and I'll pick up the tab. Then "friend Bill", who I suspect I am going to know rather well, can repay me at a rate that won't endanger the show. Who knows, I may even develop a taste for financing musical revues and other theatrical extravaganzas.'

'Amadine has really got to you, hasn't she!'

'Much good it has done me. She has refused to marry me, if that's what you are wondering.'

'I am sorry to hear it, and surprised – I thought she was an intelligent young woman. But you won't take no for an answer, surely?'

'I'm not about to go on my knees and beg,' Pierce said drily. 'I'm not the type, and I doubt if Amadine would respect a man who was.'

'So is this it? Now that you have solved our mysteries, you will vanish into the night, as it were?'

'I still have a vague sense of unfinished business – the gunshot, and the stalker; and there was another incident in Washington. I must take no for an answer, but I cannot vanish into the night, not until I know she is safe.'

Chapter Thirty-Two

Susannah was pregnant again. Theo was surprised that such important news had not been mentioned in her letters, then relieved – because, if her first pregnancy was anything to go by, she would refuse to sleep with him until after the birth – and finally frightened by the creation of another innocent life that might be ruined by him.

In addition, Susannah was in a cold, martyred mood and Theo knew that it was all his fault. Joining the tour had seemed such a reasonable request at the time. Wanting a few months to himself, to learn about the theatre and possibly get it out of his system, had not appeared to be unduly self-indulgent, but now he could see it from Susannah's point of view. She was a pretty young woman of good Philadelphia family, who thought she had married a lawyer of good Philadelphia family, not this . . . this . . . well, whatever or whoever Theo had become. He ought never to have married her but, when he courted her, he did not know what, or who, he was. And if he had not married her, there would be no Emily and he could never regret that. Of all the people, things and experiences in the world, Emily came first and her future happiness took precedence over everything else. Even the theatre. Even *Barbara Frietchie*.

But Emily gave him a blank stare and turned away, burying her face in Susannah's shoulder. He was a stranger to her, and perhaps it was better that way. Emily needed a real father, a proper father, just as Susannah needed a proper husband. They both deserved better than Theodore Wingfield Davis, of peculiar habits and perverted tastes.

Banished, as he had hoped, to the single bed in the dressing room, he worked on the play. He was determined to complete it: Emily was his masterpiece, but, in case she grew up to despise him, he would leave something else by which he could be remembered. And when at last the finished manuscript lay before him, to his humbled astonishment, it was not bad, not bad at all. When he reflected on his former obsession with the fancies of the Philadelphia School, he was amazed at how far he had come.

And he was horrified at how far he had travelled away from Philadelphia, and family and home. He did not belong here any more: that much was clear from Susannah's remote coolness, the strained disappointment of his parents, and the way Emily fixed him with a wide-eyed stare of disinterest. No, he did not belong here, but neither did he belong in the theatre. He sensed a gulf opening between him and his colleagues on the tour, and began to doubt that he had ever been one of them. The upheaval of Jay Johnson's death, and the revelations that flowed from it, provided a cast-iron excuse to rush back to the city from Chestnut Hill and mingle with the crowd at the theatre, to exclaim and gossip and marvel. Yet, seated at dinner with the usual crowd, Theo's sense of alienation grew. Partly this was due to the return of Laurie Knight who, quite understandably, became the focus of attention.

His left leg had healed so well that he could walk a few steps with the help of crutches, but the continued fragility of his right leg recommended the occasional use of a wheelchair. He had been staying in Boston with Miss P on Beacon Hill, but now felt that he was sufficiently mobile to manage the train. And, almost as important as his mobility, his facial wounds had faded to faint scars that did not detract from his good looks. It really seemed that Laurie would be able to work again one day, and Amadine was relieved beyond measure.

'When dinner is over, I'm going to push you upstairs in that chair,' she teased him, 'and undress you, and massage your wasted muscles before helping you into bed.'

'Now, there's an offer no sane man could refuse,' Hal laughed.

Laurie clutched Hal's arm melodramatically. 'Don't leave me alone with her,' he pleaded. 'I'm saving myself for marriage.'

Only Blanche, who had saved herself for the prize worth the price and been rejected, failed to smile.

'Theo, old man, I hope you won't take offence, but we'll have to ask you to relinquish your private quarters on the train,' Hal said apologetically. 'That room was intended for Laurie's use originally, and he needs it more than ever now.'

'I quite understand,' Theo assured him. 'Of course Laurie's need is greater than mine.'

'We could share,' Laurie offered generously. 'Plenty of room for two.'

'Oh no,' Theo said hastily, 'that wouldn't do at all. I always knew my occupancy of the room was only temporary. I'll doss down in the men's car – I can use Jay's . . .'

There was a short pause, as if no one knew what to say, or had anything more to say, but in fact they were only gathering their thoughts: how, why, wasn't it awful? Who would have thought it – Jay of all people, such a nice man! Again Amadine, rather wearily, answered the questions and tried to interpret Jay's motives. This was where Theo felt his opinion diverging from that of his companions. Instead of condemning Jay as a murderer and a thief, they seemed intent only on understanding how and why he had done it, plumbing the depths of his psyche, and analysing his character and personality. For Theo matters were much more cut and dried. The man had committed the most appalling crime – although Amadine persisted in maintaining that Constance's death was an accident, it didn't make Constance any less dead, did it? – and deserved to be punished. It must be his legal training that enabled Theo to assess the case coolly and impartially, and he was somewhat startled to find himself thinking that perhaps he ought to have stuck to the law: he might have been better at it than he had realised.

He felt out of step with everyone and everything, as if he were existing in a no-man's-land between his family and his friends. Instead of having a foot in both camps, he was falling between two stools, if that wasn't mixing his metaphors.

Staying silent during the discussion about Jay, Theo swung his mind back to his last remark. He would be sleeping in the men's car on the train, exposed to the sights and sounds and smells of male flesh preparing for bed. Suppose he had to share a berth with another man? Jay had been allocated a bed to himself, but circumstances could change and Theo might be asked to double up. His heart began to thud dully and persistently in the base of his throat. He no longer trusted himself to behave properly. He could not guarantee that he would be able to keep his hands to himself.

Was this to be his future – groping young men in washrooms, or wherever the opportunity arose? Theo was repelled by the idea. He did not want to be that person, any more than he wanted tales of such behaviour to filter back to Philadelphia.

He became aware that Amadine was wheeling Laurie from the table, and he nearly left at the same time. Only mental apathy kept him sitting in his chair, a reluctance to return either to Rittenhouse Square or Chestnut Hill.

'I didn't want to raise this while Amadine was here,'

Frank was saying to Gwen, 'but why did Pierce Radcliffe indicate to me that you knew his father's likes and dislikes better than he did?'

'I knew Sam Radcliffe when I was with McVicker,' Gwen responded cautiously. 'Pierce and I met in Chicago to clear up a few outstanding matters regarding Sam's death.'

'Not another mystery!' Blanche exclaimed. 'I can't bear it!'

'No, I'm happy to say that this turned out to be an accident,' and Gwen told them how Samuel had been run over by a train. 'We were greatly relieved that it wasn't suicide,' she concluded.

'You were lucky to clarify the matter,' Hal remarked. 'There must be similar tragedies where the doubts are not resolved.'

'I think a lot depends on the person concerned,' Gwen asserted. 'In Sam's case, the possibility of suicide never crossed my mind. He had seemed his usual optimistic self when I saw him last, and he simply wasn't the type to take his own life.'

Theo made a superhuman effort to rouse himself. 'I must be going but, quite honestly, it isn't a huge sacrifice to wrench myself away,' he said cheerfully. 'Can we talk about something other than death tomorrow? In a moment someone will say that tragedies come in threes!'

'We could count Laurie's accident as the first,' Gwen suggested.

'What about the fire in Baltimore?' asked Blanche. 'Or Amadine's accident in Chicago?'

Theo held up his hands in mock horror. 'Stop it, or we'll still end up with unfinished business. Goodnight all.' And, with a casual wave and a smile, he went home.

'I think we cheered him up,' Gwen announced with satisfaction. 'The poor boy has been looking distinctly peaky lately.'

'It's being in Philadelphia,' Blanche declared sagely.

'Being on home territory is a most disconcerting experience while touring, don't you agree, Gwen? I am always extremely disturbed by it, and thoroughly relieved to see Baltimore disappearing from view.'

Gwen agreed. 'Theo will be himself again when we leave here at the weekend.'

Despite the late hour, Theo drove to Chestnut Hill and went straight to the nursery. A light was glowing faintly in the corner of the room, so that the little girl did not wake to find herself in the dark, enabling Theo to bend over the cot and gaze at his sleeping child. Gently he caressed the peach-bloom of her skin and the silky brown curls, and she stirred slightly, her eyelashes fluttering.

Looking at her, and thinking of the unborn child in Susannah's womb, Theo knew that no sacrifice was too great to guarantee her future and keep her safe.

Kissing her forehead – hastily, or her skin would be damp with his tears – he knew what he must do.

On Saturday Theo was positively sparkling with good humour. He chaffed his brother, was gallant to his mother, respectful to his father and tender towards Susannah. For a few hours, at Chestnut Hill it was quite like old times.

'Not long now until I'm home for good,' he exclaimed at dinner. 'If you'll have me back!' and he cast a teasing smile at Susannah as he reached for her hand.

'Is theatrical life not all it's cracked up to be?' Robert laughed.

'It has been a fascinating experience, even with all the offstage drama, but I wouldn't want to live like that all the time,' Theo answered sincerely. 'I really believe that I have purged my system of that strange restlessness, and I'm ready to settle down to being a staid, respectable lawyer for the rest of my life.'

'No more playwriting?'

'I have written something that has possibilities – I want to show it to Hal and Amadine next week. So, with Susannah's permission, I might do a little more writing, but only as a hobby.'

Susannah smiled, a glow of hope filling the emptiness behind her eyes and, without the sadness, she looked young and pretty again. That night he went to her bed and, although there was no sexual contact between them, they curled up close together and achieved a real feeling of peace. Such peace that, almost, for a little while Theo wished he could change his mind . . .

He left for the station before anyone else was up, knowing that Frank wanted to make an early start and might be awaiting his arrival. In the April dawn he saw the city with the relaxed, detached eye of a stranger, and appreciated afresh its dignity and charm, imprinting its gracious buildings and quiet streets on his mind for the last time. As soon as he was aboard the train, his good humour resurfaced buoyantly.

'I am a new man,' he informed Frank. 'I have finished *Barbara Frietchie*, and feel as if a huge weight has been lifted from my shoulders.'

'When can we see it?'

'In a day or two. What I would really like is for Amadine to read it first, and then Hal, and then for everyone to sit round the table in the Palace Car and read it aloud. Do you think you could arrange that?'

'With pleasure,' promised Frank, happy that the rift between him and Theo was healed. 'Although I fail to see why you can't arrange it yourself!'

They were setting out on one of the longest journeys of the tour, travelling to Jamestown in New York State, and then spending a few days at Buffalo and Niagara Falls. There would be no performance for two consecutive nights and, while the memories of Jay and Constance lingered on, an irrepressible holiday spirit pervaded the company. After

Niagara, it was downhill all the way to New York City, and for many of the participants the end of the tour could not come soon enough. However, today was also Hal's birthday, and a few treats had been organised. In a festive atmosphere, no one in the Palace Car noticed that Theo placed his bag in a corner, behind an armchair, instead of claiming his berth in the men's car. On top of the bag he balanced a neatly wrapped parcel addressed to Amadine. All day he maintained that cheerful, optimistic mood and, if at times his manner seemed a little forced, it only coincided with the feelings of his companions. Amadine especially was struggling to put a brave face on things; not only was she grieving for her friend, but Pierce had not attempted to speak to her privately in Philadelphia, nor had he said goodbye. There was a sporting chance, she supposed bleakly, that he might surface in Boston or New York, if only out of courtesy, but she could not expect him to waste any more of his valuable time on the affairs of the Smith-Sinclair company. It was as though there was a huge hole where her heart should have been, but she smiled, teased Hal about a crop of grey hairs that she swore had not been there the day before, and sat down at the piano to play and sing.

In the evening, they pulled into a small, wayside station and were shunted into a siding to refuel and partake of Hal's birthday feast, food and drink being provided for the entire company. The celebration could not have come at a better time, Hal thought with relief; it would help everyone to overcome recent events, and give a feeling of a fresh start as spring began to blossom in eastern America.

To his considerable surprise, Theo ate well. He had been dreading this part of his plan because he was sure he would be unable to swallow a thing, but the food and the company were excellent, his talented companions vying with each other in their efforts to entertain. The end of the meal came all too soon. Slowly Theo stood up and walked to the door. In the vestibule he paused and glanced back at the table, at the handsome, animated faces, and at the haunting beauty of Amadine in particular. Then he left the train, and walked slowly along the track.

Bobbing pinpricks of light, like fireflies in the darkness, denoted the presence of other men from the company, strolling and smoking in the fresh night air. Theo lit a cigar. After the rigours of the Midwestern winter, the evening was chilly but not uncomfortably cold and although he shivered slightly, he did not want to go back for his overcoat. Purposefully, although he tried to make it look like an aimless stroll, he made his way towards the small station building. Behind him, as the others milled around close to the train, he could hear male voices and the occasional deep chuckle.

In case anyone was watching, he produced his notebook and pretended to make a few entries, in the hope of appearing to be lost in thought and deep in plans for the future. But Theo had only one plan for the future, and that involved the time of the next train along this stretch of line. He really did not want to use the company train. Not only was he afraid that Frank would do a head count in order to make sure that no one was left behind, but he did not want to leave his friends with that dreadful memory and equally awful guilt. He was determined, and fastidious, about that. Yet he dared not ask the time of the next train. Whatever else happened, this must look like an accident. Everything he had done and said in recent days had been geared to make it look like an accident. Gwen had put him on the right path: '. . . the possibility of suicide never crossed my mind. He had seemed his usual optimistic self when I saw him last . . .' Everyone would be able to say that. His children would grow up with the legacy of a tragic loss, but not with the burden of disgrace and shame.

The cigar was pungent and pleasant, and down the track the actors still circulated in weaving patterns of light. Theo felt a rush of affection for them, an impulse to hold out his hand, but then remembered that he did not belong with them, or with anyone else. Lifting his eyes from his notebook, he observed the station master stroll out of his office and stand, hands clasped behind his back, looking down the track.

Theo's heart quickened.

The station master looked at his watch. Obviously he was expecting something.

Then it came, floating on the still night air, a faint rumble, a throb, a movement bursting out of the blackness. Theo turned, ears attuned to the sound and, jettisoning his cigar but keeping notebook and pencil in his hands, he walked to the middle of the track and began his journey into the heart of that force of sound and movement and power.

In the Palace Car, in the siding, the lights shone, the wine flowed and the songs continued to be sung. Amadine was dizzily aware of drinking too much, admitting defiantly that she was deliberately seeking forgetfulness. To put back the clock, how wonderful that would be! But to where – to one of those nights in this car when Hal was trying to seduce her? If she had surrendered, so many things might have been different: Constance might still be alive, and Jay, and she would never have gone to bed with Pierce Radcliffe.

With a feeling close to tenderness, Amadine crouched beside Hal's chair. 'I wish,' she said, looking up into his face, 'I wish . . .'

'What?' Hal said, smoothing her hair from her face.

'That I could have cared more, and made everything all right for everyone.'

Hal was slightly drunk, too, as he bent his head and kissed her brow.

Out of the corner of her eye, Amadine saw the calculating

look on Blanche's face as she watched them. There was
beginning to be something rather irritating about Blanche,
and for a moment Amadine was tempted to spike her guns,
or at least to tease her. Her hand slid up to caress Hal's
cheek. For a split second she reflected on the advantages of
doing this for real, but she smiled at Hal and, as one, they
said: 'Too late now', and laughed.

Laurie was beginning to shift uncomfortably in his seat,
and Frank went to move an armchair from the corner of the
room into a more prominent position by the table. As he
was helping Laurie into the chair, Amadine noticed the bag
and parcel. She peered at them curiously and, seeing her
name on the packet, perched on the piano stool to open it.
The manuscript of *Barbara Frietchie* lay on her knee and,
with it, a letter.

> Darling Amadine,
>   I wrote this for you in the (probably vain) hope
> that you might play Barbara one day. If you do, I'll be
> watching. This is a free gift, and you can do what you
> like with it, but I'd be very pleased if the first matinée
> could be for the benefit of Constance's children.
>   My love always,
>   Theo.

Amadine flipped through the manuscript with eager fingers, but then read the letter again. 'Frank,' she said
urgently, beckoning him over. 'Where is Theo?'

'I haven't seen him for a while. Why?'

She gave him the letter, and watched his expression as he
read it.

'I don't like it,' he said in a troubled voice. 'It sounds as if
he doesn't expect to know whether you play Barbara or
not.'

'It sounds,' said Amadine, 'like goodbye. So where is he?'

'He has been so cheerful and happy . . .' And then Frank

remembered what Theo himself had remembered – what Gwen had said about Samuel Radcliffe, and the manner of the man's death. 'Oh God,' and Frank plunged for the door.

Pausing only to toss the manuscript and letter on her bed, Amadine followed. While Frank checked the men's car, she jumped down to the track and looked around. Several members of the company were near the train and glanced at her curiously, but no one spoke. Frank appeared at her shoulder, indicating that Theo was not on the train, and they hurried towards the station building. Then they heard the sound of the approaching train, and at the same moment they saw Theo. Head bent over his book, apparently absorbed in thought, he was wandering along the track in the path of the express that was thundering down on him. Frank and Amadine froze, unable to move or speak. Amadine tried to shout a warning, but only a strangled gurgle escaped her throat.

'*No!*' Frank bellowed and, managing to force his paralysed limbs into action, he ran into the centre of the track, launching himself at Theo only seconds before the train bore down on them.

As it swept past, Amadine could only stand and stare at the spot where she had last seen them, and wait, wondering what she would see when the blur of coaches had cleared. What she saw was two prostrate figures on the far side of the line, lying motionless, limbs and torsos tangled together. Fearfully, dreading what she might find, Amadine crossed the railway line towards them.

Slowly the tangled heap moved and began to unravel, sorting itself into two heads, two sets of arms and legs, and finally into two men struggling to their feet. They were white and shaking but, as far as Amadine could make out in the darkness, intact.

'You shouldn't have stopped me,' Theo was sobbing. 'It was better that way!'

'Keep quiet,' Frank said roughly, holding him upright, 'and come back inside.'

Amadine took Theo's other arm, and together she and Frank helped him back to the train and into the Palace Car. 'Don't mind us,' she said to the others. 'Theo's had a bit too much to drink. Haven't we all!' and she steered him into her room and shut the door. While Frank watched, she sat down beside Theo on the bed and put her arms around him.

Over the top of his head, she looked at Frank. 'That's two lives you have saved,' she remarked in a matter-of-fact tone. 'If I stood the slightest chance of success, I would propose marriage but, in the circumstances, I hope that I can be the hero's friend.'

'Perhaps we should make a marriage of convenience,' Frank suggested, in a shaky voice, watching the back of Theo's head buried against Amadine's shoulder, 'to protect you against unwelcome advances and me against . . . well, you know what against!'

'What do you need protecting against, Frank,' Theo demanded, 'other than my fist right between your eyes? Damn you, you've ruined everything! Now I'm going to have to go through all this again, and next time it might not look like an accident!'

Frank and Amadine exchanged a glance, as both reached the same conclusion regarding the reason for Theo's suicide attempt.

'I am a homosexual, Theo,' Frank said bluntly, 'and therefore I live a lie. You might be surprised how many of us there are, and just how much of it there is about.'

'You?' Theo looked at Frank in astonishment, but then he groaned. 'You know about me, don't you!'

'We made an educated guess,' Amadine consoled him.

'You realised when you saw me with him in the washroom.' Theo's eyes never left Frank's face.

'It takes one to know one,' Frank replied gently, 'and I

feel sure that no one else has realised, just as no one else knows what you tried to do tonight. This is between the three of us, Theo, and it can stay that way, so tell us exactly why you did it.'

There was nothing to lose, so he told them everything.

'One kiss,' Amadine gasped, 'and for that you want to abandon your wife and children!'

'They would be better off without me.'

'They most certainly would not!'

'You are worried about living the lie,' Frank said, with infinite understanding, 'but it isn't so bad. One gets used to it. And although a gap is left in one's life, it's better than having no life at all.'

'But think of Mrs Wilde and her children – I don't want to do that to my family.' Theo's agony was made worse by the announcement, only a few days before, of Mrs Wilde's sudden death at the age of only forty.

'That was Oscar's fault. Until attitudes and opinions change, he should have been more circumspect. All you have to do, Theo, is make sure that you never put yourself in a position where temptation can get the better of you. Never let the heart rule the head.'

'If it was merely a matter of the *heart*, I wouldn't be so worried,' Theo replied.

And for a brief, crazy moment, Amadine had a wild desire to laugh.

But Theo was swaying as the wine, and the shock and strain, took its toll and, as he toppled against her, she stretched his unconscious form on the bed.

'Fetch his bag,' she told Frank, 'and tell the others that he has passed out and is going to sleep here. I'll be fine on the sofa in the parlour.'

'You can have my bed.'

'In your room, right next to Hal? I don't think so. Blanche would have a heart attack, and we'll have another tragedy on our hands.'

Frank grinned, but then their smiles faded and suddenly they were in each other's arms, holding each other tight and trembling.

At last the train was under way again, and the company was asleep. Only Amadine was awake, lying on the sofa and wrapped in a quilt, reading *Barbara Frietchie*. She read it from beginning to end and when she did doze, towards dawn, a slight smile was playing around her lips.

She awoke to find Frank watching her, the manuscript in a neat pile on the table in front of him.

'Theo?' she asked.

'Still sleeping peacefully.'

'Have you read the play?'

'Not all of it, but enough to know that it's good.'

'Good!' exclaimed Amadine. 'It's brilliant, and I want to do it. However, first we must show it to Hal, and then we'll all gather here for a reading.'

'There is only one copy.'

'We'll *manage*. We always do.' She sat up, and took the coffee he handed to her. 'We have to hope that Hal likes the play as much as I do, because Theo is likely to believe I'm only trying to be nice to him. If we can convince Theo that Hal knows nothing about last night and genuinely admires his work, that would really give Theo a reason for living.'

'I'll leave that in your capable hands. I think my role is to persuade Theo that his feelings are by no means unusual, and nothing to be ashamed of.'

'But he is a married man. What would you suggest that he does about that?'

Frank drank some coffee, and then heaved a sigh. 'It is 1898, and I believe that the manners and mores of the age require Theo to go back to Philadelphia and his family, and live the lie. I also believe that course of action requires even more courage than trying to commit suicide.'

'I agree, and I also agree that he does have a duty to put his children before his own happiness. At the very least, he ought to try. Frank, do tell him that we will help him in any way we can.'

'We will be leaving America in a few weeks from now,' Frank said grimly.

Amadine stared at him. 'We cannot think that far ahead,' she said at last. 'Not on this tour. On this tour anything can happen!'

By lunchtime that day Theo, pale and uncertain of himself, was being swept along on a tide of enthusiasm, which at one time would have surpassed his wildest dreams and expectations.

'Is it really any good?' he kept asking. 'Do you truly like it? Honestly?'

'I'm only furious that you gave it to Amadine and not to me,' Hal assured him.

'I started out hoping that you would do it together.'

'We could attempt a very rough-and-ready matinée in Boston, to establish copyright. How about asking Laurie to read the part of Barbara's wounded brother – he does a very convincing limp!'

So instead of being taken back to Philadelphia in a wooden box as he had intended, Theo spent the day in the Palace Car listening to clusters of actors, craning their necks to see the script in Amadine's hand, sight-reading his play.

The experience was strange and exciting, but Theo was not altogether sure that it was enough to make him want to carry on. It took days of patient counselling by Frank to persuade him that he could make good those brave promises to his family, and that he could go back to Philadelphia and try again. He tried to believe that his emotions might have been heightened by the hothouse atmosphere of the train, and the tour in general, and that things might seem different when he was back in his old, familiar surroundings. And he needed no persuading to give the men's car, and the washroom in particular, a very wide berth. On the pretext of working on *Barbara Frietchie* at all hours, Frank and Theo took it in turns to occupy Frank's bed or the sofa in the parlour.

Between them, Frank and Amadine tried to ensure that he was never out of their sight.

It was just a pity that, in the absence of Pierce Radcliffe and with the changing kaleidoscope of relationships in the company, no one thought to keep an eye on Amadine.

Chapter Thirty-Three

From Jamestown their route took them along the shores of Lake Erie to Buffalo's great grain elevators and iron-works, where they were to give six performances. To Amadine, the town was the gateway to Niagara but, to her immense frustration, she was forced to wait for an opportunity to view this great natural wonder. The company arrived in Buffalo on Wednesday and had to settle into the theatre, while Thursday brought a matinée of *Trelawny*, and so Hal promised a full-day's expedition to the Falls on Friday.

On Thursday night Amadine lay in bed re-reading some descriptions of Niagara, and became acutely aware of another dimension to the place. Here were not only enthusiastic accounts of torrents of bright-green water, of foam and spray, of rainbows and the thunder of the cascades, but clear indications of a spiritual experience. The travellers wrote movingly of their feelings of peace and wonder, and of communing with their inner self. Amadine read, and read again, Anthony Trollope's account of his visit:

> You will hear nothing else, and think of nothing else. At length you will be at one with the tumbling river before you. You will find yourself among the waters as though you belonged to them. The cool green

liquid will run through your veins, and the voice of
the cataract will be the expression of your own heart.
You will fall as the bright waters fall, rushing down
into your new world with no hesitation and no
dismay; and you will rise again as the spray rises,
bright, beautiful and pure. Then you will flow away in
your course to the uncompassed, distant and eternal
ocean.

Amadine felt a great need to rise again 'bright, beautiful and
pure', and longed for the sensation of waterfalls rinsing
away her sin and showing her the way forward. Also, she
knew that this was not an experience she wanted to share.
She wanted to go to the Falls alone, to sit quietly and think,
and try to rediscover that still, calm centre on which she
had relied during the worst moments of her life.

The next morning she rose early and, after sending a
short message of explanation to Frank, set out for the Falls
alone.

Keep an eye on Theo was the general gist of Amadine's
note, and Frank grimaced as he read it. It would be only too
easy to stage an 'accident' at the Falls. He recalled that
poor old Bill Terriss had nearly met an untimely end there,
when he slipped and almost fell, during a tour with Irving
some years ago. No doubt about it: if Amadine had gone off
on a jaunt of her own, he would need to keep not only an
eye but a very firm grip on Theo.

Then he realised what Amadine had done, going off
alone like that, and that if she slipped there would be no
one to catch *her*. And then he remembered what Pierce
Radcliffe had said about unfinished business, and keeping
Amadine safe. Frank stood, twisting Amadine's letter in his
fingers, as he wondered what he ought to do. He could not
go after her himself, because that would leave Theo at risk.
Hal was not dressed yet. Laurie was not fit. Ida . . . now,

that was a possibility. If Amadine was up and dressed, the likelihood was that Ida would be, too.

He found Ida talking to George White and, ignoring the other man, challenged the girl about Amadine's movements. 'You will have to go after her, and find her,' Frank said, after explaining the situation, 'and stay with her until the rest of us arrive.'

'But I don't know where . . .' Ida began.

'I can go,' George interrupted, 'if you can spare me from the theatre this morning. I'll take the next train.'

'Good man.' Frank dug in his pocket, and handed over some loose change for the train fare. 'Find Amadine and pin her down in one place – a safe place – until the Chief and the rest of us join you. On no account let her go too near the edge, and keep your eyes open for suspicious characters.'

'Will do,' and George virtually touched his forelock. 'You can rely on me.'

Frank watched him go, and breathed a sigh of relief. One problem solved . . .

Ida, too, watched George hurry away, but her feelings were very different from Frank's. Ida felt guilty and afraid. She knew that she ought to tell someone that she suspected the intruder to Miss Amadine's room that night had been George. It had to be George. It was the only answer that made sense. But she was frightened to tell anyone, and most of all she was frightened of mentioning it to George. There was a suppressed violence in him which Ida, brought up in a humble home in London's East End, had begun to recognise and knew better than to arouse. A wise woman avoided giving aggravation to a man like that.

But what was his interest in Miss Amadine? Surely to goodness he could not imagine that she would look twice at him? So why, if it was him . . .?

*

Amadine was standing on the parapet at Prospect Point, gazing at the American Fall, standing so close that she could almost touch the rushing water. On this sunny April morning, the bright green of the water and the colours of the rainbows were intense, and Amadine was stunned by the wonder of the spectacle. She did not know what impressed her most: the awe-inspiring torrents of the Falls themselves or the powerful surge of the rapids before they hurled themselves over the edge.

Slowly, glad to be here before the crowds and without the need to make polite conversation, she made her way to the bridge that spanned the river to Goat Island. The bridge seemed insubstantial and Amadine negotiated it cautiously, but the view from it was so breathtaking that she paused. Then, leaning over the flimsy railing, her gaze was drawn down to the raging river beneath her. It was true what people said: one experienced an almost irresistible impulse to throw oneself in, and follow the great flow and become a part of it.

Transfixed, Amadine did not know how long she stood there, but then her reverie was broken by the sensation of a shadow falling across her, and she realised that someone was standing next to her. Disturbed by this intrusion, she resumed her journey to the island, unaware that she was being followed . . .

Frank was going into breakfast when he stopped, and did a double-take. For a moment he thought he was hallucinating but, no, it *was* Pierce Radcliffe.

'Good Lord,' he said. 'Can't you keep away?'

Pierce had been in New York, where he boarded the New York Central train to Chicago. The first part of the journey traversed New York State, via Albany, to Buffalo and, as that town came closer, Pierce became more and more thoughtful. He knew full well that Amadine would be in Buffalo when his train passed through and admitted

ruefully that, subconsciously, he might have timed his journey to coincide with hers. As Frank was to do, Pierce also
reflected on the spectacular opportunities offered by the
Falls for murders, suicides or accidents; but surely, he
argued, an attack on Amadine at the Falls was something of
a cliché! However, her stalker might not be the most
sophisticated of men and, besides, Pierce had the same feeling about this as he had had about the possibility of Hal
seducing Amadine on the train: opportunity was everything, and there was plenty of that at Niagara.

He reached for his bag. His own firearms were at home
in Chicago, but for some reason he had held on to Jay's
gun. He checked it, found that it was loaded and put it in
his coat pocket. At Buffalo, he left the train.

'I wanted to see Amadine,' he told Frank.

'No can do. She's made an early start for the Falls, but
don't worry,' as Frank saw the alarm on Pierce's face, 'she
isn't alone. Someone is watching out for her.'

'Thank God for that,' and a relieved Pierce accepted the
invitation to breakfast.

'Do you remember George White from the old days at
the Lyceum?' Frank asked Laurie, apparently apropos of
nothing in particular.

'Name doesn't ring a bell.'

'Fair-haired chap, very good-looking, but not unduly
gifted. Was at the Lyceum on and off for years.'

'Did he do Guildford in *Henry VIII*?' Laurie said doubtfully. 'Hal, you were there.'

'The production where you were playing Henry, and I
was Buckingham? Yes, I've a vague recollection of a pretty
blond. Mind you, he was no spring chicken by that time.'

'And his name wasn't George White,' Laurie announced
decisively.

'Really?' queried Frank. 'But you think it was the same
feller who was walking-on ten years earlier?'

'Gilbert West,' Laurie asserted. 'And I'm sure it's the

same chap. Caused a distinct flutter among the female cast – *and* a fair number of the men, who were more than somewhat miffed when he turned out to be a real ladies' man. Made more of a career out of pleasuring ageing leading ladies offstage than he did playing opposite them onstage.'

'Good God, you're right,' Frank exclaimed. 'Our George is really Gillyflower – he was called Gilly for short, and some wag added the flower because he was so pretty. I wonder why he is calling himself George.'

'And I wonder why you are making him a major topic of conversation,' Laurie commented.

'He's here, in the company. Rather reduced in the good looks department, and down on his luck as well, but he's been helping me behind the scenes most efficiently. Dyed his hair red – going grey, he said, but I've noticed he seems to be letting it go back to its original colour.'

'Fascinating,' drawled Laurie, 'but why is he such hot news over breakfast in Buffalo?'

'He was on my mind. It was him I sent in hot pursuit of Amadine.'

Pierce's fork dropped to his plate with a clatter. 'You did *what?*'

'Sent George – or Gilbert – to look for Amadine.'

'I wish to God that it had been anyone but him! There is something about him that I . . . To be honest, I had him down as my number-one suspect for Amadine's stalker until you reassured me that all the stage staff were at the theatre at the time of the incident.'

Frank leaned back in his chair, and looked at Pierce oddly. 'And I wish you had made it clear that your interest was in George,' he said quietly, 'because he only joined the company in Chicago.'

'And now he is alone with Amadine at the Falls.' Pierce pushed back his chair and stood up.

'We don't know that he means any harm,' Hal broke in

placatingly, but did not continue because Ida was sidling up to the table. 'Yes, Ida, what is it?'

'It's about George.' To Ida's surprise and concern, absolute silence greeted this announcement. 'I feel I ought to tell you that I think it was George who was in Miss Amadine's hotel room that night. I didn't mean no harm, sir, honest, but . . .'

'We know now,' Pierce said grimly, making for the door.

'I'm coming with you,' called Frank.

'So am I,' said Theo.

Frank paused. 'No, Theo, that isn't a good idea,' he said, very quietly.

Theo eyed him steadily. 'I won't do anything silly – you have my word of honour on it. But I must help Amadine, and you will need extra men. We don't know where she is, and may have to split up to search for her.'

'Very well, but if you aren't sound in wind and limb at the end of this, I'll –' Frank sought the most dire punishment he could think of '– so help me, I'll burn *Barbara Frietchie*!'

Stretching her legs in that long, effortless stride that had stood her in good stead in her native dales, Amadine walked swiftly to the little bridge that crossed the Centre Fall to Luna Island. After gazing again at the superb view of the American Fall, she returned to Goat Island and hesitated for a moment. She wanted to walk down Biddle's Stairs and pass under the Centre Fall but, on reflection, decided to delay that experience until she was joined by her companions. She would use the privilege of solitude for moments of quiet introspection, not sight-seeing.

Traversing the north-western end of the island, she passed Terrapin Rock and the great Horseshoe Fall on the Canadian side of the river, but pressed on in the hope of finding both a vantage point and an isolated sanctuary.

Then she saw the very spot – the three tiny islands known as the Three Sisters. Connected by bridges, the little rocky islets formed a promontory jutting out from Goat Island into the rapids above the Horseshoe Falls. At this time of day most visitors were congregated at the tourist attractions near the Falls and so, this area being deserted, Amadine ventured on to the first bridge and walked to the farthest point of the outermost islet.

She sat on a rock only a foot or so above the river and watched the strange patterns made by the currents, the water seeming virtually motionless directly below her and yet, only a few feet away, roaring towards the Falls with terrifying force. As she looked upstream, the waters appeared to be bearing down on her with such primeval power that she felt they must surely sweep her – insignificant creature that she was – from the rock, and indeed send both her and the rock itself spiralling over the Falls. But at the very last minute the waters parted and raced past on either side, leaving Amadine with a dizzying sense of awe at the power and beauty of God's creation, and a strange sense of peace and tranquillity in the fascination of the water. Colours, light, ripples, patterns . . . always different and yet always the same; Amadine could have watched it for ever.

But then, as one sometimes does, she became aware that she was not alone. She did not look round at first, but when the prickle of unease persisted, she turned and saw him. He raised his hat and gave an ironic, exaggerated bow.

And then Amadine saw who he was, and nearly fainted.

On the opposite side of the island, assured by observant officials at Prospect Point that Amadine had crossed the bridge, Pierce decided that the group must separate. He despatched Frank and Theo to the Centre Fall, instructing Theo to go to Luna Island and then under the Fall, while Frank carried on to the Horseshoe Fall. In the meantime he would set off to the other end of the island, round the point towards the Three Sisters. But they must hurry because Amadine, and George, had a good start on them.

There was no one about, but this only increased Pierce's concern. If Amadine called for help, not a soul would hear her. As he ran, he kept hoping that Frank or Theo had found her and that this frantic anxiety was needless. They would all be laughing about this tonight. Bloody woman, he thought; if I find her, I'll kill her myself! At last the path wound down towards the Three Sisters. Pierce paused and, narrowing his eyes, focused on the outermost island. Yes, there were two figures, a man and a woman. He could not be sure of their identities at this distance but, frankly, it was unlikely to be a coincidence and his gut feelings pointed him straight down the promontory.

Moving lightly and quietly, Pierce set off across the bridge.

Amadine had listened to his initial tirade with more scorn than fear. Recovering quickly from the shock, she tried to control him with her superior intellect and use of language, but in the end there was no reasoning with him.

'You must be mad,' she said. 'You and me – *together*! In your dreams!'

'But I love you,' he protested. 'I have always loved you. That must mean something.'

'Not to me.'

Then he tried a different tack.

'So it's my money or my life,' Amadine said cynically. 'Either I spend my life with you, or I pay you to stay away. What planet are you on, Gilly?'

That was when he produced the gun, and for the second time in as many weeks Amadine looked death in the face. The difference was that this time she really was frightened. For a split second she dared to glance back towards the main island, and for a moment, just the minutest moment, she thought she saw a movement. Keep him talking, she thought. Even if I was mistaken and there isn't anyone there, someone might come along.

'Now you are being ridiculous,' she said scathingly.

'You'd better be careful what you say – from where I'm standing, it is the person without the gun who looks ridiculous.'

'What does pointing a gun at my head achieve? Come to that, what did your violent streak ever achieve?'

'For once in your life, stop talking and listen.' His voice was shaking with anger, and the hands that levelled the gun at her head were trembling. 'Even you must be able to see that if I can't have you, no other man will!'

He meant it. She was in no doubt of that. She stood up and faced him.

'You won't get away with it. They can do tests, like they did with Constance. They will know that your gun fired the fatal shot.'

'But they won't find a gun. I don't see anyone diving into that,' and he pointed at the raging river, 'to retrieve it, do you? Come to that, they are very unlikely to retrieve *you*.'

'Someone must know that you are here.'

'Frank sent me, with strict instructions to look out for suspicious characters. My little exploits in Boston and Philadelphia must have come to his notice, and they'll come in very handy again. Yes, my dear Amadine, the nasty man did come to get you, and unfortunately I was just too late. I couldn't find you anywhere.'

'Perhaps we can work something out, after all,' she pleaded. 'Perhaps . . .'

Pierce was close enough to hear her voice, but the roar of the waters drowned her actual words. George, or Gilbert as he must learn to call him, was standing sideways on, but his gaze was riveted on Amadine and he had not noticed Pierce's approach.

Pulling the gun from his pocket, Pierce crept a little closer and then took aim. He was not prepared to risk shouting a warning. The man's finger was on the trigger, and sheer reflex action could send Amadine spiralling into eternity.

Pierce was a good shot, if somewhat out of practice. He aimed for Gilbert's right hand, and the gun . . .

'Perhaps nothing, Amadine,' Gilbert said. 'You ruined my life, and now I'm going to end yours.'

At the sound of the shot, Amadine flinched and cowered to the ground. Then, to her astonishment, she found that she was not hurt. Instead, Gilbert had toppled to the ground. He twitched a few times and then, almost in slow motion, slithered into the water and was swept away.

Like Jay, Amadine thought. Like Jay.

Dazedly she watched Pierce approach. 'Good shot,' she whispered.

'No, it was a bloody bad shot. I was aiming for his hand, not his heart. Not my gun, you see. It was Jay's.'

Yes, Amadine thought. It would be.

'He was the gunman, and the stalker,' Pierce said, standing several feet away from her.

'He was more than that,' Amadine said, in a strange, flat voice. 'He was my husband.'

Chapter Thirty-Four

'You must understand that I was very young when I met him,' Amadine told Pierce later, 'not only in years but in experience. My family moved in a small social circle, and I led a very narrow and restricted life. My brothers went away to study, but I was stuck at home, watching the river race down to the sea and wanting, more than anything in the world, to go with it. However, the situation improved somewhat after my eighteenth birthday. My uncle was acquainted with the local aristocracy – he undertook legal work for the estate – and I began to receive invitations to receptions at the Castle. I was convinced that this was my big chance and that I would meet a man from London who would take me away.'

'With your looks, I am only surprised that apparently it did not turn out that way,' Pierce remarked.

'They found me pretty, and I was a popular turn at Castle parties. Dressed in my best – oh my God, home-made satin, I look back and *cringe* – I met any number of admirers. And then, after about a year, there was one admirer in particular. Here he is, I thought, my escape route, my passport out of this place. But in the end he only wanted what all the others wanted and, when he didn't get it, he went away. The difference was that, that time, I felt even more frustrated and imprisoned than before, even though I knew I deserved nothing better – I didn't love him, I was only using him in much the same way as he wanted to use me.'

'Were there no men in your own social circle whom you could have cared for?'

'None. Isn't that terrible? Just how fussy can one girl be! But there were not many to choose from, and I found all of them dull and boring.'

'I bet they didn't find you dull and boring.'

'No. In retrospect, I think I may have been rather unkind.'

'Young women often are.'

'You didn't discover that from personal experience! Anyway, where was I? Oh yes, local men. My family had chosen one for me: a friend of my father's, who led a reclusive, and doubtless blameless, life in a large mansion nearby. I couldn't believe that my father would even consider the idea. I mean, Mr Knightley this man was not – do you know *Emma*? But then I realised that everyone was in deadly earnest, and that Pressure was being Brought to Bear.'

'You seem like the last person to be forced into something against your will.'

'But young women are in a very difficult position. Where could I go? What could I do? I would have had to go on living in my father's house, in an unpleasant atmosphere of guilt, with a reproachful father who genuinely thought he was doing his best for me, and a furious mother who accused me of being ungrateful, vain and stupid.'

'And at this vulnerable moment, when one escape route had clanged shut, and another prison door was opening, you met Gilbert West?'

'My younger brother, Richard, was at home, and he took me and my cousins to the theatre in Leeds for a birthday treat. Gilbert was playing one of the leads. I thought that he was the most beautiful thing I had ever seen.' Amadine paused. 'He was extremely good-looking and well dressed in those days,' she said, rather apologetically, 'and I didn't know that he was playing those leading roles in a third-rate touring company, and had risen to those dizzy heights only as a reward for services rendered to the middle-aged leading lady. I thought he was a famous actor from London's West End, an impression he did not exactly go out of his way to correct. It so happened that my brother had a slight acquaintance with him – Richard was studying for the church, but never allowed that to come between him and a rather louche existence in London – and he invited Gilbert to join us for a late supper after the show. I was even more smitten. Gilbert could put on a very convincing display of being the perfect gentleman, and to me he was the epitome of sophistication – if anything, more lifelike than the real thing I had met at the Castle. And he was from *London*. That clinched it. I was determined that this was one opportunity that would not pass me by.'

Amadine paused, and smiled sadly. 'So naïve, and so stupid! He came to the dale when the tour ended and went on walking trips with my brother, while we met in secret. Then I had an awful quarrel with my father about the marriage he wanted me to make, and stormed out of the house. When I met Gilbert later in the day, he tried to make love to me – as usual; and I said no – as usual – but this time I went on to say, "Only after we are married." He agreed that we would marry, and we ran away to London the next day. My father died without forgiving me, and to this day none of my family has acknowledged that I still exist.'

'Not even the brother who introduced you to Gilbert?'

'Oh, Richard is a typical example of male double standards – Gilly could be his friend, but was unsuitable to keep company with me. Mind you,' and Amadine grimaced, 'he was right. It didn't take me long to realise what a ghastly mistake I had made. I soon discovered that there was London, and there was *London*. Gilbert shut me away in dingy lodgings in Islington. We were always short of money and what little we did have, he drank. My next

lesson, learned the hard way, was that he had a nasty temper
and became abusive when chided. Why he married me, I
did not know.'

'If you were half as beautiful then as you are now, the
reason is not hard to find,' Pierce said gently.

She smiled wanly. 'Half of him wanted to parade me in
front of his friends – after all those ageing mistresses, look
what he had won! The other half was jealous and scared of
losing me. He never introduced me to any of his theatrical
connections, or allowed me anywhere near the theatre
where he was working. Even so, it didn't take me long to
twig that he wasn't the big star I had believed him to be. I
reached rock bottom when I received a note – just two
lines – from my brother, telling me that my father had died
of a broken heart.' Amadine struggled to compose herself.
'By the time I recovered from that, it was January 1892 and
I had been in London for nearly eighteen months. I knew
that an influenza epidemic was decimating the casts in
London theatres and, being desperate for money, I screwed
up my courage and presented myself for an audition. I got
the job.'

'Now, there's a surprise! And Gilbert's cup of enthusiasm
for your enterprise did not exactly run over?'

'He hit me.'

'He knew that he was going to lose you.'

'That was the moment he did lose me – until then, I had
felt a measure of sympathy for his failings, and his failures.
I stayed for a few more months because I had nowhere else
to go, months when Gilly came home drunk, and hit me,
and . . . Let's not talk about that. Then, in the autumn, I
was given a job at the Criterion, by dear Charles
Wyndham, and it paid enough for me to afford a room of
my own – as long as I didn't eat! I moved out, and I didn't
give Gilly my new address. He found me, of course, and hit
me again. But he never came to the theatre. Funny that. At
first he never acknowledged me in public because he was

afraid of losing me. Then he never acknowledged me
because he had lost me.

'Apparently my success grew in exact ratio to his failure,
and I now know that he blamed me. According to him,
everything in the garden was lovely until he met me, and
the West End was at his feet. I pulled out the rug from
under those feet, and ruined his life. Wonderful, isn't it, the
fantasies that the mind will conjure up! For years I was on
tenterhooks in case he turned up but, here in America, I
thought I was safe. I never gave him a thought. It was just
bad luck that he had been touring in Australia, and was
working in California when our first notices appeared.'

'What did he actually want?' Pierce asked.

'From what I could gather, his motivation changed as
time went on. At first it was "Amadine Sinclair is a star, and
she is my wife, and I want the whole world to know." Then
he decided that he could hitch his wagon to my star and tag
along – manager, power behind the throne, that kind of
thing. He even went through a phase where he deluded
himself that we could have a full and proper marriage again.
Finally, if none of those ideas worked, he would blackmail
me into paying him enough to keep quiet about my youthful indiscretions.'

'Why didn't you divorce him?'

'Oh, Pierce, do you know so little about me! You are
forgetting that I am the rector's daughter. To my father, a
divorcee was little more than a scarlet woman. I don't know
what the situation is in America, but where I come from,
divorce is not acceptable – morally or socially. Now, I may
not care about the social graces quite as much as my publi-
cists would like, but I was brought up to care for my moral
and spiritual welfare, and to believe in the gospel and the
teaching of the Christian faith. I defied my father over my
marriage, but I could never defy the Christian principles
and virtues that he instilled in me from the day I was born.
"For better for worse, for richer for poorer, in sickness and

in health, to love and to cherish, till death us do part." Or, I've made my bed so I must lie in it; or, marry in haste and repent at leisure. Gospel, proverb or cliché, the end result is the same. I could not divorce Gilbert.'

'And that is why you would not marry me.' When he had discovered that she was not a virgin, Pierce thought, the possibility that she might have been married never occurred to him. It ought to have done.

As if she was reading his thoughts, Amadine leaned forward and covered his hand with hers. It was a rare gesture. They never seemed to touch any more. 'I was a virgin when I married Gilly, and since then there has been no other man but you.'

Pierce retained her hand. That assurance brought a rush of pleasure, but he still did not know what the future held. Her husband's death removed an obstacle but, if he knew his Amadine, she would take a while to get over it, and by then she would have returned to London.

Via Rochester, Syracuse, Utica and Albany, the company returned to Boston for two weeks at the beginning of May. Theo had travelled on ahead, in order to arrange an informal and inexpensive matinée of *Barbara Frietchie* for copyright purposes. Keeping costs to a minimum was all-important, so he set about borrowing scenery and costumes – Yankee and Confederate uniforms being top priority – and away from the hothouse atmosphere of the train, he began to feel more his old self. He could see that matters had got out of proportion as well as out of control, and that it need not be like that. He was still frightened of the future, but glad that he had one.

Amadine had indicated that if the performance went well, she would do *Barbara* in London. As her only worry so far was the authenticity of her American accent, Theo was optimistic enough to think ahead and to imagine taking Susannah to England to see the play. Now, that would be something! And he was encouraged by the fact that Susannah was the only person, apart perhaps from his brother Robert, with whom he could envisage travelling.

At the end of that magical, unreal afternoon in Boston, Amadine and Hal led him on to the stage, to applause and shouts of 'Author!', and he conceded that Amadine was right when she whispered, 'There, aren't you glad you didn't miss it!' However, he knew, too, that picking himself up while his friends were around him was one thing. Returning to Philadelphia without any support was another. One of the most important things would be to keep busy.

Theo began casting around for an idea for a new play.

Despite the tragedies, Gwen was sorry that the tour was nearly over. She was uncertain what the future held. Would Hal's profits finance a London season and, if so, would he invite her to join him? Might Amadine's plans include her? Was the health of her mother such that Gwen could put the width of the Atlantic between her and her responsibilities yet again?

The hotel being situated near the theatre in Boston, she decided to go back there for tea after the matinée before returning for the evening performance. A man was standing outside the stage door, staring at her. Shades of Jefferson City, she thought ruefully, but on this occasion the man approached and politely raised his hat.

'Miss Hughes,' he said. 'Gwen. It's me, Nicholas Lang.'

He was nothing like the tall, lean patrician she had envisaged. Nicholas Lang was no more than medium height, with rosy pink cheeks, and although the hair was grey, the top of his head was bald.

'There,' he said, looking worried. 'I'm not what you expected. I'm a disappointment, aren't I? I'm not tall. People always expect me to be tall.'

'You aren't small either,' she said politely.

He smiled, and she noticed that his eyes twinkled behind the spectacles. 'You didn't read my letter, did you?'

Gwen had stuffed the letter into her bag in Chicago, where it had remained ever since; more a case of cowardice than forgetfulness.

'I had a bad fall in the snow,' Nicholas said, indicating his right leg, 'and was confined to bed for several weeks. I arranged for a message to be sent to St Louis . . .'

'It didn't arrive.'

'My manservant failed to send it. I do apologise. I was immensely distressed when I found he had forgotten, and I imagined you waiting – if you did wait – if you went to the tearoom . . .'

'I went. And I waited.'

'I am so sorry.' Evidently his leg was troubling him because he leaned heavily on his walking stick, and gave a little grimace of discomfort.

'I'm going for a cup of tea now,' Gwen said kindly, 'if you would care to join me.'

Nicholas brightened and limped along eagerly beside her, sitting down in the tearoom with a sigh of relief. 'I'm getting old,' he said sadly, 'and it is beginning to show.'

'Growing old is not for the faint-hearted,' Gwen agreed. 'The only good thing that can be said for it is that it is preferable to the alternative. But only just.'

They laughed, and settled down comfortably.

'I never dared to hope that you would forgive me,' he said.

'But you dared to approach me outside the stage door.'

'Only after failing to find the courage on several other occasions.' As Gwen stared at him uncomprehendingly, he went on, 'I've been following you for a while. Ever since I got back on my feet, in fact, but I was afraid of being snubbed. I wanted to ask you to dinner. I don't suppose that this evening . . .?'

'I think I would like that very much.'

And it was only afterwards that Gwen realised that not once had she wondered if she was a disappointment to him.

She was not looking for a husband, she thought, but, oh, how she would like a friend! Someone of her own age with whom she could relax and be comfortable, and share outings and experiences and jokes. It was much too early to say for sure, but there did seem to be a chance that she might find this with Nicholas Lang. If only there was as much chance of finding some financial security for her old age.

But, unknown to Gwen, other forces were at work. Pierce Radcliffe took the Panhard out of storage, and drove to the top of Beacon Hill. While Amadine sat with Gwen's mother, Pierce took an overwhelmed Miss P for a drive round the perimeter of the Common and a discreet conversation.

'There's your answer,' Amadine had announced, having been apprised of Gwen's history with Pierce's father. 'That is how you pass on some of your father's money to Gwen, without her knowing it.'

'I knew I could rely on you to find a way,' Pierce said, with mingled admiration and sarcasm.

'All you have to do is buy Miss P's house – or another house on Beacon Hill if her landlord doesn't want to sell – and give it to her, along with a regular income. Then Miss P pretends that she has an inheritance from a long-lost relative, and tells Gwen that she would like her to have it when she dies. In fact,' continued Amadine, warming to her theme, 'it is a perfect plan, because it enables you to help Miss P as well. She would never accept "charity" for herself, but she will take the money if she thinks it is really for Gwen.'

Pierce was concentrating hard, marvelling at the machinations of the female mind. 'I wonder if Machiavelli was really a woman,' he said thoughtfully, 'or probably he took a lot of advice from Mrs Machiavelli.'

'The important thing is that Gwen should not find out

that you are behind it. My father always used to say that one must do good by stealth, from a genuine desire to help, not for gratitude or any earthly reward.'

'My lawyer can fix it.'

'As you didn't touch the money for so many years, he might be a bit surprised.'

'After *The Philadelphia Girl*, I think he is shock-proof. Mind you, his son, Oliver, to whom I spoke in New York, did mutter something about hoping that automobile manufacturing would become profitable before I ran through all my father's millions, and into debt. Going from one extreme to the other was more or less the general gist. I said that he hadn't met you, and that if he did, he would understand.'

'Why, what's to understand?' she asked, perplexed.

Pierce looked at her tenderly. 'It's difficult to explain.'

By Brooklyn, in the middle of May, the tour had only three weeks to run, and Hal's mind moved forward to London and the autumn season. Pierce's injection of cash, in repayment of the money Jay had stolen, meant that the tour was showing an excellent profit. Even after sharing the proceeds with Amadine, and setting aside a suitable contribution for Constance's children, he could afford to finance his own company.

He began cabling London, searching for a suitable theatre, and mulling over the choice of plays for his repertoire and the casts to perform them. His first consideration was his leading lady. He had been so convinced that he would return in triumph from the United States with a besotted Amadine in his company, and in his bed, that he had not sought an alternative. Of course, he had promised a place to Blanche, but not necessarily the number-one slot. She would not object if he brought in someone over her – she would be grateful for whatever he cared to offer. The thought made Hal remember her suggestion about just how grateful she could be, and he groaned. Celibacy did not suit him. Sex, or the lack of it, preyed on his mind and drained his energy, blunting his creative talents. What he needed was regular, easy sex with no emotional complications. In fact, what he needed was a wife.

Such a pity about Amadine, but perhaps Blanche could substitute, as she had done on the stage, and very adequately, too. For several days Hal watched her and found himself increasingly attracted by her pretty face and curvaceous figure. She was always willing and cheerful, reliable and professional. Equally important, he felt that she could be moulded to his ways, on and off the stage.

She always seemed to be there. Wherever he looked, or sat, or walked, Blanche was never far away, and accordingly his method of courtship was more casual than the approach he had tried with Amadine. He simply walked into her dressing room, closed the door behind him and kissed her. Distinctly unsubtle, but she did not seem to mind.

'Do you still feel like coming to London with me?' he whispered.

'What do you think?'

'And do you still feel like showing your gratitude?'

Blanche tensed slightly with surprise, and then tightened her arms around his neck. 'Only if you feel like showing me how to do so, because I've never done it before.'

As far as he could recall, Hal had never done it with a virgin before. His interest, and a few other things, perked up remarkably.

He proposed the next morning, was accepted and a date for the wedding was set. Then they settled down to plans for the forthcoming season.

'I would like to include Laurie in the company,' Hal said.

'Ye-es,' Blanche agreed doubtfully, 'but his range is a bit limited at the moment, isn't it? It might be better to wait until he is fully fit. Amadine is still talking about doing

Barbara in London. Laurie would probably be better off staying with her.'

'I suppose so.' Hal felt faintly guilty, as if he was letting down his old friend, but Blanche was right – Laurie might not be able to stand through an entire evening's performance for a while yet. Best to play safe. 'And then there is Frank to consider.'

'Oh, I don't think we want Frank.' Blanche was decisive, and utterly determined on this point. She did not know the whole story about the money, and was basing her abhorrence of the idea purely on her prejudice against homosexuals and her general antagonism to Frank. 'He hasn't been an outstanding success on this tour, and your brother can't hang on to your coat-tails for ever, or you'll find he is holding you back.'

Hal did not know the whole story about the money, either, and he remained in ignorance of Frank's sexual preferences, but he had been worried by Frank's handling of the tour finances. Without Blanche's intervention, he would probably have forgiven his brother and given him another chance but, with a young lover to impress and keep happy, he was easily swayed.

As Hal agreed that they would dispense with Frank's services, Blanche smiled. She knew what Hal thought about her, but he would soon learn who was moulding whom . . .

The June wedding of Hal and Blanche, at the Little Church Around the Corner, was not an occasion that aroused unalloyed joy in all the participants. Blanche was happy and Hal was content, but profound cynicism prevailed elsewhere. Theo, whom Blanche had asked to give her away, was inclined to give the pair the benefit of the doubt, but Frank, as his brother's best man, was appalled. He could see why Hal was doing it – fear of another Constance would provide prime motivation – but there was another side to Blanche Villard and Frank felt fairly certain that Hal would see it before too long, but too late to extricate himself. As for the professional partnership, Frank felt that Hal could have done better; on the other hand, Blanche was a quick learner and, with Hal as her mentor, would improve rapidly. With luck, Frank thought philosophically, Blanche would be clever enough to get her own way while still keeping Hal happy.

He was in no doubt what his own position would be. He did not like Blanche, and knew that she did not like him. Even without Hal's reservations about his financial aptitude, he would be out.

A tight, dull despair gripped him at the prospect of searching for another job. He was only in his early thirties, and would find something in the lower echelons of a company in London or New York, but the awful spectre of Gilbert West loomed before him. He could see himself in a similarly seedy and run-down state a few years from now, a figure of pity and ridicule as people compared him to his brother, and remembered that even that brother had not thought enough of him to stick by him.

'Cheer up,' Amadine said, at the reception at the Waldorf after the ceremony. 'Anyone would think that it was you who had just married the fair Blanche.'

He smiled, and wondered how Amadine was feeling about the wedding. Incredible to think that she had been married to Gilly West. Frank was the only person, apart from Pierce, in whom Amadine had confided her secret, but he still found it a difficult subject to raise.

'I thought it might be Ida for whom the sound of wedding bells induced gloom and melancholia,' he remarked, in an oblique reference to the man.

'Ida is bearing up remarkably well. In fact the whole affair was such a shock that I think Walter might be in with a chance after all.' Amadine glanced across to where Ida was adjusting a stray lock of Blanche's hair. 'Bearing that possibility in mind, and taking into account how close she is becoming to the bride, I have little doubt that Ida wants to work for Blanche next season.'

'Pity I can't apply for the job as your maid,' Frank said lightly and, as Amadine arched her eyebrows enquiringly, he explained, 'Hal finds it possible to struggle through next season, and all his other seasons, without my amazing gifts and talents.'

'You're joking!' Amadine's eyes swivelled back to Blanche. 'Hm, you're better off out of that, in my opinion, and anyway it's the best news I've had all day.'

'Thanks a lot,' Frank said gloomily.

'Would you consider working with me? I haven't mentioned it before because I took it for granted that you would be with Hal, but I could face forming my own company with much more confidence if you were there to help. I'll pay you whatever Hal is paying you – hell, *more* than he's paying! I'm not ashamed to offer a bribe in such a good cause!'

Frank was aware of a cloud lifting, and of the sun shining on him again. 'You would do that, for me, after everything that . . .'

'Oh, *that*!' Amadine dismissed the past with an airy wave of her hand. 'You have more than made up for that, and you really are very good at your job, so there is precious little altruism involved. I am considering putting on *Barbara* at a small theatre – the Royalty, for example – for a limited season, while preparing a new production for the West End. What I want is a repertoire that I can bring back to America on another long tour – if you could bear it!'

'I'd love it.'

'You don't think I'm a jinx?'

Her tone was jocular, but he knew her well enough to sense the anxiety that lay behind it. 'I think that you are a bloody miracle.'

'I can see us now in our Palace Car on the next tour,'

Amadine said mischievously. 'One stateroom for you, and one for me, so that neither of us can be led astray!'

'Pierce would be happy with the arrangement,' Frank laughed. 'It would relieve him of the necessity of carrying out constant checks on the activities of handsome, hetero-sexual leading men. And, while we're on the subject, have you anyone in mind?'

'Laurie must come with us, of course. I thought,' Amadine said tentatively, 'that we might try *Antony and Cleopatra*. If he thinks I'm up to it.'

'You are up to it. Believe me. What about Gwen?'

'Hal offered her a place, but she turned him down. Gwen wants to spend more time here, concentrating her work in New York and Boston, because she says she needs to put down a few roots, make friends, make a home. She appears to be making rather a good start,' and she indicated where Gwen was talking animatedly with an elderly man of almost Pickwickian appearance.

Then, by mutual, unspoken consent, they both looked at Theo. Amadine laid a hand gently on Frank's arm.

'Are you over him?'

'Just about.'

'You won't have a relapse if and when Theo arrives in London for the opening of *Barbara Frietchie* with his wife on his arm?'

'Lord, no, but I might have a very nasty turn if he arrived with anyone else.'

Amadine took his point, and smiled. 'It hasn't been all bad, has it, this tour? Some good has come out of it?'

Frank looked at the bridal pair, and scowled. 'Let's put it this way: everything will have been worthwhile if you marry Pierce Radcliffe.'

'Oh, *him*. He's another story.'

'No, he isn't. And to prove it, he has just come into the room and is heading this way.'

*

'I wish it was us,' Pierce said, as he looked at Hal and Blanche in their wedding finery.

'I cannot afford to make another mistake,' Amadine said simply. 'If I marry again, it can only be after a long period of reflection, when I am sure I am doing the right thing.'

'In which case I will be pushing you down the aisle in your wheelchair.'

'The only thing you ever push is your luck! Anyway, I'm younger than you, so it will be me in charge of your wheel-chair.'

'I will be making my annual visit to England, to see my mother, in a week or so, but I cannot stay in Europe as long as usual because of getting the new business up and running.'

'You do see that the Atlantic Ocean is the other problem? Your business interests are here. My career is, and is likely to remain, based in London. I can visit America, and tour here, but I cannot be sure that I want to live here perma-nently.'

'We are on the brink of the twentieth century, and the future is here,' Pierce said confidently. 'You are ambitious and forward-looking, so surely this country, where the best is yet to come, is the best place for you to be?'

'I concede that the twentieth century is likely to belong to America, but I *love* London. It is a wonderful place in which to work, almost as though there is something in the atmosphere that is conducive to creativity. I can't explain it – perhaps it's the weather! Perhaps it is the tradition that permeates every brick and cobblestone and enables an artist to know who he is and what he is, and build on it. All I can say for sure is this: only in London can I do my best work.'

'And you want to go on working? No, don't answer that – it was a rhetorical question. Of course you want to go on working, and I wouldn't dream of trying to stop you. Sometimes I hate sharing you, but more often I'm so proud of you, I could burst.'

'Thank God that is one choice I don't have to make! If we could work out a geographical compromise, we could be more than halfway there.'

'Would you agree to an engagement, while we try to achieve the best terms for a transatlantic alliance?'

'An official engagement?'

'Very,' and Pierce produced a small box from his pocket.

Amadine hesitated, the diamond ring blazing in the box, while not only Pierce but everyone in the room watched and waited for her answer . . .

The Plays

Some licence has been taken with the plays in the repertoire. While it is feasible that Amadine Sinclair could have taken over the lead in *The Second Mrs Tanqueray* in London, after Mrs Patrick Campbell left the cast, Mrs Pat was responsible for introducing American audiences to the play during her 1901–2 tour.

Trelawny of the Wells was first produced in London on 20 January 1898 with Irene Vanbrugh as Rose Trelawny.

Having decided the tour itinerary and repertoire in advance of my research trip to the United States, I was somewhat spooked to discover that E.S. Willard played *The Physician* at Wallack's Theatre, New York, at the same time as the Smith-Sinclair company.

Barbara Frietchie was written by Clyde Fitch, and opened in New York on 24 October 1899 with Julia Marlowe in the leading role.

A revue called *Miss Philadelphia* was staged in Philadelphia in 1894 by George C. Tyler, financed entirely by kite-flying. It was an unqualified success.

MY BEAUTIFUL MISTRESS

Carolyn Terry

THE SCENE

Murdered on the stage of his own theatre, Vere Cavendish
has died as he lived – surrounded by beautiful women.
He is one of the most famous actor-managers in the
thriving London theatreland of the 1880s, a man in love
with every kind of drama. They are the stunning Leigh
sisters. All, in their own way, were Cavendish's lovers,
but only one became his murderer . . .

THE SISTERS

Marion, desperate to feed her impoverished household,
turns to the immoral occupation of the stage, achieving a
little fame and fortune, but great suffering at
Cavendish's hands.

Frances, while profiting from her sister's career and
connections, is a gifted pianist for whom Marion's success
is an endless source of shame and frustration.

Charley, the star-struck teenager who becomes Cavendish's
leading lady, prepared to do anything to protect the status
she has fought so hard to achieve.

And Arabella and Imogen, the beautiful twins sharing a
guilty secret behind an impassive façade . . .

With its vivid characters, unfolding suspense and climatic
dénouement, *My Beautiful Mistress* is a delightful insight into
the decadent world of the Victorian stage.

FLOWER OF SCOTLAND

Emma Blair

'Emma Blair is a dab hand at pulling heart strings'
Today

In the idyllic summer of 1912, all seems rosy for Murdo
Drummond and his four children. Charlotte is ecstatically in
love with her fiancée Geoffrey; Peter, the eldest, prepares for
the day when he will inherit the family whisky distillery, while
Andrew, gregarious and fun-loving, is already turning heads
and hearts. Nell, the youngest, contents herself with
daydreams of a handsome highlander. Even Murdo, their
proud father, though still mourning the death of his
beloved wife, is considering future happiness with Jean
Richie, an old family friend.

The Great War, however, has no respect for family life. As
those carefree pre-war days of the distillery fade, with death,
devastation, revenge, scandal and suicide brought in their
wake, the Drummonds are plunged into the horrors of
the trenches in France. Yet those who survive discover that
love can transcend class, creed and country . . .

<u>HALF HIDDEN</u>

Emma Blair

The news of her fiancée's death at Dunkirk was a cruel blow
for Holly Morgan to suffer. But for Holly – forced to nurse
enemy soldiers back to health while her beloved Jersey
ails beneath an epidemic of crime, rationing and the worst
excesses of Nazi occupation – the brutality of her war
has only just begun.

From the grim conditions of the hospital operating theatre
where Holly is compelled to work long hours alongside the
very people responsible for her grief, unexpected bonds of
resilience and tenderness are forged. When friendship turns
to love between Holly and a young German doctor, Peter
Schmidt, their forbidden passion finds sanctuary at
Half Hidden, a deserted house deep within the island
countryside. A refuge where traditional battle lines recede
from view in the face of more powerful emotions, it
nevertheless becomes the focus for the war Holly and Peter
must fight together – a war where every friend may
be an enemy . . .

THE ITALIAN HOUSE

Teresa Crane

Secretly treasured memories of her grandmother's Italian house, perched high upon a mountainside in Tuscany, are very special for Carrie Stowe; for not only do they recall and preserve the happy childhood summers of the golden years before the devastation of the Great War, they are her only escape from the mundane and suffocating routine of her life with Arthur, her repressive and parsimonious husband.

When she discovers that she has unexpectedly inherited the house Carrie sets her heart upon going to Tuscany alone to dispose of the effects of Beatrice Swann, her eccentric and much-loved grandmother.

Arriving late at night and in the teeth of a violent storm she discovers that she is not the only person to be interested in the Villa Castellini and its family connections. A young man, an enigmatic figure from the past, is there before her: and as the enchantment of the house exerts itself once more, Carrie finds herself irresistibly drawn to him . . .

<u>COCKNEY FAMILY</u>

Elizabeth Waite

London, 1936. There was a time when Patsy Kent thought
she might never belong to a real family, when her mother
died and she was nearly sent to the orphanage. But the
market traders of Strathmore Street stood by her and Ollie,
Florrie and all the others became the best relatives anyone
could wish for.

And now Patsy has a husband and four children of her own,
and life is full of the cares and joys of motherhood. Alex
and David, her sons, always seem to be getting into scrapes
while the twins, the prettiest little girls on Navy Street, are
a constant source of delight. But war is in the air, and as the
fateful events of September 1939 unfold, London will be
shaken by air raids and food shortages, children evacuated,
men called up. And though the cockney spirit never burns
brighter than in times of trouble, Patsy wonders if her family
can survive the war intact . . .

Tugging at the heart-strings throughout, Elizabeth Waite's
moving portrayal of Patsy and realistic depiction of
wartime London make *Cockney Family* a worthy sequel to
Cockney Waif.

Other bestselling Warner titles available by mail:

☐	My Beautiful Mistress	Carolyn Terry	£5.99
☐	Flower of Scotland	Emma Blair	£5.99
☐	Half Hidden	Emma Blair	£5.99
☐	The Italian House	Teresa Crane	£5.99
☐	The Raven Hovers	Teresa Crane	£5.99
☐	Cockney Family	Elizabeth Waite	£5.99
☐	Cockney Waif	Elizabeth Waite	£5.99
☐	Nippy	Elizabeth Waite	£5.99

The prices shown above are correct at time of going to press, however the publishers, reserve the right to increase prices on covers from those previously advertised, without further notice.

W

WARNER BOOKS

WARNER BOOKS
Cash Sales Department, P.O. Box 11, Falmouth, Cornwall, TR10 9EN
Tel: +44(0) 1326 372400. Fax +44 (0) 1326 374888
Email: books@barni.avel.co.uk

POST and PACKAGING:
Payments can be made as follows: cheque, postal order (payable to Warner Books) or by credit cards. Do not send cash or currency.

U.K. Orders	FREE OF CHARGE
E.E.C. & Overseas	25% of order value

Name (Block Letters) _____

Address _____

_____

Post/zip code: _____

☐ Please keep me in touch with future Warner publications

☐ I enclose my remittance £ _____

☐ I wish to pay by Visa/Access/Mastercard/Eurocard

Card Expiry Date

_____